HASTINGS

HASTINGS

BRITTANY WYNNE

The Rock On Series • Book One

This book is a work of fiction. Any references to historical events, real people, or real places are used fictitiously. Other names, characters, places, and events are products of the author's imagination, and any resemblance to actual events or places or persons, living or dead is entirely coincidental.

Cover Design: Murphy Rae

ISBN 979-8-9903637-2-4

For my dad.

You've always believed in me, Daddio, and made me believe I could chase my dreams.

P.S. Don't read this one. As you would say, it has parts.

Note From the Author

Dear reader,

Music is a huge part of Jaxon and Cambri's story. Each song listed was chosen carefully to convey words or emotion between them. If you aren't familiar with a song, I encourage you to give it a listen!

I cannot wait for you to travel down this road with them. So, crank up the volume and find a cozy spot to crack this story open! Enjoy the moment. Just Today.

Rock On!

Brittany

Prologue

Cambri

Before

The wind blew through the open window in my bedroom right as I flipped my pencil around to use the eraser. Reflexively, I reached up and tucked the hair that blew in my face back behind my ear. Brushing away the pink bits that were left on the paper, I got back to it.

"You need a starting point, sweetheart," my dad had said the night before when I told him my grand plans. I was going to apprentice at the record label and then I would start my own company, from the ground up, just like he had.

I am going to be just like him. I want to be the next Norwood that takes the music world by storm.

A knock sounded on my door right before my dad popped his head in. His eyes scanned the room, a grin stretching from ear to ear when he found me sitting at my desk. He strode over toward me, resting against the tabletop, peering down. "What do you have there?"

I gave a shrug. "My starting point."

"Always so determined, my love."

"If I'm going to run my own record label by the time I'm thirty-five, I am going to need a solid foundation. It's like you always say, Daddy. Dream big. Work harder."

He had that twinkle in his eye as he watched me move my pencil around the page. "I have no doubt that you will accomplish everything you set your mind to. I'm going to be working for you someday." He reached over and ran his hand across my head.

"Dad," I laughed, smoothing my hair back into place.

He crossed his arms in front of him as he chuckled. "Tell me about this starting point that you are working on."

I opened my mouth to explain what I had been sketching in my notebook, when movement from outside my window caught my eye. My cousin Sarah was running up the lawn, waving her hand when she saw me noticing her.

I whipped my head toward my dad, and he glanced out the window before meeting my eyes with a resolved grin. He knew what I was going to ask before I even uttered a word.

"Go on. Get out of here." He motioned with his head. "I'm just about to head down into the recording studio to listen to some new tracks that got sent over anyway."

I was practically bouncing. I gathered my notebook and pencil and rushed toward my bedroom door, pausing before I stepped out of my room. I quickly made my way back to my dad's side and gave him a kiss on the cheek. "Thanks, Daddy," I beamed.

He held out my cell phone that I'd forgotten, and I slipped it into my pocket. "I expect a full report on your business plan later."

I nodded. "Yes, sir."

I couldn't wait to show him. He never made me feel silly for having big dreams and big goals. He made me feel like I could reach the stars if I wanted to. Him and his smile that made you feel like the most important person in the room.

When I'm older, I'm going to do business exactly the way he has. He will be right by my side the entire time. He told me so.

"Love you, Cambri. Have fun with Sarah."

"Love you too, Dad!"

I ran down the hall and the stairs. Briefly stopping in the kitchen to grab an apple for Sarah and I to take.

"Hi, Mom. Bye, Mom," I said grabbing the fruit, carefully maneuvering one into each hand so I didn't drop my notebook.

"Darling, where are you off to in such a hurry?" she asked with amusement in her voice.

"To the field with Sarah!" Before she could ask, I added, "Dad said it was okay."

Her mouth closed, swallowing the question I'd already answered. "Alright. Have fun." She grinned. "Wait. What do you have there?" she asked, noticing my notebook as I turned toward the back door.

I glanced over my shoulder. "The first phase of my business model."

She lowered the spoon she was using to stir the pot against the rim. She was giving me that look.

"I know. I know. I'm such an old soul," I said, adopting a British accent to give my best impression of her.

She grinned so big, her eyes got lost in her smile. Holding the spoon up like a magic wand, she moved it in the cadence of her words. "I've said it once, and I'll say it a thousand more."

That's when I realized it. Halting my forward momentum. "Are you cooking? Where's Eliza?" My mom is a lot of things, but a chef is not one of them. My tastebuds were still recovering from the last over salting, when she attempted a birthday dinner for my dad. I shuddered at the thought.

Her shoulders dropped. "Emery is sick. She is home nursing that sweet toddler."

I tried not to grimace, but when the fate of my meal was in my mom's hands, that was a difficult task. She looked from me, to the spoon, and then back to me. "Pizza?" She laughed.

"Pizza." I nodded along. My relief palpable.

Adjusting my notebook in my arms, I took a breath. "Can I go now?" I asked excitedly.

"Sometimes I don't know where your dad stops and where you begin," she teased. "Go have fun in the field. Be a kid!"

"Thanks, Mom. Love you, Mom," I said, hurrying out the door.

"Love you too, Cambri," she called out as I made my exit.

I met Sarah down at the bottom of the steps.

"What took you so long?" She asked.

"Sorry. Here, I got one for you." I tossed her one of the apples.

Catching it, she smiled. "Thanks! Let's go!"

We took off across the stone path until our feet hit the grass. Cutting through the crepe myrtles, we dashed toward the field, pausing near the pavilion to check on the baby bunnies we'd found a couple days ago. They looked more like furry little balls than bunnies. Satisfied that they were snuggled in well, we took the last set of steps before reaching the door that would take us to the field behind my house.

I undid the heavy iron latch and leaned into the large wooden door, pushing it open. This was our favorite way to get to the field because it felt more like we were entering a magical realm than simply a field behind my house.

We walked out the door, careful to latch it behind us, and made our way through the red oaks and into the clearing. Sarah pulled out a blanket she had in her bag and spread it out. I immediately plopped down and opened my notebook.

Sarah placed her hands on her hips. "What's that?"

"Step one of becoming CEO of my own company one day."

"Of course, it is," she grinned. "Okay, fine. You work on that for a little bit and I'm going to gather us some flowers."

"Sounds good." I began adding to what I had been working on.

"Cool." She danced off, gathering all the wildflowers she could find.

I worked in my notebook, my father's words urging me on. "Go get 'em, Cambri. Dream big. Work harder. There's nothing you can't achieve." He meant it. I could tell by the way he was looking at me when he said it.

My parents have always said I'm a daddy's girl. I love my mom like the air I need to breathe. She is essential, but they are right. I am a daddy's girl. He actually hung the moon. How could I not be?

"Cambri!" Sarah said, exasperated, like this wasn't the first time she had said my name.

I glanced up from my notebook, a smile stretching across my face. She had both her arms out, twirling in slow circles, head tilted toward the sun.

She collapsed on the blanket beside me. "Are you done yet?" She removed the crown of flowers she had made and adjusted one of the stems.

"Almost." I hugged my notebook to me. It wasn't ready to be shared.

Her shoulders and her head dropped. She gave me that look. The one that said she was no longer taking no for an answer.

Sarah reached out and took my pencil, setting it down on the blanket before carefully taking my notebook and closing its pages. I released it because I knew she wouldn't look at it until I was ready to show her.

"Let's make you one. I'll show you how." She placed the flower crown back on her head before reaching over to what was left of the pile of flowers she had collected earlier.

I watched her carefully choose each stem, weaving them in and out, creating my crown.

"Here." She handed me what she had gotten started and then a couple of the spare flowers. "Now just stick them in the openings and loop around the stems until you can tuck in the last little piece. That's the most important part. You don't want your crown to look like it is made of thorns with all the little ends poking out."

I did my best to follow what she had done. There was no point arguing against it. That was the thing about Sarah: she lived life and expected that I live it right along with her. She was always telling me that I was trying to grow up too fast. That I needed to slow down and enjoy right where we were.

I guess I really was an old soul. Sarah always managed to get me to take a break from my plans and live a little, as she would say.

I loved her for it.

Sometimes it felt like I didn't know how to act my age. I certainly felt different than other kids my age. I was focused on what I wanted to become. Sarah helped make sure I lived in the moment, right where I was.

She stood up and reached down for me. I placed my hand in hers, letting her pull me to standing. She gave me a tug that almost knocked me off balance. Our eyes met and we both broke out into giggles.

She took off running, and I followed closely behind. Laughing, we ran and twirled through the field.

Eventually, we tired out and made our way back to the blanket. We landed on our backs with a whoosh. Her hand reached out for mine. I set mine on hers as I let my head fall to look at her.

She grinned.

I grinned.

"Just today," she said, like it was a lifeline.

"Just today," I repeated back, breathing in the moment here with her.

I hoped it was always like this. I needed it to always be like this. She made me feel alive in a way that I couldn't seem to manage on my own.

Sarah sat up and reached over for her bag, taking out her phone and starting her current playlist. "I've added a few new ones that you have got to hear. They are so good." She laid the phone between us before laying on her back, touching the top of her head to mine. I placed my hands on my chest, listening to the music she shared, thinking how much I loved this.

The music played as we watched the clouds take shape, shifting into different forms as they drifted by.

"You going to show me what you were working on?" Sarah's voice cut through my thoughts of oddly shaped cloud creatures.

"Maybe. When it's done." I continued to watch the clouds, particularly enthralled by one that reminded me of one of those creepy creatures Winnie the Pooh was frightened of. What were they called again?

Sarah rolled over, making us lay side by side. "Don't be such a nincompoop. I want to see what you were working on so hard that kept you from picking wildflowers with me."

I eyed her, letting the silence speak for me.

"I guess I will just have to tell Ronald Asterly that you would in fact like to be his date to the ice cream social at school."

I pushed to sitting, looking down at her with an aghast expression.

"You wouldn't dare!"

Ronald Asterly, Ron, had asked me to go to the ice cream social fundraiser at school with him a week ago. No one else my age was coupling up, yet Ronald had decided we should go together. Citing his reasoning that we were the only two redheads in our grade. Like that was a good enough reason to go to a school event with someone named Ronald, of all things.

My family's trademark red hair had really gotten me into a pickle this time. Though I actually quite like my bright strawberry-blond hair. It is definitely more of the red hue than blond, but I am certain you couldn't lump my red and Ronald's red together. His was a dark sort of orange that was rather dreadful if I am being honest.

She didn't respond.

"Sarah!" I shrieked. "You know how I detest a grouping based on something as simple as our shared hair color. Besides, it would be rather dull to attend an event with anyone but you. Plus, you know Daddy would have an absolute fit if he were to find out I was meeting a boy at the social."

I circled my finger on the spot beside me, needing a moment to calm my racing brain before I rambled on further. "Come, have a sit, will you? Let's talk logically about the whole sordid idea."

"You're doing it again." She wore an amused grin as she pushed to sitting.

"Doing what exactly?"

"You're starting to use more British English than American English. It always happens when you get excited or flustered after you get back from visiting your mom's family in London."

I crossed my arms in front of me, letting out an exaggerated "Hmph."

Sarah rolled her eyes. "Listen, Cambri. I won't say anything to Ronald. I swear. I just want to see what you have been working on." She nudged my shoulder with her own. "You know, to see what ideas are going to make you the future CEO of your own company."

I swiveled my head her direction with a grin. "Fine. But promise you won't laugh. It's not done yet."

She held out her pinky. "Pinky swear."

I hooked my pinky with hers and then reached over for my notebook.

"Wow. This is really good!"

"Yeah?"

"Yeah! Future CEO material for sure!"

I grinned larger. "You don't even know what it is."

"Doesn't matter. If you dreamed it, it will be great. I don't know anyone else so headstrong and determined. That counts for something."

I tucked my knees underneath me. "Well, right now I am determined that you won't catch me." I tagged Sarah and then pushed up and fell into a dead sprint across the field. It took mere seconds for her to follow, both of us giggling as we ran.

Her laughter stopped, gaining my attention. I turned to see Sarah slightly hunched over, grasping at her chest.

"Sarah?" I took a step toward her. "Sarah!" I ran back to her side, grabbing onto her for support while she took a shallow breath. "Hold on. Stay right here. I'm going to call for help!"

Frantically, I ran over to grab my cell phone, fingers fumbling as I tried to navigate to my dad's name. He answered almost immediately.

"Daddy. It's Sarah. We are in the field back behind the house. Out the left door. Hurry! Please."

Sarah had had episodes before, but something in my gut told me this one was different.

When the ambulance arrived, they tried to separate us, but they couldn't remove me from her side. I rode in the ambulance the entire way to the hospital, her hand in mine.

"Cam, tell me about your company. The one you are going to build."

"I don't care about the stupid company. I just want you to shake this off, okay?"

"I will," she grimaced. "I just want you to help take my mind off it until I do. Okay?"

I nodded. "Yeah. Okay." I nodded several times, trying to piece my thoughts together. I didn't like seeing her like this. My larger-than-life cousin, my best friend. Seeing her strapped to a gurney was terrifying.

"Um…" I searched for the right words. I couldn't seem to find them. She squeezed my hand, drawing my attention to where we were attached. "Daddy said you have to start somewhere." I swallowed. "Today I was working on my logo. It's not much, but it's a start. I definitely want to work in music. Just not in the traditional sense."

I brought my other hand up to my mouth like I was letting her in on a secret. "I haven't quite figured that part out yet."

We hit a bump in the road, sending me backward enough that I had to let go of her hand to catch myself. I reclaimed her hand instantly. It was just a bump.

"We. You and I. Are going to search out talent. We are going to discover music, like you do now. You know how you find these amazing bands and then share them with me." She nodded. "It's going to be like that. But we will be drab and old."

She shook her head. "No. Absolutely not. We will get older, for sure. But you and I will never be drab. I simply will not allow it."

I grinned, nodding along. "Deal. We will age like timeless beauties. Luring unsuspecting musicians in with our charm and trapping them in our lyrical webs."

We both giggled.

"Yes. We will trap them in our webs, and then we will captivate them, becoming their muse," she elaborated. "We will inspire great love ballads, and live life on the road, and then fall in love with another musician and do it all over again."

My grin stretched from ear to ear. "Yes. Yes. And there will be pizza. Lots and lots of pizza!"

"Because tour busses require pizza."

"Exactly! Oh – and dancing!"

Her eyes got lost in her smile she was grinning so big. "So much dancing!"

We both giggled and then took in a breath. The reality of the situation, where we were headed, sinking back in.

"Promise me. Promise me you will chase your dream. Find your musicians. Go on the road. Live."

Sarah wasn't much older than I was, but sometimes she seemed so much older. This was one of those moments. I think when you're sick, it forces you to grow up in a way other kids aren't capable of.

"I will. We will. It will be wonderful. We are going to make you better, and then you will go home and we will be unstoppable. This is just a bump in the road."

"Just today." She searched my eyes.

"Just today." I squeezed her hand. "Tomorrow we will be back in the field behind my house making more of those flower crowns."

When we got to the hospital, they finally tore me away from Sarah. Taking her back so they could make her better. My dad met me right outside the hospital, catching me in a hug as they wheeled her inside.

Sarah's parents got there seconds later, running up to us when they saw us. My dad directed them into the doors, telling them they'd just taken her inside.

It felt like hours passed before they let me see her, but I eventually got to go back.

"Hey," I said, walking up to her bed.

"Cam, you gotta hear this song. One of the nurses told me about it when we got to talking about music."

"Of course, you would find new music while at the hospital." I laughed.

She moved her fingers over her phone and played it for me. My eyes lit up and met hers.

"Right?" she asked excitedly.

"I mean. It is really good."

We finished her song and let the silence spread between us, taking in the effects the music left behind.

"When do I get to bust you out of here?"

"They want to keep me overnight for observation and stuff." She shrugged.

"Cool. I'll bring breakfast."

The following morning, Daddy and I called in a to-go order of biscuit sandwiches from our favorite breakfast spot. My mouth was watering just thinking about the biscuits I held in the bag the entire drive.

Bag in hand, the two of us were waiting outside when Sarah, my mom, and my aunt and uncle came through the doors.

Our eyes met once she spotted us, grins spreading across both of our faces. She turned to look at my aunt, who gave a nod, before making a quick route to where Daddy and I were waiting.

I threw my arms around her. "Let's never do that again, okay? You scared me."

She gave a nod. "Deal." She gave a weak smile that made my own feel forced, with a pit settling in my belly.

"One of those for me?" Sarah pointed to the bag I was holding, the label indicating what was waiting inside.

"Of course! We need to make sure you are well fed to get you back up and running," I said, feeling happy to have her out here with me and not stuck in a hospital bed, hooked up to all the beepy things.

She laughed. "I'm not dead yet."

I froze. Her comment reigniting the sense of dread I'd felt since that moment in the field. No, she wasn't dead yet. But both of our parents have been very up front with us about the reality of Sarah's life.

It sounds incredibly morbid, I know, but Sarah's parents wanted her to live as normal a life as possible, not having to make her feel like she lived in a bubble. To do that, they made sure we both knew the reality of her situation. That was one of the reasons why they gave us the freedom they did. They trusted that in a less than ideal situation, we would be able to get her the help she needed. Like how I knew to instantly call for help, not wasting valuable minutes.

I handed over one of the biscuit sandwiches. "Daddy ordered all the bacon well done again." I rolled my eyes. Sarah liked her bacon as flimsy and chewy as possible.

"We will let it slide. Just this once." She winked, taking the butcher-paper-wrapped biscuit from my hand.

I nodded several times. Yes, I was definitely glad she was coming home today. I don't know what I would do without her.

She peeled open the wrapper of her biscuit before taking a bite, nudging my shoulder with hers. "Come on, let's go find a new album in your dad's submission stack."

I looked at her with wide eyes, scanning the distance between her and my dad, hoping he hadn't heard her. I don't think that he did. At least, he gave no indication that he did.

That is something we did from time to time. We'd comb through a box of new artist hopefuls and listen to their music. Some were really great. Others sounded just like everyone else and would get lost in the stack. We always put them back when we were done.

Sarah giggled and started walking to our car. "Mom, I'm riding with Cambri."

We both turned to see her reaction. Aunt June hesitated for a moment but then gave a curt nod with a smile.

"Why don't we all head back to the house?" Dad suggested. "We can put on a pot of coffee. I know I sure need some."

"Perfect idea," Aunt June agreed, squeezing my uncle's hand. "We will see y'all in just a bit then."

I watched as everyone dispersed to our cars. I was a step behind Sarah the entire time, thankful for biscuit sandwiches and an aunt and uncle who seemed to understand how important it was not to separate us right now.

Then again, even if they would have said no, she would have found her way to me sooner rather than later. That was just Sarah. She was headstrong, and full of life, and never wasted a minute doing something she didn't want to.

She was fearless.

She lived with intention.

She was what I sometimes wished I could be but didn't know how.

That time Sarah went home.

The next time she went into the hospital, she didn't come out.

A part of me didn't either.

Chapter One

Cambri

I placed a practiced, polished smile in place as I held the folder in my hands containing the business proposal for why I should be assigned the PR manager for a band that had just signed to the record label. I sat in that first meeting, held to discuss who Mitch referred to as his newest rising stars, and had to fight the urge to shake my head in disbelief. It wasn't that I disagreed with the description. The music sample I'd heard was lights out. It was that Mitch referred to all his new clients that way.

I, however, knew they were different. They stood out. There was something about their sound that I couldn't shake.

They brought a rock edge to country music which, in my opinion, was a welcome change to the pop style country the industry had steered toward lately. Their sound had my Spidey senses tingling. I knew they were special. I could feel it.

I wanted to be the one to represent them.

This band was going to shine. Don't ask me to explain how I knew they were going to make it. I just did. I had an ear for these things, it was innate.

The moment I heard their music sample, I knew that this was the band that was going to be my ticket to the promotion I had been gunning for.

I wanted to be the one that made them light up the whole country music scene. They were going to boom, and I planned on riding that momentum all the way to the top.

I was ready to represent a sound that moved you. That could make you laugh, cry, or fall in love just by listening. That was these guys. I was certain. There was a certain angst in the lead singer's vocals that cut straight through to your core.

Goosebumps.

He gave me goosebumps.

I had prepped for this meeting. A little digging pulled up a story about a college town band's rise to small town celebrity. Their faces weren't clear in the picture from the article, but I could tell their overall look would be an easy one to sell.

I had a major morning news outlet on board, ready to book an interview slot for Reckless as soon as I gave them the green light. I didn't usually like to name drop, but desperate times call for desperate measures. This band was new, and no one wants to waste airtime for artists that aren't guaranteed ratings boosters. However, with the Norwood name backing my call-in request, I was able to get this new band a place in line.

The *Nashville Times* was also willing to run a story on the band with my headline "Fall Recklessly in Love". The local paper more willing to accept my pitch, without having to use a name drop. Selling something with just the power of persuasion always felt like a bigger victory, like I was doing my job right.

I had several ideas ready to go on the social media side that would give Reckless exposure as well. A fan favorite has always been an Instagram takeover. Giving the group a day to take over the label's page would give people a chance to know them on a personal level.

The content would be perfectly curated material by yours truly, of course. It was never a good idea to let the unexperienced go rogue when the press was always ready to chew you up and spit you out. I swear they could smell fresh, easy-to-take-advantage-of meat a state away.

If they could spin a scandal, a scandal they would print. Then I would spend two weeks putting out bad press fires. Mitch would never give me the PR promotion I had been trying to land if that happened.

I have been stuck, for far too long, with a position title that doesn't reflect the quality of the content that I'm creating. The results I'm producing are better than some of those that are two levels above me. I have worked hard for this. I'm ready to be recognized for what I do and for the results I produce.

I am done making coffee runs and copies before meetings. I've always put in the work, however it was asked, pay your dues and all. I no longer want to be the one that gets saddled with the grunt work.

I want my responsibilities to reflect what I'm capable of and the value I add to the company.

Mitch refuses to see that I can handle more. I was already doing the more, just without any of the credit. Higher-ups ran with my pitches and got the recognition for it. I'm done with that. I've never thought myself a push-over, but somewhere along the way I began flirting with that line because it was disguised as respect.

I wanted to be taken seriously and be given the recognition I deserved. I wanted the promotion, which Easton Davenport thought he was a shoo-in for. I shook my head at the thought. I swear it would be easier to be a man in this industry. I ran circles around Easton, yet he still was given bigger accounts and was probably not wrong to assume the promotion was his.

I wasn't going down without a fight. I was determined to make Mitchell Norwood see that I was the better fit for this position. The numbers proved it. What I had done with my clients proved it.

Easton was literally handed golden opportunities and wasted them away. He did the bare minimum PR for his clients. Not a one of them had topped the billboard charts, and not because they didn't have the potential to. Good PR is everything.

I watched the elevator numbers climb. I took in a calming breath, ready for my moment to present my pitch outlining why I should be able to take point on representing our new client's public relations. The fact that I had already gotten people willing to book the band, without even being their official representation or the companies knowing much about them, proved I could do this. Half the battle is making someone want to say yes, even if they don't know why.

This was my world. I was born for this. I was a Norwood after all. I was ready, I could feel it. The excitement I felt kept bubbling up and it was all I could do to stifle it so I didn't appear the giddy little girl my dad had trouble seeing past.

I stepped into the meeting confident. Too confident. I managed to share the good news about the morning news outlet and per usual my dad cut me off, assigning my success to, wait for it, Easton Davenport.

Sure, Easton has worked PR for Norwood Records for longer than I have been here, but not a day goes by where I haven't fanaticized about wiping his smug grin right off his stupid face.

I was prepared for this though. I knew how my dad operated and I had planned an assertive but respectful way to jump back into the conversation when this happened. I was not losing these clients when I was the one who put in the legwork. I could pretty much guarantee the only thing Easton had done regarding these clients was listen to the music sample that was played in the meeting.

Predictably, Easton piped up. "I will plan on reaching out to the band and the morning news outlet soon and make sure everything is squared away."

He had nothing new to add and didn't even acknowledge that I had been the one to secure the media spot. I clamped my lips together.

Nope. I was not going down without a fight.

With a smile, I put myself back on the table. Giving one more nugget away, not wanting to reveal all of my cards right now, in the event this didn't pan out in my favor just yet. I didn't want Easton to end up taking the credit for my work – again. The thought made my skin prickle with frustration.

I explained what I thought we should do and then confidently suggested I be the one to do it. I informed the room that I was ready, that I'd prepared for this. I met the eyes of several people around the table who I had helped out in the past and who knew exactly what I was capable of. In return, I was met with nods and approving grins from around the room. I sat up a little straighter, proud of the support I was receiving from people I respected.

I turned toward my dad, ready to see his approving nod, signifying that these clients were mine.

I deflated.

He was wearing a thought-provoking expression that in no way said he was about to hand over this project to me. He tapped a pen on the table. Pressing his lips together, he gave two nods. "Cambri, I can see you put in some effort here." Some effort? I dug my nails into my palm, working to keep a neutral expression on my face. He turned to Easton. "Easton, include Cambri on this. Let her get her feet wet."

Include Cambri? Let her get her feet wet? What was he not seeing when everything was laid out so precisely in front of him?

Easton's shocked expression almost matched the one I felt internally, but I'm sure for a different reason. I doubt his was over me getting a hand-fed snack while he got the main course.

Easton cut his eyes to me and I gave a professional grin, not letting the frustration I felt inside spill out. "I look forward to working with you on this." *For now.* I finished the last part in my mind. Neither of them had any idea that for me, this wasn't over.

"Likewise." Easton recovered. "It will be a pleasure to have you assist with this one."

I sat back in my chair. My smile staying in place as I gave a curt nod. Not missing the way he enunciated the word "assist" as he spoke.

This wasn't over. Nothing was official – yet.

I know my dad wasn't trying to insult my competence. Not getting to take lead on the bands PR wasn't personal. He knows what I am capable of bringing to the table. Our conversations in his office at home while he sips his brandy are a testament to that.

He knows I can do this. Somewhere deep down, he knows I deserve these clients and the promotion. It's because I am his daughter. A part of him will always see me in long strawberry braids and a flower crown, just like the picture on his desk.

My dad is soon going to realize that it has been a while since I have worn braided pigtails and that I am ready to be given what I have earned.

I am ready for this.

He knows it and I know it.

My dad has always told me to dream big, work harder. Well, he is about to discover exactly how big I can dream. Even if the journey that gets me there is a bit – unconventional. Go big or go home. You have to be willing to fight for what you want in this life.

I exited the meeting with the same polished poise with which I'd entered. My calm, cool, collected shell not giving away the frustration clawing its way up inside.

Walking into my office, I closed the door behind me in one smooth motion, without missing a stride. I needed something to ground the emotions I was feeling. I sat in my chair, popping in my AirPods and putting on one of the most respected women in Nashville.

I pressed play on Reba McEntire's "Fancy" and let the grit in her voice and song's fighting spirit take over. Yeah, the lyrics are morally gray and some people get hung up on the working girl part of the song. What they miss is that that girl was a determined fighter that didn't quit until she had exactly what she wanted.

Chapter Two

Jaxon

Nashville. We made it to Nashville. I seemed to be having trouble finding the same enthusiasm about it that my bandmates currently possessed.

I brought my amber colored companion back to my lips and took another hefty drink, hitting the large square ice cube against my teeth as I did.

Despite knowing that we were here, and instead of just being drunk on this incredible opportunity, I was holed up in a bar alone. Commiserating my person not being enough while my bandmates were out celebrating.

I was aware of my self-induced pity party situation, but the past summer had messed with my head. I couldn't figure out why I was the guy that's so damn easy to leave behind. What was so inherently wrong with me that made me so easy to walk away from?

I'd decided that I would give myself tonight to clear my mind. I would give myself one motherfucking night to deal with my demons and get it together.

I just needed a night.

Something about how things ended back in Texas just shook me. It made me feel out of control, and I didn't like that. I had felt more on top, more in control of my own life than I ever had going into that summer. Hell, maybe that's what did it. I thought I'd learned how to be untouchable. The faux control allowing my fear to creep back in undetected.

I gripped my glass a little tighter. I was not a helpless little boy anymore. I could take care of myself. I didn't need anyone. I just needed myself and the music.

For me, it has always been about the music. The music will never leave me behind. No, the lyrics, the melodies, they've intertwined themself so deeply into who I am, they can never leave.

Clinging to the music has always been safe, reliable. The music has never let me down.

Tomorrow, I will let the effects of the booze seep out of my skin, taking with it what my twin sister calls my undealt with childhood trauma. I brushed condensation off my glass with my thumb. Assigning labels like that is just another way of dealing with your problems. Jade has her way. I have my amber colored one.

I swirled the remaining remnants around in my glass, watching the way it curved up the sides as I did. Tomorrow I will get my shit together, or at least act like I have as we move out of a hotel and into a house that we will rent for the next year. Tonight, I will fight off my demons the best way I know how, drowning them one tilt of my glass at a time.

I signaled the bartender for another drink as I took the last swig of the numbing elixir inside my glass. Perhaps I could just drink the summer straight out of my memories and be done with the whole thing. Wonderful, even my thoughts sounded like a damn country song.

I sat my glass down as the barstool two down from me screeched back before being filled with a redhead who plopped down with a thud, thumping her elbow on the bar and then placing her chin in her hand before emitting a sigh.

I reckon I was staring harder at her disheveled state then I realized because she flipped her long auburn hair over her shoulder, whipping her head my direction.

"You know, if you took a picture, it would last longer." She plastered on an annoyed grin before turning to the bartender, crossing both her arms on the bar in front of her, capturing my attention with her unexpected attitude. "Bill, will you make me one of those drinks I like? And make it strong."

"Sure thing, darlin'," he nodded, setting a glass in front of me and then getting started on her drink.

I watched the whole sordid scene. She slumped down on her stool without giving me a second glance.

In my experience, females came to bars to dance with their friends or find a cute guy, and they rarely came alone. This one had not only come alone but appeared to want to be left alone as well.

She was intriguing. Her feisty little comment was amusing, and now I was curious as hell to see what her mysterious drink was.

"A splash more, por favor." She held up two fingers, indicating to add a little extra of the vodka being poured as she squished up one side of her face.

I chuckled into my glass as I took a drink, causing her full head of red hair to turn back toward me. I glanced her direction, her forehead rising and eyes going wide. Her reaction caused another chuckle to escape my lips.

"Seriously?"

I held a hand up. "I didn't mean to offend."

She scoffed. Literally scoffed. I wasn't aware people actually did that in real life.

"Yeah – okay," she quipped.

An amused grin crept out the corner of my mouth. This was new. I didn't think a female had ever taken this much attitude toward me. At least not before they realized I was exactly who I said I was.

I don't do anything that could be construed as serious. I broke that rule this past summer and look where that left me.

Leaning forward, I placed both elbows on the counter, glass in hand. "That was amusing is all. No offense intended." I gestured with my glass.

With a look that said she wasn't convinced, she turned away and watched the bartender, who I now know as Bill, finish making her drink. I shook my head, turning my attention back to my own beverage with no intention of reengaging the lovely human next to me. Then Bill set her glass down in front of her and I couldn't help myself.

"A cosmo? You ordered the most basic drink there is and couldn't remember what it was called?"

Gasped.

She audibly gasped as she turned back toward me. "What's with you? You say you didn't mean to offend, but that sounds a little judgey and offensive. Truth be told, you judging my drink choice is why I hate ordering them out loud. Yes, I am aware this is a cosmo. It is also my favorite drink. Are we going to have any further opinions about that?" She took a healthy gulp of her drink.

I'm fairly certain that I have never been more amused by another complete stranger of a human being. She was as fiery as the hair on her head.

"No." I shook my head.

"Good."

"Great." I grinned as I brought my glass to my lips.

She turned her gaze back to the bar, but it took me a moment to do the same. Watching her was like trying to look away from a car accident on the highway. You knew you should focus ahead, but it was too damn tempting not to assess the damage.

I watched as she snuck a few glances out the corner of her eye before shaking my head and glancing forward, focusing my eyes away from the fiery wreckage before I was singed.

She sighed. Yes, actually sighed. Her audible expressions alone were entertaining.

I slowly glanced back over at her.

"Listen." She waved a hand in the air. "You caught me on a bad day. I don't normally snap at random people sitting near me in a bar."

I wanted to say, "How about the poor souls outside of the bar?" but something told me to keep that one to myself.

I raised a brow. She was intriguing, I'd give her that. Everything about this girl so far was intriguing. "This you apologizing?"

The bartender, Bill, cleared his throat, causing me to briefly glance his way just long enough to catch his subtle shake of the head warning me to stop.

He knows her. Well. Interesting.

I lifted my glass her direction. "Apology accepted…" I paused, waiting for her to insert her name.

"Oh, uh," she said, realizing I was waiting for her name. "Aspen." She cleared her throat and snuck a glance at Bill that she tried to hide in her drink.

"Okay… Aspen," I said, peeking at Bill to see his questioning reaction, confirming my fake name suspicion. "Tell me, why am I catching you on a bad day?"

She gave a faux grimace. "If I told you, I'd have to kill you. Then I'd have to go into witness protection, move to the Himalayas, join a tribe of snow monkeys, and be forced to never shave my legs again to properly assimilate so my primate family would think that I was one of them." She sipped her drink and gave a shrug of her shoulder.

"Yikes. We can't have that, can we now?"

"Yeah. No." She looked at me for a moment. "What about you? Why are you sitting at a bar all alone?"

"Oof." I reclined back and let my eyes go wide. "Well, if I told you, then I'd have to kill you and then join witness protection, of course."

"Of course," she chimed in, sipping her drink.

"Then I'd have to move to the Galapagos Islands, where I'd be taken in by a family of indigenous iguanas. Only later to find out that I was merely a food source for their colony."

She grimaced. "Yeah, better not say."

"Better not," I agreed.

Smiled. She gave me her first genuine smile of the evening and it was hypnotizing. Curious.

Who knew one smile from a stranger could draw you in so intently that you had no idea how long you had been staring? I sure as hell didn't. It was completely unexpected, and if I was being honest, a bit troubling. I had no idea how long I had been staring at her like a complete moron.

This time it was me making an audible expression as I sucked in air, trying to snap myself out of the effects of her gaze.

She cleared her throat, being the first to blink. "You never told me your name," she said, casually. Like she was unaware of my insane reaction to her smile. She either was used to throwing men off in unexpectedly extreme ways or was as lost in this moment as I was. It had taken her a minute to blink too.

"You never asked." I swirled my drink, watching the amber colored fluid in my glass so that I didn't keep staring at the captivating redhead beside me. She was dangerous. Watching her was starting to feel more like a compulsion. That was the last thing I needed. The only thing I needed, the only thing that mattered, was the music.

"Well now I'm asking."

I turned back to the auburn siren. Dang it. No. I cannot let my mind go there. Not a siren. Just an oddly interesting female stranger whom I need very much to peel my attention away from.

"Frankfurt," I said matter-of-factly, causing her to spit her drink back into her glass. I mentally counted to three as I reminded myself to start working on the peeling-away-from part. "But my friends call me Fronk," I added. I couldn't help myself.

After a beat of me not saying anything, she set her glass down. "Oh crap, I'm sorry. You're being serious."

"As serious as my new friend, Aspen," I winked. Stupid. Why did I wink? I am failing at wrapping up this interaction. One little smile has ignited that primal instinct from within. I am no better than a wild peacock displaying my feathers to allure the female species. She's definitely dangerous.

Understanding washed over her face. "Well, Fronk," she said, playing up a German accent. *Well fuck.* "It's lovely to make your acquaintance."

An accent. She used an accent. Peeling myself away from this confident, feisty redhead was proving more difficult every time she opened her mouth.

"Likewise."

She laughed as she held up her glass, her eyes drawing me in like a moth to a flame. "Cheers."

What the hell is happening? "Cheers," I replied, leaning over to clink my glass to hers. Unaware of who was having more trouble peeling their eyes away first.

"Watermelon Sugar" by Harry Styles started playing in the background and her eyes lit up.

"I love this song."

"Yeah?"

"Yeah. The beat and the melody are so good. It can be chill, it can focus you. It can even be sexy. It's incredibly versatile."

I chuckled. "Okay. Point taken."

"Mmmm," she let out, enjoying her song. She swayed to the beat as she downed the rest of her drink before signaling Bill for another round.

Bill glanced at me, and I nodded for another as well. What the hell? Might as well. It's just a drink.

"Is this your favorite genre of music?"

She didn't reply immediately. She was with the music. I understood that.

"No. My favorite is music."

"Music?"

She smiled as she nodded.

"Like all of it?"

"All of it," she agreed. "Music is so much more than a sound. It's a feeling. It's a vibe, you know. Like something you can feel down in your bones. There's a place for all of it. A time for all of it.

And yes, before you ask, I do have favorite songs. But as a whole, music is a reflection of who and where we are at the time. We are constantly growing and changing, and music is right there with us the entire way." She paused and stared at me for a second. "Anyway, you don't have to get it. I just have a very deep connection to the music."

I got it. All of it. So completely. For me it had been all about the music for so long, I didn't even know who I was without it. I couldn't stop staring at her because her words connected with me. I felt understood by her. I felt understood by this complete stranger sitting next to me. Maybe she really was a siren song.

I had to will myself free from the transfixed stupor. "No. I get it. I completely get it."

"You do?" She looked at me like she wasn't convinced.

I nodded. "Music is like breathing. It gets into your lungs and molds itself into your being. It's essential."

"Yeah," she nodded.

Bill set our drinks down and she quickly grabbed hers. Holding out her glass she said, "To the music."

"To the music," I responded, meeting her glass with my own.

"So, Fronk," she said with that dang German accent again. "What is one of your favorite songs?"

A grin crept up the side of my mouth at her use of "Fronk."

"Easy. 'Have You Ever Seen the Rain.'"

Her jaw dropped. Actually dropped. I felt myself smiling in response.

"Look at you dropping a little CCR. Okay."

"Don't look so shocked."

"I'm…I'm actually not. I just wasn't expecting that song choice. I totally pictured you as a little rock and roll and a little moody. But there's," she waved her hand around in my general direction, "a little country in there too. But that's probably just the boots."

I glanced down at my boots and then back at her and she winked. She winked. Damn it. I faced forward and took a sip of my drink. If I knew what was good for me, I would stand up right now, wish her a good night, and walk away without looking back. This was…I don't even know what this was.

"Yeah," she said like she had been sitting there analyzing me. "You're like a moody rock and roll cowboy."

I had a type to her. Perfect. Just perfect. *Walk away, Jaxon. Walk. Away.*

She grinned and I knew I was in trouble. Good thing I've never been great at staying out of trouble.

"What song did you expect me to say, ASPEN?" I dragged out her name causing her to pull her bottom lip between her teeth, trying to hide the amused grin from taking over her entire face.

"I don't know, something like 'Going to Mars.'"

I couldn't hide my surprise. "She knows Judah and the Lion. Color me impressed. But they aren't country. Like at all. And I don't think I'd classify them as rock and roll either."

"I said you seem a little country. And you asked what I thought you'd say your favorite song was. Something you could vibe to. I definitely see you blasting some Judah. And they one hundred percent have some rock to their sound. Maybe more alternative rock, but rock nonetheless."

I just stared at her, not able to form a reply.

"I told you. Music is life. I could shock you with my lyrical knowledge."

"And here I pegged your feisty self as a simple Swiftie."

She looked aghast. "Simple Swiftie?" She narrowed her eyes at me. "Aren't we all?"

"Meh."

"No, no. Even if her original stuff isn't your vibe, her post-*Lover* phase fits the whole moody thing you have going on."

I let out an amused laugh. "'Exile' has made it onto a playlist before."

"Moody Swiftie. I knew it."

I took another drink in response.

"What got you so into music, Aspen?"

"My cousin."

"Your cousin must be pretty great to have instilled a love of music in you."

"She was."

"Oh. I'm sorry. Is that why you are here tonight?"

"No. It's okay. That was a long time ago. But um, she's why I got into music the way that I did. Not that I think I could have ever really escaped it. Music is kind of…a big deal in my family."

Bill let out a laugh that he tried to cover with a cough, stealing both of our attention. There was more to this story.

Dragging her eyes back to mine, she went on. "Music was always a special link between my cousin and I. She was magic and her enthusiasm made music magic. She was big on living life to the fullest because she knew nothing was guaranteed. The only guarantee we have is right here in this moment. Music has a way of making every moment come more alive. Ya know?"

She studied me for a second like she was trying to decipher whether or not to say what was sitting on her lips. I guess I passed her examination because on her next exhale she said, "Whenever things got hard or just generally sucked, we always repeated the phrase 'just today' to each other."

"Just today?" I managed, the words trying to get stuck in my throat.

"Yep. Those two words could mean so much. If you were having a particularly terrible day, it would remind you that it was just a day with the promise of a better tomorrow. If something was hard, it meant it was just for the day, because it would get a little better the next." She smiled at a memory. "But it could also be really good. Like an epic summer day where everything just lined up. We could look at each other, utter our phrase, feeling all the wonderful things in that moment, and the other one just got it."

"Deep," I uttered, thankful she'd missed the frog in my throat.

She let out a laugh as she shook her head. "That is why you should never talk to strangers in a bar. Especially ones who have been imbibing vodka." She held up her drink.

"Nah. I'm invested. You should put that on a T-shirt." I fanned my hand across the air: "Just today." I grinned, slipping into the stage charm to counteract the emotion I was feeling.

"You know, Fronk. You might just be onto something."

Our eyes met and I got lost in hers. Her blue eyes sparkling with amusement. I could have stayed right there the rest of the night. A thunk onto the bar stole both of our attention.

"Loaded tots! Bill, you're the best!"

"I thought you might need a little something to mix with all those drinks you like." He smiled fondly at her before grabbing two cups and filling them with water.

She smiled at him and then plopped a tot into her mouth before turning to me. "Want some? They're amazing." She placed another one into her mouth and moaned. The girl literally moaned as her head tilted back in visible pleasure. Turning back to me, she licked salty remnants off her pointer finger. "I swear, you will not regret it."

After that display, the only thing I would regret was the large boner that I would now have to adjust. Scooting over to the seat next to her, I grabbed a tot and placed it into my mouth. She watched me expectantly. "You're right. These are pretty great."

"Right? So good. They are always perfectly salted and somehow crunchy despite all the toppings."

I smiled at her for a moment. Placing another tater tot in my mouth I asked, "Who are you really, Aspen from the bar?"

She inhaled. "Who are you really, Frankfurt whose friends call him Fronk?"

Our eyes held each other's in some unspoken standoff.

Neither spoke.

We both turned toward the bar on a grin.

We each ate a few more tots.

"What if for tonight, we were just Fronk and Aspen?" she asked.

"You saying you want to be Fronk's Ass?"

She snorted. She laughed so unexpectedly that she snorted.

I loved it.

We finished the tots and then got refills for our waters, allowing the H_2O to rinse down the salty snacks. Setting down her glass, Aspen asked Bill for two half glasses of soda water before bending down and rifling through her purse, holding up two packets in her hand when she was done.

"Want one?" she asked with a mischievous grin.

"Eh, what is it?" I asked, unsure of what the packet in her hand contained.

"Electrolytes."

I couldn't help it. I laughed out loud. "Electrolytes, huh?"

"Yes, my good man. Electrolytes. I cannot bring my A game to work tomorrow if vodka is seeping out of my pores."

"And the soda water?" I gestured to the cups Bill set in front of us.

"I swear it makes it taste better."

I laughed again. "Alright." I held out my hand and gestured for her to hand over one of the packets. "I'll bite."

She gave a triumphant grin as she dropped a packet into my outreached hand. "You will thank me when you wake up."

I'll thank her all right. Every time I visualize her licking salt off her finger.

She ripped the top off her packet and poured it into one of the small glasses. I followed her lead, using my finger to stir it in.

She lifted her glass in the air. "Down the hatch it goes."

I watched as she chugged the mixture, my eyebrows inching up my forehead as she lowered the empty glass from her mouth, using the back of her hand to catch a stray drip.

Setting down her finished drink, her eyes met mine. "What?"

There were no words. I shook my head and then lifted my glass like she had. "Bottoms up."

I set my glass on the bar, swallowing the berry flavor down as I turned to see her blue eyes sparkling, watching me consume my drink.

I choked.

I literally choked on the artificial berry flavor. One glance at her pair of blue eyes and I forgot how to swallow a damn drink. Most of it went down, as I tried not to die of embarrassment. Please God, don't let my obituary read "Rising country star dies while taking a shot of electrolytes in a bar." A fate so stupid, it wouldn't even make it into a country song.

"Oh my God, are you okay?" She reached out, wiping away the spray that spewed from my mouth with her thumb.

We froze. Our eyes locking together at the feel of her skin on mine. Forget choking to death. Her touch was going to suffocate me by stealing my oxygen.

I'd come here tonight to be alone, to get away. This girl, Aspen, came out of fucking nowhere. Now all I knew was that I didn't want to leave alone. I was enjoying her company, despite the fact that I knew I shouldn't.

I couldn't go down this road. I did not need anything to distract me from the music. Yet, I couldn't peel myself away. I'd add her to the list of things I need to file away in the morning.

I don't know why I said it, but I told her another song that spoke to me. No explanation, just the song. "'Find Another Reason Why' – Judah and the Lion."

She nodded, retracting her hand from my face like she hadn't just stolen the air from my lungs. "I feel that one."

She didn't need anything other than a song title. She just got it.

"'Castle on the Hill' – Ed Sheeran."

I nodded. "Reminds you of your cousin."

She smiled. "Yeah." She ran her fingers through her hair. "Tell me the last song you listened to on your current playlist."

That was easy. I'd had it on repeat basically all day. I'd never admit it to my sister, but maybe there was something to her inner child mumblings. This song had been one that carried me through the years like a comforting blanket. Though currently, it sounded completely embarrassing to admit to another adult. I didn't want to say it out loud. I just stared at her.

"What?"

"I don't think I'm going to answer that one."

"Come on. Now you have to tell me."

I ran my hand through my hair. "You're gonna laugh if I tell you."

She shook her head. "Nope. Pinky swear I won't."

She held out her pinky. She actually held out her pinky.

"That's because you haven't heard it yet."

She tilted her head forward, sitting there staring at me with her pinky outstretched toward me.

"Ugh, fine. But remember. You said you wouldn't laugh."

I locked my finger with hers. Startled again by the way her skin felt against mine, the words fell straight out of my mouth. "'I'm Gonna Be Somebody.' Travis Tritt."

Her shoulders dropped, her pinky floating down to her lap.

Ah hell. There was a twinge of sadness in her eyes. I would have rather her laughed than look at me like this. Of course she would pick up that there was something deeper about the song for me, that it wasn't a chauvinistic message of male success.

She got the music on a deeper level too.

"Okay fine. You can laugh." I tried to lighten the mood, turning on my stage charm.

She searched my eyes, and I watched the resolve settle in hers, her easy smile from earlier slipping back onto her face, like a practiced stage trick.

"See. I told you there was some country in there," she announced like she had just won a prize.

Who are you, Aspen from the bar?

We grabbed our waters and took a drink.

She glanced at her watch. "Okay, next song decides our fate."

Wait. What? I gave her a questioning look, hoping like hell that she wasn't about to end our night as two strangers that remained strangers. I wasn't ready to end our charade. It had yet to strike midnight.

"You give me a song, and if I know it, we find another adventure. If I don't, we call it a night."

I studied her face, taking in a slow breath, not wanting the dread I was feeling about this abrupt ending to show through. "You ready to get rid of me so soon, Aspen?"

She shrugged a shoulder. "Who says I'm getting rid of you?"

"You're leaving the rest of your night to chance."

"I'm leaving it to fate."

"Fate?" I said in disbelief. I wasn't sure I believed in fate. Fate was like magic. It wasn't real. It is more so that we make our own way with our own choices. Like hers on whether to call it a night or not based on a guess.

"Yes, fate. What's meant to be, will be. But nothing is guaranteed."

"Just today?" I held her gaze steady and a hint of a smile threatened her face.

"Exactly." She nodded.

"What if I don't like the end result?"

"Come on, Fronk. Live a little. Right here in this moment."

I let out a breath. I couldn't believe I was going along with this. I sucked the top corner of my lip in while I thought.

"'Don't Threaten Me with a Good Time.'"

"I'm not," she said. "I'm just asking you to live a little."

I deflated. I'd picked one of our favorite covers to do as a band. It always got great crowd participation, but Aspen had no idea what I was talking about.

She cracked a smile. "Thomas Rhett," she said like duh you idiot. "I was hoping you'd make it a little harder than that."

"You just said to give you a song. I can't help that you have a vast database of lyrical knowledge."

"We're in Nashville! Like I wouldn't know Thomas Rhett." She playfully reached out and nudged my leg as she laughed.

Instinctually, I captured her hand with my own, my body needing the moment to last longer. Her eyes snapped to mine. She was no longer laughing. Her breaths were deep and slow. I could see them with each rise and fall of her chest.

"Maybe there's more country to you than I thought."

Cambri

Who is this guy? Hot. He's definitely set your skin on fire from just a glance hot, but where did he come from? Him and his shaggy blond hair and honey-brown eyes, making me lose track of time.

He was an interesting puzzle with a relaxed V-neck top and jeans that got tucked into one of his cowboy boots down below, like he had left wherever he had come from in a hurry.

The way he kept looking at me, like he was trying not to. It drew me in and pushed me away at the same time. I couldn't quite place how he made me feel. This stranger in a bar. There was something about him: he was alluring, creating this unexpected warmth that made him hard to look away from. Hard to ignore. I tried. God knows I tried.

Nothing today had gone as planned. Not at work and certainly not tonight. Fronk, whoever he really was, was like the first snow of the season; unexpected. I'd thought I would pop into my favorite spot, have a drink to unwind, and then head home to prep for my next move at work. Not in my wildest dreams did I imagine myself living under an alias with a man that sent electricity through me with a single touch of his skin.

Despite needing an evening to myself, my engrained manners wouldn't let my rudeness prevail. My parents' early indoctrination of southern hospitality never could resist bubbling up like a true southern belle. Right when I thought I would be able to ignore the unexpected individual beside me, I could hear my mother's voice in my head: "You know darling, you can catch more flies with honey."

On a sigh I found myself laying out a plate of honey. Somewhere between witness protection and eyes that felt unexplainably familiar, I found myself getting stuck in the sticky sweet. Much to my surprise, I looked up to realize that I didn't mind that I was. This shockingly charming stranger, whom I'd pegged as just another trying to make it musician in an already saturated town, completely took me by surprise.

I recognized something in him. He got it too. He felt it too. The music. He felt the music on a deeper level like I did. It was in his blood like it was mine. I could see it. And it wasn't because he recognized me and was trying to schmooze his way into getting a meeting with my father. It was genuine. It was refreshing. It was a part of him in such a way that it made me feel less alone.

But he was a stranger, and it had to stay that way. If he was in fact a musician, once he found out who I was, who my father is, his self-preservation would take over. It always did. I've seen it happen too many times.

After all, he was most likely a musician. By the looks of him he was a drummer simply by the way he held the beat in the natural flicks of his wrist on the countertop without even realizing it. Maybe a singer. He had the smooth confidence of someone used to commanding a stage.

For now, this was simple. Smooth. Enjoyable. Too easy to mess up by asking more questions. I learned a long time ago to enjoy the moment while it lasts. In a blink everything can change and often does. So, for now, I lived. Riding the high of this interesting connection I felt with this mystery man next to me.

I felt the buzz I had wearing off thanks to the tots and H_2O, making it easier to resist the urge to bury my hands in his perfectly tousled hair. I allowed my head clearing to assist in shaking off that thought. I didn't need to be thinking about tangling my fingers in his hair, even if it was begging me to.

I reminded myself that the increasing sobering clarity was a good thing. He was intoxicating enough without the booze. I needed all the help I could get to stay focused. The way his eyes kept dropping to my lips before looking back up at me, like he'd rather I be shoved up against a wall, did dangerous things to my mind. I was not this girl, but he was making it easy to be.

I wanted to remember tonight like this. The way he made me want to completely throw caution to the wind. I didn't want to taint the memory I was going to have of him with the creep of sobering clarity that got more pronounced by the minute. I wanted to remember the night like this when I came into my favorite escape. I decided I would let fate decide if I should walk away once we left the bar or risk a little more time together.

I asked him for a song and he took a chance, he played along. It only made me like him more. He chose 'Don't Threaten Me with a Good Time' by Thomas Rhett. Ironically, that's exactly what he was doing to me. He lit this fire inside of me. The thought of this handsome stranger igniting these feelings both scared and excited me.

I'd promised her in the end that I'd always choose to live in the moment. For every moment I got that she didn't. So instead of letting the fear stop me, I jumped right in and embraced it fully. When he held his hand out for mine, I took it. I took every feeling that he ignited and breathed more life into it.

It might just be for the night, but for tonight I'm going to set the world on fire. I'm going to embrace every race of my heart from the way he looks at me, every rush from his touch, all of it.

Tomorrow it will all vanish like the lifting of a veil. So, for tonight I live. Right here in this moment.

Just today.

Chapter Three

Jaxon

Our eyes were locked.

I dug my card out and handed it to Bill.

He paid us out.

I stood up and held out my hand to her.

She took it without hesitation. Her eyes never leaving mine.

She slid off the stool, our fingers interlocking.

I glanced down at our hands, not sure what in the hell I was doing. I came to get away from it all. I came to be alone. I came to clear my head.

I didn't come to preoccupy myself with something new.

Someone new.

I definitely didn't come out tonight looking to add any complications to my life. But this didn't feel complicated. This was the promise of two strangers getting lost in a connection that didn't cross over into the morning light. It was the uncomplicated pull of

Aspen and Fronk. It was giving in to whatever this was, knowing that tomorrow Fronk's Ass would be behind him where it belongs.

My eyes found hers. "Nothing is guaranteed."

A ghost of a smile gave way from the corners of her mouth. "Just today."

We left.

Hand in hand.

Ready to live in this moment, if only for tonight.

We walked. We laughed. We jumped in a puddle and splashed a spray of water around us. We walked some more.

She pulled me up to an ice cream shop where you walked up to order outside.

"This place is closed," I informed her.

She gave a sly grin. "Not to us."

She began to knock on the window. Then she started banging on the window. The shop owner came from a back room with a frown until he saw her. His shoulders relaxed and he unlocked the window. "What do I owe this surprise…"

"Aspen," she interjected quickly. Cutting him off before he could end the mirage of her alias. "And this is my friend, Fronk." He eyed her strangely with an amused grin.

"Okay, Aspen and Fronk. What can I get you two?"

Aspen turned to me.

"Rocky road for me."

Her entire face lit up. "Even your ice cream is moody. Vanilla please, Stephen," she said, addressing the second man who apparently knew her this evening.

He nodded and then closed the window to go get our creamy indulgences.

She turned to me and then quirked her head. "What?"

"First a cosmo, and then a vanilla ice cream."

She lifted her shoulders up, holding them there for a moment before lowering them back down. "I like what I like. Both flavors are smooth and enjoyable. Simple yet satisfying."

I watched her for a moment, just taking her in. "Like you."

"Like me?"

I grabbed her hand and ran my thumb across the top. "Smooth and enjoyable." Releasing her hand, I leaned against the window wall. "Definitely satisfying."

Her chest rose slowly. I didn't miss it. It was difficult to look away after. I could see the outline of her right breast with how her shirt was currently pulled. She saw me looking but made no move to fix her top.

The window opened, stealing our attention. She adjusted her shirt and we each grabbed our cones. I reached back for my wallet, but Stephen waved me off. I wondered how many other names I would learn tonight.

"On the house."

Aspen tasted her ice cream, licking her lips clean. "Thanks, Stephen."

He gave her a fond grin, like one a father would give a child. "You are most welcome. Now y'all don't get into too much trouble tonight."

"Me?" she said with mock offense. "Never."

He chuckled and then closed the window. Locking it back up.

She turned back toward me, ice cream on her lips. Lowering her cone, she again licked her lips clean. My restraint to not do that for her growing weaker with every flick of her tongue.

I tilted my head toward the street, and we fell in stride.

"First a bartender, and now the owner of an ice cream shop."

She looked at me, licking that damn cone. "What do you mean?"

I tore my eyes off her lips. I wondered if she knew the torture she was inflicting on me. "These people know you."

"I grew up here. Stephen has known me since I was a child. My dad would bring me to his shop on Fridays after school and anytime we were celebrating something. Bill is more of an adult acquaintance."

"I would hope so," I teased.

She laughed and I grinned. A concerning level of satisfaction settling into my chest at the sound.

We strolled slowly down the street. Both of our feet subconsciously gravitating toward the street musicians playing on a corner. They had quite the gathering.

I pulled out my wallet and took out a few bills, placing them into the opened guitar case. I knew what it was like doing what you loved, waiting for lightning to strike, waiting for the big break.

We stood and listened to them play while we enjoyed our treats. A few couples started dancing. I wondered if she knew how serene she looked as she watched them dance.

I took her free hand and pulled her into a dance of our own. Her grin reached ear to ear as we danced to the beat, careful not to drop our cones. I took her by surprise as I spun her at the same time that she took a lick of her ice cream, causing some to end up on her bottom lip.

I stopped moving and stared right at the drip of sticky sweet cream resting on her plump bottom lip. With her hand that was in mine, I pulled her closer until she was staring right up at me. The twinkle in her eye urging me to live right here in this moment.

I leaned down and took her bottom lip between my teeth, swiping my tongue across it. Her arm looped around my neck, and I gave into it. I gave into all of it. I dropped my cone and cupped both of her cheeks in my hands as I kissed her like tonight was all that we had. Because tonight was all that we had. Tomorrow, the illusion of Fronk and Aspen will have dissipated into the recesses of my mind.

A few people around us started whistling and cheering. I pulled back, both of us grinning like idiots. She grabbed my hand and pulled. We half walked, half ran to an alley with brick buildings on either side, both bent over laughing behind the cover. We righted ourselves and our eyes met. The laughter dying under the intensity of this pull between us.

It was as thoughtless as breathing, us moving toward each other, lips crashing together. I was high on the rush that was Aspen. My hands were everywhere, trying to commit her to memory, needing something to remember her by once we said goodnight.

Her hands seemed to have a similar agenda; I was acutely aware of every placement of her fingertips. Her hands made it into my hair, and she grabbed on tight causing me to emit a low growl which only seemed to make her more determined.

I memorized it all.

Every corner of her mouth, the curve of her neck sloping into her shoulders. The feel of her waist moving out toward her hips. The smooth firmness of her back. The way my hands fit around her jaw, holding her steady for my tongue to explore her mouth. That fiery siren song of a mouth.

The kiss ended, our foreheads touching, both of us breathing heavy. I couldn't do it. I couldn't end tonight and let this be my last moment with her.

"My hotel isn't far from here." My words danced across her lips.

Her hands crept up my chest. "'We Are Young' – Fun," she uttered.

"'Lover of the Light' – Mumford and Sons."

She grinned.

We stepped out to the street, and I led her hand in hand around the corner and down the block to my hotel.

We rode the elevator up silently, each on an opposite wall, watching the other.

The door to my floor opened, and I motioned for her to go first.

We walked down the hall, our fingertips dragging along opposite walls, stealing glances out the corner of our eyes. She bit down on her bottom lip, and I almost shoved her against the wall right here.

The key flashed the light green and the door swung open.

She stepped inside wearing a silent grin that made it difficult not to usher her forward and speed up this slow burn I was feeling.

I walked in and the door clicked shut behind me, my eyes trained on her.

She turned to face me and then stepped backwards until she was leaning against the wall. Me never more than a couple steps away from her. This pull between us not allowing me to be further than an arm's reach from her.

My hand found her waist, my other arm resting on the wall above her as I peered down and whispered, "'Georgia' – Vance Joy."

Barely above a whisper, she sang her next words. A section from the song. Dead. I'm dead.

My lips found hers and I got lost in her. Aspen was every part of my wildest daydream.

Wall kisses turned to moving kisses. Turned to clothes being shed one slow layer at a time as our lips kept crashing back together; they couldn't stand to be apart one second longer than they had to be. I heard a crashing sound when we bumped the table, but the sight in front of me stole all my attention.

Lace.

A matching red lace set is what she was wearing under her other layers.

I took a step back and drank her in. She was mesmerizing. I wanted to devour her body, ravage her breasts, which parts of me were convinced were my own personal buffet, and then do it all again.

She reached back to unhook her bra and I intercepted her action.

"Leave it. You look like winter wrapped in fire."

I ran my fingers down her arm, enjoying as she shivered under my touch.

I feathered my lips across hers and over her jaw, tasting the nape of her neck as I trailed across her. The press of her fingertips into my arms as I did had me reflexively flexing under her touch. I was completely swept up in her.

She moved, I moved. Lips tasted, mouths consumed.

"Fuuuuck," I called out, and not in a good way.

Aspen took a quick step back at my reaction. Initial confusion turning into shock as her hands cupped her mouth.

"What? How?" she asked, assessing the situation.

I dropped down and picked up a large piece of glass as Aspen snatched a towel from the bathroom to wrap my foot, which was spilling blood at an unexpected rate.

She laughed. I looked up questioningly. She laughed harder.

"I'm sorry. I'm sorry." She tried to suppress her laughter. "I'm not laughing at you. It's just this…us…what is happening?"

She laughed again and despite the fact that my foot was oozing blood and the moment was totally ruined, the infectious sound of her laughter had me laughing along with her.

I got the bleeding under control while Aspen slipped my shirt over her head (and damn she looked good in my shirt) before finding a few more pieces of glass by the wall. My brain registered the sound I had heard when we bumped into the table. We must have knocked over the glass and then kicked over the piece my foot found during our disrobing process.

Problem solved, our bodies naturally gravitated back toward one another.

Our eyes met. I breathed her in.

Knowing full well that I risked sounding completely pathetic, I've lived fully in the moment up to this point, so why stop now?

I slid my hands across her waist, fisting handfuls of my shirt, resting my cotton filled hands on her hips. "Is it wrong if I say I still want you to stay?"

I stared into those blue eyes as her hands rose up my chest, eyes studying me right back. I felt her inhale. Her next breath drawing me in as her eyes fluttered closed.

My lips brushed hers, but her mouth didn't part open.

It took me a second to realize that her hands on my chest were a wait instead of urging me forward. I leaned back and was met with her conflicted eyes.

"I um," she bit down onto her lip. "Whilst you might be the sexiest man, I'm not this kind of girl. I needed that piece of glass to snap me out of – you." I watched a light bulb go off in her mind. "You are a mind haze."

"A mind haze?" I asked, amused. I wanted to deflate over not getting to have my way with this gorgeous siren song of a woman, but she kept opening her mouth and intriguing me all over again.

"Yes," she insisted. "You and your moody, rock and roll, country boy self can get a girl entirely swept up in the moment, sir."

She was flirting with me despite letting me down easy.

I grinned as I reached up and tucked a piece of hair behind her ear.

"You telling me I got you to live in the moment, Aspen?"

She gave me a lips-pressed-together smile. "Oh yes, Fronk. I don't normally do one-night stands." She made a faux grimace. "Except for that one night in college. Naturally, there was lots of booze involved."

"Naturally," I agreed with an exaggerated nod. Earning me one of her full-face grins. God I was going to miss this girl. Which is precisely why we couldn't shed our aliases. There was no room for complicated.

"I think I just got caught up in…"

"All of my sexy?" I finished for her. She narrowed her eyes while trying to suppress her amusement. "What? Your words. Not mine. You said I was sexy. Correction, you said I was the sexiest man."

"I was going to say caught up in the moment, Fronk." She exaggerated my name to make a point and I loved it. I also loved the blush that crept across her cheeks.

I couldn't help myself. I reached up and ran my thumb across her blush. She leaned into it, into my touch. I didn't think Aspen could get sexier but bashful Aspen proved me wrong.

"I'd tell you that you were sexy too, to even the playing field, but that doesn't quite cover it. You're more of a captivating siren song that is impossible to look away from."

The look on her face made me wish that this night wasn't coming to an end. I wanted to know what was going through her head. I needed to know if she was sharing in the disappointment I was feeling.

"Tonight was – unexpected," she said. Her face completely unreadable.

"What? You didn't go into tonight planning to be Fronk's Ass?"

She looked down while letting out a laugh. Wearing an amused grin, she brought her eyes back to mine. "No. I did not plan on being anyone's ass tonight, I assure you."

I reached out for her hand. As I lifted it toward my mouth I said, "Well Aspen," before placing a kiss on the inside of her wrist, "the pleasure was all mine." I let go and she retracted her hand, staring at me intently. "I've never had such a fine ass. Must be all those squats."

She nodded along seriously. "Must be."

I noticed as she ran her fingers across the spot on her wrist that my lips touched. "I'm glad neither one of us had to end up in witness protection tonight," I informed her, delaying the inevitable a moment longer.

Her eyes went wide as she nodded along again. "Another solid point, Fronk. Yet I fear that if we don't get our clothes back on one of us just might."

"Well, we can't have that."

"Quite right," she said, slipping my shirt off over her head. Killing me slowly with the action. Handing me my shirt, we both held on, eyes locked for a moment more before she turned and began stepping toward her shed items, picking them up one by one.

She held her clothes in her arms and we held each other's gaze. Neither seemingly able to break our stare.

I rubbed the back of my neck. "This feels kind of terrible, doesn't it."

She forced a grin. "Just today."

"Just today," I repeated.

She got dressed and then opened the door to leave, pausing briefly to look back over her shoulder, popping her hip out. "Thought you'd like one last look at Fronk's Ass."

"'You know it'...Colony House."

She gave one last beaming grin and then she was out the door. I stood there frozen, cementing that last gaze into my memory. My beautiful siren song.

Cambri

The door closed behind me and I pressed my back against the wall outside his room. I took a breath in as I reminded myself why

I didn't have room for more than what we shared tonight. I reminded myself that I didn't get involved with musicians.

Assuming that he was in fact a musician. There were subtle things he did all night that pointed to that conclusion. Down to the tattoo that ran up his side.

I ran my thumb over the tips of my fingers, remembering the way his skin felt as I traced the bar of notes that spilled onto his abs, disappearing into the cut V. Abs like that didn't exist in the real world, they shouldn't exist. I shook my head. Too messy. Too complicated. My family name made it too complicated.

I have dreams, and goals, and a name to make for myself that is all my own. I can't do that and entertain any sort of romantic connection that could interfere with the path I have been working so hard to carve out. Especially not with someone that is this hard to walk away from after one night.

I released a breath. Why was he right? Why did leaving him tonight feel terrible?

I looked over at his door and had to force myself not to knock and tell him that I changed my mind. That I would stay.

This is nuts. You don't know him. You don't even know his real name.

I shook my head and then pushed myself off the wall and down the hall to the elevator.

Sleep.

I needed sleep and then everything would feel better in the morning light.

It always did.

I watched the elevator doors close on tonight and on Fronk. To whoever he really was.

Chapter Four

Cambri

It's official. This might top the list as one of the dumbest things I've ever done. It's just that I love this industry, the music. I love the energy it creates, the way it moves you, that it brings people together, the high you feel leaving a concert, all of it.

The buzz. The electricity. I will never get enough.

Sometimes you have to make your own luck, think outside the box. If you're not willing to fight for what you want, then who will? After that meeting…I had to do something. I had to do something before my dad just handed Easton Davenport this account.

Not this time. Not when they were going to be my ticket to the promotion I have been aiming for.

I gripped the steering wheel of my car as nerves about how I went about this crept in. I took a deep breath. Can't back out now. It's already in motion.

I may have called in a favor at the label and had a team assistant email the band on my behalf. Outlining that though normally we like to bring them into the office, we wanted to get a jump start by sending a PR rep to them. The band thought I was coming out to see if they'd settled in, to be there in person to answer any questions they might have, and to give them a lay of the land. They also might have been led to believe that they got a say in their PR representation rather than have someone assigned to them.

It was a bold move, I know. My dad always said dream big and work hard. I took a huge swing here, knowing full well that this was risky, but some risks are worth taking. After all, if my dad's newest rising stars had a request for representation, why would he deny them? It might just be the push he needed to let me take the lead.

I flipped open the mirror on my car visor and smoothed down my hair, double checking my appearance one last time. I grimaced. I also may have changed my last name on the email sent to them. They were expecting a Cambri Evergreen.

I couldn't have them requesting me simply based on my last name. I wanted to earn their representation, even if I went about it in a more – creative way.

You can do this. One day you'll laugh about this. I nodded a few times at my own reflection and then swiped on some clear gloss to make my pink lips shine.

Flipping the mirror lid down, I gathered my things and stepped out of the car. The heel on my red bottoms slipped on the gravel, causing me to stumble slightly. I gave a quick look around, thankful I was the only one present for the misstep. Off to a great start.

Closing the car door, I continued on. *Your name is Cambri Evergreen* I repeated one last time in my head, walking up to the residence the label had on file.

I gave a firm knock on the door, smoothing down my pencil skirt and adjusting my posture, ready to bring my A game. I had one shot to make a killer impression.

The door swung open and a tall guy with red-tipped hair and a cigarette between his lips stood in front of me, eyes trailing down my person. With a smirk, he brought his eyes back to mine, crossing his arms and leaning against the doorframe.

He put out his cigarette on the doorframe. "Hello there, doll." He let his eyes scroll down me once more, making no effort to hide his action as he flicked the cigarette butt into the yard. "What can I do for a pretty little thing like yourself?"

I mentally fought the urge to tell the guy off. Some artists think they are entitled to ogle a girl just because they are in a band. I have grown up with his type. I'm not impressed. I'm certainly not interested. I plastered on a polite smile, choosing to ignore his entire demeanor.

"Hi, I'm Cambri Evergreen. I'm here to meet with the band about PR representation."

He lost interest the moment I didn't bite. Standing up straighter, and looking half bored, he said, "Right. Come on in. I'll assemble the guys."

By assemble the guys he meant calling out, "The PR chick from the label is here," as we walked through a living area.

I followed the red-tipped hair guy into a room with chairs set up that allowed the band to sit together and me across from them. He gestured for me to take a seat before giving me another once-over. "You sure you're in the right place, doll face? We're a country-rock band. And well, you look a bit prim and proper."

If he was trying to get a rise out of me, it wouldn't work. Like I said, I have grown up around his type. Without batting an eye, I replied, "I'm aware of the music you perform. I'm also aware of what good PR can do for a band trying to break out into this industry. How about you worry about your image, and I'll worry about making sure people care about that image. Sound good, doll?" I crooked an eyebrow up and settled my hands in my lap.

I was waiting for his reply when I heard a low whistle come from the door. "Can we hire her for no other reason than the fact that she can put Everett in his place?" someone asked in a voice meant to carry behind him.

I glanced up to see a guy wearing a backwards ball cap and a boyish grin standing in the door watching our interaction. Great, smashing first impression.

"Time to rock and roll guys!" he called over his shoulder before making his way to me.

Forcing my face to remain calm and collected, I gave a confident smile as I rose to shake his hand, aware of the movement behind him as the rest of the band stumbled in.

"The remaining band members I presume?" I began as they approached to meet my outstretched hand. "Cambri Evergreen. Nice to meet you."

"Cambri is it?" an amused voice asked, causing my eyes to snap in its direction.

That voice.

My eyes bulged.

Oh my God.

Fronk.

I cleared my throat, shaking off the surprise I felt.

"Yes," I said, attempting to remain polished and professional despite my heart speeding up at the sight of him. "And you are?" I asked. Your move, Fronk. How are we going to play this?

A smile escaped his lips as he stepped toward me. "Jaxon. Jaxon Hastings." His eyes held a playful amusement as he held out his hand for me to shake.

"Nice to meet you, Mr. Hastings." I placed my hand in his, giving a firm handshake. I stared up into those honey-brown eyes of his as we held each other's gaze, wondering who would blink first. His shaggy blond hair perfectly tousled today, I wanted to bury my hands back in it. In the light of day, he was still incredibly handsome.

"Likewise, Miss...Evergreen."

I pressed my lips together, fighting back the smile that threatened.

I freed my hand, pulling it back before I did something stupid, like use it to propel me into him.

Jaxon glanced down as I did, his amusement growing. "Before I forget, let me ask you something. You know we are new to the area. Would you happen to know the best drugstore nearby? In case we need to grab something quick like toothpaste or a – band aid in the event of an untimely flesh wound."

My mouth opened, but no words came out. Snapping my mouth shut, a small laugh escaped.

"I will make sure someone from the label reaches out with a full list of helpful things you might need to know as you acclimate to Nashville."

He ran his tongue over his bottom lip, and it took everything in me to keep my eyes on his.

"Thank you, Cambri," he said enunciating my name. "We would be so grateful." He moved to join his bandmates, leaning over and whispering, "The image of you standing in red has been burned into my mind," as he passed, letting his fingers graze my skin.

I stood there for a moment. You are going to be trouble, aren't you, Jaxon Hastings.

I turned toward the band and the guys exchanged glances. It didn't take much to see that they were missing something. Especially with my erratic breathing that I needed to get under control. Jaxon was going to have to keep his thoughts to himself.

We made introductions. After meeting Ridge Salinger, drummer, and Stellan Harrington, lead guitar, I learned that the red-tipped hair guy was Everett Declan, bass guitar.

Then there was Jaxon. I was right that he was a musician. But not just any musician. He was the lead singer. The one the article had described as having tantalizing hip movements. The one whose vocals gave me goosebumps.

Wonderful.

With that realization, I did what I do best. Dove into work. I could not get derailed by Fronk, er, Jaxon, or his goosebump-inducing vocals.

I took my seat and gestured for them to do the same.

Snapping into work mode, we had a smooth meeting. My years growing up in this world getting to shine as I walked the boys through it all. They may have been small town celebrities, but they were very new to the Nashville scene. I got the feeling that they were quickly learning the Nashville game was on a totally different level.

"That about covers it. Do you guys have any questions left for me?" I was met with blank stares that said definitely no. "If not, I will plan on hearing from you soon. I look forward to getting the chance to work together."

The boys shared a glance and then all turned to Jaxon. He was obviously the guy in charge. "I think that about does it. Thank you, Cambri. We will be in touch," Jaxon said.

"Great." I stood, brushing my hands down my skirt to smooth it down. "Let me give you my direct number." I pulled out a generic company business card, careful not to give him my own as to not give away my name, quickly jotting down my cell on the back. Acting like that wasn't always part of the plan.

"We have a few PR representatives at Norwood Records, and we want to make sure you feel like y'all have the right representation for your brand and vibe. You can come straight to me if y'all decide I am the right fit for your representation. I appreciate the opportunity to have met with y'all." I walked my number over to Jaxon.

"The pleasure was all ours," Everett informed.

I opened my mouth to reply, then pressed my lips together, letting the corners curve up into a placated grin.

As I turned back to Jaxon, he gestured for the door. "I'll see you out."

I made my way to the exit. Jaxon a step behind me the entire way. I was hyper aware of each step, every swallow I took, as I made my way to the front door.

I placed a hand on the doorknob and then just stood there. Frozen in my indecision. I found myself needing to know if his mind was spinning a thousand miles per minute like mine was. If the other night replayed in his head like it did mine.

I got my answer as I felt him step up behind me, so close I could feel his breath on my neck. The sensation sending a shiver running down my spine. I turned my head toward him, his fingers trailing down my arm. Gooseflesh forming at his touch. It was one night, but my body craved him like I'd known him forever. Humming to life in a foreign way.

His fingers pressed into my palm, gliding down until our hands were pressed together.

"I can't get you out of my head."

"You shouldn't..." You shouldn't what? What was I going to say? Touch me. Say that. Stop...

"Jax," someone called out as footsteps approached. "Burgers or wings? You're the tiebreaker."

We stepped apart right before Ridge made it to us. His eyes darting back and forth between us. "Oh. Sorry. Am I interrupting?"

"No," we said at the same time.

"Cambri was just leaving," he said with a practiced ease.

"Cool," Ridge let out, eyeing us both.

Jaxon stepped around me, opening the door as he turned back toward Ridge. "Wings," he said easily, like Ridge hadn't just walked into the room watching us jump apart. Like he was oblivious to the moment the rest of us were living in.

"Cool," Ridge said again, taking a step backward. "I'll just, uh…go tell the guys."

Ridge turned, leaving us standing in the silence that remained.

Our eyes met, both of us letting out a small laugh.

"That's my cue." I nodded toward the open door.

Jaxon smirked, holding the door open for me.

"Thank you for your time, Ms. Evergreen. We will be in touch."

My eyes widened as I inwardly cringed at the last name. "Yep," I said, popping the P, making my exit.

Back in my car, I shut the door and then let out a breath as I stared out the front window.

Crap.

That was definitely an unexpected twist. Well played, universe.

I sat there for a moment, just watching the front door. I don't know what I was expecting. I started the car and drove to my condo.

Home, I walked in and up to the second floor where I threw my stuff on the table, and then walked over to the fridge. I grabbed a diet soda and then flopped down onto the couch. I cracked open the can, taking a drink as I stared at a black TV screen. What were the chances? Apparently, pretty great.

Jaxon Hastings. The name fit him. He looked like a Jaxon Hastings. He also looked like trouble. But that might just be the way he made my heart beat faster with just a glance.

"You look like winter wrapped in fire." I played his words and the tone of his voice as he said them over and over in my mind. His touch on my skin sure felt like fire, like I was going to melt under every delicious stroke of his fingers down my arm, back, neck. I blew out a breath and then took a drink of my soda.

I can't do this. I cannot get consumed with thoughts of him. He is a musician. He is signed with the label. And my name complicates everything. I turned on the TV and turned up the volume, drowning out every thought of Jaxon Hastings with the sound.

A day went by, no word from the band. Toward the end of the second day, I decided I would give them 'til tomorrow until I contacted them to follow up on our meeting. It went well, and if they didn't want me to represent them, I wanted to know why. Surely Jaxon wouldn't let the whole Fronk and Aspen thing stand in the way of good PR representation.

I was pondering the reasons why I should give it one more day before I contacted them when my phone rang.

I immediately answered. "You've reached Cambri Evergreen…"

"Hi, honey," my mom's voice cut in. "Sorry to call you last minute, but…wait…what's evergreen?"

I pinched my eyes shut. I made a mental note to check who was calling before answering the phone. "Hey, Mom. Sorry, I thought my…" I looked around for a moment, "florist was calling me back." I winced. That was terrible. I didn't even have a florist.

"Oh yes. Quite right. Well, sorry to call last minute but your father wanted me to ask if there was any way you could come to dinner at the house tonight. He has something he wants to discuss."

"Dinner tonight?" I glanced down at my watch. "Sure. I'll be there." I didn't have plans and when my dad has something he wants to discuss it always works out best to just get it over with. I have learned that one firsthand. Though I wondered why he hadn't just discussed whatever it was with me today at the office.

"Perfect. Your father will be thrilled. I'll let him know that you will be attending as soon as he's out of his meeting. Got to run. Love you."

The call went dead, and I deflated. I was so hoping that the phone call was the one I had been waiting for.

That's it. If I didn't hear from them by lunch tomorrow, I was picking up the phone and calling them myself. If they didn't want my representation, I wanted to know why. I set those thoughts aside and changed out of my work attire and into something more relaxed.

Glancing into the mirror, my thoughts drifted back to Jaxon. The way his fingertips felt against my palm before he pressed his hand against mine. I closed my eyes and shook my head. I have got to stop. One night. It was one night. I cannot lose my head over one night.

Stepping away from the mirror, I grabbed my purse and made my way down the stairs to my garage.

Walking into my parents' house, I flung my purse onto the entry table and then ran my fingers through my long red hair as I wondered what could be so important that my dad had my mom call and invite me last minute to dinner to discuss it. Rather than just add it to tomorrow's calendar.

"Good evening, Miss Norwood," Francesca, my parents' housekeeper, said as she stepped into the room.

"Francesca," I smiled. "Please call me Cambri," I said lightheartedly, trying to drive home that the formality really wasn't necessary.

"Of course, Miss Norwood," she agreed, still not mentioning my first name. "Your parents are already seated in the dining room if you care to join them."

"Thank you, Franny. I will head straight there."

Francesca was a sweet lady, but my parents' new housekeeper took her role far too seriously. Interacting with her felt like stepping into a period film.

Walking toward the dining room I said, "Mom, will you please tell Francesca she can call me Cambri, or Cam," I teased, smiling back at the sweetheart of a lady who really didn't need to keep up all the formalities. It is never how my parents have run things.

Stepping into the room I froze. I wasn't met with the two pairs of eyes that I was expecting. I was met with six pairs of eyes. It was my parents' plus one set for each of the band members that I had just met.

Oh. Crap.

"We have, honey. Francesca insists she likes to perform all her tasks with the utmost professionalism. She takes great pride in it. And we want all of our staff to do whatever makes them feel most comfortable in our home." She paused and took in my demeanor. "Speaking of feeling comfortable, why do you look like you've seen a ghost? And what in heavens are you wearing?"

I looked down at my ripped cutoff denim shorts, heather gray V-neck T-shirt, and my favorite pair of Converse before looking back up at the group. My mother looked horrified, the guys looked confused, aside from Jaxon who remained completely unreadable, and my father was smiling wildly. No doubt he had already put together this whole sordid mess.

"You asked me to come to dinner, Mother. I was unaware that this was a business meeting." I said the last part through gritted teeth.

My mother looked aghast. With a small gasp she said, "Oh no. Surely I didn't happen to leave out such an important detail as that." She gave a polite grin that said so much.

And then I knew. This was a setup. This whole thing was a setup. The poor band members were merely pawns in my parents' twisted game. Sitting ducks, if you will, with no clue as to the immense pleasure my parents were receiving through my embarrassment. It was demented really.

I looked at Jaxon, trying to get a read on him. He looked as neutral as Switzerland, doing a double take when he noticed me studying him intently. He was wearing an amused grin, sitting there quietly. I wished I knew what he was thinking.

It was my father who spoke up next. Stealing my attention from the cardiac-arrest-inducing head of shaggy blond hair sitting at my parents' dinner table.

"Do have a seat, Cambri. Jaxon here was just telling us about a PR rep the boys were considering going with at the company. A real ball buster, they said. Did I get that correct, gentlemen?" He turned to Jaxon, clearly enjoying this far too much.

"Yes, sir," Jaxon swallowed down his amusement. "That is what we said."

This was just great. I had a sneaking suspicion that I had just lost the boys as clients. Because this whole situation made me look insane. Who in their right mind would want a crazy person to represent them?

No doubt they had all made the connection of who I really was. I mean, it would be kind of hard not to when I walked into the room addressing my mother. I had a feeling they were all well aware that my last name was not Evergreen.

Dead. I'm dead.

This was a lot. My parents' little scheme. I'm sure the guys all felt terribly uncomfortable. I know I certainly needed a minute to get over walking into this scene.

Jaxon cut his eyes over to mine as my father continued. "The guys almost gave her a call back yesterday, but I had them hold off.

As the head of their record label, I thought I would inquire about this unknown PR representative we must have hired unbeknownst to me. Don't you think that was a prudent decision, sweetheart?"

"You are…right as usual, Dad," I replied, hoping my voice didn't reveal all of the mortification that I was feeling.

My father placed both elbows on the table. "A Miss Evergreen I believe – "

"Okay," I cut him off. "You got me. I wanted this account. You always say dream big. So, I went out and fought for that dream. Because I'm the right choice for this account, not Easton, and you know it."

My father's grin grew at my outburst. I had wanted to make him see that I could do this. That I was ready to take the lead on this account. But the only thing I managed to successfully do was further my dad's belief that I wasn't.

I chanced a glance at Jaxon, who had a finger pressed against his lips as he clearly was still suppressing his stupid amusement.

Out of the corner of my eye, I caught Everett, sitting there looking like he was enjoying this, maybe more than my parents. Of course, he would love this. Love my childish outburst opposed to my polished professionalism I presented at the meeting.

I clamped my eyes shut and grimaced.

At that my father burst out laughing.

"You should have just told me if you wanted to represent them, Cambri. Although, you were already on the account with Easton. Why all the hubbub?"

I took a step back, throwing my hands in the air. I mean, this couldn't get any worse than it already was – why not. "I did. I did tell you. That's the trouble. And you still handed this account to Easton. You said I could help. Get my feet wet." I forced myself to stop rambling.

Embarrassed by this whole thing, I turned toward the band. "I am flattered that you were previously interested in my representation. However, after this display I completely understand you wanting to go a different route. I will let you all get back to your dinner."

With that I turned and exited the dining room. The moment that had just unfolded taking the cake for top embarrassing moment of my life.

I made a mental note to never subject my future children to this level of embarrassment. I shook my head in disbelief because both of my parents, my own flesh and blood, seemed to be enjoying that cluster far too much.

I rounded the corner when I heard him.

"Cambri, wait," Jaxon let out. I kept moving. "Aspen." I slowed, letting him catch up to me. "Please don't leave without hearing what I have to say."

I stopped midstride and clamped my eyes shut. I wanted this whole thing to be done with but apparently, I was trapped in a nightmare. Opening my eyes, I turned toward Jaxon.

"I'm really not sure there's anything left to say after that." I gestured with my hand toward the direction of the dining room.

A grin turned up on one side of his face as he crooked his head to the side. "I can think of quite a few things actually. Off the top of my head, is this a typical family dinner for you?"

I'm dead.

I'm dead. I'm dead. I'm dead.

"Cute." I turned to go.

"We've got to stop this."

I craned my neck around. "What?"

He gave this look like he couldn't believe I didn't know. If I wasn't so embarrassed, I might have cracked a smile at his antics.

"This whole you keep leaving me thing. I mean, its exhausting. You come. You go. You come. You go."

I bit the inside of my cheek. "When did you know? When did you figure out that my last name was Norwood?"

He pretended to think about it. "Well, you waltzing in talking to your mom was a dead giveaway."

I just stared at him.

"There was also the big family portrait when we walked inside that your dad was pretty proud of."

I scrunched my nose up. These guys probably think I'm a psycho.

"Honestly, I probably should have connected the dots sooner, but it has been such a whirlwind for us since arriving here. It feels like I've hardly kept my head afloat. The only night I took for myself, to slow down a moment, was when I met you."

"Aren't you glad you did?" I asked sarcastically, looking away.

"Yeah. I am actually. That was a fucking great night."

My eyes snapped to his.

"Don't try to say it wasn't. I was there. I lived it with you. If it wasn't for that stupid piece of glass, maybe I would have learned who you really were."

"No. You wouldn't have. Jaxon, I could tell you were a musician."

He rolled his eyes up in faux annoyance. "Ugh. It was my tattoo, wasn't it?" He brought his eyes back to mine with a look that rippled through me. "Such a dead giveaway."

I pressed my lips together in a line. How was he making jokes right now? "I couldn't let you know who I was. Especially if you were involved in music. It just makes things so incredibly…" I trailed off.

"Complicated." He nodded. "I know."

"Yeah."

We stood there holding each other's gaze. What do you say in a moment like this?

"I don't regret it," he said, breaking the silence.

"Jaxon." I shook my head.

"Cambri."

I was unable to ignore the tenor of his voice, or the way it felt to hear my name on his lips – it was concerning really.

"I would be lying if I said I felt anything other than fucking elated when I walked in that room and saw you sitting in the house we are renting." Glancing down, he gave a humorless laugh. "And I know how that sounds." He sounded nervous for the first time since I'd met him. "But when you left that night… it really did feel terrible. I can't explain it. And I don't normally ramble on like this."

He reached back, running his hand across the back of his neck like he needed something tangible to focus on to stop his words.

"Just today," I uttered.

"Yeah," he said in response, and my heart rate picked up. The intensity of his stare making it difficult to take in air.

His words did something funny to my insides. But this couldn't happen. We couldn't happen. The reasons were too many. The big one being that he was signed to the label that contains my last name. I knew enough to know that you don't shit where you eat.

I needed to put some distance between the two of us so that I could think clearly.

I took a step back. Finding my center and reminding myself what put us here in the first place. The job. The career. The life I had desperately been trying to build for myself. There was no room for this. And nothing productive comes from dwelling on a missed opportunity. I just needed to find the path forward.

Starting with getting the heck out of this house.

"Tonight – was humiliating. And I do apologize for you guys having to be subjected to that. But I'm going to go, and I hope that we can both forget about this evening, and everything else, sooner rather than later. Norwood Records will make sure you have representation assigned to you next week."

I turned to leave.

"No. I don't accept that."

"Excuse me?"

"I can't just forget. Just like you can't forget. It doesn't work that way. I also am not okay with just being assigned to some random direction at the label."

"Easton?" I tried not to let the smile spread as I said his name, clarifying the "random direction".

"Easton, Weston, whatever. I'm not interested."

"Jaxon," I said with a surprising amount of humor in my voice.

"Cambri," he enunciated my name.

I bit down on my lip, attempting to tamper the ridiculous amusement he was inflicting with his words.

"Easton will…" I paused. He will what? Give them mediocre representation? No, I can't lead with that. "Well, he certainly won't put you guys in this type of situation." That much was the truth.

He looked at me. He just stood there and looked at me for a second.

"Does he love the music like you do? Is it essential for him like it is for you? Is he going to chase this thing down because it is woven into the fabric of who he is?"

I couldn't move.

I couldn't even breathe.

Nobody would see this through like me. There was no me without music.

But I couldn't say either of those things.

"How could you possibly not want to go with different representation after what you just witnessed? It was incredibly embarrassing and not at all professional. This is the start of your careers. This can't be how you want to begin."

“I’m Gonna Be Somebody,” he uttered, starring directly into my eyes, and I knew I couldn’t walk away.

The song from that night. The one he was embarrassed to share. The song that when he said it, he said with such conviction, I don’t even think he realized the emotion he put behind it. When he revealed it that night at the bar, I could feel how special it was to him, that it propelled him forward. It was more than just a song for him.

I got it.

“Okay,” I agreed.

I can’t explain it. This connection, this tether, whatever this was. A chance encounter at a bar, connecting two souls, fused by the music. The moment he uttered that song, I knew I couldn’t walk away.

I looked at him for a moment. “What about the other guys? I won’t blame them for wanting to run the other direction after tonight.”

“We were all in agreement after you left the house the other day. You know your stuff, yes. But there is a fire in your spirit. There is a determination that is so evident, it’s infectious. That’s what we want.”

“You say that like you know me – you don’t.”

He didn’t say anything in return. He just looked at me with his penetrating stare.

I took a moment. “You need to be really sure that this is what you want. What happened tonight, I can’t guarantee that something like this won't happen again. My family is complicated, and my dad has already decided to give you to his golden boy."

"Easton? Nah. I can't do it. Consider this my first diva moment. I am refusing to sing under his representation."

I bit down to suppress a grin. "You haven't met this guy. He's a shark. He thinks he's got you in the bag."

"You're saying he's better at his job than you?"

"Hell no! That weasel. I have no idea why my dad is so charmed by him, but I run circles around that guy. He's managed to get by, by riding the coattails of people around him. Always managing to shine in the right moment. Nothing would make me happier than exposing who he really is to my father, and Norwood Records getting to wash our hands of him."

I clamped my mouth shut.

"That," he said as he pointed at me. "That's what we want. When the wolves circle, we want that fiery, take-no-crap determination."

I was stunned. Not the reaction I was expecting after that confession.

"I need you to be mentally prepared for what it would look like moving forward with me as your representation. I really can't guarantee that my father won't handle future interactions similarly when I'm involved. You need to take a minute to think about that. I don't want any unnecessary drama getting in the way of our professional relationship."

I wasn't trying to sound repetitive, or like I didn't want to take them on. I just didn't want this band to look up and feel like they'd made a mistake over something as ridiculous as family drama. At the end of the day, this isn't personal, it's business.

"I know a little something about the complexities of the family dynamic. In any relationship, the only person you can control is yourself. Are you confident that your relationship with your dad won't get in the way of your work?"

"The things he decides to do are on him. It would never affect the job I do. That I can guarantee you."

He shrugged a shoulder. "What about at a press conference or another public arena?"

I knew what he was asking. "He would never," I said with confidence. "He would never say or do anything without the utmost professionalism in the face of the public."

"Then it sounds to me like we've found our PR representation."

I began nodding before I found my words.

"Okay."

"Alright then. Welcome aboard, Miss Norwood?" He questioned my name.

I pursed my lips together. "I'm going to regret this aren't I?"

"Nah. Well, probably not."

"Oh," I laughed. "That's reassuring."

He grinned and I shook my head.

"How would you like to proceed from here?" I asked.

"Yeah, uh." He scratched the back of his head. "As my new PR rep, I kinda figured that would be your job."

"Yep. Fair enough. Let's start by making sure we are all on the same page. After you." I gestured toward the dining room.

We barely took a step before Jaxon turned toward me.

"For the record, you earned every one of our votes before we knew who you were. I just wanted you to know that."

I tried not to let the emotion his words caused to spill over onto my face. "Thank you," I managed. I don't know if he realized how much his confession meant to me, that they wanted me, even without the Norwood name.

He nodded. "You said you could shock me with your lyrical memory. Let me feel your spark, Cambri."

My breath hitched at his words, and I watched him, stunned, as he made his way back toward the dining room. All I could do was stand there for a moment, unblinking.

I followed behind him, watching as he rejoined his bandmates, slipping back into his role as their leader; the cool, confident demeanor he wore so easily. I don't know what his demons were that led him to the bar alone the other night, but this role he played well. The strong leader of a promising rising band.

It was my turn to slip into the role I wanted to play. I am ready for this. I was born for this. This is my chance, my opportunity to prove to my father what I can do.

I took a seat and stared straight at my dad. "I believe that you and I have business terms to work out in regard to our newest clients at Norwood Records."

My father's head cocked to the side, as he glanced back and forth between Jaxon and I. A smile stretching across his face as his eyes settled on me. "I suppose that we do."

Chapter Five

Cambri

Dinner went – well. Honestly, it went better than I thought it would. Jaxon apparently wasn't kidding when he said this would be his first diva moment. He was polite, of course, but laid it out very plainly that it hindered his artistic ability and creative focus to be placed with a direction he wasn't going. He needed north and Easton's name was too lateral.

I'd be lying if I said it wasn't incredibly flattering. Knowing the whole production was because he – they – wanted me. The wink he threw my way after he stated his case sent a flutter through my chest, making it difficult to contain my grin.

My father was a bit stunned, but I had to believe he saw the potential of these guys the same as I did because it didn't take much for him to cave and let me take the lead. It was slightly off-kilter as Mitch Norwood has a smooth-talking way of getting what he wants. And truly speaks to the boys' talent because my father isn't usually swayed by a diva moment. But I wasn't going to question it. I ran with that momentum.

I was practically humming with the hopeful anticipation I felt about this opportunity. When this is all said and done, I was going to make him see that I was the right person for the promotion.

There was a moment toward the end of dinner where I sat back, watching the conversations and laughter from around the table, and just took it all in. I was going to represent this band, and together we would chase down everything we were after.

I couldn't wait. This felt like my moment.

I stepped into my parents' foyer after saying goodnight to them. I'd used the guys' exit a few moments prior as my exit cue as well, but I stayed behind long enough to allow the guys a moment alone on their way out. There was a lot that they needed to discuss. A bunch of new information was thrown at them tonight. I figured a moment to chat about some of it would be appreciated.

I was emotionally exhausted after this roller coaster of an evening and was ready to crawl into my bed. I could only imagine how the guys felt. My parents' little stunt aside, they had to make some big decisions; decisions that would affect their career.

Deciding that I'd allowed enough time, I grabbed my purse off the table and headed out the door. Stepping outside, I was surprised to see Jaxon still standing there on the front porch, head buried in his phone. He didn't hear me walk closer to him. Whatever he was looking at had his full and undivided attention.

Stepping up beside him, I couldn't help but notice what had him so distracted.

A girl.

Of course, it was a girl. And not just any girl, she was gorgeous; long blond hair and bright green eyes that popped, you couldn't miss them. To have him this distracted, she clearly meant something to him.

I didn't get the "I'm taken" vibe from him the other night. Not in the slightest. I'm not that girl, the one who gets involved with someone else's guy. Not that we were involved, it was one night. But why was he this enthralled with the picture of her if there wasn't something going on? What did I miss?

"Who's the girl?" I asked, catching him off guard.

"No one." He shoved his phone in his pocket. "No one important anyway."

I blinked twice, taking in the way he quickly discarded his phone and bold face lied to me.

"Okay..."

"Not a topic for discussion." He said it with finality in his voice. Something about this picture had struck a nerve.

Wonderful. Several alarms went off in my mind and slipped me right into problem-solving mode. I was silently hoping that this mystery girl wasn't going to be the first PR fire I would have to put out for the band.

She clearly was not someone of zero importance. But the picture didn't seem like anything special or crazy. It was just a girl in the photo, and she was beaming while her feet were hanging off a dock, toes dipped in the water. So, what was the issue?

"Jaxon," I began. Goal number one was to be as disarming as possible so we could get to the root of why he was zoned out on my parents' front porch. Not to be dramatic or anything, but if this were a horror movie, he would be dead.

"Is there anything else I can do for you, any more questions you might have for me?"

"Don't. Don't do that." He stared off into the night.

"I'm just following up with you. There was a lot to sift through tonight and you were out here alone. I'm just making sure you weren't lingering because you needed to talk to me."

He swung his head in my direction. "Just because I sing in a band doesn't mean I'm stupid."

Whoa. I held my hands up defensively. "I wasn't trying to imply that you were."

"If you have something you want to say to me, just say it. Don't tiptoe around it."

Maybe that diva moment earlier wasn't as big a production as I thought. "Okay fine. Have it your way. If you'd like me to be more direct with you, then I will be."

"Is this Miss Norwood speaking right now? Because I'm getting the impression that there's a difference between her and Cambri. The latter is a girl who's not afraid to speak her mind."

My jaw tensed. "The girl from the picture. She going to be a problem?"

He smirked. "There it is. There's that fire."

I mentally counted to three. "You're avoiding my question." I did my best to stay calm in my reply. If my voice raised, this would escalate, he was teetering on the edge.

He made a point to recoil back. "It's a little bit like Dr. Jekyll. Weirdly calm, a fiery snap, then that unsettling calm again. I'm not sure which personality to address. What should I call you?"

I stood there, lips pursed together, speechless. There was something about him that made it difficult to not let myself get engaged in the argument he was trying to provoke.

I gestured to him. "And what should I call this?"

The smugness on his face grew. "Pure gasoline."

Yeah. He knew what he was doing. Stoking the fire and pushing the right buttons. I looked down and squeezed my jaw shut, trying to keep my lips in a neutral position.

I brought my eyes back to his. This was my job. To tame the artists and make sure things run smoothly. My role was not to get drawn into the drama. I was the one that's supposed to make sure there was none.

Why was he getting under my skin so easily?

I forced a polite smile onto my face. "You asked me to be direct, and I will respect that. In return, I ask that you answer my question."

The corners of his mouth turned up into a mocking grin. "And I'm asking you to drop it."

"I'm just trying to do my job."

"So do it."

"I'm trying!" I snapped.

He shrugged. "Try harder."

My jaw dropped as I watched him exit the porch and make his way to his car.

I followed after him.

"Are you serious right now?"

"As a heart attack," he called over his shoulder.

I picked up the pace. When he reached for his door, I shoved my hand out, preventing him from opening it.

"Why are you acting like a child?"

"I've been accused of worse."

I let out a slow steadying breath.

"Can we please. Have a conversation about this?"

"I told you she was no one. Drop it, Cambri."

"You can see how I don't believe that."

He turned to face me. "Why can't you just drop it?"

"Because your decisions don't just affect you anymore. Your choices and actions reflect the band, your label, and everyone involved. That's the business. If you want to make it in this world, you have to let me do my job. Or this industry is going to eat you alive."

I paused a moment, letting my words sink in. "It's my job to make sure everything runs smoothly. And I do my job best when I am aware of all potential no ones and nothings. No curveballs, Jaxon. Got it? The press will latch onto anything that they can and spin it in whichever way makes them the most money."

He shifted his body toward mine. "And why do you care so much?"

"It's my job to care." I made myself focus on his eyes and not the way everything seemed to change when his body was this close, angled toward mine.

He leaned in, placing his lips near my ear. "That the only reason?"

I shivered involuntarily at the feel of his breath on my skin. The corners of his lips turning up deviously.

Shut it down, Cambri. That's the job.

"We both represent Norwood Records," I said firmly.

He caged me in, slowly placing one hand on either side of me on the hood of his car. "You didn't answer my question. Now who's not playing nice?"

I couldn't think straight when he was this close to me, even if he was being a bit of an ass, but we didn't need to point out every little observation.

"I simply need to know if she is going to be a PR crisis that I need to address. The earlier I get a jump start on something, the better."

He pulled his bottom lip between his teeth, and it took everything in me to pretend that I didn't notice, pretend that I didn't have to force my breathing into a steady, non-erratic pattern.

The smugness melted off his face, and he rested his forehead on mine. "What is this, Cambri? What is it about you?" He didn't need to elaborate. I felt it too. This tether between us.

"I don't know." I answered honestly. Because I didn't.

"Tell me how I get you to stop messing with my head."

"I don't know," I said again. How could I answer that question for him when I couldn't answer it for myself? This whole thing, this electricity between us. Between two strangers. I didn't know how to place it, label it.

"We can't do this…"

"I completely agree…"

The conversation we should be having. I shouldn't be watching our lips inch closer together with each shallow breath in my chest.

"Tell me about the girl," I managed before his lips connected to mine.

He let out a whisper of a laugh, dropping his head.

"She's just a girl. From back home. I knew her for a summer. She won't be any trouble for the band or the label. I guarantee it." He sounded defeated as he pushed back and reached for his car door.

I moved to the side, letting him open it while I attempted to process this pendulum swing of emotional back and forth. It was messing with my head.

"Okay." I nodded. "If you're sure, I'll let this go..."

"Let it go, Cambri."

I nodded once more, and he slid into his car.

If he said I could let this go, I wanted to take him at his word. The trouble was, he looked haunted as he spoke. If I know anything, it's that you can't outrun a ghost.

I watched him drive away as I wondered about the girl from the picture, whoever they were to each other.

Details.

They mattered.

That was the job.

He was the job.

I reminded myself of that before I could get any crazy ideas about him being anything other than that.

He was dizzying and I was going to have to find a way to steady myself in his presence before he knocked me over.

Jaxon

I slid into my car, and then gripped the steering wheel with both hands. My mind was ping-ponging back and forth between the picture from my phone and this unexplainable thing that existed between me and Cambri.

I should not have checked Instagram on my way out of the house. If I hadn't have seen that damn picture. Well, I wouldn't have ended up closer to Cambri than I should have been after learning that she was essentially my boss.

I don't know. I'm not sure yet how the whole PR representative and Norwood line is drawn; the web of who works for who is intertwined so intricately that I don't know which cord belongs where. But something tells me I need to figure that one out sooner rather than later.

Freaking McKenzie. The girl I left back in Texas. Though that's not even technically what I did. She was never mine. You can add that to the list of complicated.

Cambri found me just staring at her. Like some sort of obsessed stalker.

What was I thinking?

I wasn't supposed to bring her here. Nah. She needed to stay across state lines.

If only I'd unfollowed her on Instagram, I could have avoided this mess. But I didn't because we're supposed to be friends, and friends don't unfollow friends, and here we are.

It's all beginning to seem more complicated than it should be.

I don't need complicated.

The band doesn't need complicated.

Complicated gets messy and I'm tired as shit of cleaning things up.

This has to stop. Whatever this pull is between Cambri and I, it ends here. It has to. We have to figure out how to sever this connection before it all gets more convoluted.

This life comes first.

The music comes first.

I ran a hand through my hair. Why does it feel like that is going to be easier said than done?

I glanced up, seeing her standing there, watching my car as I searched for any explanation that made sense as to why I would feel so drawn to her. This woman whom I barely knew. What could possibly explain why it felt terrible separating that night at the hotel or the relief I felt when I found her sitting in my house afterward?

Maybe she really had hypnotized me with a siren song. Every myth has to be rooted in some sort of truth, doesn't it?

I started my car and pulled away from the Norwoods'. I cranked up the music and just drove. I needed Cambri out of my mind and my line of sight before I did something stupid. Like march right back up to her and capture her lips with mine.

She fogs my memory and makes everything else dissipate while I'm too distracted to notice. She is concerningly consuming and not at all what I or the band needs right now.

It's terrifying. This bewilderment. I should be on high alert due to her maddening way of throwing off the balance and creating this perplexing state.

It makes no sense why she is able to mess with my head like she does.

I'm going to need to man up and get my shit together – to figure all of this out.

I meant what I said earlier. We want her to represent us as a band. So, I'm just going to have to figure it out. How to be around her. How to let us both just do our jobs without her mixing up all of my logical thought.

When I realized who she was, so many things clicked into place. She was Mitchell Norwood's daughter. Of course she was passionate about music. It was literally her whole world. She was a Norwood, as in Norwood Records. Names don't get bigger than that in this industry.

Regardless, seeing her walk through that dining room door tonight made me feel more than it should have. I'm going to need to get it together. I'm going to need to forget about Fronk and Aspen. They weren't real. But this life is. This opportunity is.

The guys know nothing about the night we met. It's going to stay that way. I don't want to add any worry to their minds about where my head is. We made a pact before we left Texas, to leave it all behind and only look forward. To attack this opportunity with everything that we have. That's why I took a night to myself in the first place. To clear my head and embrace this opportunity. To give me and the guys our best shot of breaking out into this industry.

We are not in Kansas anymore. That was made abundantly clear the first time we stepped foot into Norwood Records. Nashville is worlds away from our small town in Texas. Each of us had better have our head in the game.

And I didn't just mean me and the guys.

I don't know exactly what happened tonight between Cambri and her parents. I was honestly a bit surprised by the whole thing.

The look on her face when she exited the dining room, I thought there was a good chance that we were going to lose her as representation. But that hunger I recognized inside of her, that thing that lights her on fire, that makes her determined to succeed. The thing that made us want her to represent us – it won out, despite the apparent humiliation she felt.

I saw it in her eyes the moment she decided to take us on as clients. Then she walked back into that room and owned it like I knew she would.

After that initial bump in the road tonight, everything went smoothly. We got back on track and had a productive evening.

Until McKenzie.

Of course Cambri would leave her parents' house right after I opened my phone to a picture posted by McKenzie. With some caption about the perfect day. I should have kept my phone in my pocket. I should have done a lot of things.

You can't change the past.

You can only learn from it, choose to move forward.

Mack taught me that.

I grinned thinking about that old man. I hope we make him proud. He's done so much for me and the guys. He helped us get started. If this career works out, I want to make it up to him. I want to repay him for everything, because I owe him everything.

Chapter Six

Jaxon

Before

I waited. Waited for my friends to leave with that practiced easy grin I have adopted. Life is great. I am chasing my dream, singing one night away at a time. Drinking one night away at a time.

Normally, by this time, I have secured a warm bed to sleep in for the night. But some nights, ones like this, I just don't have the energy for the charade. The carefree wannabe rock star who charmed his way between a beautiful girl's legs to secure a place to rest my head for the night.

Not that a pretty girl taking you home is a bad thing. Most of the time it is where I want to be if I'm being honest.

It's not that I'm totally homeless. My sister would let me crash on her couch if I asked. And sometimes I have. But other times my pride didn't want to appear like I wasn't capable of taking care of myself.

This was a temporary situation and one completely self-created. My mom's place also wasn't too far from here. But if I lived there, she would just worry. She'd worry when I came home late, when I didn't come home at all, and when I came stumbling in smelling like the whiskey on my breath. I didn't want her to worry.

She had worked so damn hard for so long, working two jobs just to take care of me and my twin sister. To make sure there was food on the table and that we had what we needed. The last thing I wanted to do was add stress to her life when she thought we were finally getting the life she always wanted for us. And my sister was. Jade was attending Texas A&M on a scholarship for being brilliant, and she had a job that paid well to help out where the financial aid stopped.

My life was on a slightly different path. I mean yes, I also got a scholarship to school. But my dream wasn't to attend a big university. My heart was in music.

I enrolled in just enough hours to satisfy my scholarship requirements so I could tell my mother that I was taking classes and doing great. She wanted this so badly for us, I didn't have the heart to disappoint her. Plus, school had never been super tough for me. It was easy enough to make the grades I need and then spend the rest of the time with the music, doing what I love.

While my sister had the reliable job, that covered living expenses and what not, my cash flow directly depended on how many shows I could book. As it would turn out, I was not the only college-aged male fighting for a spot to play.

I was close to having the money for my own apartment, but then I spent it on new stage equipment. A necessary evil since money from shows is how I would get the money to pay for an apartment in the first place. The better the equipment, the better the sound, and then the better jobs I could get. The better jobs pay more and well, it comes full circle.

Tonight, will just be another night I sleep in my car with all my gear and be damn thankful that I even have that. It's only temporary.

Besides, one more whiskey and I'd sleep like a baby anyway. It wouldn't matter that I was stuffed in the front seat of my car.

I made my way to the bar, bumping into a burly looking fellow in the process.

"My bad, man." I stepped to the side, creating enough space for us to both keep moving the direction wc were going.

The guy whipped around wearing the kind of grin that either said he genuinely didn't give a shit or that I was about to get my ass kicked. He just had that look about him.

He used his fingers to spike up his blue-tipped hair while he sized me up.

Instinctually, I rolled my shoulders back, readying my posture. I wasn't necessarily in the mood to get in a fight, but I also wasn't going to be somebody's punching bag either. A corner of his mouth turned up and I relaxed a little.

"Nice set tonight." He pulled out a cigarette and put it between his lips.

This place was a smoke free vicinity, but I wasn't about to throw that out.

"Thanks, man. Appreciate it."

"You ever need a bass guitarist, let me know. I've been playing in a garage band with my boy for a while. It could be chill to breakout of the cave eventually."

That is certainly not at all what I was expecting to come out of his mouth.

"Cool, man. How many guys you got? What kind of music do you play?"

He shrugged. "Just me and my buddy. My first mistake was letting him know I could play. He's a bit obsessive about playing his guitar. But I don't really mind. It's something to do. And the ladies love it." He wagged his brows.

This guy was a character alright.

"Anyway, we play a little bit of everything. You mainly stick to this country stuff?"

"Yeah. It goes over well here, and I like the sound so." I gave an indifferent shrug.

"I dig it."

"Thanks, man."

"Don't mention it. Anyway, I'm outta here. Maybe I'll run into you again sometime."

"Maybe," I said like it was an actual possibility. I'd probably never see this guy again. He was kind of a strange dude.

A devilish smirk spread across his face. "Just don't look for the blue. Tomorrow these babies will be red," he said, working his hair between his fingers. "Fits my whole aesthetic more, dontcha think?"

"Right on." I nodded.

"See ya around, singer dude."

He turned and walked away as I gave a two-finger salute.

Shaking my head, I climbed onto a barstool. There are some interesting characters in this world. That's for damn sure.

"What'll it be, son?" Mack, the old man behind the counter asked.

I perked up, not sure what to say because he was also the one signing my check tonight. I wasn't sure if he was aware that I wasn't quite twenty-one yet. I decided to play it cool, like I sat at a bar ordering drinks all the time.

Damn it. I should have had one of my buddies order me something before they left.

"Whiskey on ice. House is fine."

He poured my drink without asking for ID.

Placing the glass in front of me, he bent forward, crossing his arms on the bar. "In my day, if you were old enough to vote and fight for this country, you were old enough to have a drink in a damn bar. You vote in the last election, son?"

"I – I did."

He gave a curt nod. "Great show tonight."

"Thank you, sir."

"You usually stick around solo after you play? Good looking young man like yourself, I'm surprised you didn't leave with your friends."

I didn't necessarily want to lie to the old man, but I didn't want to get into my situation with him either. That's awkward.

"I just needed to wind down a moment. Clear my head." I kept it simple.

"I can understand that. Needing time to settle after a performance. After a show like that, I'm sure I'd need a quiet moment to myself too."

I gave a polite grin, bringing my glass up and taking a sip.

"Whenever you're ready to settle up, you let me know. I'll just be in that back room there."

I gave a curt nod myself and then watched the old man walk away. I took my time finishing my drink, not necessarily ready to go sit alone in my car for the night. It was a different kind of lonely, being cramped in a parked car.

I sat my empty glass down, and then slid off the stool, making my way to the back room. I used two fingers to knock on the back of the opened door.

He swiveled around in his desk chair.

"You ready to settle up then?"

"Yes, sir," I said with a nod.

"Go on then." He gestured to the old couch along the wall. "Take a seat and I'll get you a check written." He swiveled his chair toward his desk, stopping before he got turned all the way around and craned his neck back to me. "Unless you prefer cash."

"Either is fine." And it was. It would be going straight into my bank account anyway. I'd need a check to present to the apartment complex when I had enough to cover rent.

He pulled out a checkbook and scribbled across the front of it. He tore it out before turning his chair back to me, reading the amount out loud. I struggled to keep my eyes from bugging wide. It was more than I had anticipated.

"I know we didn't cover your pay before you played, but I reckon this is a fair amount for a young talent like yourself. I didn't subtract your drink, that one's on the house. Figure it's fair since you'll be bringing those ladies back for more business when they see your name on the calendar again."

I swallowed trying to tamper my excitement. No one had booked a follow up show without me asking for another spot. This was a first and it felt like a big deal.

Nodding, all I could manage was, "Yes, sir." He seemed like the kind of old man that wouldn't take anything short of a sir attached to my response.

"Alright then, it's settled." He studied me for a moment. "If you're going to be playing my bar again, might be worth knowing a bit more about you. You from around here?"

"Not too far from here. My mom's still there in the house I grew up in."

"You driving back there tonight?"

"No, sir," I said, hoping he didn't ask me too much more about it. I didn't really want to admit that I would be sleeping in my car tonight.

He continued to look at me with this piercing look that I didn't know if he could see right through me with, or if it was just one of those things that came with age.

Either way, it made me shift uncomfortably in my seat.

I was saved by a creaking noise that predicated the AC unit kicking on. It sounded normal to me, but Mack looked up, staring at the exposed duct work like it was a cause for concern.

"That old thing has been soundin' weird here lately. I hate leaving it at night in case something happens before I can get it looked at. But I can't stay here and babysit the AC unit and be home to take care of the mutt at the same time. You see my dilemma here."

I nodded in agreement even though I really didn't. Like I said, it sounded fine to me, but he seemed concerned about it.

"Here's a crazy thought. No need to feel obligated but it would be helping this old man out. Think you could stay overnight and keep an ear out for me? That couch isn't too uncomfortable, and it looks about big enough for you to stretch out on. I'd offer you a blanket but I'm afraid I don't have one."

I just looked at him at first, not sure what to say. Stretching out on a couch with access to a bathroom would be a huge upgrade from being stuffed into the front seat of my car. Plus, it'd been hot today.

I didn't want any charity, or I'd go to my sisters'. I didn't think I'd given any indication about my lodging. Temporary lodging. But I also didn't want him to think too long on his offer and decide against it. Especially when it allowed me to stretch out and grab a glass of water. I didn't think he'd mind if I helped myself to a glass of water.

"I don't mind keeping an ear out. Anything in particular I need to be listening for?"

Mack gave me a sort of grin. "Nah. Nah. Just anything soundin' real off. I'll stop by in the morning and get your assessment."

"Yes, sir. I can do that."

"Alright then. How about you help me get this place shut down, and then I'll let you get on your babysitting mission while I go let the dog out."

We made our rounds, Mack showing me which light switch did what and how to shut down the sound system as his bartenders prepped the bar area for closing. I helped him wipe down all the tables and while he let out his last two bartenders, I did an extra sweep of the floor. An offer like this didn't come around too often and I wanted to make sure he didn't regret giving me a place to crash.

I locked him out like he asked and made my way to the back room with the couch. The AC unit kicked on again and I listened for anything out of the ordinary. Again, it sounded normal to me but who was I to argue with a couch to crash on in exchange for listening to that old system.

I didn't know it then, but Mack would find random odds and ends for me to attend to overnight over the course of the next year in this bar. Always somehow lining up with nights I would have ended up crashing in my car. Somehow, he knew. I didn't know how, but somehow, he knew.

As the band grew from just me singing and playing guitar to a couple more guys willing to risk it all for the music, Mack made sure we were taken care of. From sleeping on that worn couch to putting us on the regular schedule until we became hard to book in town.

I owe a lot to him.

Me and the guys owe a lot to him.

That's why when he needed a band to fill a spot for him, we played. Helping him out when he asked because he was always there for us.

Chapter Seven

Cambri

Some days you wake up with an edge of excitement in the air. That's studio days for me. I love the smell of the control rooms, watching artists find their groove, and listening to the music evolve into an album-worthy track.

It also always feels a bit like time travel. Being in the same room that some of the greats recorded in. It's like you feel their presence and approving nods when you get it right. Then, there's the way the sun shifts between the time you walk in and the time you leave. It's arguably disorienting, but I find magic in the entire process.

I met Reckless in the studio for the first time today and, dare I say, the air was buzzing with more electricity than normal. I was ready for this. They were ready for this.

I wanted two things out of today. First, I wanted to hear them live and see how they worked together. To begin to understand their chemistry and how they vibed, so I could best represent them.

Secondly, I wanted to go over the terms of the contract. Give everyone a chance to speak their piece and get everyone's expectations out along with any questions that may be remaining.

Sitting down with them today in the studio was meant to eliminate any surprises that could pop up on contract signing day, when I was assigned as their official representation. That way all we had to do is briefly go over the fine print, per HR, and then put the pen to paper when the time comes.

"Cam, Cam! Bri! The Bri-ster!" Ridge greeted when I walked into their reserved space.

I stopped walking and stared at the baby of the group for a moment. "Did you get all of that out of your system?" I asked him.

Ridge was wearing the same boyish grin that he had worn every time I had seen him. Except this time his smile was a bit bigger, probably because he was sitting behind a drum set.

"Nah," he let out. "But don't you worry, Cam-star, I'll find the right nickname for you yet," he insisted, then smacked the drums a few times.

"No." I shook my head.

He pointed one of his sticks at me. "Yeah," he said smiling, nodding along.

I quickly glanced away, trying to hide the amusement on my face before he could get too sidetracked with this. There was something endearing about Ridge and his boyish charm. That was going to be great for publicity.

My phone beeped, and I quickly dug it out of my purse to turn it on silent. I was shocked at myself that it wasn't already. That is walking into a recording studio 101.

I glanced back over at Ridge, and he was still grinning. A smile broke out across my face at the sight. Ridge was impossible not to like. He brought the right balance to Jaxon's angst and Everett's special cocktail of a personality. Stellan, I would need to figure out more. He was quieter and the hardest to read of the group.

I took the next moment to scan the room and take everything in; the guys, and the way they operated. Ridge was beginning to play around with beats on the drum set. Stellan was tuning his guitar, and Everett was taking a sip of water. But no Jaxon. Everett seemed to catch on that I was looking for him and pointed to the control room behind the glass.

Jaxon had on a pair of headphones and was saying something to the audio engineer. He glanced up and saw me staring at him. A fluttery sensation floated through my chest when his eyes met mine. I scolded myself for having that reaction, but some things couldn't be helped.

I drew in a breath, slightly nervous because the last time I saw him we parted on – interesting terms. He smiled an easy grin and I relaxed as he gave me a head nod in greeting before signaling for me to join him.

Excusing myself from the studio, I made my way toward the control room and to him.

"Cambri, take a listen to what we recorded yesterday. Tell me what you think," Jaxon said as I walked into the room. He was in work mode, which made it easier to stay that way myself without my mind wondering off onto – other topics.

He set the headphones down and asked Mike, the audio engineer, to play the track back. I listened for a moment before signaling for Mike to kill the track.

"The bass could be turned down a bit. It's coming in too heavy right at the start. What if we start it here," I reached down and started the track, signaling at the moment in the music I was talking about. "And then slowly fade the bass in heavier right about here," I said, adjusting the knobs to let them hear the difference.

The boys exchanged a glance.

"That is basically the same thing that Jaxon was just saying," Mike explained. "I told him I thought it sounded fine but," he paused and chuckled to himself. "I'll go ahead and order lunch in for us all. I've worked with Cambri enough to know a perfectionist when I see one. We're going to be here for a while," he teased.

"Mikey, you know I just love creating sounds that feed the soul. Good things take time." I insisted.

I looked up at Jaxon. "Why don't we play it both ways for the guys and see what they think?"

He gave a small nod of approval cueing Mike to call the others in to join us.

Mike played the intro of the song both ways for the group. Stellan was the first to speak up.

"I didn't notice it before, but once you adjusted the sound, y'all are right. It sounds better with the bass turned down at first."

"Cambri's idea," Jaxon said nonchalantly, giving me the credit.

I eyed him questioningly as Ridge threw a hand up to give me a high five.

"Alright! The Caminator. Coming in hot."

A ridiculous smile took over my face as I met his hand in the air.

"Still no, Ridge."

"We're gonna get there," he wagged his finger at me. "You just wait."

I gave a little laugh. "Yay," I let out.

Jaxon looked at me with a lifted brow.

"Don't ask."

"Alright," he said, staring at me in such a way that I felt it in my chest.

"What?" I asked when he didn't look away.

"You told me not to ask."

"Well, now I'm telling you not to stare."

"You sure like doing that, don't you? He smirked in response. "Where would you have me look while we're conversing?"

"Oh, that's what this is?"

He cocked his head to the side. "Last I checked."

I shook my head on a small laugh. "You are somethin' else."

"And you like telling me what to do."

"That is my job."

He didn't flinch. Neither did I, refusing to be the first one to look away. Not being able to be the one that severed this feeling that he had buzzing in my chest.

"Ah geez," Everett chimed in, drawing both of our attention toward him, breaking the spell-like trance Jaxon had created.

"What?" Jaxon and I said at the same time, glancing briefly back at each other before turning back toward Everett.

I rubbed at my chest as the sensation of his gaze holding mine slowly dissipated.

"You two standing there making eyes at each other. This one," he said, thrusting a thumb toward Jaxon, "is still recovering from the last girl that made eyes at him." He said it in jest, but at the mention of who I was assuming was the girl from the picture, there was a noticeable shift in Jaxon. "How bout we stick to the music, yeah buddy?" Everett finished, giving a few firm pats on his back.

Everett was obviously just razzing him, but I could feel the change that occurred in Jaxon. When he looked at me next, there was a hollowness there. The electricity that had existed between us, severed by cold indifference.

Though simply looking at him you couldn't tell. He still presented that cool, untouchable demeanor that he wore so well.

I watched him, intrigued. Wondering how a person could shut something off inside as easily as Jaxon had.

"Always, bro," Jaxon said with an effortless grin. "The music always comes first." He offered his fist for Everett to tap with his.

"Yeah," Everett let out. "The music first, always."

At that they all started howling and chanting "Always the music" while making their way back toward the studio.

No one even noticed as Jaxon uttered, "Always," under his breath like a silent prayer.

The guys may not have noticed Jaxon's near undecipherable word, but I did. I noticed the shift in him, noticed his quiet whisper, and I noticed as I became just another person in the room, no longer feeling the warmth he created when his eyes met mine.

I noticed that I noticed. And then I tried not to notice. He was my client. He had his music, and I had my dream. That should be the only thing that mattered.

It had to be the only thing that mattered.

Jaxon

The moment we signed with Norwood Records, we had a plan. We were supposed to get to Nashville, record some demos, and then be the first opener for Back to Texas on their tour. But once we got here, everything changed. We recorded our demos, and then Cambri got ahold of them. I don't think we could have been prepared for what happened next.

One minute we were in the studio recording the demos. The next, Mitchell Norwood was personally calling us, explaining that a video of our band had gone viral. Because of that, we now had a larger fanbase and a greater opportunity if we ran with the momentum.

We went from being the first opening band for Back to Texas, to the only opening band. We were originally only going to play four songs, and now we had one hour of preshow to fill. It felt like a landslide and things began moving very quickly.

Tour planning was in full swing, and we needed someone to be a direct line of contact to the label, someone to help organize the setlist, a tour manager, a social media coordinator, and someone to be in charge of a million other little tasks.

The guys looked to me for a lot of things, but I knew in the long run it would be in the best interest of everyone if there was a designated person in charge other than me.

I don't mind being the frontman. It goes with the territory of being the lead singer. But we are who we are because of the group. Our presence collectively, how we work together, and what we each bring to the table. I don't want to end up as one of those bands that falls apart right when they are at the top of their game because of internal issues. I have bigger dreams for us.

Insert Cambri.

She commands a room in an impressive manner and manages to get the guys to shut up and listen. When she opens that fiery mouth of hers, you quickly learn that she is an all business, take no bullshit from anyone type person. She is a viper and someone you want on your team in this industry.

And she happens to be a Norwood.

It wasn't what made us want her to represent us, she did that all on her own. But it sure as hell doesn't hurt. Having Mitchell Norwood's daughter as our PR rep gives us another leg up. It's as if the stars had aligned and the gods looked down upon us, giving us their blessing.

Cambri became everything that we needed. I don't know when it happened exactly, but she went from PR representative to our one-stop-shop for the tour.

It was as natural as breathing, her weighing in on the setlist, organizing tour prep details, and then handling everything on the Norwood Records side of things. I don't know if she even slept pre-tour because she was constantly working on something. She was like watching a wildfire grow and take down everything in its path. She was a force. A wild, beautiful being.

I had liked Aspen when we met. I was attracted to Ms. Evergreen. But Cambri Norwood, she was electric. She solidified that no matter how she appeared in my life, I would be in awe of her, want her. I was just going to need to be able to separate that want from need. I wanted her. But we, the band, needed her and everything she brought to the table. Nothing could get in the way of this dream, the music.

I had not come this far to fail. I was not stopping until we were selling out shows and headlining our own tours. I wanted platinum records on the wall with shelves full of other awards. I wanted it fucking all.

When Everett gave his not-so-subtle warning that day in the studio, I wanted to smack him upside the head. But I needed to simmer down and be thankful for his redirection, for keeping me on course. He knows better than anyone, how much this is in every fiber of my being.

I know starting something with Cambri isn't an option. But pretending like whatever this is between us doesn't exists is pointless. It's there. We simply have to find a way to navigate around it.

It's doable.

We will figure it out.

We both have a common goal – the music.

I just needed to focus on the music. Always.

After Everett's comment that day, I dug deep and forced myself to refocus. I shoved it all down because I didn't have time to deal with it. If it could hurt the band or the music, then there wasn't a place for it.

I can't do anything about the chemistry between Cambri and I. It's not something you can just turn off. Or trust me, I would.

People let you down. Whether they mean to or not, they always end up letting you down. The only person who's going to look out for you in the end, is you.

The only thing that hasn't let me down is the music. It's been with me the entire time and it hasn't failed me yet.

So, I'm just gonna need to make a deal with the god of the sea that this siren isn't going to be the end for all of us. 'Cause if my ship goes down, I take the whole crew with me.

Chapter Eight

Jaxon

Before

I can't believe it. The sperm donor, because you lose the title of dad when you abandon your family, wants to help us out.

Financially at least.

Apparently, Jade, and her never-ending hopeful optimism, found him and reached out and invited him to her art show.

Jade is crazy talented. The art teacher at school entered her work in a competition an exhibit down in Houston is putting on to display the who's next in local talent. Obviously, her work was chosen to be put on display. They would have been crazy not to have chosen her for their exhibit.

Much to our mother's chagrin, Jade managed to dig up our sperm donor's information and called him. I don't know exactly how that phone conversation went, but according to Jade he was glad to hear from her. It took everything in me to fight the eyeroll that came so naturally and to keep a pleasant smile on my face when she shared this information.

It took even more when she hesitantly shared that the reason he could make it was because he lived down in Houston. With his new family. His new wife. And his new son that he bothered to stick around for.

That particular piece of information made me feel off kilter. It stung more than I thought it could. I didn't think I could harbor any more resentment toward him. Turns out I was wrong. Finding out his new son was someone he gave a crap about…that news was a different brand of hurt.

One I didn't know existed.

I didn't want to be the one that rained on Jade's parade, but I knew I would be the one who ultimately held up the umbrella when life threw her a sucker punch for believing the man who abandoned us would want us now. But I said nothing. I held my tongue and kept the smile that was getting easier to summon on my face.

Smiling was just easier. It kept the questions, the unwanted helpfulness, the good intentions, and so on at bay. Every good intention had a good excuse when it became tiring or inconvenient.

This one surprised even my cynic heart. The sperm donor said he would be at the show. I didn't know how I felt about it. My emotions on potentially meeting the man who helped bring Jade and I into this world were a bit all over the place. But I held that smile on my face because my sister was excited. She was happy about this. Who was I to take that away?

Jade hardly said a word the entire drive to Houston. Her excitement palpable.

My mom had managed to get someone to cover her shift so she could be here to see Jade's achievement. She tried to make small talk with my sister during the drive, but Jade could barely manage one-word replies. The hopeful smile on her face and rigid posture she sat in making her appear more like one of the art pieces we were driving to see.

I drove both the girls to the event. Because that's what I did. I took care of my family. Getting to drive my mom and sister to Jade's art show felt like I was doing my part, taking care of them.

I had never driven downtown in a big city before. Navigating around the first time felt like driving through a maze. I managed to get us parked and headed toward the building on foot without showing the strife I felt inside. I appeared calm as a cucumber.

Walking inside the building, I hadn't realized that I had come to an abrupt stop, jaw dropping open, as I took in the talent scattered across the room. Everywhere you looked there were amazing pieces. This was so much more than I expected out of a high school art show. I knew my sister was good, but to see the work she was selected amongst, I didn't have the words.

I was so proud of her.

A bitter feeling tried to rise from deep within. The thought of him getting to be here, getting to share this with her when he had missed our whole lives up to this point felt like cheating. He didn't deserve to see her shine like this. This was a privilege that he forfeited the day he walked away.

"You going to just stand there all night or are you going to come see my work?" Jade teased, smiling brighter than I'd ever seen.

It was easy to picture her here. An artist debuting her work in a proper gallery like this.

I shook off the emotion that was fighting to surface, wrestling it back down where it belonged.

"Lead the way, sister of mine."

We found the spot where her art hung and I put my arm around her, pulling her into a hug. "So proud of you," I whispered in her ear.

She turned her head to look at me, beaming with a pursed lip grin.

We heard a sniffle and we both turned toward our mom.

"My baby is hanging in an art gallery." She brought a tissue up to her eye and dabbed.

Jade's shoulders melted like butter. "Mom." She walked over and wrapped our mother in a hug.

"I'm sorry. I don't mean to embarrass you on your big night. I'm just so proud of you Jadelyn."

"You're not embarrassing me. I'm so glad you got to come tonight. I love you."

"I love you so much, my girl."

"Care to see any of the other work?" I asked. Not sure what the plan was. I didn't know if Jade wanted to stay here and wait for the sperm donor or walk around and see any of the other art.

"Oh. Um." My sister glanced at my mom, visibly torn between waiting for the sperm donor and seeing the other pieces.

"You two go. I'll stay here and eavesdrop on what others think about your masterpiece."

I raised a brow. "You sure?"

"Absolutely." She shooed us away. "I'll let you know how much everyone loves it, and won't hurt anyone that doesn't." We turned and began to make our way to another art piece. "Too bad," she said under her breath.

"I heard that." I called over my shoulder, glancing back at her. She held her hands out and shrugged her shoulders.

Nearly an hour later, and we were circling back toward Jade's piece for a fifth time. I made eye contact with my mom as we approached, and she gave a small shake of her head. I felt my fists balling up at my sides. He wasn't coming.

Jade turned toward me. "Maybe he's just running late."

"Jade."

"He said he'd be here."

"Alright."

The end of the night rolled around, and the last few people began to trickle out of the doors. I watched as Jade stood there, watching the door, waiting for him to come running through.

He never did.

I hated him more in that moment than I ever had in my entire life.

He managed to dim my twin sister's light. I didn't know that was possible. Seeing the disappointment on her face as she fought tears out of her eyes, the only color I saw was red. I hoped he didn't walk through that door. He wouldn't be walking out as intact as he came in.

"I'm just going to use the bathroom before we head out." Jade's voice cut through before she turned toward the ladies' room. My mom placed a hand on my arm, meeting my eyes with hers before following after my sister.

"Jaxon?" A man's voice stole my attention. I didn't have to ask. It was like looking in a mirror. It made my stomach knot wondering how my mom must feel every time she saw my face.

"Son?"

"No," I said forcefully. "You don't get to call me that."

"You're right," he stammered. "I should have just mailed this, but since I'm here…"

I took the paper he held out. Holding it in my hand, I saw that it was a check, with more money than I'd ever seen written on one. It was laughable, seeing this amount after managing to barely get by for my whole life.

"I wanted to be here earlier, but this was the first I could get away," he said sheepishly. "And well, I thought it would be better, simpler, to come at the end. You understand."

My eyes snapped up to his. "No. I don't." Then something in me cracked and a lifetime of hurt and frustration spilled out. I couldn't stop it. "Simpler? How was it simpler to leave two children behind? Struggling to keep food on the table." I waved the check in the air. "When you clearly had more than enough. I hope you have lived comfortably in your nice house, with your new family, not thinking twice about the one you left behind." I scoffed, shaking my head, not even trying to hide the disgust I felt for him. "Stop making excuses and just admit that you were too chickenshit to be here."

"Son."

"No," I barked. "You don't get to call me that. You haven't been here. You weren't there when the power went out one winter because we couldn't afford it, when we all shivered in one bed trying to stay warm. You sure as hell weren't here tonight, watching Jade wait for you to burst through those doors like some kind of knight in shining armor."

I tore the check down the middle, letting it fall to the ground. "We don't need your guilt money. We've managed until now and we will continue to manage without you. Run back to your new family while I pick up the pieces of this one."

"At least let me write you another check. Let me help."

I let out an incredulous laugh. "Get out. Leave. Before you can do any more damage."

He looked pained but he didn't try to say anything more. He turned and headed for the doors, stepping through them not a moment too soon.

The girls walked up right as he was leaving. My mom took one look at his departing form and gave me a knowing look.

I gritted my teeth. "Let's get to the car."

The drive home was a quiet one. No one tried to make small talk and Jade's earlier excitement had dissipated. I kept my mouth clamped shut, knowing good and well that opening it would unleash this resentment that was raging inside me.

I felt murderous. My anger brewing like a storm on the horizon. It took everything in me to keep it from swarming out.

I stayed silent.

The rest of the night.

The following morning.

On the way to school.

My heart ached when my sister spoke to me but all I could give her was a weak attempt at recognition. The look on her face in response, made it all feel worse.

I felt like a tightly coiled spring, ready to explode under the pressure.

I made it halfway through the school day before I snapped. Clocking a guy in the jaw for his smart-ass comment. He had it coming.

"Jaxon, my classroom. Now," the world history teacher commanded from his doorway. His words intercepting the fight that was to ensue.

I slung my backpack over my shoulder and made my way to the door.

"This ain't over, Hastings," the dickhead called from behind me.

"Didn't think it was."

I paused. My history teacher stood there in the doorway with a look that said I was most definitely getting suspended. Moving, I walked to the center of the room.

The door clicked shut and I watched as Mr. Agerthy walked to his desk, crossing his arms across his chest as he leaned back, resting against it.

"Mr. Hastings, you are aware of the school's zero tolerance for fighting policy."

"Yep." It was all I could manage, so it's all he got. I was ready to get my slip written and be sent to the office to receive my punishment. I adjusted my backpack on my shoulder, hoping this would be over sooner rather than later.

"Would you like to explain yourself? A chance to plead your case."

"Nope," I said, popping the P.

Mr. Agerthy stood there watching me, pulling his top lip between his teeth. I wished he would get this over with.

He uncrossed his arms, placing his hands on either side of his desk.

"Your paper you turned in, it was well written and had a clever angle. I was impressed."

That was unexpected. I wasn't sure where he was going with this. But I'd prefer to skip whatever life lesson he thought he could impart to me and get this over with.

He continued when I didn't say anything in return. "Meet me in the staff parking lot after school. Three-thirty."

"What?"

"The staff parking. I assume you know where that is."

He made his way around his desk, straightening a pile of papers as he did.

"You're not sending me to the office?"

He glanced up at me. "Would you prefer that I did?"

"No, sir." I shook my head. That was the truth. It would crush my mother if I got sent home for fighting.

"Then I'll see you after school." He nodded to the door. "You better hurry so you're not late to next period."

Dumbfounded, I hustled down the hall, stepping into the cafeteria as the bell rang. I ghosted through the line and the rest of the day, confused why Mr. Agerthy didn't send me to the office and have me sent home in line with the schools anti-fighting policy.

At three-thirty sharp, I walked into the staff parking lot, scanning the rows for Mr. Agerthy. I found him standing against a car that I wasn't sure how he afforded on a teacher's salary.

"You made it."

I shrugged. "I wasn't aware that I had a choice."

Lips pursed together, he nodded.

"You want to tell me about what happened today?"

"Bryce is a dick. That's what happened."

His eyebrows went up as his head tilted to the side, but he didn't say anything.

"You're a bright kid, Jaxon. I'd hate to see you throw away your future because of a stupid mistake."

"Can we skip the lecture?"

He went on like I hadn't just given him attitude.

"What they don't teach you here," he gestured toward the school building, "is that in life there are gray areas, and that everyone fucks up from time to time."

My eyes widened, but I kept my mouth shut. I'm pretty sure teachers aren't supposed to use curse words. Mr. Agerthy went on, like he didn't just drop an F bomb in casual conversation.

"You like music?"

I shrugged again. "Yeah. Doesn't everybody?" I didn't really feel like getting into that it was more of a necessity.

"I assumed you were a musician."

I narrowed my eyes in confusion. "I'm not."

"I just assumed. You always keep a casual rhythm on your desk. Interesting thing to do as a not musician."

"It helps me focus, getting the beats out of my head."

He stared at me for a minute.

"I have something I want to give you." He turned and opened the back door of his car, pulling out a large case.

My eyes bugged out. Was he serious?

"I – I can't," I stammered, realizing what it was. A guitar. Those weren't cheap and I couldn't afford it.

"I figured you might have more use for it than I do right now. I don't have much time to play lately, and I hate to see it sitting in the corner not getting to do what it was made for."

My head started shaking before I found my words.

"Mr. Agerthy, I can't take your guitar."

"Maybe it will help you focus. Let you get more of those beats out of your head."

He handed over the case. My eyes scanning the hard black container before finding their way back up.

I tried to hand it back. "I can't afford this."

He held his hands up. "You don't normally need to afford something that's given to you."

"Fine. I can't accept this."

"Why don't you look at it as a loan."

I watched him for a moment with a slack jaw. "Why are you doing this?"

He paused, giving a knowing look. "Let's just say I recognize something in you."

I scanned my eyes over his car. "I doubt that."

"Looks can be deceiving. You know those gray areas… Well, let's just leave it at that, shall we?"

"I don't understand."

"Not everything has to make perfect sense. I'll see you tomorrow in class."

I watched as he made his way to the driver side of his car, pausing to look over at me before he climbed inside. "Oh, and Jaxon. Next time you feel like taking a swing at someone, put that energy into the music. Who knows? You might just find you like it better." He gave me one more look and then disappeared inside his car. I watched, dumbfounded, as he drove away.

He was right about one thing, not everything makes sense. I stood there completely confused as I watched his taillights disappear while I remained there holding the guitar case.

Chapter Nine

Cambri

Scrolling through the list on my iPad, I felt confident about where the guys stood. They'd nailed their first press interview. Though I had held my breath when the interviewer began pressing about Jaxon's love life.

I don't know why that became such a focal point because Jaxon had stayed on topic and in no way deviated to allow the interviewer's interrogation. She was asking high pressure questions that were not in the prep list we were given. I watched the interview, unable to look away as Jaxon navigated around her prying claws until she finally relented.

I let out a sigh of relief that the mystery girl hadn't become an issue and that nothing slipped about our chance encounter. The way she went in for the kill, I would not have been surprised if something had popped out in a nervous panic or just to get her off his back. Oh, the story that would have been. Front man of Reckless dating Mitchell Norwood's daughter and head of the group's PR.

It didn't have to be true. It just had to sell.

Jaxon handled it like a pro. Even managing to charm a blush right across her face at one point.

I continued making my way through the list of upcoming things to do. Photo shoot for the single we would be releasing prior to the tour, local news interview, and figure out who mystery girl was and why he was so fixated on her.

Okay, that one isn't officially on the list, and it shouldn't be something I have given a second thought. He is the job. I don't get to care about the details of his love life unless they pertain to image control.

But when I'm around him, it's hard not to. I reached up, placing my fingers against my lips. Knowing what whiskey on his breath tastes like is hard to forget.

However, it's not my job to think about that. It's my job to set up all the things and make sure they look good for the press.

I'm their voice behind the scenes that helps them do and say all the right things. It's my job to make them shine. And shine they have.

Somewhere in this process the line of what I do for them exactly has blurred and I have become their musical lifeline. It has all happened organically, one thing leading to another, and I looked up to find PR isn't my only role for this band. When my dad told me I was going with them on the tour, my jaw dropped. It's what Sarah and I had always dreamed about.

"Cambri?"

"Mmhmm," I said, rejoining the brainstorming session.

All eyes were on me waiting for me to expand on whatever they were talking about.

What were they talking about?

"Your thoughts on the set playlist?" Jaxon prompted.

"Right," I said looking down, pulling up the playlist we organized yesterday.

"We were thinking that this should be the finalized setlist for the tour. Do you agree?" Jaxon asked.

"Mmm…no," I said, pointing my finger for emphasis. I sat back in my chair, arms extended out in front of me, palms flat on the edge of the table. I tapped my finger a couple times. "The more I thought about it, I think y'all should end with 'High Dreams'. It's catchy. It has the right vibe and energy. I think it's the perfect way to go out."

My eyes connected with Jaxon's, and I knew that he agreed. From just a look, I knew that I'd said exactly what he was thinking.

What was I supposed to do with that?

"Alright, I'm convinced," Stellan chimed in, stealing my attention. "Jax said the same thing earlier." My head snapped back to his direction, and I felt his gaze in my core; warmth spreading like a wave. "If it has Cambri's vote too, then I'm sold." He reclined back, kicking his feet up on the table.

Jaxon broke my gaze to address the other two group members who hadn't voiced their opinions yet. The loss of his stare scooping away the warm feeling so quickly it left an emptiness in its wake.

A string of colorful words rippled through my mind at the realization.

I mentally chastised myself over the absurdity of it. My head and my heart were on two different wavelengths. The latter was going to need to figure out how to get with the program because this couldn't happen.

Jaxon turned to Ridge, lifting a brow in question.

Something I'd learned quickly about Jaxon is that he is without a doubt the leader of this motley crew, but it is a democracy, not a dictatorship. He likes everyone's voice to be heard and they make collective decisions together.

Though there are definitely times that I notice the other group members tend to just fall in line. Even Everett Declan, despite his rough around the edges demeanor, seems to understand the importance of a good leader.

"Yup," agreed Ridge, throwing a playful wink at me before turning to Everett.

I let out a small laugh before waiting to hear the last vote.

"Alright." Everett threw a hand up. "We will go with Cam's guidance. She hasn't steered us wrong yet."

Mutters of agreement were uttered around the table, and I took in a breath of relief. It was not like me to lose focus like that.

Despite my mind being all over the place, we'd still managed to conquer what we set out to do in this meeting. But I was going to need to find a way to get Jaxon out of my head. Jaxon, Fronk, they have taken up too much space in my mind. They have to go. Both of them. I need to be able to operate as business as usual without any further distractions.

The moment our meeting was over, I decided it was best to head straight out. Out of the building, out of Jaxon's presence, and away from the air-stealing effect he seems to have whenever the two of us cohabitate in the same space.

Stepping out of the building's double doors, I took in a large inhale of fresh air. I stood for a moment, letting the sun hit my face before slipping my shades on. Then I pulled out my phone and clicked the first number in my favorites list.

It only rang once before she picked up.

"Mal!" I greeted her.

"Hey girl. How was the meeting?"

"Oh, you know, worked down the list and got all of our ducks in a row. I think we have something really special on our hands. These guys are special, Mal. I tell you I can feel it in my bones."

"That's what you keep saying. When do I finally get to hear their new stuff?" she asked excitedly.

That's one of the things I loved most about my best friend Mallory. If you were excited, she was excited. If you were happy, she was happy. She was my favorite person to share news with because I knew without a doubt that she would be genuinely pumped for me.

"Soon. Very soon. They are almost done with the mini record they're cutting under the label. I know it's a crazy fast turnaround, but they had a lot of great material already. And though it's a smaller album than we would like, Mitch really wanted something to be able to sell on the tour."

"Mitch?" she interrupted, amused.

"Yes. Mitch. I've decided it's best to refer to my dad as 'Mitch' during business hours, because 'Dad' doesn't seem to land as professionally."

"Right." The humor in her voice was palpable. I could literally feel her amusement.

"Anyways, these guys have put in tons of late nights and early mornings to make this happen. Once I can get my hands on a demo track, I'll give you an early access sneak peek!"

"My girl! Coming in clutch with the hookup!"

"Perks, ya know?" I teased. "Any who, what are you up to tonight?"

"Oh, nothing too exciting. Some laundry and maybe some takeout if I'm feeling extra spicy." She paused. "Why? What were you thinking?"

"Want to go hear a band?"

"Your boys are playing tonight?"

"No. I've actually been thinking it would be good for me to have some space from said boys."

"Said boys or said boy?"

I clamped my eyes shut for a moment. I'd told Mal a brief version of the whole Jaxon situation so she wasn't totally clueless about it all.

"Boys," I clarified, enunciating the S on the end. "I've been catching wind of this girl that is playing all the bars downtown. She's getting quite the following on social media. Want to go check her out with me? You never know, maybe I'll get her signed under the label if her live show is as good as the rumors say."

"Are you ever not working? Like, does your mind even have a wind down function?"

"Listening to music in a bar isn't work." I attempted to defend myself.

"For most people, no. For you, yes, it is one hundred percent work related."

"Are you coming with?"

She let out an exasperated sigh. "Yes. Fine. I will be there supporting your workaholic ways."

"You know you love me."

"Which is why you will understand when I force you into a work-life-balance intervention."

"Come on. I'm not that bad."

She paused. I didn't have to ask if she was giving me the look. I knew she was.

"You need a night off. You've been working around the clock. Your brain needs a minute to decompress."

I said nothing.

"Seriously, Cam. Since you've met those boys of yours, you are all about the J.O.B. I have barely seen you!"

"I know. I know. Things have been crazy getting ready for the tour and Jaxon is arguably more dedicated to work than I am."

"Speaking of, how is that leader singer of yours?"

"A problem. A really big problem." I pinched the bridge of my nose.

"But like a really smoking hot problem. Right?"

"Not helping," I laughed. "I lost focus in a meeting today."

"I think your best course of action is to wash him out of your mind. Just one hot night so that you can be done with it. Right now, he is this elusive, forbidden anomaly. And forbidden always appears so sweet. Especially all wrapped up in lead singer sex appeal!"

"Mal! He is my client. They are my clients. And I…"

She jumped in, cutting me off. "Need a drink and a stiff one!"

"Mal!"

A brief moment of silence occurred before we broke out into giggles.

"You know I don't date musicians. Too tricky. Too messy. Plus, I don't have time to date anyone right now. I can't commit to a relationship when all of my attention is on building my career."

"Who said anything about dating?"

"You're relentless."

"And you need a night where you aren't conquering the music world and can simply relax. Say it with me – relax."

"Relax? What does that mean?" I teased.

She let out a small laugh. "I'm just glad I don't have to go up against you. I can confidently say that you are scary determined when you set your mind to something."

"Glad you noticed."

"You're a mess. You're a workaholic and a mess, but I still love you."

"Aw, love you too, Mal."

"See you in a bit, Cambri."

"Okie – bye."

"Bye," she laughed.

Chapter Ten

Cambri

I was sitting at a table when I got the text from Mallory that she was walking in. I glanced up and spotted her right away. Lifting an arm into the air, I waved my hand to signal where I was sitting. She walked over and yanked her crossbody purse off before plopping down into the seat next to me.

"This for me?" she asked, sipping on the drink I had waiting for her.

"Of course. See, I'm relaxed."

She gave me a look before settling into her chair, stirring her drink with the tiny straw. "So, when does this girl go on?"

"Right after this group. But it doesn't look like they are slowing down. So, who knows?"

"Okay. What all do we know about her?"

"Uh, not much actually." Mal gave me a look so I went on. "That's part of her appeal. She's got this mass following on social media. Yet, she's gotten everyone that has videoed one of her sets to just film her shoes."

"Her shoes?"

"Yeah. And from what I can tell, she's got quite the collection."

Now Mal was really looking at me strange. "She nuts or somethin'?"

"No. It's brilliant. It certainly got my attention. Her music is good, but so is every other musician in Nashville. People come here to be discovered. To be a star. I wanted to hear her live specifically because I was intrigued. There is something quirky about her and her sound that just works."

"Alright then. Here's to random shoes," she said, holding out her glass.

I met hers, clinking it with mine.

The band on stage kept playing and Mal signaled the waiter to bring another round. I eyed her as she sucked down half of her drink.

"Tough day?"

"Not at all. We just haven't done this in so long. Those boys of yours have you clenched tightly in their grimy little fingers right now. Who knows when we will have another work-induced girls' night? Especially if you poach another client tonight. I figured we better make this one count," she smiled wickedly.

"Oh no. I've seen that look before," I teased. "I hope you Ubered here."

"Ya girl definitely came prepared."

"I would expect nothing less."

We clinked our glasses together again before each taking a sip.

Mal was right. It had been too long since I've seen my best friend. I'd almost forgotten how good it felt to swap stories and laugh along with her in person.

She gave me the download on this new guy she was seeing and told me not to be too upset that she was just now telling me about him. That she didn't know if it was going to go anywhere, and that she couldn't tell me about every overconfident musician that thinks they can get a date just because they play in a band.

I waved away her apologetic explanation.

"I know I said that I would never go for the musician type – again," she began. "But this guy, there is something different about him. The way he kept coming back and refusing to take no for an answer," she smiled as she took another sip of her drink.

I raised a brow at her, eliciting a creep of a blush across her cheeks.

She held up a hand. "I know. I know. That sounds totally creepy. But I swear it wasn't. It was…nice. Ya know? I feel like guys don't want to put in the time to woo a girl anymore. Or who knows, maybe they just don't know how to anymore or simply don't give a damn to try hard enough. Anyway, he is sweet, and charming, and my God Cam, he is so drop dead sexy." She fanned herself, eyes widening.

She paused as the waiter delivered our next round, smiling as she thanked him. I threw up a "Thanks" before returning my attention to her.

"And?" I let out. Needing to hear more about this persistent, sexy man.

She sat back in her chair, the corners of her mouth turning up. "And I agreed to go out with him. And so help me all mighty deity I am smitten. I don't want to be that girl, but he has kind of made me that girl."

She sat back up, twirling the straw around her glass. "We've gone out a couple times, but it's always sporadic and when he can fit it in. His band is swamped. They are trying to get started. And…I don't need to explain that part to you. You are currently living the hectic music schedule life right now too." She took a drink, crimson spreading up her face. "It's just, I can't make myself stop thinking about him."

The corners of my mouth twitched, and I chomped down on my lower lip to keep my reaction from fully taking over.

"I know what you're going to say," she jumped in before I could say anything. "I'm giddy-school-girl ridiculous. And I am. You're absolutely right."

This time it was me sitting back into my chair, mouth agape. "Oh my God, Mallory. You slept with him. You've already slept with him!"

She placed her elbows on the table and dropped her head into her hands. "I totally have," she grimaced. Looking up at me, she went on, "I know this isn't like me. I'm not acting like myself at all. This guy has just taken me by surprise and..." She paused for a moment and then asked me, "Am I the worst? Have I turned into a slutty groupie?"

I leaned forward and took both of her hands in mine. "Of course not."

"Really?"

"Really! I'm so happy for you that you met an exciting, sexy musician that swept you off your feet!" I squeezed her hands before relaxing back in my chair. "This guy pursuing you, making my careful best friend throw caution to the wind and get lost in a whirlwind romance, is everything that you deserve! I hope he woos and swoons the heck out of you!"

"Really?" she asked again, with an edge of excitement in her tone.

"One hundred percent! When do I get to meet him?"

"Okay," she let out, looking visibly relieved. "I was hoping you would ask that!"

My watch vibrated, but I ignored it. I wanted to give Mal my full attention to share her news.

Mallory preceded to give me all the juicy details about the first date. Including the fact that that was when she slept with him.

My watch buzzed another time, but again I chose to ignore it.

"I have never experienced anything like him," she admitted. She was gushing and I was smiling so big that my cheeks hurt.

"That's it," she said, wrapping up her retelling of this guy. "He's been the most fun phenomenon. I can't wait for you to meet him."

"I will certainly cheers to that," I said, holding my drink out to her.

"Though, between your two insane schedules, that moment might be between now and never."

As if on cue, my watch vibrated again, and this time I finally looked. I wasn't about to disrupt Mal's story for whatever or whoever could wait at the other end of the message.

I glanced down to see that it was Jaxon wanting to know why I wasn't responding to my text messages. *I swear he has the patience of a toddler. And boundary issues when it comes to work.*

I rolled my eyes before reaching for my phone to send him back a quick reply, so he'd stop with the obtrusive pestering for the night.

C: Out with my bestie.

Call you in the morning and we can talk about the album.

And so I can have a moment where you aren't being thrust into the forefront of my mind.

I placed my phone into my bag and then looked over at Mal. "Sorry about that. The lead singer has trouble turning off business mode. And would you believe me if I said it has gotten worse the closer the tour date gets?"

"Noooooo…" Her expression feeling a bit accusatory. "Someone else obsessed with work?"

I narrowed my eyes at her, and she laughed.

My watch buzzed again, and I glanced down briefly before again picking up my phone.

J: Where are you? We can come to you.

I shook my head at his persistence. *Jaxon, you are killing me.*

C: Jaxon. You guys are my top priority right now. I swear I will get in touch with you first thing tomorrow. But this conversation is going to have to wait until then. TOMORROW.

I hit send and watched as those three little dots immediately appeared.

J: We will be fast. You won't even remember we were there in the morning. Just a few minutes of your time.

I pinched my eyes closed and then let my head fall backward. Taking in a breath before I looked back over at Mal. "Would you mind terribly if the guys ran up here for a second? That lead singer is refusing to take my morning meeting redirect. Apparently, whatever it is simply cannot wait."

She giggled before saying, "It's fine. Besides, I've grown a soft spot for the brooding artist type."

"Thanks. You're the best."

"Tell me something I don't know."

C: You can have five minutes. Make it quick!

He texted a thumbs-up and then I sent him the location of the bar we were at.

After trying, and failing, not to watch the door awaiting their arrival, the guys finally walked in. I took a mental picture of the carefree way that they did.

They had a sizeable fan base from their hometown and surrounding area. When the label released their name for the tour, and their social media presence ramped up, it grew their fan base even more. But in a city full of musicians, they currently could still just causally walk into a little bar without their lives being disrupted.

As head of their PR, I hoped they were able to enjoy the simplicity of that act. Because after the tour and all the press that would come along with it, these boys would not be able to just walk inside a bar, unattended, without being mauled by a sea of fans. Their world was about to drastically change, and I hoped they were ready for it.

Now, as the girl out with her best friend trying to distance herself from said boys, I was shooting daggers out of my eyes at them. Had they, and by they I mean he, no shame?

I was about to give Mal a heads up that the boys had just walked in when her eyes got big. "Don't look now."

"What?" I asked, flustered. Distracted by the warmth that spread throughout me at seeing Jaxon enter with his confident swagger. I attempted to swallow down the unwanted reaction.

"He's coming."

I wanted to inquire more about her sudden onset of nerves, but the oxygen in the room began to dissipate. My chest feeling tight with my own dose of nervous energy. Stupid betraying body. Whose side was it on anyway?

"Who's coming?" I finally managed.

Mallory uttered something under her breath before shoving her face into her glass.

"Cam, thank God you answered your phone," Everett exclaimed. Dragging my eyes away from Mallory and her odd reaction, he went on. "Was worried that this one was going to spontaneously combust," Everett said, thrusting a thumb in Jaxon's direction.

Jaxon ignored him.

"Hey guys," I smiled. Thankful for Everett and his distracting way of talking about people like they weren't standing a foot away from him.

I turned my attention to Jaxon. "Jaxon, what was so urgent that this couldn't wait until tomorrow?"

I didn't miss his eyes trailing up and down my body, taking in my night out ensemble before coming back up to mine on a swallow. Well, if that didn't further induce an internal frenzy of absolute chaos.

I focused on releasing a slow, steadying breath.

"The timing isn't right."

That's for damn sure.

He held my gaze, my heart about bottoming out. "For the hook, on track two," he stammered. I let out a whisper of a laugh. Of course, that's what he was referring to. "It throws the whole flow off. I tried talking to Mike, but he insists it's fine. I figured if he won't listen to me, then he will listen to you."

My head dropped a notch, eyes staying on his. "Seriously? That is what couldn't wait? And you couldn't have just texted me that?" *Do not stab him with a tiny cocktail straw. Do not stab him. With a tiny straw.*

He didn't miss a beat.

"For whatever reason, Mike's not too worried about fixing the track. If you give him a call, I know he'll get on it. Then it will be ready to go for us first thing when we get to the studio tomorrow. And based on your lack of communication tonight, I knew you would be more inclined to give him a quick call if you had incentive to get me out of your hair."

Something I have learned about Jaxon is that he is all business ninety-nine percent of the time. Which, to his credit, will serve him well in this industry. The music biz is part talent, part luck, and a whole lotta hustle. So, I get it.

However, I would also get if he ever needed point two seconds to stop and catch his breath. Or at least give me a minute to catch mine.

I pursed my lips together. There is certainly irony in the perfectionist being out-perfectioned. It was hard to turn it off. I understood. I really did.

I blinked a couple times. "If I do this, you'll leave the same way you came and let me and my girl finish our drinks?"

"Absolutely," he said earnestly.

I stared at him, trying not to laugh at what I knew to him felt like a true emergency, but to me felt like a slow form of torture.

"Okay, Jaxon. I'll give him a quick call. But then y'all are out." I made a shooing motion with my hand to drive my point home.

He gave me a thumbs-up as I took out my cell.

A quick call later, and I had upheld my end of the bargain. Mike was going back into the studio despite being clearly frustrated about it. I grinned as I put my phone back in my bag, unable to not feel proud about a job well done. It was a special kind of high, achieving what you set out to do.

Turning my attention back to Jaxon, I said, "All done. You guys can rest assured that the studio will be ready to rock and roll as soon as y'all get there tomorrow." I paused for a moment, but no one thought my pun was quite as amusing as I did.

"Sheesh, tough crowd," I said, glancing around to the others for the first time. It didn't take long for me to put together that while Jaxon and I were caught up in what we were doing, the others were caught up in something else entirely.

Ridge's reaction to what was taking place between Stellan and Mal was pure enjoyment. Everett looked annoyed. Stellan was at a loss for words and Mal was slightly wide-eyed with her lips pressed together.

It took me a second to get my bearings, but then everything fell into place. "Stellan? Mystery guy is Stellan?" I asked Mal. Truly, I did not see that coming.

Jaxon being all business meant that by default so was everyone else. I was genuinely shocked that she'd had time to meet him and go on a couple dates without me somehow knowing about it. Apparently, the group did not always do everything together.

A smile broke out across my face. "Stellan Harrington, you truly are a mystery man."

Nothing. No response. It was Mallory that spoke up next, and not to me.

"This is your little startup band?" she asked, looking directly at him, but getting nothing back. She smiled, but it was more of a crazed sort of grin. "Startup is playing in your basement, maybe a bar or two. You guys," she paused, looking at me and gesturing with her hand I assume for emphasis, "are about to go on tour. You're opening for Back to Texas. Your band is far from being a garage band. Is everything else you said also a lie?"

Oh no. This wasn't good. I could feel my friend about to self-detonate. The rising tension was almost palpable, like you could actually hear the countdown ticks of a bomb that was about to go off.

Mallory is careful by nature. She is not a risk taker, and like she told me earlier, doesn't date musicians because there is lots of instability there. Not to mention a certain level of trust is required to date or be with someone who is in the spotlight. It is not for everyone.

She took a chance with Stellan to basically feel lied to right off the bat. Knowing Mal, she is feeling validated in why she doesn't date the artist type. She also doesn't like to be made to feel stupid and right now I have a feeling that Stellan has made her feel just that. And she has been drinking. This could get ugly.

"Mallory," Stellan began.

"Don't." She held up a finger. That reaction making it apparent that she really had managed to quickly fall for the guy. And by the look on his face, the feeling wasn't one sided.

"Mallory, I didn't lie to you," Stellan said in his ever-present calm demeanor.

Honestly, if Mal was going to fall for a musician, it makes perfect sense that it would be Stellan. He is a musician in the ways that it counts. He loves music, loves what he does. It is his world. But like my best friend, he is the cautious type. He's not your typical musician with the cocky attitude or the take advantage of all the groupies kind of guy. If Stellan gave her the time of day, it's because he thought she was special.

For Stellan, it's not about the fame. He just loves to play. If his heart wasn't in music, he'd be the perfect dependable guy with the steady nine-to-five job. If I were to have met him outside of Nashville, I would have guessed he was an edgy accountant or something. Physically speaking, the only thing that separates him from your fantasy accountant is the sun tattoo on the top of his hand and the lack of glasses.

"We are a startup band. These guys are my closest friends. We started in a college town. Everything that is happening right now is a stroke of luck. And I can't say that I'm not honestly stoked about it all. But we are just getting started in this town. I'm grateful for this journey. Wherever it may take us. Yes, we are about to go on tour. And yes, opening for a big band could open lots of doors for us. But no matter how far we go or don't, these guys are my brothers. That fact will never change. Everything that is currently happening feels incredibly surreal."

Nothing. She said nothing. Mallory just sat there looking like she was one wrong word from storming off, crying, or both.

Stellan took a step toward Mallory. "I didn't mean to make you feel like I lied to you. Clearly your perspective is very different. But for me, this still feels like we are just getting started. This still feels like the small-town startup band trying to get a spot to play at the local bars."

He said it all so humbly and sincerely. I was trying not to gush for her. Meanwhile, I noticed as Jaxon rolled his eyes out of the corner of my mine. Eliciting a curious look from me.

Everett slapping Stellan on the shoulder is what broke the silence that followed. "Yeah, yeah. But just for now," he said wagging his eyebrows.

I palmed my head. "Seriously?" I said looking at Everett. "Read the room."

Sometimes I just wanted to reach out and clamp his lips shut. Everett is just...Everett. Full of confidence and gumption. He is ready to embrace everything he feels he deserves. Frankly, his moxie will help get him there. He is harmless – mainly, but it wouldn't kill him to dial it back sometimes. Like I told him, read the room. The juxtaposition between the two guys is humorous really.

"You lied to me," she said finally.

"Mal," I cut in. "I really don't think he meant to."

Stellan gave me an appreciative nod before turning back to my friend.

"Can we just go talk for a minute?" he asked her.

Mal glanced at me and I gave her look that said, "I would." Turning back to him she nodded once. Then stood up and collected her bag before following him away from the group.

"I'll be at the bar," a visibly annoyed Everett said gruffly. "Looks like we're gonna be here a while after all," he uttered under his breath.

Shaking my head at him as he made his exit, I thought to myself, "Mainly harmless. But oh, so special."

"Think that will end well?" Jaxon asked me, nodding toward Mallory and Stellan as they stole away to try to figure it out.

"I do," I said confidently. "You've got two fairly levelheaded people who obviously like each other. They just need a minute to sort a couple things out."

Jaxon didn't say anything back, he just absorbed what I said.

We stared in the direction that Mal and Stellan took off in.

"They met at the grocery store, you know."

I nodded. "I know."

"He saw her inspecting apples and approached her at the lemons." I looked up at him and he glanced down out the corner of his eyes. "He couldn't take his eyes off her as we made our way through the store. By the time we got to the frozen section, he was getting her number. Those two just kept making eyes at each other, just happening to look at the same items. It was amusing."

"I think it's sweet." He glanced back down at me. "What? I do," I assured him. "And I mean, why would my best friend not happen to meet a member of your band at a grocery store that just happens to be between the two of your houses. Like fate really couldn't help itself."

"There you go with that fate stuff again," he grinned.

I let out a laugh. At the absolute coincidental absurdity of it all. I could feel Jaxon's eyes on me. And the laughter built.

He turned toward me looking confused. "Are you okay?"

I laughed harder.

He shot up a brow.

I swiped under an eye to remove the tear forming from laughing so hard. "I don't even know where to start. Or how to explain."

How does one explain this situation?

"Cambri?" He looked concerned.

"Yes, Fronk?" The name just slipped right out. My brain didn't even register what I said at first until his face took on a pained expression. Then it sunk in. What I said. And the laughter ceased. Completely and immediately.

We both froze, neither of us able to move or speak.

The music in the background faded and we both lost the ability to perform the most basic tasks. Talk, move, blink, breathe.

I swallowed, needing to end this painfully uncomfortable moment. Maybe if I could push past this one slight, we could go back to pretending that I didn't remember the way he felt against my skin.

I found my voice. "Seeing as our plans have taken a slightly different turn for the evening, care to take a seat?"

"Right now?"

"You don't have to. You can continue just standing there if you want."

Chapter Eleven

Cambri

Jaxon stood there for a moment. "Cambri Norwood," he said matter-of-factly. "Why the hell not." He held my gaze, sliding back a chair and taking the seat next to me.

I suppressed the grin that was threatening, never breaking eye contact. Another standoff. Another shallow breath. Another part of me, though I'd never admit it aloud, starting to enjoy this twisted carousel we were on. Going round and round, stuck in a nightmare I couldn't wake from.

Trying to figure out how to hold on tight enough to not get thrown off. Or allow myself to believe this could be anything more than a haunted memory.

Because I can't. We can't. Nothing can distract from the music, the job, the dream. I won't let it.

A throat cleared. "I'm going to join Everett at the bar." Ridge made his way toward Everett, leaving me wishing I could protest that decision, but not having a reason to without making things more awkward.

He left me. Alone. With Jaxon.

"That was kind of weird."

"I…" Jaxon had perked up, sitting on the edge of his seat, his own protest dying on his lips.

He relaxed into his chair. The suave musician slipping back over him like a garment he wore so well. "You know those artist types. So moody," he teased.

"And vexing." I pressed my lips together before I could say more.

His eyes narrowed at me. "You find me vexing?"

"Don't flatter yourself. I was speaking of Ridge."

A brow went up. "You find Ridge vexing?"

Sweet, happy go lucky Ridge. Whom absolutely no one found vexing.

"You're insufferable."

He couldn't hide his amusement

"Do go on."

I shot him a look.

"Truly, Cambri. I find this word game of yours rather entertaining. I'd love to hear what other words you'd use to describe me."

"I bet you would," I said under my breath, picking up my drink and taking a sip.

"Still drinking those drinks you like I see."

Paralyzed. I momentarily forgot how to move.

Slowly, I forced my drink back down, setting it on the table.

Did we not just recover from the last slip?

Fine. If that's how he wants to play it.

"And I had to order it by name," I grimaced.

He grimaced right back. "I'm sure that was difficult."

This is what's difficult. Slipping back into Aspen and Fronk. How is this not killing him like it is me?

I nodded. "Truly."

Jaxon reached over and placed his hand on top of mine. "How did you manage?"

I managed by slipping my hand out from under his. Fine, more like yanking it away because the contact from his skin felt like an electric jolt. It was hard enough sitting here alone with him, no work to distract us, without him physically touching me.

If I'd blinked, I would have missed it. His exterior slipping. The expression that briefly crossed his face. He recovered quickly, relaxing into his chair.

"What are y'all doing in a dive bar tonight?"

I studied his eyes for a moment. This back-and-forth momentum, it wasn't as easy on him as he first made it appear.

"Came to hear a girl that's taking the town by storm. Girl power and what not."

"Cambri Norwood, I thought we were your main focus and that we had your 'undivided attention'. Are you here for another client?"

I gave a tilt of my head. "Potential client. I wanted to see her live first. Then I'll think about approaching her with an offer of representation. But rest assured, there would be nothing official until after the tour. You dorks still have my undivided attention."

He shifted closer. "Here I thought you were trying to replace us. I might have had to seriously consider the Galapagos in that case."

Heart. Beat. Thud. Why was he doing this?

"Oof. Thank goodness we avoided that. Or I would have had to start growing out my leg hair to begin assimilating with the snow monkeys," I informed him, without missing a beat. Refusing to let him knock me off balance with his comment. "I simply could not remain in civilization if I drove a rising star to his death by iguana."

I don't know what he was playing at, but the smirk that stretched across his face at my words was lethal. Boom. Dead. I was dead.

Lost in reminding myself to breathe, I missed the girl I'd come to see taking the stage. Her voice greeting the crowd snapping my attention to her.

"Here's your girl," Jaxon said, reclining back in his chair. "Let's see what she's got."

The music started and she opened her mouth, cueing Jaxon to look over at me and give an approving nod right off the bat. She was young, but she had IT. That special something that made her stand out. She captured my full attention as excited adrenaline set in.

"This girl is somethin'," Jaxon said, leaning over to me. Chuckling, he went on. "By the look on your face, I don't have to be telling you that. You have this little twinkle in your eye that requires me to ask this next question."

I glanced at him.

"Do I need to hold you back when she's done? Because you look a bit crazed."

The music taking over, soothing me to my core, caused a genuinely carefree laugh to escape my lips. I stuck my tongue out at him in response.

"Oh, it's gonna be like that?" He scooted his chair closer.

"Yeah," I insisted. "It's gonna be like that."

"Well, Ms. Norwood, I may just have to speak to HR about feeling harassed in the workplace."

I picked up my drink and gave a slight shrug. "Your complaint will be noted on file and addressed in a timely manner. I assure you." I sipped my drink.

He opened his mouth to say something, but she broke out into the chorus of an already catchy tune, stealing both of our attention.

I'm scoopin' corn and mashed potatoes on your plate.
Don't really wanna know what's makin' you late.
I'm watchin' that back door boy yeah, I'm ready to play.
There's more than just corn and mashed potatoes on your plate.
Come have a taste.

We both sat there, mouths agape.

I finally found my words. "Did she really just sing about corn and mashed potatoes?" I asked loud enough for him to hear me.

"Yup."

"And make it crazy catchy?"

"Yup."

I dragged my eyes to Jaxon who was still sitting there watching the stage, perplexed.

As if he could feel me, he met my gaze.

"What the hell just happened?" he asked.

I shook my head side to side. Bringing my arms up in a shrug. "I genuinely. Do not know."

She sang the chorus again and Jaxon scooted his chair closer, leaning over so he didn't have to shout.

I was hyper aware of his close proximity. His breath trickling across me as he spoke. "Did she poison him? Or is that a come-hither moment?"

It kind of sounded more like a woman scorned to me. It was upbeat, catchy, with a hint of poison. I loved it. I turned my head with a reply.

He was still turned too close to me. A centimeter more and I would have brushed his face with my own.

My breath hitched. Neither of us moved.

His hand reached out, fingers wrapping behind the base of my head as his thumb brushed along my jaw.

My heart started beating erratically, the air feeling thicker, harder to take in.

"Jaxon," I whispered. "What are you doing?"

"I don't know," he whispered back, so close I didn't know where his breath stopped and mine began.

I glanced at his lips.

"'Iris' – The Goo Goo Dolls," he breathed.

His lips touched mine and everyone else melted away. I felt his tongue asking for permission and my lips parted in response.

"Get a room." The sound of Everett's voice broke through my thoughts bringing me back to the reality of the situation. I pushed my chair back with a screech, causing Everett to bark out a laugh. Jaxon pinning him with a death glare.

I looked back and forth between the guys and shot out of my chair.

"I need a drink," I said, making my way over to the bar.

What was I thinking? Line. I am crossing a line that does not need to be crossed. We are about to go on tour. We don't need any hiccups along the way. This is a big moment for all of us. We need to be one hundred percent focused. On the music. Only on the music.

Jaxon

If looks could kill, mine would certainly do the trick right now.

"Come on, man. Don't look at me like that," Everett laughed. When I didn't say anything, he threw his hands up in defense. "What? I'm doing us all a favor. That has disaster written all over it. Besides, we don't need two lovesick puppies going into this tour."

He glanced around. "Speaking of lovesick puppies. Where the hell did Stellan run off to?" He brought his attention back to me. "Whatever. We need you to have your head in the game. You're the glue that holds us all together."

"You think I don't fucking know that?"

I sat back in my chair, running a hand through my hair. I didn't like it, but he was right. I hated that he was right and even more that he knew that I knew it. I didn't ask for this position. It just happened.

"My head is in the game. This – was just a momentary loss of judgement."

Everett arched a brow.

"Stop looking at me like that. I said I got this, okay?" I looked away from him, unable to look my friend in the eye knowing he would see straight through my bullshit. As much as I would like it to be true, I really didn't have a grasp on any of it when it came to Cambri. It was incredibly frustrating.

I didn't know what I was doing tonight. Or where my head was. It got muddled so quickly. I came here for the band. To make sure that we were where we needed to be so that we could be successful in the studio tomorrow.

There's just something about her. I can't explain it. It's frustrating that I can lose my head around her, get swallowed up by her orbit. It's a problem. A really big problem that I need to find a way to handle.

She was killing me in her night-out getup. Her long legs stretching out from that leather skirt. Her scent breaking through, pulling me into her like a moth to a flame. Beckoning me toward her until it was too late. She was too close, and I was debilitated. Held captive by her energy that seems to draw me in.

My inhibitions were lowered. The music playing, weaving through the air, wrapping around us like an invisible thread that pulled tight. Drawing us toward each other. Drifting closer together until I could feel the heat radiating between us.

I tasted her lips. The feel of her touch igniting a fuse. I was gone.

Everett poured a bucket of ice water over us. Putting out the flame before we could burn this whole place down.

I should be thankful. I shouldn't want to deck my bandmate, my friend, square in the jaw. I shouldn't want a lot of things.

I felt his hand on my shoulder. "Come on, man, I just don't want to see you all bent out of shape over her. Like after McKenzie."

I jerked away from him. "Fuck off, Everett."

He gave me a look that had me deflating into my chair.

I ran a hand down my face, practically whispering the next words. "This isn't the same thing."

I don't know how to explain that to him when it doesn't make sense to myself. It's a feeling. I just know. I thought I was falling in love with McKenzie. In reality, I think I fell for winning her. Needing her to love me back. Needing her to choose me over him. Like I said, it doesn't even really make sense to me.

A shrink would probably sum it up as some sort of daddy abandonment issues.

Cambri came out of nowhere. It was unwanted and unexpected. Kenz told me one time that Ryan felt necessary. I didn't get it then. I get it now. Though everything in me wishes that I didn't.

It was scary, and inconvenient, and didn't fit at all into my carefully constructed plan. Cambri was a hazard I needed to figure out how to safely move around.

"How is it then?"

I met Everett's stare straight on. "I don't have the slightest damn clue." I don't think either of us blinked. "Sometimes I just want to walk away." That was the most honest thing I could've said, and it made me feel uncomfortable. I ran my hand across the back of my neck.

"So, walk away. We walk away."

As tempting as that sounds, walking away from Cambri would be turning our backs on this opportunity. I wouldn't do that. I wouldn't jeopardize all of this, for everyone, because of my own shortcoming.

I shook my head. "I can't. We can't. That would be incredibly stupid."

He knew that just as much as I did. And though I appreciated the sentiment, I wasn't dumb enough to piss on this opportunity.

"I just need her to stop being her." That for sure didn't make any sense. "To stop with the come-hither glances and biting down on her fuckable lips." I tried to clarify, but only made it worse. So much worse.

Again, Everett raised a brow, the prick not even trying to hide the amusement on his face.

I'd hit a new low; I was confessing things to Everett that I had no business confessing. I closed my eyes for a moment. "Shit. Please forget everything I just said. Immediately." I tried to laugh it off.

I'd told myself that I would never admit out loud how I felt about Cambri, how she managed to get under my skin, in any capacity.

Saying it out loud made it too real. Real makes you vulnerable. Keeping my feelings inside is what I needed to do. For everyone's sake.

Everett's eyes went wide. "Shit. You are all sorts of fucked."

I released a breath, reaching for Cambri's unfinished drink on the table. "You have no idea," I admitted before shooting it back in one gulp, causing Everett to bark out a laugh.

Setting the glass down, I stared at it. "Huh." These are delicious.

Everett took the seat next to me, shaking his head with a smirk on his face. "What's the plan?"

I looked at my bandmate. "Shove it down and try my darnedest to ignore it."

"Because that's going well for you."

I sat back in my chair, clenching my jaw.

He was right. I needed to refocus. Get out of my head and channel all my energy into the music and what makes us great.

"You know, you're right."

"Of course I'm right. But specifically, why?"

"I need to forget about anything other than this band, the music. Get through the tour, capitalize on the exposure, and grow our fanbase. Revisit all of this…never."

Everett clapped me on the back of the shoulder. "Yeah, good luck with that, man. That's what you need to do and should do. Something tells me that brunette over there has a better chance of going home without me than you do avoiding Cam for the entire tour."

I raised a brow.

He gave a smug grin. "Spoiler. She ain't goin' home alone."

"Thanks for the vote of confidence, Ev."

"I've said my piece. You know what I think. The rest comes down to you, brother."

It was at that moment that I realized Ridge hadn't come back to the table with Everett. I used that to divert away from hammering the Cambri subject any further.

"What happened to Ridge?"

Everett tilted his head to the side. "Left him over at the bar." Both our lines of sight followed the direction of his head tilt.

There was Ridge.

Sitting at the bar.

With Cambri.

Laughing.

She brought her glass to her lips, and I was surprised at the way my chest tightened watching her from across the room. The sight of her throwing her head back laughing shouldn't make me jealous, shouldn't make me want to carry her out of here and beat my chest like a caveman claiming his prize.

Everett looked from me to Cambri, shaking his head. "Like I said," he cut through my thoughts. "Fucked."

I stood from the table abruptly and stomped to the door, Everett barking out a laugh as I went. I felt Cambri's eyes on me as I made my exit, but I didn't let myself look over at her.

Not a once.

Chapter Twelve

Jaxon

Before

The ride home felt longer than usual. But that could have been due to the awkward silence.

I wish she'd just yell at me. Tell me that she was disappointed. Anything would be better than the silence, her eyes focused on the road ahead.

I opened my mouth, sorry poised on my lips, but I clamped my mouth shut before I could get it out. Sorry didn't feel like the right word. I didn't know what that was.

I rested my elbow on the door and laid my head in my hand, staring out the side window as we drove.

I followed my mom into our home. The silence eating me up inside. She's never at a loss for words. I hated the way this felt.

I hated that I was the reason she was this upset.

She pointed to the couch as we walked by and said, "Sit," before walking into the kitchen.

I did. I sat on the couch, hands in my lap, waiting for whatever was to come.

"Here." I looked up and saw her holding out a frozen bag of peas. "It will help with the swelling."

I didn't question it. I took the frozen peas and held the package up to my eye.

She took a seat next to me, folding a foot underneath her, and taking in a deep breath.

Here it comes. The disappointed speech. The lecture. My sentence.

"Did you win?"

My head snapped to her. That, I wasn't expecting.

I swallowed. "The other guy looks worse."

"At least we know you can defend yourself."

I lowered the peas to my lap, my jaw going slack. "You're not mad?"

That was the wrong question. Her eyes got big, a humorless smile stretching onto her face, as she held a finger up.

"I'm processing. There's a difference." She ran her teeth over her lip. "I want to say that I'm disappointed, but I think you know that."

I nodded. There it was. That word.

She placed an elbow on the back of the couch, resting her head against her hand. "Jaxon, what happened?"

I shrugged a shoulder. "He landed a punch. Hence, the black eye."

"Don't try to be cute. It will not help your case while I'm trying to decide if you will ever see the light of day again. If I lose my job, having to leave mid-shift, you might not."

I winced. I felt terrible that the school made her pick me up for this.

"I'll ask you again. What happened?"

"Nothing. It's stupid."

"Having to pick you up for fighting is not nothing. I'm going to need you to elaborate."

I sighed. "Justin was being clingy and emotional. He was acting like such a chick with his 'I thought we were friends' speech. I told him that's what he gets for thinking. A few more things were said and then he swung." She didn't need to know what those few more things were. That would lead to an entirely different chat.

Her eyes widened in surprise. "I thought you were friends with Justin. What could you have possibly said to make him take a swing at you?"

"I mean, we were chill. But then he got all weird about me being his best friend and that's just bull..." She gave me a look. "Crap. I don't have a best friend. I don't need a best friend. I have you and Jade."

Her shoulders sank, her face taking on a saddened expression.

Please don't cry. Please don't cry.

Mom let out an audible sigh. "Honey. It's okay to let someone in. Justin is a good friend. You guys just need to work it out."

"Was. He was a friend."

The sadness on her face grew.

I stared at her, not knowing what to say. I knew what was going on in her head. We'd had this conversation before. That she thinks my inability to let someone in stems from my dad leaving. How it breaks her heart.

She's begged me to talk to the school counselor about it. That's a hard no for me. I'm not going to go fill some school counselor's head with why I'm angry at a father that has never been there. It doesn't change anything. I don't even look at him as a dad. A dad is someone who is present. Mine was just the sperm donor who helped create us.

There's a difference.

Her lips pressed into a thin line as she reached out, smoothing my hair down with her hand.

"Not everybody leaves, my sweet boy."

I said nothing. I didn't want to have this conversation again. I gave a curt nod in response. Because this was one time my mother was dead wrong.

Everybody leaves. At some point or another, everybody leaves.

She checked her watch. "I have to get back to work. Are you going to be okay here alone?"

"Yeah, Mom. I'll be fine."

"Your sister will be here in a couple hours. You should meet her at the bus stop before I decide fresh air is reserved for those who don't get sent home for fighting."

I honestly couldn't tell if she was making a joke or not. That scared me.

She rose from the couch, and I followed her lead. "You sure you'll be alright alone?"

"Yes, Mom. I'll be fine. I'm not a little kid anymore."

"I know. But no matter how big you get; you'll always be my baby." She stepped forward and placed a kiss on the top of my head before making her way to the front door.

"Love you, Jaxon. I'll be home in time to make dinner."

"Love you too, Mom. And, sorry about today."

She paused, giving me a smile. "I know. Thank you." She walked over and gave me a hug, placing another kiss on my head. "Lock the door behind me."

I nodded, watching her walk out the front door before turning the lock like she asked. I walked over to the couch and laid back, stretching out across it, leaving a foot on the ground.

I stared up at the ceiling. She says she wants me to have friends, to let people in. But I don't know how to do that. I don't want to do that. I've seen the wreckage of that kind of vulnerability.

Mom works two jobs to keep this roof over our head. Two jobs that still manage to put ramen on the table in a fairly frequent rotation. She always has a smile on her face and a positive attitude, wearing them both like protective armor.

She doesn't know that I hear her cry behind closed doors at night. Doesn't know that we are aware of how hard this life is on her. She does her best and we love her for it.

I don't know if she sees how hard this is for us too. Seeing her hide in a shell of herself. Always wondering if this month we'll be okay or barely scrape by. She opened herself up and look where that left her. I'm never setting myself up for that type of vulnerability.

I wasn't going to lie here and dwell in the depressing. I walked to my room and grabbed the CD I'd found in my mom's old stack, the one I hid away so no one could find it. I took it with me to the living room and put it in the CD player.

I would never admit how much this song speaks to me. How it makes me feel like I can do better and not have to ever eat another ramen noodle in my life. I will never tell another soul that this song lets me cling to a bigger hope of a brighter future. I would sound so lame. Who even listens to country music anymore?

But when it's just me, I will put it on and let it take me to a place away from here. Where I can be anything I want to be. Somewhere that I'm not cast in the shadow of a dad who left us behind.

What my mom doesn't know is that this was my third offense since school began. Three strikes you're out. That's why they sent me home this time.

It's not that I necessarily want to get into fights. But I'm also not going to let anyone talk smack about me or my family. Someone has to stand up for us, and I'm the only man in this family who can.

I pressed play on "I'm Gonna Be Somebody" by Travis Tritt and let the melody and the lyrics make everything better. If only for a little while. If only for just today.

Chapter Thirteen

Cambri

I woke up the next morning immediately regretting all the cosmos the night before. I reached over and smacked my alarm, accidentally knocking the thing onto the floor. With a groan, I kicked a leg out of the covers. I had to wake up. I had to get going.

Duty calls.

I was meeting the guys in the studio in an hour, so I had better get a move on it.

I sat up and swung my legs over the side of the bed, stretching my arms out wide up and over my head. Last night ended – differently than I thought it would. Mallory never came back with Stellan, and I ended the night drinking cosmos with Ridge.

How I managed to talk to Alyssa, the girl I had gone to see, and tell her to send in some demos to the label is beyond me.

Jaxon.

I groaned, falling over onto my pillow. What the heck happened with Jaxon last night? He wasn't even supposed to be there. Next thing I knew he was stealing a kiss and then storming out without acknowledging me at all.

I have no idea what I'm supposed to say to him today.

I forced my way off my bed. Slipping on my favorite cutoffs, a V-neck, and some Converse before pulling my hair back into a ponytail since today would be full studio and no office. I swiped on some mascara and lip gloss and was out the door.

Starting an awkward morning with coffee in hand was definitely my best option. Texting Ridge, I got everyone's order and then was on my way.

Ready to start the day.

Yay.

I entered the studio, armed with the liquid gold, and found myself hiding behind everyone's caffeine fix like it was a protective shield I could actually hide behind. That lasted all of six seconds before the guys grabbed their coffees.

All except for Jaxon, who was standing on the other side of the room reading through a page of notes.

He looked up, and our eyes met. His gaze doing a funny thing to my chest.

I straightened my shoulders and then made my way over to him.

Holding my arm out, I offered his cup to him, telling myself not to blink as his honey-brown eyes pierced through mine.

I was about to give him the same morning greeting that I had given everyone else when he took the cup of coffee, our fingers brushing in the process, making the words get lost on my lips.

He cleared his throat. "Thank you. For this."

"Sure. Don't mention it."

He held my gaze as he took a sip of the drink, then brushed past me. Leaving me standing there facing the wall confused.

I clamped my eyes shut, taking in a steadying breath. *This is ridiculous. You're being ridiculous.*

With my best grin, I turned and faced the group. "Okay guys, the clock is ticking down. We are mere weeks away from the start of the tour."

Grunts and cheers filled the room, coffee cups raised like beer mugs.

Giving a pleased nod, I raised my cup back at them in acknowledgment. They'd earned every ounce of respect I could give. The work they had put in to make them tour ready in the short time span we were given was impressive.

"Let's try to wrap up studio time this week. That gives us more than enough time for finalizing meetings and such with Norwood Records. As well as a little wiggle room if we need it. Sound like a plan?"

I was met with hoots and cheers in response.

"Okay then. I'll be behind the glass if you need me. Let's do it!"

A few late nights gave way to early mornings in the studio. Once our studio time was completed, we were pretty much living in

Norwood Records for meetings and interviews. I managed to put together a pop-up show where the guys performed in a parking lot, garnering fan excitement in pre-tour momentum. At one point, I think I went more than twenty-four hours without sleeping or showering.

But we did it. We made it to the day of the tour!

Stepping up onto the tour bus, I took a minute to take it all in. This was happening. I helped put this together, and I could not wipe the smile off my face or erase the feeling of accomplishment I felt if I tried.

We were all exhausted, but at the same time, I had never felt more alive. In this moment, it felt like we had endless opportunity and potential in front of us. The feeling of stepping up onto this tour bus was an adrenaline high that I had never experienced before.

I was ready. The boys were ready. This was the first day of the rest of our lives.

I couldn't wait.

Then I saw him. Walking up to the bus, bag hung over the back of his shoulder. Hair styled in that perfectly imperfect tousle that begged my fingers to dive in. Wearing his jeans, graphic tee, and shades in a such a way that I swear he was trying to kill me.

He gave me a nod as he stepped up onto the bus and then brushed past me. Fingertips hitting mine as he passed, causing a wave of electricity to shoot over each one up into my palm. Leaving me wondering if that was intentional or because of the lack of space entering the bus.

"Cambri," he nodded in acknowledgement as he passed by. A lifeless greeting that was a mere formality.

Since the moment he up and left the bar that night, when Ridge and I stopped our conversation and watched him leave like the building was on fire, he has been different. A wall has gone up and I honest to God don't know why. I've thought about it more times than I should.

If anything, I guess I should be grateful. It has helped us stay focused and not get off track during the last leg of tour prep. Not. A. Once.

I didn't get a chance to spend too much time on that particular train of thought because I was wrapped in a bear hug from behind before being hoisted up into the air by Ridge.

"Caminator!" Ridge said my nickname that he'd settled on excitedly.

I tried to veto that one, but he insisted on it because I "terminated" all issues that popped up. Bless.

"Let's do this thing!" he exclaimed.

Laughing, I greeted the playful baby of the group. He sat me down with a satisfied grin before trudging to the back of the bus. "I get top bunk!" I heard him shout excitedly.

"Cam, you think you can get ahold of that before we take off?" Stellan asked with a grin, stepping up onto the bus.

"Oh no. That's all you," I teased. "Welcome aboard, sir!" I offered a high five that he eagerly met.

"Saving the best for last I see." Everett's voice cut through as he stepped up onto the tour bus, wearing a wicked grin and rock star style shades.

"Nice shades," I laughed.

"You like?" He wiggled them up and down. "I thought they made me look mysterious."

Laughter bubbled up from inside me. "So mysterious," I agreed.

"You laugh now, Cambri. But these are gonna be my chick magnet. You just wait and see." He said confidently.

"Mmm hmm," I nodded dramatically. "I think they are working." I took slow steps toward him. "I am so drawn to you right now."

He gave my arm a playful shove causing me to step back, laughing.

"Ha ha. Very funny," Everett said, making his way to the back of the bus.

"I can't. Stop. Moving. Closer to you."

He turned and shot me a grin over his shoulder before walking away with a shake of his head.

All alone, I sunk down onto the couch with a satisfied sigh. Mentally running through my checklist one more time before we drove off, starting the first leg of the tour.

Eventually my thoughts drifted back to Jaxon. My head subconsciously turning toward the back of the bus as I wondered what he was doing. What he was thinking. Was it about me? Or had he figured out how to stop his thoughts from turning to me, the way that mine did to him. If only I could be so lucky.

A couple hours into the drive, I found Ridge at the table eating a pack of Oreos. I squished in next to him and reached into the container.

"Hey!" he said in protest. "What gives?"

I snuggled into him, smearing a big goofy grin onto my face. "Aw, thanks, Ridgegans," I said in a cartoony voice. "You're the bestest." I took a nibble of the cookie.

He watched me with narrowed eyes before melting into his marshmallow of a self, matching my goofy grin with his own.

"Fine." He surrendered, tilting the package toward me, offering up his sweet treats.

Grinning, I reached down for another, popping an entire cookie into my mouth. Ridge's eyes went wide, and a laugh escaped his lips.

"You know. If this music thing doesn't work out, we could start a spectacle show of other random talents you possess."

I opened my mouth to retort with a witty comeback, but a sound floating up from the back of the bus had it dying on my lips. A guitar. The melody filling the space, stealing all of our attention before blending with the sound of Jaxon's voice.

I paused, looking up to meet the remaining band members' eyes.

"Well, that's new," I said.

"He's always working on something," Everett let out before drumming on the back of the couch with a pair of drumsticks.

"Hey! Be careful with those," Ridge called out, sitting up straighter as Stellan popped an AirPod into each ear.

A mischievous grin took over Everett's face as he began drumming more wildly. Ridge's features morphed into genuine concern. He started making his way out of the booth seat, forcing me out on his way.

I stood up, a laugh threatening as I glanced over at Stellan who was completely oblivious to the situation, or just generally didn't care. Eyes closed, and fingers tapping to the music coming through his headphones. Always so serious, that one.

The guys all preoccupied, I let my feet wander in the direction of the melody, making my way to the back of the bus to where Jaxon was sitting on a bottom bunk, strumming a couple cords and then pausing to scribble notes on a piece of paper. He was with his music.

I noticed the moment he knew I was there. Mid-strum he froze and then glanced up my direction.

"Hey." I gave a small flick of my hand.

"Hey." He nodded.

"What's that?" I asked, leaning against the wall.

"Something I'm workin' on." He shrugged my question off like it was nothing.

"Obviously."

His eyes met mine and he ran his teeth over his bottom lip.

"It's fiction."

I raised a brow.

"The song. It's called 'Fiction,'" he clarified.

"You must tell me more," I insisted. "What is this fiction?"

He narrowed his eyes, an amused glint passing quickly over his features.

He considered for a moment. "Come here." He motioned to the spot next to him with his head. "I'll show you."

I walked over and took the seat beside him on the bed.

"A little closer. I won't bite…too hard."

There it goes. That shiver that starts in the base of my neck and then ripples down my spine.

I scooted over and he moved the guitar onto my lap. I gripped the neck with my left hand and then draped my right arm over the top.

He leaned in, scooting behind me in such a way that he could place his left arm around me to assist my fingers.

"Press here and here like this," he instructed, guiding my fingers. "Now strum down with your right hand." I followed his instruction. "Good. Now again."

He took my hand in his, pressing my fingers into a guitar pick, and started strumming to the cadence of the song he was working on.

Letting him guide my hands, we played the parts of the song he had written. His body pressed into mine. I closed my eyes and let him take over. Giving in to the music. Giving in to him. If only for a moment.

He began to sing the words of the song, his breath on my neck sending a new wave of chills throughout me. He stilled. He felt it. Of course he felt it. I could feel every part of him pressed into me.

"Cambri." My name left his lips on a whisper.

I turned into the sound of his voice, my face brushing up against his. Slowly, ever so slowly.

"Cam!" Ridge's voice cut through, breaking me out of the spell Jaxon had put me under. A whisper of a laugh emerging from my lips as I pulled away from Jaxon. "The driver wants to know when we plan to stop for grub!" he shouted.

We moved apart, but our eyes stayed locked.

I stood up and took a few steps backward. I could still feel his gravity pulling me in. It made it hard to think straight.

"Don't worry," he said, excusing me from having to try to explain this moment. "It's just fiction," he informed me, picking up his guitar and getting back to work.

I blinked a couple times.

Fiction.

The song he was working on. The word he used to describe the moment that transpired between us. That keeps transpiring between us when I manage to slip behind that wall.

I turned and made my way to the front of the bus. I didn't have the head space for this right now. I was here to make sure things ran smoothly on this tour, and right now I was needed at the front of the bus. To do just that. To do my job.

Jaxon

I watched her go. Leaving the air behind her stirred up like a live wire.

I'm not sure what it is about her. What draws me in, sneaks past my defenses. Like a siren and her sea.

The look on her face, when I gave her an out, letting the word fiction slip off my lips, was like she'd seen a ghost. And maybe she had. I certainly feel like a shadow of myself.

Cambri Norwood was the last thing I needed and everything I needed all at the same time. She was the biggest threat and the ticket to this all piecing together.

She was the lyrics of a song all mixed up so that you don't know where it starts or ends.

After this tour, when we aren't forced together, it will settle. She'll leave, focused on her next endeavor, allowing me to clear her out of my head once and for all.

I just need to keep all interactions on a need-to basis until then. Get through this tour, and then on with the rest of my life.

I wasn't expecting her to seek me out on the bus tonight. Look at me with that way of hers, making the back of my throat dry. The way she felt, settled into me…no, I'm not going there. Nothing good can come from thinking about the way she fits into me like a missing puzzle piece.

She's here to organize this tour and make sure it runs smoothly. I just have to remind myself of that whenever my head gets other ideas. She's here to do her job. She'll be gone the moment we land on the other side, chasing down the next big thing.

I turned back to my guitar and soothed my mind with each strum of the strings. Getting lost in the lyrics as they formed in my head. Giving an outlet to the things I was feeling in the only way that I knew how. In the music.

I poured all my emotions into my craft. I have learned that there is a lot you cannot control in life. It has not always been easy for me to express emotions or deal with them. But I could put them into a song. Into melodies and lyrics.

I wrote my first song when I was old enough to comprehend that my dad not being around was his choice. I didn't realize then that it was a song. Back then it was just words on a page. A way to deal with the heaviness of it. It wasn't until a teacher gave me a guitar and ended up teaching me how to play it when I tried to give it back, that I understood it for what it was. It was then that I realized I could sing those words on the page. Put a melody behind them.

It was healing. It was powerful. I couldn't stop.

Music has been vital for as long as I can remember, even before I could play guitar. Before I realized that people liked the sound of my voice. It's been there for me when nothing else was. It's something I have always been able to turn to. Getting lost listening to a song. It has pulled me out of dark moments. Music has been something that has saved me time and time again both figuratively and literally.

The first time I heard one of my songs on the radio, it was like being shot up with a dose of adrenaline. It felt huge. I felt alive. I immediately went out and had my favorite lyrical melody from the song tattooed up my side. A bar of notes from that first aired song runs from the top of my thigh up to my shoulder.

It was a way to celebrate. It was also an F U to my dad. A way to say you left us, but we didn't need you anyway. We're doing just fine without you. Here's the proof.

Music is how I met the guys in my band. My brothers. These guys, we have slept on random couches when we didn't have a place to stay. We have done odd jobs to pay for the band equipment we began with. We truly started at the bottom with nothing but a love for music.

Now we are on a friggin' tour bus, signed by a record label, about to open for one of the biggest bands in country music. I didn't need that sorry excuse of a sperm doner. I've never needed anything from him. All I need is the music. All I've ever needed was the music.

People say the truth will set you free. I put my truth, what I know, into my songs. It's how I process, it's how I move forward, and it seems to resonate with those that hear our music. The words meaning as much to them as they do me.

I put everything in my head into a new verse. I purged all the emotions, cleansed them right out of me and turned them into something beautiful; something I could understand. I let them become lyrics on a piece of paper and turn into the only thing that makes sense.

I'm grateful as hell that others feel the same. That our music reaches them and allows us to take what we love and make it a career.

I didn't realize that we stopped for food at some point. It wasn't until Everett leaned against the wall, giving it a knock with his knuckle, that I looked up and saw him holding a bag of food.

I set my guitar aside and welcomed whatever was wafting the smell that made my stomach rumble. I hadn't realized how hungry I had become.

"We called for you when we left the bus to eat. There was no response. Figured we'd give you your time to flush it all out and do your process," Everett informed me.

I unwrapped the burger and popped a fry in my mouth. "Yeah," I said, shoveling more food in. "I didn't even notice."

"Figured." Everett crossed his arms across his body.

I held up the burger. "Thanks for this." I took a bite, savoring the greasy goodness as it hit my taste buds.

"We gotta keep our frontman fed." He shrugged a shoulder. "When do we get to hear this new one?" He nodded toward the guitar.

"When it's done."

"Which will be?"

"When it's done," I said again.

"Touchy. You thinking about adding it to the set playlist?"

"Probably not. But never say never."

Everett nodded. "Yeah."

Silence passed as I ate my meal. Everett keeping me company by just being there.

"You good, man?"

I looked up at him.

"Sorting everything out that you need to?" he clarified.

Popping the remainder of the burger into my mouth, I chewed, taking a moment to think. I swallowed it down. "Yeah. I'm good."

"Alright. If that changes…" He let his words trail off.

I gave a curt nod that he returned.

I loved Everett like a brother. He can be a real dick, but underneath it all, he is as good as it comes. He's been with me through a lot of the ups and downs. He puts up with my shit. He always seems to know when I'm wrestling with my demons and has his way of checking in.

"I'm gonna hit the hay. You know where to find me." He climbed up into his bunk, pulling his curtain closed. I picked up my guitar, strumming softly until I heard the soft snore indicating that he'd passed out.

Stretching out on the bed I was sitting on, I pulled my guitar into me and closed my eyes.

Chapter Fourteen

Cambri

Two days on the road and we were almost ready for our first stop of the tour. I was itching with the anticipation of the first show. I could only imagine how the guys were feeling.

It didn't take me long to decide that drumming to a drummer was like breathing for the rest of us. Ridge had carried around his drumsticks almost constantly since boarding the bus. Thankfully, drumming on mostly soft surfaces so there wasn't a constant clanging reverberating through the air.

That would have been a lot harder to ignore. I didn't want to interfere with his rhythm, possibly throwing off the whole vibe.

They were artists.

I wanted to respect their process.

However, after the fourth time Everett baited Ridge, taunting him about those wooden tools that were apparently his lifeline, I found myself escaping to the back of the bus before I got stuck playing the role of a parent interfering in sibling rivalry.

I plopped down on an empty space.

The brooding-angsty one, immediately slipping out of his own hiding spot to escape to the front of the bus after sensing my presence. His MO since the whole "Fiction" conversation went down. Which let me tell you, is not the easiest thing to do when stuck in a relatively small space.

"I'm not kicking you out of your spot. You're not bothering me any." I held up my iPad to show that I could still work just fine with him back here.

He glanced over his shoulder. "I know."

He turned and began his trek back toward the front. I let out a breath as I placed my iPad down.

"Jaxon, you can't avoid me the whole tour."

He looked back at me. "I'm not."

I crossed my arms, giving him a look that said I didn't buy that. "What would you call this then?" I challenged.

He shrugged. "I'm hungry."

I shook my head. If he didn't want to talk about this, I couldn't force him to.

But he was going to soon realize that I was correct. I couldn't do my job and be avoided by him the entire time. It didn't work that way.

He took a step.

"Whatever I did to piss you off, you gotta find a way to shake it off."

"There you go making T-shirts again."

I swallowed the smart remark that wanted to fly out of my mouth. Scolding myself that I keep allowing him to get under my skin in the first place.

"Forgiveness is a powerful thing, Jaxon," I called out in a manner that could arguably be explained as childlike. However, the message was true.

He held a thumbs-up in the air before closing the door to the back of the bus.

I fell backwards with a groan.

Artists.

He is so frustrating.

Despite his general broody presence thus far, I wished him luck the same as everyone else as the boys prepared to take the stage the first night.

Then I was blown away. My body humming with excitement.

I was not prepared for the show they put on.

Electric.

The energy the boys create on stage is electric.

The crowd went nuts after their first song ended. They loved them.

I was standing backstage watching the whole scene unfold smiling wildly. The way Jaxon commands the stage is an experience all its own.

Watching them perform isn't merely something you do. It's something you experience – feel. A feeling like that isn't easily ignored or forgotten.

They came off the stage that first night a sweaty mess and all smiles. I greeted each of them with a high five, applause, and praise for a job well done.

You could feel their energy. It was contagious. It was like they had shot up with pure adrenaline and were riding out their high.

I felt everything right there with them.

It was amazing.

Jaxon sauntered off the stage with the swagger of a rock legend. He knew he owned that stage. The charisma oozing off him like it had to run its course before he could return to being a normal person.

When his eyes found mine, something was different. I could feel it. I was still laughing after celebrating with Ridge when he held out his guitar to a stagehand, his gaze trained on me as he stalked my direction.

The way he moved toward me, with determination, had every nerve ending in my body responding. Too quickly he stopped right in front of me, sending a million different sensations in every direction. My breath hitched as I peered up into his eyes, so close that I could feel his breath on my skin.

"Hi," he breathed.

"Hi," I managed.

He peered down into my eyes, and it was suffocating, the intensity of the way he looked at me. The way he looked coming off stage. His hair wet with sweat, his skin glistening from it. The surprise I felt in wanting to lap my tongue over his skin, tasting him in his postshow state.

I was aware of every rise and fall of my chest with every deliberate inhale I took in. His smile crooked up, want in his eyes. I bit down, pulling my bottom lip between my teeth.

I could have sworn my name ghosted on his lips, but with the feel of his fingers brushing against my hip, I could have imagined it. A phantom of a touch before letting his hand fall back to his side. Leaving my body burning with the lingering sensation of him.

It was dizzying. Being with him like this after their show. I forced air into my lungs, his holding stare making each draw of breath feel thick, hard to take in. All of me was aware of his closeness, wanting to have him grab onto me and not let go. My fingers itching to reach out.

Instead of giving in to the urge to reach for him, I managed to find some rational thought.

I brought my hand up, averting his attention to the waiting high five I gave everyone else. Allowing me to take a step back, where I managed my first full breath since he stood in front of me.

He let out a low, humorless laugh before brushing past me. The attitude I have come to associate with him slipping back into place. I lowered my hand as I worked on steadying the onset of nerves his presence brought on.

"Did you see that, Cam? It was incredible," Ridge called from behind me. Turning to meet his excitement, I smiled back at him. It was impossible not to. "Performing for an audience that big…there's nothin' like it. You can feel their energy up on the stage and it urges you forward." He paused to search my eyes. "I want to do it again."

I let out a laugh. "Good thing. Because you get to do it again tomorrow night, and the night after that, and the night after that."

He was beaming. A multitude of emotions radiating off him.

Off all of them.

It was incredible.

Thus began our postshow ritual. Celebrating with each of the boys as they came off stage. I had a high five ready or a little dance that looked absolutely ridiculous. It didn't matter. It was amazing, thrilling, perfect.

Jaxon continued to torture me each postshow exit.

The adrenaline rush he felt sending him straight toward me, until we were breathing each other in. Like he needed me to come down from the high. His eyes holding mine until he would brush past, disappearing backstage. Leaving me standing there as I slowly exhaled his presence. Letting the rush he created after he stalked toward me dissipate.

One by one the guys would vanish to shower, change, and come down from their high before reappearing to finish the Back to Texas show from the sidelines with me.

And then we ate. Usually a burger joint, but always something fried and greasy. It was wonderful. Life on the road.

I never wanted it to end.

Any of it.

* * *

Travel day.

These, I was learning, were the days that everyone seemed to disappear into their own little pod and do their own thing. It's not that the guys ignored each other the entire time while traveling. It was more like they took time to recharge and have as much quiet time as one bus would allow between performance days.

That's not to say it was totally quiet either. They each did what they needed to do before getting amped back up to play their hearts out.

Stellan, of course, was always the most quiet. Calmly reading through his sheet music or engrossed in his phone, texting Mal, in one of the swivel chairs he claimed as his own. It was sweet really. And only a matter of time until she texted me later gushing about it all.

Everett, surprisingly enough, was the second most Zen in nature between shows. I found that amusing since preshow he would get pretty amped and tended to pester the dickens out of Ridge. Travel days, he would stretch out on the sofa and just chill.

Ridge was just happy to be here. Happy to be along for the ride. Honestly, if it weren't for those darn drumsticks always beating on something, he would just be a happy little presence radiating joy to the rest of us. Happy to be in his little nook in the booth seats where he always had a snack. That he would share with me when I scooted in his space. Which was more often than not.

Then there was Jaxon. He was a recluse on travel days. He'd barricade himself in the back, his presence never being seen as much as heard. His soft guitar music floating up playing pretty melodies for the rest of us.

I made a point not to bother him on days like this. Especially because the music made his eyes gloss over in a way that made my stomach flutter more than usual in his presence. It was better to just not.

I busied myself as much as possible on travel days. It was a full day where I could focus on getting stuff done without really being bothered or having to put out preshow fires. I still had responsibility at the office, though my main focus was obviously this tour and the band.

I was in my own head, bouncing from one item on my list to another, when I realized I needed something from my bed space. I stood up to retrieve what I needed, humming to a tune in my head.

"What is that?" His voice instantly snapped me out of my thoughts and brought my focus back to the bus. To him.

"What is what?"

"That tune. What you're humming."

My cheeks flushed a light rose. I hadn't realized I was humming aloud.

"Nothing." I continued on my path, hoping he would leave it at that.

But he had that darn guitar in his hand. He strummed a chord and then tweaked it. Nodding his head when he recreated the sound.

"Like this?"

I paused. He has mastered pretending I don't exist on this bus, but I hum one little tune and he can't let it go.

"Jaxon, it's really nothing. I was barely paying attention to what I was doing." I silently begged him to leave this alone. No such luck.

"Hum it again." I looked at him. "Please?" he added.

I closed my eyes for a second, giving a slight shake of my head. He was annoyingly persistent when it came to music. I knew he wasn't going to let this go until I relented. "Ugh. Fine. One time. And then you can do with that what you will."

"Deal," he agreed easily. Like having a casual conversation with me wasn't out of the norm. Then again, this was about the music. In this instance, I guess it wasn't.

I loved music. I loved listening to it, being around it, but I did not produce it from my person for anybody besides myself.

This was terribly uncomfortable.

I looked him dead in the eye, not wanting him to pick up on how unsteady this made me feel. I took a breath in and hummed the way I always heard the melody in my mind. I closed my eyes and focused on the tune, seeing the way it moved. Like the rhythm was a tangible thing I could reach out and touch. Getting lost in the process.

Finishing, I gave a quick smile, then attempted to snatch what I needed and be done with this moment.

He fiddled with the notes, managing to quickly get a grasp of my tune. Musicians.

"What are your words?" He was strumming chords out, his eyes slipping from his strings to me.

I froze. *Why, Jaxon? Why can't you leave this alone?*

I looked back over to him. "No words. Just my little tune." It was mainly the truth. It was a fragment of a song, with only a string of words to go along. It was just something I hummed to myself from time to time.

He arched a brow. "This is what I do. This is what I know. You don't just hum a pretty little tune without playing words in your head that go along with it."

"Has anyone ever told you how fixated on something you can become?"

"Your words, Cambri."

I grunted. "It's hardly a tune. It's like a little snippet of something that plays in my head."

He just looked at me.

"It's personal." I deadpanned.

"Music usually is."

"You are incredibly frustrating."

He smirked and my insides did a little flip.

"Okay fine." I found myself agreeing to distract myself from the way his look affected me.

This time I focused on a space to the right of him. I could not share these words and have his stare holding me in place while I did.

"I don't fit. In this little role. In this tight packed mold. I'm feeling the pinch." I hummed the parts I truly didn't have words for, then continued. "Who I am. Who I want to be. Sometimes I get tired just tryin' to find me. Running fast as I can, after my big dreams. Wondering if it's ever going to happen for me."

I stopped, slowly moving my eyes his direction and giving a dramatic shrug of my shoulders. "That's all I got."

He lowered his hand from his strings, just looking at me.

"Just say it," I said, not wanting to stand here in a quiet so uncomfortable it was prickling my skin.

"It was personal. You let me see a piece of you."

This didn't feel good. I did not like the way this felt.

"I told you I didn't want to share it." I moved toward my little space, still needing to retrieve what I'd come back here for.

"I'm glad you did. Honestly, I think you could have something there."

I looked at him. "You don't have to say that."

"I know." He held my stare. "In my experience, when something feels vulnerable and scary in your music, it usually makes for the best kind."

I inhaled. I wasn't prepared for that type of feedback.

"Thank you." I swallowed. "For not laughing or making me feel stupid. Singing is not what I do."

His eyes grew comically large. "Oh, I know. The singing was a bit like a dying cow squawking."

My jaw dropped. "Well, you're being a bit cheeky, aren't you?"

He bit down on his bottom lip, trying to suppress a grin.

I crossed my arms, standing there.

"Why do you do that?" he mused.

I narrowed my brows. "Do what?"

"You become all British when you get flustered," he informed me, adopting a British accent.

I opened my mouth to insist that I didn't but promptly closed it. I had just said cheeky. Instead, I said, "My cousin used to tell me that too."

He gave a nod. Like he knew that was a better reply than "I'm sorry" or something equivalent.

"I really do think you're onto something with your little tune."

I raised a brow.

"No. I'm serious." He thought for a minute then strummed his guitar, singing. "When you're young you think you know just what to do."

His voice. It made the song come alive and I heard words in my head. "Hindsight sure can feel just like a bruise."

His eyes danced with excitement. "Oh, I love that."

"I'm surprised you could get past the squawking of a dying cow."

"I didn't say it was easy."

I pursed my lips together. "You can be a bit of an ass."

"Cam, I can be a lot of things," he said with a wicked grin.

My stomach dropped. I hated this. When we slipped into this easy banter like everything wasn't stacked against us. Like we could be an us. And I hated that I didn't hate it.

"Come on." He strummed his guitar again. "Let's keep this momentum."

"No. Absolutely not. I don't write songs."

"Coulda fooled me."

I shot him a look. "You fancy yourself so clever. I know what you're doing."

"Oh?" He strummed a chord as he let out a hum, and then mumbled words. Like he was working something out in his head. "…hardens to stone in end. To hell with your good intentions." He cut his eyes back to me.

I crossed my arms, shaking my head. "No. I said no."

He sang the part I had intended as a chorus.

I stood there, watching him. His smirk growing with each tweak he made with his guitar. Literally working out more of a tune right in front me. Like it took no effort at all.

He was messing with my words.

My song.

"Ugh. Fine." I took the couple steps required to enter his space bubble.

He arched a brow.

"Well, I can't let you mess it up," I said in way of explanation.

"I thought you didn't write songs."

I pinched my lips into a thin line, uttering dryly, "Normally I don't."

"You just couldn't pass up an opportunity to work with an artist like myself?" he quipped, giving a tilt of his head.

"Like I said, I couldn't have you messing up my baby."

"So, you are a songwriter." He said like he'd proved a point.

It took everything in me to grit my teeth and not give into the reaction he was trying to produce.

I forced a grin. "We will just have to agree to disagree."

"We sure will," he smirked.

I inhaled, about to tell him to forget about it. But then he strummed. Asking me how I felt about the chord he played.

I watched it happen. His focus shifting from messing with me to completely on the music. Any thought I'd had about leaving got swept away. I sank into the wall behind me and watched him radiate pure magic.

Later, I don't know how much later because I'm not certain when I came back here in the first place, but we had the makings of a real song.

"Okay. Let's take it from the top. You go."

"What? No. You're the rock star here."

"Darlin'," he drawled. "As much as I'd like to disagree with you on that, I cannot. However, this is your baby. From the top."

"I would hate to affect your precious ears with my squawking."

"Come on. You're not – that bad." He couldn't even get that out without cracking a grin.

I nudged him with my foot as I laughed because somewhere along the way, we ended up sitting across from each other on the floor in front of the bed pods, legs stretched out in front of us. It was tempting to leave my foot resting against him, but I rolled it back over because sitting here like this, creating music with him, already felt intimate enough.

"Fine. But it's your funeral." I sat up straighter, tucking my hair behind my ears. He gave a small laugh before strumming his fingers down his guitar.

I listened to the melody we had pieced together, coming in after he nodded my direction.

Verse 1

I don't fit
In this little role
In this tight packed mold
Yeah, I'm feelin' the pinch

The weight of your looks
And your words
And your expectations

They're too freely given
Like you think it's what I want
But it's not
Didn't ask for any of it

To hell with your big opinions
Slammin' me like a hit and run

Chorus

Who I am
Who I want to be
Sometimes I get tired
Just tryin' to find me

Running fast as I can after my big dreams

Wonderin' if its ever gonna happen for me

Years pass by, slippin' through my hand

Am I gonna like who I am in the end?

When I look up and all I see

Is the reflection staring back at me

Verse 2

Why's it seem so thick?

Decisions made, pavers laid

And honey finds a way to stick

Was I misguided by the sweet of it?

Time marches through

And hindsight sure can feel just like a bruise

You learn to stop listening to

All the dos and the don'ts

And the yesses and the nos

Chorus

Who I am

Who I want to be

Sometimes I get tired

Just tryin' to explain me

Running fast as I can after my big dreams
Sometimes this life ain't what it seems
Years pass by, priorities change
The person staring back sure feels strange

When my times up and all I see
Will I be able to recognize me?

Bridge

Life's a funny thing,
and the jokes can sting
You learn it can all change in a blink

Gray areas bleed through,
your tears were black and blue
You just had some growing up to do

Perspective comes with age,
the memories start to fade
Gray begins to dissipate

Chorus

Who I am
Who I want to be
Sometimes I get tired
Just tryin' to be me

Running fast as I can after my big dreams
The only person I ever owed was me
Now I keep a blank face, wisdom comes with age
And I smile as I turn the next page

It's no longer red
I have crimson intentions
That fade without a hint of regret

Cause when I look up, all I see
Is the woman staring back at me

Jaxon strummed the last chord, letting the sound fade around us. "Damn."

"That a good damn or a bad damn?" I asked him.

"It's a you had a whole lot of stuff packed into that head of yours damn." He ran his hand across the back of his neck. "How do you feel?"

I let out a small laugh. "Like I just bared my soul and couldn't take it back if I wanted to."

"Do you want to? Take it back," he clarified.

I started shaking my head before words formed. "No. No I don't think that I do. I feel lighter." I paused, running through it all in my mind. Searching for any part of me that wished I could take my words back. I couldn't find it. "I know that probably sounds stupid."

"It doesn't," Jaxon said with such conviction my eyes snapped to his. "It's never stupid to give into the music, let it move you. Heal you. There's no one formula for how that process works."

I gave a small nod in response, our eyes locked on one another's.

The air began to feel thicker, and I knew we needed some distance before we did something we might regret. Before I quit thinking so damn hard about everything and acted purely on what I wanted. What I felt.

Making music with him was confusing in a way I didn't know how to explain with words. It felt wonderful. Natural. Freeing. It was messing with my head.

If I continued to let myself be held captive by him, with the way he was looking at me…well. We both just needed some space.

Songwriting session over.

He knew it too because when I stood up, he didn't try to stop me. I ran my hands down my shirt, smoothing down nonexistent wrinkles, needing something to do with my hands.

I took a step toward the front of the bus, stopping when he said my name. I turned back, glancing down at him.

"You forgave yourself in your lyrics. For growing up. For changing. For becoming who you are. That wasn't stupid. It was inspiring."

There it went.

My breath.

My mind.

My heart.

All of it.

I swallowed. "Forgiveness is a powerful thing."

I was frozen in his gaze, unable to move. Then he gave a curt nod, freeing me from my standstill, and I propelled myself forward. Away from him and this moment without another word.

I realized I never got what I'd initially gone to grab, but there was no way I was going back to get it now. Not after that.

I sank down into a chair, watching the lights go by out a window. Only glancing back when I heard the sound of his guitar drifting up again.

He doesn't quit.

He was playing our song. The one we created together.

My head fell back, and I let out a breath. Now we had a song.

That felt messy and complicated.

Crap.

Chapter Fifteen

Cambri

"Caminator!" Ridge said excitedly from across the table one night after a show.

I sipped my milkshake as I lifted my brows, wordlessly asking him to go on.

"Did you like what we did up there tonight? That change in the fourth song."

I pulled my cup away from my face. "I did in fact notice your little drum solo improv tonight."

"And?" he asked eagerly.

"And I think it's great to let the music take you where it will. To enjoy the ride. You guys vibe well enough that it doesn't throw a kink into your show. Everyone just gets it. Rolls with it. The chemistry y'all have up there makes for a fun live show. And the fans agree. People are going nuts over the video I posted of your impromptu moment." I reached for my phone, pulling up the video, revealing all the likes and comments. "You guys are creating quite the buzz."

My eyes were pulled to the pair of honey-brown ones directly across from me. Watching me. Intently. I inhaled and dragged my eyes back to Ridge's, putting my phone down.

"How'd it feel? The drum solo."

"It just took over. The adrenaline. The beat. The energy from the crowd. The music as a whole, and I just started whaling. It had to come out of me. Like I couldn't have held it in if I tried. Ya know?"

"It's the power of music."

He cracked a grin. "Yeah. The power of the music."

I was focused on Ridge, but I could feel Jaxon's eyes on me. Not releasing me until I turned my attention away from Ridge, back to my shake. Taking in a long deliberate drag of the creamy indulgence. I tried to prevent myself from looking back up at him. If I did, I would capture his attention again.

I couldn't be held captive by his stare again, have the feel of his eyes on me. It was too much. He had a way of making me feel him everywhere.

It was getting harder to ignore.

He was getting harder to ignore.

It was like writing a song together changed something. When you put your vulnerabilities out in the open like that, letting them create something beautiful, you share something that's hard to explain.

Back on the bus, I tucked myself into a corner, needing the distraction of work to keep my mind from drifting to a particular lead singer that was inhabiting the same small space. AirPods in, I tapped on the screen of my iPad, bringing it to life. I opened the band's Instagram. Taking time to comment and engage with the fans who had flooded their page since I posted the video earlier.

I made my rounds on all social media platforms, making sure fans felt seen and heard. Engaging with as many as I could on the guys' behalf.

After the tour, my plan was to have a few surprise pop-up shows where the guys could meet and mingle with fans in a more intimate setting. It would be excellent exposure and a great way to keep up their momentum. I'd created a spreadsheet that allowed me to log where large clusters of fans resided so I could narrow down potential pop-up locations.

Right now, it was all about garnering their fan base. I poured all my energy into cultivating that aspect of their careers.

An hour or so passed and I lowered the iPad. The drain of the day catching up to me. I rubbed at my eyes that had been focused in on the bright light in front of me and scanned the bus. The guys were either out like a light or zoned out, relaxing.

I stood up, placing the iPad down, and made my way toward the bathroom, snatching my toiletry bag and PJs. Taking my time behind the closed door, stretching my arms up, brushing my teeth, and washing my face before exiting back to the shared space.

My mind was already spinning with new ideas on how to gain exposure for the guys. Lost in my thoughts, I wasn't anticipating the honey-brown eyes that were right in front of me as I walked out of the bathroom.

Giving a slight start, I released a breathy laugh as I watched amusement light up his eyes.

"I was not expecting to see you there."

"Clearly."

We stood there a moment, holding each other's gaze. My chest doing that funny little thing it did whenever he looked at me like that. The easiness that dances through his eyes when I catch him off guard before that mask of self-preservation catches up to him.

I didn't want to let myself spend too much time on that thought or the fact that he was still looking at me like he wished our paths had crossed at a different time. One where we weren't focused on chasing our own dreams. Where he wasn't signed under my family's label. When it wasn't all so damn complicated.

I inhaled. "You headed to bed?"

"Yeah." He ran his hand over the back of his neck. A move I had come to know as so keenly him. "I'm wiped."

"I bet. You guys put on a great show tonight."

Pride and a sense of accomplishment radiated off him. There was no smugness there, just appreciation in being recognized for a job well done.

"Thanks, Cambri." He meant it.

I nodded in response as the bus hit a few bumps, jostling us side to side. The bathroom door swung shut a moment before my back smacked against it. My stomach bottoming out as I expected to be thrown into the floor behind me.

I didn't get to process the relief of hitting the door instead of landing on my butt as I sucked in a breath. Taking in the body that was hovering inches from my own.

Jaxon had shot a hand out on either side of me, preventing his body from smacking into mine, but pinning me between his arms in the process. His close proximity responsible for each labored rise and fall of my chest.

His eyes slowly scanned down, no doubt seeing the dramatic way my chest filled with air with each new breath. I clutched my clothes and toiletry bag tighter to my chest, trying to hide the visible evidence of how he affected me. I dug my fingers into my items, clutching them tighter, as I needed something to focus on other than the way he was looking at me.

This would be so much easier if I wasn't so naturally drawn to him. If my body didn't crave him with every thought that passed. The way it reacted to him was completely beyond my control, like a magnet caught near another. The strength of that pull demanding to be put together, begging for us to give into the force, letting the two sides rest where they wanted to be.

I tried to shake my head clear as he dragged his eyes back up to mine before I sunk further into his honey-brown haze. His words from that first night played back through my mind. "This feels terrible, doesn't it?"

Why does this have to be him? Why now? When I don't need any distractions. When I'm so close to having what I've always wanted.

We stood there, unable to move, unable to speak. Until he ran his teeth across his lower lip.

"'Photograph.' Ed Sheeran."

My heart slammed into my chest. I clamped my eyes shut as I reminded myself of all the reasons why the timing wasn't right. Why I shouldn't reach up and pull him against me and say to hell with it all.

I began to shake my head in a last-ditch effort to not give into how badly I wanted him. Because I did want him. I just wanted my career more. Or I'd at least wanted it for longer. It had been my sole focus for so long. It was what Sarah and I always talked about. I was on my way to reaching the goal I told her I would achieve. That's the narrative I had built for so long that I didn't know who I was without it.

"I know," was all he said before pushing off the wall and walking away. Saving me from having to try to explain the chaos swirling around in my head.

I watched him go the short distance to his bunk, climbing inside and disappearing into the security of the small space. I stood there, just watching where I knew he was. Torn between being thankful he'd walked away and wondering if we were doing the right thing.

I let my head fall back into the door behind me, staring up and letting out words so faint that they almost weren't. "I wish you were here. I wish you could tell me what I needed to do." I glanced down, shaking my head. "Is it too much to send me a sign? Something. Anything."

The strum of a guitar filled the space and I straightened. Collecting myself and making it back toward the front, scooping up my iPad and powering it off for the night.

* * *

A thunderstorm.

Who knew a flipping thunderstorm could throw so many kinks into a show schedule?

First of all, we were running late because it was raining so intensely that the bus was practically crawling down the highway.

Second of all, the electricity in the air had everyone in a mood and I was seconds away from strangling each one of the four musicians.

I sat, listening to the patter of rain hit the bus as I rubbed my temples. Reminding myself that murder was a felony, and that part of the job description was putting out fires in whatever way they presented. Including when everyone was just tired of sleeping on a bus and being crammed into a shared space for days on end.

Don't get me wrong. None of us would trade it for the world. But it does start to wear on you. Not having a minute to yourself to simply sit in quiet and think.

The rain finally eased as we pulled into the venue scheduled for that night. I glanced at my watch, letting out a sigh of relief at the realization that as long as we didn't hit anymore kinks, we could pull off setting up in time for the show to go on as planned.

Then we stopped.

Too soon.

I looked out the window to see that we were a good distance from the unloading zone and found myself digging my fingernails into my palms. I walked to the front of the bus where Bear was sitting, hands wrapped around the wheel.

He looked up at me, his head already shaking. "We're blocked for the time being."

Looking out the front window, at the barricades that were still up, probably because of the rain, I frowned. "I can see that."

"Want me to try to back out and find another way to get us closer?"

I glanced around the parking lot, surveying our options. "No. I don't think it would do any good and might complicate things more trying to get back here eventually."

He nodded in agreement. "What's the plan?"

"I'll get the guys inside. Get them settled and warming up the best they can. If nothing else, allow them to stretch their legs and try to work out the nervous energy surrounding everyone. You just get to the unloading zone when you can. Call me as soon as you're close."

"You got it, boss."

I shot him a look out the corner of my eye, giving a curt nod. Then I was walking the length of the bus, telling the guys to grab what they needed and to prepare to walk a bit.

Ridge was perched on the couch, his forehead pressed against the window. "Aw, Cam," he whined. "In the rain?"

I placed a hand on my hip, giving him a look. "It's drizzling. Don't tell me you're afraid of a little rain."

Everett popped up from the back, drumsticks in hand. "I dunno. Maybe he'll melt," he said in a hopeful tone, causing me to suppress a grin.

Ridge, still pouting, turned to nod in agreement before noticing what Everett held.

"Hey! I told you to stop messing with those!"

A mischievous look took over Everett's face. "You want them? Come and get them," he said before giving me a quick wink and making his way out of the bus.

Ridge looked at me and I shrugged. Ridge's shoulders dropped, eyebrows narrowing in frustration as he stood up and strode after Everett.

I made my way to the back to collect the other two. Stellan and Jaxon were hunched over a sheet of music. Of course they were.

"Come on guys. Let's take it inside." I thrust my thumb behind me.

"Yeah. Yeah. We're coming," Stellan said, standing up straight, shuffling the papers together.

"Grab what you need for now and we will get the rest unloaded when the bus can get closer."

That got their attention.

"Closer?" Stellan asked, Jaxon just standing there with a questioning look.

"Barricades are still up. Probably because of the rain. Bear will get to the unloading zone as soon as he can. For now, let's get inside and warm up."

"With what?" Stellan piped up again.

My lips pulled into a line. "Let's just get inside, get a feel for the place, stretch our legs, warm up vocals, arms, fingers, toes, whatever you need to. I'm sure you can figure something out."

Stellan's eyes narrowed. He isn't easily rattled, unless it interferes with the music. This, I'm sure, was killing him.

"Who knows? The instruments might already be inside. The equipment trucks did leave before we did. I just can't get a text out to confirm their status."

"Here," Jaxon said, holding out his guitar. "Take her. I'll warm up once they get yours unloaded."

Stellan nodded once, taking the guitar and walking to the front of the bus.

The three of us filed down the steps and made our way halfway to the venue entrance.

"Crap," I said out loud, gaining their attention. "I forgot my iPad."

I turned and headed back toward the bus. Making quick work of climbing the steps up and snatching my bag that contained my lifeline for this tour. I was so focused on getting the boys out that I'd forgotten to grab it.

Climbing back down the stairs, I noticed that the guys had waited for me, and a smile crept up the corner of my mouth at the sight.

Steps from the bus, the rain picked up. My eyes widened, snapping to Stellan, who looked panicked before shielding the guitar with his body and sprinting for the door.

I picked up my pace, clutching my bag in front of me in a similar way that Stellan had cradled the instrument. Jaxon barked out a laugh at the sight of the two of us scrambling, but he didn't budge until I reached his side, falling in stride with me as I moved.

I felt his amused glances the entire way to the door. Irritating as they were, I didn't give him the satisfaction of looking his way until we were safely inside. Both of us shaking off like wet dogs.

He laughed again at the sight of me, and I scowled.

"What?" I eyed him, still clutching my bag to me.

He laughed again.

"You afraid of a little water, Cambri?"

"No. My iPad however, isn't much of a fan."

"I feel confident that the rain didn't penetrate through your bag the way you wielded your body into a human shield." He made a show of arching his head toward my back. "The back of you however…" He let out a low whistle.

Irritated, I smoothed down my wet hair with my free hand.

"Disheveled and wet isn't a bad look on you. Just so you know." He reached out and tucked hair behind my ear. The humor falling from his face at the contact. His eyes peering into mine.

I scowled at him despite the wave of heat that burned through my body at his touch.

"Ugh, let's go," I grumbled, stalking off. Muttering "rock stars," under my breath.

Recovering, he barked out another laugh as his footsteps sounded behind me.

Sooner than I anticipated, they got the barricades moved and everyone sprang into action. People were moving so quickly it was almost disorienting. Boxes were unloaded, cords were stretched across sections of the floor and tapped down securely, sound began humming to life and I thanked the music gods that we had such a great crew.

My name kept bouncing in every direction, my body following the sound, putting each piece together as I went. I silently cursed each crossing of the floor because without fail, some part of me kept brushing against Jaxon. Everybody was just moving so swiftly, you'd shift to dodge one person just to bump into another.

All my shifting and dodging had me pivoting into the one person that I'd rather not. Once, I turned right into him and he caught my shoulders with his hands, the breath whooshing right out of me. I felt like I might burst right out of my skin if I had to endure anymore touches or brushes from him today. I needed this madness to end so that I could slow down and put a safe distance between us.

And then it was over. A new type of energy swirling around as the venue came alive, filling with footsteps and voices.

I took my time adjusting my headset and scanning through the notes for the evening. Then someone spoke into my ear, and I grinned. Looking up I announced, "Five minutes! Let's head to the stage."

They filed toward the door, shoulders shaking out, jumps in place, lips vibrating as breaths were released. One by one, they each did what they needed to do to expel energy as they exited the room.

Showtime.

The guys took the stage the way they always do. Then, they went out there and just owned it.

There was something different about tonight. Despite the hiccup this morning. And who knows? Maybe blame it on the rain. The energy of the place was palpable, like you could actually feel it trickling through the air.

They were amazing onstage tonight. This was them at their best. At one point I saw a girl on the front row crying. Crying. Actual tears in a preshow. Because of the way the guys made her feel.

Coming off the stage they were hyped in a way I hadn't seen before. They felt it too. The energy buzzing around them, propelling them forward. They were a tangle of sweaty, endorphin high, adrenaline filled rock stars. They took a preshow and made it their moment.

I was giddy right there with them. Even Stellan was more animated than I have ever seen him. Everett started beatboxing and Ridge and I began dancing around to the beat. Laughing and twirling.

And then my eyes found Jaxon.

The way his eyes locked onto mine felt predatory. He handed off his guitar and stalked across the floor with a determined swiftness. And despite my best efforts to keep him at a distance, to not want him, the look on his face caused a delicious warmth of anticipation to spread through me.

Blame it on the strangeness of this day, but my heart sped up and I barely had a moment to take him in before his hands found my face, crashing his lips into mine right there in front of everyone.

And I didn't care.

I was too high on the postshow adrenaline.

I gave into it, reaching out for him, digging my fingers into his sides as I fisted handfuls of his damp shirt into my hands, pulling him closer. We kissed like we needed the other one to breathe. And who knows, maybe in that moment we did.

The crowd was still going wild, but all I could feel and hear was Jaxon. He consumed every space in my head and I welcomed it. Welcomed the way my body clung to him, molded to him like it was meant to be there all along.

The guys, witnessing it all, started whistling and cheering at the sight.

Nothing mattered.

In that moment, nothing else mattered but me, and Jaxon, and his lips on mine.

Jaxon

I kissed her.

I walked right up to her and kissed her. This feeling of needing her.

It was unexplainable.

It was consuming.

It wasn't an option. It was necessary, like there was something bigger than us that decided to pull us together.

The rush I felt after this show, seeing her feeling it too as she danced around with Ridge. I couldn't help it, help myself. All I wanted was her.

To hell with it. To all of it. If this was a mistake. If this was crossing a line. I'd pay for it later. I didn't care. I just needed her. And before I could think twice about it, I gave into every instinct I had whenever I looked at her.

My lips found hers, and it was like the rest of the world orbited around us. The feel of her hands digging into my skin had an uncontrollable grin creeping up the corners of my mouth. She pressed herself into me, claiming me just as much as I was claiming her.

Releasing a low growl at the feel of her perfect body against mine, I let my hands slide back, curling my fingers into her hair, tasting every part of that mouth I enjoyed so much.

The kiss slowed, our breathing attempting to as well. But damn, the way this felt. The way she felt. I was completely consumed by her.

My hands cupped her face as she peered those bright blue eyes up into mine.

"Hi," I breathed.

"Hi," she whispered back.

My grin stretched from ear to ear. I let my forehead fall to hers. My smile somehow growing larger when I realized her grip on me hadn't loosened either. Like neither of us could let go if we wanted to.

Something passed between us. Maybe it was the rain, maybe it was the tour, or some music-filled energy, but there was no going back. It was just different. We were different.

When I was off stage, we were together. My arm around her, her hand on my leg, our fingers intertwined.

But no kissing. Except for moments right after the show. When I needed her to come down from the performing high. It was this line that we didn't cross. But one that I craved to step over every time she was near.

I've never been one for superstitions, but a part of me was worried that if I did, it would be the end of whatever this was. I couldn't fuck it up. I needed her like I needed air to breathe.

She felt too good not to have, even if I couldn't have her how I wanted. A taste was better than being completely starved.

I had no idea what it looked like for us when this was all said and done, but right now, I was going to savor every moment with her every chance I got. For as long as I got. For just today.

Last night, Back to Texas went late with a double encore. It was awesome. Getting to be a part of this experience was surreal.

Our nightly food run was later than usual, but in these big cities, there was always somewhere open late at night.

We got back to the bus later than normal, after our postshow food run, and she fell asleep in my arms. We had sat on my bottom bed laughing and the next thing I remember was waking up to her.

We had driven all night because this was going to be our first full day off on the tour. Driving through the night allowed us to have a day to just relax and unwind from the constant grind we had been going through.

Waking up in Miami gave us a full day to explore the city, the food, the music, the culture. And I got to do it with her. I couldn't wait.

She shifted in my arms and her eyes batted open, a sleepy grin forming on her face.

"Hey," she greeted me. "Wow. Sorry, I passed out last night. You must have been very cramped."

I shook my head. "Not at all. I was out." I left out the part about getting the deepest sleep that I had had in a long time. "The last thing I remember is laughing about the way Stellan came alive last night. Throwing out guitar picks into the crowd."

She gave a sleepy laugh. "Oh yeah. You guys have really found your footing. Y'all were born for this."

"I wish I could argue, but alas, I cannot."

She covered her face with her hands before rubbing at her eyes. "Okay. I need to get up and go check the iPad," she said, scooting out of the bed space and then stretching her arms over head.

"Why? Today is our day off. Let's enjoy it."

"Yes. But I have to check in and check up on all the things. Even on our 'days off'. It's why you pay me the big bucks." She winked.

I laughed, rolling to the side and propping my head up in my hand. "We pay you nothing. The label writes all our paychecks. So, you should scoot your fine ass back over here."

"Then you couldn't watch me leave."

"You're killing me, Cam."

"Y'all are killing me," Everett called out from his bed.

Her eyes locked onto mine, twinkling with the promise of trouble. A mischievous look took over her face. "Jaxon!" she shrieked in protest. I raised a brow in response. "Don't you dare try to bite my ass!"

My eyes widened in amusement as Everett called out. "Ugh. I'm going to be sick."

She stared at me from where she stood, giving me a look that had me rolling onto my back chuckling to myself.

"Alright, you scallywags," she called out in a voice meant to wake everyone if they weren't already. "Rise and shine. You don't have to get out of bed, but you're not getting breakfast if you don't. I will be at the front of the bus waiting to leave in thirty!"

"Who brought their mom on tour?" Ridge asked once Cambri stepped into the bathroom with fresh clothes and her toiletries.

"I heard that," she called from the other side.

Ridge popped his head down into my bedspace. "Sometimes, she scares me," he whispered.

I threw my pillow at his face barely missing him and then climbed out of my bed, pulling my shirt up over my head once my feet hit the floor. Leaning into Ridge's space I whispered, "Then I'd hurry up if I were you," before walking to my bag of clothes.

Twenty-nine minutes later and we all made it to the front of the bus where Cambri was sitting. She looked up from her iPad with a grin. "Y'all made it. And with a minute to spare." She looked around our group, beaming. "I have a surprise for you guys. Norwood Records is putting everyone up in a hotel while we are here since this is a multi-night stop. You each get your own room, a king size bed, and access to a mini fridge. Please drink responsibly because the show must go on."

Stellan was the first to speak up. Clapping his hands together in front of his face and giving a slight bow. "You are a goddess and a muse. When do we check in?"

Cambri leaned back slightly as a laugh bubbled up out of her. "Right after breakfast, Stellan."

"A goddess," he said again, stepping down off the bus.

Ridge was next, holding his hand up for a high five. "The Caminator, coming through again! Seriously clutch."

"You're welcome, Ridge," she giggled with that laugh she only used with him.

Ridge stepped down off the bus, Everett following closely behind. Pausing briefly as he passed by Cambri.

"You did a good thing, Norwood. A good thing."

"You're welcome too," she called out after him as he stepped off the bus.

With a content sigh, she closed her iPad and looked over at me.

"You ready?" I asked her.

"Yep! Let's do it."

She set the iPad down, extending the breakfast invitation to our driver Bear. He declined, explaining that he needed to sleep after the overnight drive. Nodding, Cambri said, "Of course," and then asked him to lock up if he decided to step out.

I climbed off the bus first, turning back to Cambri as she stepped down, and reached my hand out for hers. She gave one last salute to Bear and then slid her hand into mine. We slipped into the uncomplicated ease that had become Jaxon and Cambri as we walked to our breakfast spot.

After breakfast, we decided to do a little exploring instead of heading straight to the hotel. I'd had no idea that there was so much art in Miami. Out of all the places we could have had some time off, it worked out great that we ended up here. The street art, the culture, the food trucks, it was all amazing.

Cambri captured it all. Taking candid shots on her phone as well as posed pictures with the colorful murals in the background. She added it all to our social media page with captions about how much we loved the city, and the art, and the food.

Boy did we love the food. Ridge and Everett most of all. It was a good thing that this was our day off and that we didn't have to perform tonight because I think those two successfully ate their way into a food coma.

On our way to the hotel, we found some street performers who were using things like flipped-over trashcans for instruments. We walked up to enjoy their art and Ridge migrated close enough to them that one of the performers eventually offered up his drumsticks to the little air drummer. Ridge took them gladly and started tapping out beats. Glancing over at us from time to time with a goofy grin on his face.

Noticing the crowd his energy was drawing, we were each eventually handed something to make music with. I was given a milk jug full of beans, Everett had a washboard and a spoon, and Stellan was given metal tappers to attach to the bottom of his shoes. They welcomed us into their group, and we played our hearts out of their unconventional instruments.

One of the guys handed Cambri a large metal sheet that bent back and forth to make sound. She tried to protest but the guy and Ridge worked together to get her involved. Rolling her eyes, she jumped in and stood front a center, contorting her body as she moved the metal. I threw my head back laughing at the scene. She turned to me, and I mouthed, "Just today," causing a smile to break out from ear to ear on her face.

Our song ended and we handed back all our instruments. Thanking them for the opportunity to join in and be a part of their art. After handing over hers, Cambri walked up to me and placed both her hands on my chest. "Just today," she said back to me, peering up into my eyes and I realized she was right. Those two words had the capacity to convey all the wonderfully amazing emotions that you were experiencing in a moment.

She walked away, catching up to Ridge before casting a glance back at me over her shoulder. Smiling so fully it reflected in her eyes.

I found myself just watching her, unable to look away. I was caught up in her smile, the way she laughed so easily around Ridge. It twisted up something inside me, and I tripped over my own two damn feet at the shock of it.

I paused at the realization. Feeling like I had just been hit by a brick wall.

This has gotten out of hand. My want of her. My need for her.

The way she has been consuming my thoughts is alarming and should have been the first warning that this was on course to spiral out of control.

Despite the fact that my instinct was to catch up to those two, slip my arm over her shoulder, and join in the laughter of their conversation, I held myself back.

I have grown too comfortable in this thing that has become us. I shook my head at the mere fact that I even lumped the two of us into an us. Having fun is one thing. Enjoying the moment, her company. But letting myself get consumed with her this way is not something I'm going to continue to do.

I can't.

Letting myself get too close to someone is not what I'm going to do.

Getting closer to our Texas stop should be enough of a reminder of that. I need to pull myself back into focus. I shook my head at the absurdity of it all. I should not, for one minute, have let myself get distracted from the music.

The music never leaves.

People do.

Chapter Sixteen

Jaxon

Before

I held the crayon in my hand, taking time to carefully add color to my paper. Stopping periodically to study my creation before deciding to add to it. I smiled with each stroke of the colored wax.

I don't know why I hadn't thought of this before. It wasn't until one of the kids at school asked me why I wasn't making one of the cards my class was. I was about to explain that it was because I had no one to give it to, when I realized that I was wrong. I did. I just needed someone to deliver it for me. And my mom was the best, she helped us with everything. I knew she could help me with this.

I waited until I got home from school. Then, I went straight to our table. I took out the crayons I had borrowed from my class and the paper I had asked my teacher for once I changed my mind about needing one.

I sat down and got to work.

I took my time with each drawing that I added, making sure to copy the words my teacher had written on the board carefully. I had jotted them down on a scrap piece of paper and shoved it into my pocket before the board was erased.

This was my best work yet. I couldn't wait to show my mom. She was going to love it too. I was almost done when I heard the front door open, her keys hitting the counter.

"Mommy!" Jade exclaimed. No doubt my twin had run straight for the door once it opened.

"Hey, Jadie. How was school today, my sweet girl?"

"It was good."

"Yeah?" my mom's voice sounded from the other room. "You two getting on and off the bus okay? I'm sorry I couldn't be there today at the stop waiting for you."

"Yes, Mom!" Jade declared. "It's so easy. We walk on. We walk off. Just like you told us." My sister's voice attempted a whisper that I could still hear from where I sat. "And we put the key back where you showed us too."

"I knew I could count on you. My sweet, sweet girl. Now where is your brother?"

I filled with excitement knowing she was coming to find me, and I could finally show her what I had been working on.

"Jax? Honey," she called out.

I turned toward her voice right as she leaned against the door frame, crossing her arms as a smile grew up her face. "Well, what are you working on in here? You must be working very hard to be sitting so quiet and still."

I smiled up at her as I nodded. "He's going to love it! I just know it. Can you make sure he gets it, Mom? Please?"

Confusion took over my mom's face. "Make sure who gets what, Jax?"

"Dad," I said, like obviously. I held up my card, beaming with excitement. "I made him a Father's Day card. I thought, maybe, if he knew how much we missed him, he'd come back."

My mother's face paled. She swallowed hard and I watched her take in a breath that had her whole chest filling with air as her face changed into an expression I didn't understand.

"Put that away right now, Jaxon," she said, making me feel so confused.

She just didn't understand. I needed to explain it better. "But, Mom. Maybe he just doesn't know how much we love him. Maybe if he knew, if he just…"

"Stop it, Jaxon." I flinched at her tone. She never sounded this frustrated at me and I didn't understand why she did right now.

"Can you? Can you make sure he gets it?" I pushed on, my voice taking on a tremble. I didn't want her to be angry at me, but I just knew if he could get this card, see this card, he might come back.

"I said stop, Jaxon," she bit harshly. I had never heard my mom sound like this. I glanced down at the card in my hands, the paper stretched tightly as my confusion grew.

My chest hurt like I had fallen and hit something, but I hadn't. I was angry, I realized. Heat burned through me like I might spit fire if I opened my mouth, like one of the dragons from my story books we read at night. I just sat there in my chair, forcing my mouth to stay shut.

"Just get rid of it. Throw it away," she said in a calmer tone, but one that was still laced with anger. Like she might breathe fire too.

I forced breaths in, the act feeling foreign as I stared hard at the paper in my hands. I heard it before I realized what I had done. The drop spreading out in all directions. And then another. My heart sank. My card. My perfect card that I had worked so hard on ruined by my own stupid tears.

The anger inside me boiled and rose out of me like steam. Like I really was a dragon. Then a tear. I had pulled too hard, and the paper ripped away from the edge I was holding.

I was certain I had never felt this angry before as I smashed the paper in my hands. Crumpling it up and smashing it down hard. I marched to the trash and shoved it down until I couldn't see it anymore.

I never wanted to make a stupid card ever again.

Chapter Seventeen

Cambri

After our day of exploring, we walked back to the bus that took us to our hotel, finally checking in and then going our separate ways. Agreeing to meet back down in the lobby in a few hours to go find dinner and more adventure.

Something was up with Jaxon. He was fine one minute, and the next he was a withdrawn, moody version of himself, refusing to make eye contact with me. I tried not to internalize and overthink it. Life on the road affected everyone in different ways and he was probably just tired. Plus, the broody, angsty musician vibe wasn't entirely out of character for him. It was just different from how things had been lately – between us.

I did my best to push Jaxon and his weirdness out of my mind. I couldn't lose focus on today and its importance for the band as a whole. This was good for them, taking time to unwind and have a little fun. It was good for all of them to lay it all aside for a moment and just live.

I started my shower water and stepped in once it was hot and steamy. I enjoyed letting the water flow over me and simply how good it felt to be in a shower that was bigger than the small box the bus afforded us. Little luxuries felt so rejuvenating. Not that I would trade life on the road for anything. So far this had been the experience of a lifetime.

I stepped out of the shower, wrapping my towel tightly around me, before combing through my hair and brushing my teeth. I felt like a new woman.

I walked over to my bed and lay across it with my phone in hand so that I could take a minute to check up on my emails. An hour later, I realized I had fallen asleep in the process. Exploring a new city had taken more out of me than I thought.

I sat up, taking a deep breath as I gathered my thoughts, and then went to work on getting ready for the evening. I still had time before I needed to be back downstairs to meet the guys. Leisurely, I did a full face of makeup and hair in such a way that I just didn't have time for on the hectic tour days. Usually, I was doing the bare minimum trapped on the bus or before running around making sure we were ready to go for the day.

I took in my reflection and smiled at the finished product of my efforts. There was nothing like feeling all dolled up to make you ready for a night out. I walked over to my bag and took out the outfit that I had packed strictly with Miami in mind. It was a black leather miniskirt with a high V-cut slit over one thigh. And a black, plunge cami top with lace detail. Paired with black booties and a red lip. It was edgy feminine with a hint of sexy. I was ready for a night of dancing and fun.

I grabbed my small wristlet so I could pack my phone, gloss, ID, and credit card. Then I was off. Down the hall to the elevators I went. Telling myself the nerves that were starting to creep up as the elevator numbers hit closer and closer to the first-floor lobby were over anticipation of a fun night out.

I tried to convince myself that none of what I was feeling was about a particular lead singer and what his reaction to me might be. That I was in no way bothered by his sudden moodiness that afternoon. I had coasted blissfully this last little while by just living, and not overthinking any of it.

Right now, I didn't want to overthink where I was. Or where we stood. I just wanted to fully immerse myself in tour life for as long as we could. Remain in the magic of it all for as long as possible. Because as wonderful as each passing day had been, in the back of my mind I knew this was not real life. No, it was as close to a fairytale as one could get. All too soon the clock would strike midnight on this adventure, and we would be back in Nashville. Back to real life.

As my elevator plummeted to the bottom floor, I took in a steadying breath. I cleared my mind and focused on living in the right now, before tomorrow came and we were back to business as usual.

The elevator doors opened, and I could hear the crowd of voices in the hotel lobby where guests, including the guys, were standing around sipping beers and cocktails. I stepped out of the elevator into the mix of people and my nerves surged. I hated that this was my reaction, and I did my best to stifle it down.

I held my head high, walking confidently through the crowd, not letting myself convey the swirling nerves that I felt inside. Stellan, Ridge, and Everett's eyes went wide as I approached, and their whistles gave way to Jaxon turning to see what the commotion was all about.

Double take.

He did a double take, pausing the drink he was about to take a sip of before his brows shot up. I could feel his eyes drinking me in, but he made no move to open his mouth or come closer to me.

"Dang girl, lookin' fiiiine," Ridge teased out his compliment as I took my place by his side. Letting him pull me into a hug as he shoved his nose into my hair. "And you smell good too."

I laughed as I playfully shoved him off. He released me, making a show of taking in my appearance. "You're killing every male in this room in that getup, Cam."

"Oh, this old thing," I said, giving a quick pop of my shoulder.

He laughed, shaking his head.

"You do look very nice tonight, Cambri," Stellan said seriously.

I looked at him and gave a genuine smile. "Thank you, Stellan."

He nodded before taking another sip of his drink.

Everett barked out a laugh, stealing all of our attention, earning looks from all around.

"What? I'm not laughing at Cambri. She looks sexy as hell." He raised his drink in my direction for reassurance. "It's just," he glanced at Jaxon with an amused expression. "Ah hell, never mind." He took a sip of his drink.

"We ready or what?" Ridge asked the group.

"Lead the way, man," Stellan informed him.

Ridge looked to me, wagging his eyebrows as he offered me his arm. On a laugh, I slipped my arm through his and let him lead us out into the night. Only briefly letting myself glance back at Jaxon before giving my attention to the bubble of excitement next to me.

As we walked, I attempted not to think about why Jaxon still hadn't acknowledged me with words, but I failed miserably. I smiled and laughed at Ridge appropriately as he rambled on, but my thoughts were on Jaxon and this wall he had shoved back up so abruptly that it had a knot forming in my chest.

I rubbed at the sensation as I realized that; my head snapping back to where Jaxon walked behind us. As if he could sense my stare, his body tensed, and he focused intently directly in front of him. His active avoidance of me becoming brutally apparent.

I forced a smile on to my face as I dragged my attention back to Ridge. Fine. If he wanted to throw walls up and ignore me, that was just fine. I was not going to let him ruin this night with one of his moods.

A round of dinner drinks later, and it was becoming easier to ignore the moody rock star sitting across the table. I let myself take in the atmosphere coming from all around me. Miami comes alive at night and is a vibe all its own. It becomes a part of you, and you don't just experience it, you live it. I loved it.

After dinner, we moved to this amazing bar where we were squished together like sardines. The energy exactly what I hoped a bar in this town would be.

Jaxon and Everett brought a round of drinks to the bar-height table we were standing around, getting bumped from every direction. Spilling slightly on the table when they set them down.

Stellan looked up with wide eyes. "It's nuts in here," he grinned.

I grabbed my drink and held it up to him. "Agreed," I shouted over the noise. "Cheers!"

The guys picked up their beverages and met my glass before taking a drink. I sipped mine down a bit before holding it over my head as I danced around in place to the beat.

I found myself getting swept up in the crowd a few steps from our table, dancing with everyone in waves as we all moved effortlessly with each other. Laughing, I freed myself from the movement, finding my way back to the table.

"This is amazing!" I shouted over the music. Then swallowed a deep breath when my eyes found Jaxon's. I tore my eyes from his cold stare.

"What happened to Ev and Ridge?" I asked Stellan, before I could ask Jaxon what his problem was. Stellan motioned with his head, and I turned to find the two of them dancing not far from the other, each looking contently preoccupied with their lovely dancing partners. I smiled, drinking my drink as I watched them. I enjoyed watching the guys let loose.

A girl bumped into me, laughing as she apologized, and we ended up chatting about her fabulous lipstick shade. She introduced me to her friends, and we stood around chatting, and laughing, and dancing.

Stellan brought another round of drinks to our spot, handing me mine as another of the girl's friends approached.

"Gracias, señor," I called out to Stellan over the noise. The girl's hand on my arm stealing my attention away.

"This is my friend Liam," she said, bending my way.

I looked at him, noticing his dimples as he grinned.

"Hi, Liam," I shouted over the noise. "I'm Cambri." I sipped my drink as I held his gaze. He had a boyish charm and a grin that said he was the right kind of trouble.

He stepped closer to me, holding out a hand. "Care to dance, Cambri?"

I flipped my eyes to Jaxon, the scowl on his face deadly. His hot and cold moods were exhausting. He had the nerve to look irritated by Liam after ignoring me the entire evening. Nope.

I looked back to Liam, allowing a smile to form in place. "Would love to." I took his hand, casting one last glance at Jaxon before letting Liam lead us a few steps away from the table into the tangle of other dancers.

Getting bumped into him, I looped an arm around his neck for balance, making sure I didn't spill the drink I was holding in my other hand. Liam took that as permission to slip his hand around my waist, pulling me closer to him as we danced.

He spun me around, pinning my back to him as we moved to the rhythm of Miami, and my eyes landed on Jaxon. Somehow my eyes always made it back to Jaxon.

He looked pissed, his eyes lasered in on Liam and me. I scoffed. He didn't get to look at me like that while I was dancing with someone else. His own bad mood was responsible for him not dancing with me himself.

But if he wanted a show, I'd give him a show.

I brought my drink to my lips, taking a long sloppy gulp. Deliberately wiping away a drip from the corner of my mouth, slowly dragging my hand down my neck and chest in the process. Gripping the hem of my shirt, I pressed my backside into Liam, causing him to emit a groan as he pressed his palm into my stomach. My eyes locked on Jaxon's the entire time.

Jaxon looked as if he might catch on fire, and I grinned. I brought my free hand up, grabbing onto Liam's neck behind me, letting him move us to the music.

I finished my drink, my head feeling light and bubbly. I spun around, holding up my finished glass. Liam leaned forward, asking if I wanted another round. I shook my head no and he took my empty glass and discarded it on a table not far from his reach.

I didn't mind his absence, raising my arms above my head, dancing to the music on my own. He found me quickly regardless. His hands reclaiming my waist as we danced. He brought his mouth to my ear, and I threw my head back, laughing at his words.

I brought my head back up and Liam ran his nose along my jaw. I placed my hands on his chest, quickly realizing I had given him the wrong idea while my focus had been on Jaxon. An apologetic grimace scrunching up my face that he immediately recognized.

He bit down on his lip. "Boyfriend?"

"Not exactly."

"Taken," he clarified.

I was about to say, "Something like that." Because I had no idea how to describe what has been transpiring between Jaxon and I, despite the general off-putting aura he'd had going on since we had arrived at the hotel. But I wasn't given the chance.

"She sure the fuck is," came from behind me.

I spun around, my jaw going slack as I gasped in disbelief.

"My bad, man. I didn't know. We were just dancing."

"Well, now you do. So back the hell off."

Liam's lips formed into a tight-lipped smile. I was momentarily stunned speechless as he glanced at me, giving a nod. "Nice to meet you, Cambri."

I watched him walk away, disappearing into the crowd, before I whipped back around to Jaxon.

"Excuse you? What gives you the right?"

"He was all over you," he said as way of explanation.

My brows shot up. "And that's a problem because?"

"Because he was all over you," he said, visibly rattled.

I took a step toward him, standing up straight, peering up into his honey-brown eyes. "Someone needed to be."

His brows pinched together in frustration. I watched his chest rise and fall as he tried to hide the rage that was dancing behind his eyes.

"It sure as heck wasn't going to be you. You've iced me out since we checked into the hotel," I pressed on, noticing his hands twitch at his sides at my words. He was obviously mad. Good. Let him be. "You're hot, you're cold. Your back-and-forth mood swings are exhausting and…"

Jaxon emitted a growl before grabbing onto my face and crashing his lips into mine, and I briefly tensed before melting into him.

He pulled back. "You make me crazy. I don't know how to not want you."

"So want me."

He fisted a hand into my hair, pulling back until my jaw was arched up to him. He ran his lips over my jaw, placing a kiss at the spot below my ear, sending a shudder through me.

"You want me to want you, Cambri?" he released huskily. "I've wanted you every damn day since that night we met. I've wanted you every time I close my eyes and see your milky white skin draped in fire red lace. I've wanted you every second of every day, and I want you now. So, what are we going to do about it?"

I slid my hands up his chest. My frustrations evaporating with his words. "We live."

The blaze in his eyes cooled as he dropped his hands to my waist. "Just today," his voice ghosted over us.

"Yes. You moody, moody rock star. Just today."

He bent his head down, resting his forehead against mine. "'Pretty Little Poison.' Warren Zeiders," he said over me as I breathed him in.

Figuring out what we were lately, what we'd become. I hadn't let myself think too hard on it. Not wanting it to dissipate like a mirage.

Tonight, in this place, I had no idea what the rules were. I didn't want to overthink it. I just knew I wanted him.

"'Look I Like.' Alana Springsteen," I gave in response. Our eyes met and we just stood there, letting the music pass between us.

A sultry rhythm filled the space, and we began to move, our bodies blending together seamlessly. Like we were made for this. To move as one.

I lost myself in the beat, allowing every part of me to get swept up in this moment. In Jaxon.

The music, the atmosphere, the beads of sweat slowly meandering down my skin all had a rhythm of their own. Capturing us in the world they created.

He interlaced our fingers as he brought my hand up, depositing my arm around his neck that I gripped like I needed it to stand. The good Lord knows that in that moment, I probably did.

But it was his eyes that pulled heat within, spreading over my entire body, causing a shiver to ripple over me. It was his heated gaze that made the rest of the room disappear, leaving just the two of us. I never knew a look could be your undoing.

He pulled me close, his head brushing against the side of mine. "You've completely ensnared me in your siren song. You've made it impossible not to want you."

My fingers dug into him as I absorbed his words.

He tightened his arms around my waist as we moved, and I focused on getting lost in the dance.

It felt like we'd reached a pivotal moment. Like what happened next would change everything.

I wanted to run to it and away from it at the same time.

I reached back, gathering my hair in my hands, lifting it up and off my neck, for just a moment, before letting it fall back down as I secured my arms around his neck.

Our eyes met. He studied mine. "Come on," he said, releasing me, grabbing my hand and leading me toward the giant open doors to a patio.

I took in a deep breath, enjoying the calm contrast to the electric energy inside. My eyes found his and I grinned.

"Better?" He brushed hair off my face, as we leaned against a counter overlooking the view outside the bar.

"Much."

He stepped closer to me like the distance between us was killing him. He turned me, pressing my back into him. His chin found my shoulder as we peered into the night.

"You still want me to want you, Cambri?"

I tensed and hoped he didn't notice. Out here, in the open air, the question felt more vulnerable, intimate. It was harder to answer. But I didn't back down. "Yes," I told him.

"Good," he murmured into my ear. "Because I've never wanted anything the way I want you."

My breath hitched as I turned to face him. I brought my hand to his face, and he looked at me with those eyes.

This man. He's carefully, slowly slipped into crevices within me. Filling each one so fully, I don't think I'll ever be able to remove him from parts of me.

"Cambri," he uttered my name in a husky whisper. I was gone. The veil thin barrier of restraint we had put in place slipping away with one barely audible word.

We crashed.

Into each other.

Hard.

Our surroundings faded away as I got lost in his kiss. The feel of his hands grabbing onto me, blurring the lines of any clear thought running through my head. All I saw, felt, tasted was him. He was consuming. Right now, I wouldn't have cared if we were in the middle of a well-lit room. All I wanted was him.

He pressed me firmly into him, my body forming to his like it knew it belonged there. It made no sense, but he felt like home. I couldn't think about it long, his hand gripping the back of my neck stealing my focus. I craved him. Unexplainably so. I couldn't get enough. Of anything. Close enough. Kissed enough. Consumed enough. I needed more. Wanted more.

I fisted my hands into his hair, the way I have wanted to every time I saw his tousled locks. I pulled just enough for him to emit a growl against my mouth.

He brought his lips to my ear. "You're killing me."

I hid my smile in his neck, one of my hands digging into him. I ran the tip of my tongue over his skin, needing to taste him. Taking his skin between my teeth and sucking.

His hands gripped me tighter. "Let's get out of here," he uttered huskily, pressing into me so I could feel the way he wanted me.

I nodded.

The look he gave me sent my heart racing. Grabbing my hand, he maneuvered us inside and back through the crowd to where the guys were standing. Everett and Stellan were laughing over a drink as we approached. Stellan's eyes met Jaxon's and he gave a nod that Jaxon returned.

One look at us and a shit-eating grin spread across Everett's face. Jaxon didn't acknowledge him, pulling me behind him as we made our exit. I tried my best to hide my own grin as he led us away.

"Get a room," Everett called out over the music after us. Jaxon held up a finger without slowing down, and I heard Everett bark out a laugh.

He held onto my hand the whole way back to the hotel. His thumb occasionally drawing lazy circles in my palm before gripping my hand, firm and possessive. Neither of us speaking, not knowing how to open our mouths without finding one another's.

Our feet hit the lobby floor and you could hear each step we took toward the elevator echoing around us.

I pressed my floor's button, and he made no move to do the same. I couldn't help the smile that threatened as I watched him watch me. Appearing as if he would consume me right here if I so much as let one corner of my mouth crook up.

I hovered my finger over his floor, and he arched a brow, challenging me to do it. I was happy to oblige, sinking my hand into the button, illuminating his floor. Fire danced in his honey-brown eyes, turning them a deep amber. He was enjoying our game. From the way I felt his gaze burning through me, I was too.

I dropped my hand as the doors began to close, stepping against the opposite wall. Silently riding the elevator up, never dropping the other's gaze.

We stopped at his floor, the doors sliding apart, and he smirked as he stalked straight. Toward. Me. Caging me in as the doors again closed.

He hovered his lips near my ear. His breath tickling my neck. "Teasing me, Cambri." He ghosted his lips across my skin. "Only makes me want you more. My restraint to not touch you is growing dangerously thin."

He pressed his lips to mine and for a moment, I forgot how to breathe. I felt him everywhere.

The elevator dinged and the doors slid open. He stood up, gesturing for me to go first.

I heard each of his steps as he trailed behind me. I bit down on my lower lip, trying to still the rush of anticipation that was building.

I stepped up to my door and as I reached for my key, I felt his body press into mine. Strong hands found my waist, all restraint teetering on the edge.

We made it inside, and I spun to face him as the door clicked shut. He closed the distance between us in one move, looking at me as though he was starved and I was the only thing that could satisfy his hunger.

He brushed hair back over my shoulder exposing my neck.

"Cambri," he whispered, running his fingers down my exposed skin.

"Yes?"

He ran his fingers across my jaw. "'Shivers.' Ed Sheeran."

I fisted my hands in his shirt and pressed up onto my tiptoes, nipping at his lip. "'Lose Control.' Teddy Swims."

He groaned. "You're killing me."

I took a step back. "Not quite yet."

"What else must I endure?" He reached for me, but I stepped back quickly. Just out of his reach.

I grinned, turning toward the bed. "How about I show you?" I threw over my shoulder as I walked, running my hands up my sides.

I sank down to the edge, a smile playing on my lips as I looked up to see him watching me like he was about to come undone. I slowly reached down and undid the zipper on each of my booties, kicking them off one at a time.

He smirked, moving toward me with purpose.

I watched as he removed each of his shoes, matching my pace, kicking one back at a time. Never once looking away.

He pinned me in, forcing me back a bit as one of his arms came down on either side of me. He leaned in, our faces a breath apart, as he reached down, hooking his thumbs into the bottom of my shirt, guiding it up and over my head. Tossing it to the floor.

I grinned as I pushed him back, rising to meet him and grabbing the hem of his shirt. He raised his arms as I lifted it up and over his head, tossing it aside like he had mine.

I undid the clasp of my strapless bra, letting it fall to the ground as I pressed my bare chest to his, removing the smirk from his face.

He sucked in a breath.

He fisted my hair, pulling till his mouth found my ear. "Your plan is to torture me, is it?"

He cupped each of my breasts. "Fine. Have it your way." Slowly, he dragged his thumbs across each peak. Lowering his head, he took one into his mouth while gently pinching the other. My head fell back, a deep moan falling from my lips.

He lifted his head and as his eyes met mine, I took in a slow inhale, my jaw slack, unable to think about anything other than wanting his mouth back on me.

His eyes were glazed over as he rose up, gripping my hips and hooking his thumbs into my skirt.

He gave an impatient tug, eliciting a small laugh from me as I reached back and released the zipper. He eased my skirt down over my hips, letting it fall to the ground. I stepped out of it and then unfastened the button of his pants. Only getting as far as the zipper before his hands stopped on what was left on me.

He froze as his eyes met mine, dancing with fire.

I laid back onto the bed, resting on my elbows as his eyes scanned my body. He lowered himself over me, running his fingers over the barely-there undergarment that remained. "This is what you were wearing under that tiny skirt all night?" He grabbed my rear and squeezed. "You really were trying to torture me." He clicked his tongue. "Now I'm afraid I have to return the favor."

He began removing the last layer on my body. Sliding his hands down firmly as he went. Slowly kissing his way down and, true to his word, torturing me with each deliberate press of his lips.

Removing the delicate fabric, he held them up. "I fucking love these," he said before discarding the lace and sinking to his knees. With firm hands, he pressed my thighs apart, looking up at me with lust filled eyes. "Let's see if the rest of you tastes as good as that mouth of yours."

His mouth met my center and my head fell back. I didn't know it could feel like this. The mere touch of him going to send me over the edge. A heavy breath escaped me.

My eyes snapped open as his mouth moved to my thigh, biting down and making me squirm. God, the feel of this man.

He looked up at me with a devilish grin, gripping my thighs with his hands and then biting into my opposite flesh. He slipped a finger inside me, his eyes flashing up. "You're so ready for me, Cambri."

The way he looked at me when he said those words. I died.

Then his mouth reclaimed my center and my hands fisted in his hair, a sound erupting from my lips from the pleasure of it.

He gripped my hips with both hands, his tongue replacing his finger and my back arched, my hands grabbing onto whatever I could find. His name fell from my lips in a desperate plea, demanding him to release me from this coiled up need that was ready to be freed.

His eyes snapped to mine, a wicked grin on his face. Yeah, he knew he was torturing me. "Please," I managed. His grip on me tightened. The smirk on his face growing from my plea. He nipped the inside of my thigh.

"Say it again," he blew a cool breath against my heated skin.

"Please," I uttered, the desperation in my voice growing.

"No. My name," he instructed.

He wanted his name on my lips. The knowledge of that, that my wanting him was what he wanted. It wedged something right into my erratically beating heart.

I looked straight into his eyes. "Jaxon."

He yanked my hips up, burying his mouth into my folds. I fell back, gripping the sheets into my fists, his name spilling from my lips again and again as his tongue lavished small deaths against me over and over. La petite mort. It certainly felt like the truth.

My fingers loosened from the bedsheets, and I ran my hands down his head, landing on his shoulders.

He grinned at me, removing his pants. Then crawled up me, holding himself over me as he looked down into my eyes.

"Hi," he grinned.

"Hi," I smiled back up at him.

He ran his hand through my hair, tucking it behind my ear while he stared down at me.

"What?" I asked him.

"Just committing the way you look right now to my mind."

I swallowed. "How do I look?"

"Like my new favorite memory."

I didn't have time to process what he said as he pushed inside me, filling every inch of me with his length. I cried out with each thrust of his hips. My fingers digging into his back as everything went hazy, consuming me in the feeling that was Jaxon Hastings.

And I knew. This was it. There was no going back. I was so far gone into this man. Into this moody rock star. I felt it, inside me. This moment. The knowledge that he had embedded himself into my soul in such a way that I knew he could never be removed.

Chapter Eighteen

Jaxon

I thought the memory of her in red was a dangerous temptation. It was nothing compared to the swell of her bare breast. She was a fucking fantasy come to life.

Then I tasted her, watched her come undone, and I was a goner. I wanted to be the only one who could make her feel this way, and I did my best to make sure she'd never be able to be satisfied by another man ever again.

After, she lay in my arms, cheeks flushed as her breath evened out. She was radiant. The immense amount of pleasure I felt knowing that I did that to her put a huge smile on my face. I wanted to do it again. Have her again. I was convinced that I would never get enough of Cambri Norwood.

She fell asleep in my arms as I stroked her hair. I smiled down at the sight of her like this. Covering her up, I drifted off. I was convinced that it didn't get better than this moment right here, with her.

I was wrong.

Waking up to Cambri, the sleepy smile that formed when her eyes met mine was like nothing I have ever experienced before. I was a dead man. I brushed my lips against hers.

"Mmm," she breathed, pushing me back against the bed and throwing a leg across my waist, straddling me. "Good morning, Jaxon." She leaned down and kissed up my chest.

If she was trying to seduce me, it was working. Not that she needed to. I was hers to have.

She began rocking her hips against me slowly, a smile forming on my face as every part of me began to wake up. I grabbed onto her hips, enjoying the feel of her as she moved. Her lips parted as her head rolled back in visible pleasure. The sound she emitted had me taking over, flipping her onto her back.

She grabbed onto the base of my neck, and the way she looked up at me had a smirk forming onto my face. I flipped her onto her belly and pressed my body into hers, trapping her hands over her head.

"Good morning, Cambri," I whispered into her ear, sending a shudder through her body. I traced her ear with my tongue before nipping at the base. Holding her hands above her head with one hand, I used the other to line myself up with her entrance. I pressed in, slowly, working my way in and out until her breathing evened and a moan escaped her lips.

Our bodies moved together, dancing in a rhythm that heightened every movement we shared. The feel of her skin beneath mine was a pleasure unlike any other I've known. She cried out. My name on her lips making my body come undone.

I peppered kisses down her back, and then watched her flip over underneath me.

"Let's do it again," she said with a wicked grin.

"Cambri Norwood." I looked down at her. "You are gonna be the death of me."

Her smile reached ear to ear as she reached up and pulled my lips down to meet hers. "What a pleasant death it will be," she teased, tracing a finger down my neck.

I pushed up and looked into her eyes. "If this is death, then I will die a thousand times."

She inhaled a slow breath, her lips pressing together.

I leaned down, capturing her lips with mine. "'Not Finished Just Yet' – Bernard Fanning," I whispered.

"So moody," she grinned, running a hand through my hair.

Chapter Nineteen

Cambri

The guys took Miami by storm. Maybe it was because we had a day to immerse ourselves into the soul of the city. Maybe I was just high on life. High on Jaxon.

They exited the stage and as always, I stood to the side ready to celebrate with each one of them as they came off. I waited anxiously for Jaxon's exit, watching for him out the corner of my eye. He walked off stage, handed his guitar over, and had me up in his arms, my legs wrapped around his waist in an instant. Low whistles coming from the others.

He smiled against my mouth as one of his hands loosened enough to respond to his bandmates. The gesture eliciting laughs all around. Then his hands were gripping me firmly as he walked us away from the crowd and the noise.

I couldn't get enough.

Sitting in the oversized booth after the show, we ate burgers, fries, and shakes. My legs draped over Jaxon's. His finger drawing lazy circles over my thigh. I laughed easily at something Ridge said, and then responded to Everett's comment about my and Jaxon's current status by dipping a fry into my shake and feeding it to Jaxon. Licking shake that remained on the corner of his mouth with a dramatic swipe of my tongue before smiling back at Everett.

A surprised smile lit up his face as he threw a fry at me, shaking his head in amusement.

Stellan walked back to our table pocketing his cell phone. "How's Mal?" I asked him.

"Good. Good. Told me to tell you hello. And um… to call her back," he swallowed.

I grinned. I knew for a fact those were not the words she'd used but repeating what she said made him visibly uncomfortable. I missed her too and needed to make time to call her back. And I would. Soon.

We made our way back to the hotel, squishing into an Uber. Laughing and singing the whole way back. Postshow moments with the guys have become one of my favorite things.

Walking into the lobby of the hotel, the guys motioned for a nightcap to end the night before we hit the road again in the morning. Jaxon looked at me, visibly torn between the drink and – me.

"Come on." I pulled his hand toward the bar. "There's a Manhattan with our name on it."

A grin formed on his face. "Manhattans is it?"

I turned and looked at him. "They did say nightcap, did they not?"

He pulled me in and placed a kiss on the top of my head. "That they did," he said, looking down at me. Looping his arm around my waist, he led us into the bar. "Manhattans it is."

We ordered our drinks at the bar, and then carried them to a round table in the corner of the room. Settling in, Everett leaned back, turning his attention to me.

"Where to next, Cam? What city gets to experience Reckless?"

"It was in the emailed itinerary," Stellan chimed in, like duh, making me laugh into my drink. I gestured for him to go on. "Tomorrow we head to Birmingham, then Jackson, Baton Rouge, and then uh…Houston," Stellan finished, ducking his head into his drink.

I looked around the table, clearly missing something. "What?" I asked. No response. "Guys? What's the big deal about Houston?"

Jaxon looked at me, running his finger along my shoulder. Shaking his head with a quirk of his eyebrow he said, "Nothing."

It clearly wasn't nothing. "Y'all, seriously. What's the deal?"

"Nothin'," Everett shrugged, a smug grin on his face. "Just Jax's summer roommate who had a thing for whiskey and – him."

Jaxon cut a murderous look at Everett.

"Whoa. Down boy," I teased, trying to dissipate the situation.

Everett leaned over the table, meeting his stare. "Now that you've got a taste of both, who's the better flavor?"

Jaxon moved quick. Everett reacting even quicker, leaning back into his seat on a laugh like he'd known what was coming. I reached out for Jaxon, cupping my hand behind his neck. He turned toward me, and I placed my other hand on his cheek trying to calm the rage. His breathing slowed, and I looked across the table.

"What the hell, Everett?" His name on my lips had Jaxon tensing again. I met his eyes, staring into them as I spoke. "I think we've all had enough. Let's call it a night." I nodded at him and after a second, he nodded back, my hand gripping him tighter in response. "Let's go to bed," I said, lulling the beast back in, standing up and pulling him after me.

He didn't resist.

He let me take him away from the table, his hand firmly in mine. We walked away and I turned for one last look at the group, watching Everett's expression and wondering what the heck just happened.

I wasn't going to press Jaxon about it anymore tonight. Tonight, I would chase away his demons. We would revisit this in the light of day, when the things that haunt us shrink into a manageable size.

He pulled me into the elevator, wrapping his arms around me. "Stay with me tonight," he said into my hair.

I nodded into him. "Okay," I said into his chest. Like there was anywhere else I would be.

He pressed the button to my floor, and we rode up. Strong arms wrapped around me, securing me to his chest. He was holding onto me as if I were an anchor. I don't know what Houston held for him, but it was not nothing. And it felt bigger than a summer roommate.

He led us into my room, stopping just past the door. I stepped in front of him, cupping his cheeks in my hands, searching his eyes for answers I knew he wouldn't give me tonight.

His hands found my waist, resting there while I watched the storm dance behind his eyes. I raised up on my tiptoes and placed a feather-light kiss on his lips before taking a step back. I lifted my shirt up and over my head, dropping it to the floor as I continued to move backwards. Slowly, I reached down, unhooking the button on my pants, shimmying one side down at a time. I kicked my pants away from me, watching as his eyes took on a different kind of storm.

He said nothing, removing his shirt and throwing it back toward the door with purpose. He reached for the button of his jeans, unhooking them as he stalked toward me. The way he moved, looking at me like I was about to be devoured, sent my heart racing.

I reached back to unclasp my bra as his hand found my neck, his fingers curling into me as he lifted my chin, pressing his mouth against mine. The impact had me releasing a soft moan into his mouth, which served to urge him on.

He claimed my mouth, thoroughly kissing me breathless. Before Jaxon, I didn't know a kiss could feel this way.

I hooked my thumbs into his pants and boxers, breaking the kiss as I pulled them down his body, letting him step out before looking up to see his hooded eyes. He was ready for me, the evidence stretched out toward me in an impressive length. The sight pulling heat into my center.

I bit down on my lip as I looked up at him, knowing exactly what I was about to do. What I wanted to do. I reached out, running my hand down his length, licking my lips before taking him into my mouth slowly. I glanced up through my lashes to meet his eyes, seeing that the only thing running through his mind was this, before letting mine close.

I savored the salty taste of him, running my tongue over the tip before sucking him in hard and deep. He groaned and the corners of my mouth crooked up.

"Fuck, Cambri." He fisted a hand in my hair, rolling his head back. "You are goddamn amazing at that."

I relaxed my throat as he began moving his hips so I could take more of him in. Keeping my hand at his base so I could work every last inch of him. Making sure that the only thing haunting him tonight was the feel of me against his skin.

He let out a groan as he guided me up to him, claiming my mouth with his. "As much as I want to let you finish what you started, I want more of you."

He hoisted me up, wrapping my legs around his waist and walked us straight back until my back hit the wall. His mouth ran down my neck as his thumb found my center, moving it exactly how I needed him to. He dipped his hand lower, driving a finger into me.

His head pulled back, a smirk on his face at finding me ready for him. He added another finger and his eyebrow arched up in question. I nodded and he added a third finger, my head falling back against the wall, my breathing turning heavy. His thumb began moving in circles in tandem with his fingers, finding a rhythm that had honeyed heat pulling low in my belly before exploding all around me.

"I lied," he whispered. "This is going to be my favorite memory." My head snapped up, my eyes finding his. "Are you ready for me, baby?"

"Yes," I managed.

He carried me to the bed, laying me back and looking down at me as he ran his thumb over my cheek. "You are so fucking beautiful it hurts."

He removed the remaining barrier between us and then pushed inside me in one thrust. My fingers digging into him as we got lost in each other's bodies. Washing out the memory of Houston, if only for tonight.

I burned everywhere he placed his lips, the feel of him maddening. I needed more. And he gave me more with each thrust, kiss, and touch of his hand. Every part of me came alive under him as he worshipped my body like it was a religion.

I was completely spent and satisfied in a way I had never known. In a way that ruined me for anyone else. Nothing would ever compare to this. To him. The way he made my body hum to life.

We fell asleep, a tangle of legs and sheets. His arm draped over my torso. We were completely wrapped together. Yet we couldn't get close enough.

We climbed on the bus the next morning, and Jaxon pulled me against his side when we reached the top step. His lips brushed my ear as he leaned into me. "'Sun to Me.' Zach Bryan."

He kept walking, taking our bags and leaving me standing there staring after him. His words and the feel of them against my skin were like striking a match. He had heat blooming in my cheeks, my body craving more. I bit down on my lip as I realized that I might just be addicted to Jaxon Hastings.

Everett caught me staring and his brow went up. A knowing look on his face. I lifted a finger in response, and he barked out a laugh before carrying his bag to the back of the bus. Jaxon looked at me in response, and I shrugged before plopping down and opening my iPad.

The guys absolutely crushed the shows in Birmingham and Jackson. In Jackson, the boys covered Elle King's "Jackson" and the crowd lost it. Actual panties made it onto the stage. I couldn't blame the girls that shed their delicate undergarments during that particular performance.

Jackson allowed Jaxon's voice to cut a gritty tone that was chill inducing. That and he did this thing with his hips and also these hair flip motions that were making the females in the audience absolutely lose their minds.

Both Everett and Stellan got to take center stage at one point with guitar solos that they incorporated. The performance, as a whole, was transcendent.

Heck, I wanted to throw my panties at them from backstage.

A grin formed on my face, and I found myself shaking my head processing the moment. The boys were on fire. Actual fire.

They finished their set, and I couldn't help myself. I didn't wait for Jaxon to come to me. I walked up to him, took his guitar and handed it off myself as my free hand looped around his neck, pressing my lips to his.

Jaxon stretched his head back and peered down at me. "It was the hip movements, wasn't it?" he teased.

"Shut up," I grinned against his lips. "Maybe."

His arm tightened around my waist as his other hand brushed a piece of hair behind my ear. "Is this you telling me to wiggle like this more often?" He moved his hips against me. "Because if this is my reward, I will dance my ass off every night."

My hands cupped his jaw. "I don't care what you do out there as long as I get you all to myself after."

Jaxon leaned back in to kiss me as Everett coughed beside us. "Get a room," he finished with another cough.

"That's the intention," Jaxon responded with a wicked grin, never taking his eyes off me. "Just as soon as we get off that damn bus." He pretended to think for a moment. "Or we could just lock them out of the bus for an hour," he said loud enough for Everett to hear.

I raised a brow. "An hour?" I said in disbelief, taking a step backward. "More like five minutes. Seven maybe," I teased. "I have some pretty powerful hip movements of my own." I winked at Everett, and he barked out a laugh.

Holding up a hand, Everett gave me a high five that I met before hearing my name being called from further backstage.

"That's my cue."

I walked in the direction of the voice, casting a glance back at Jaxon who was holding his hands over his heart. "Ouch," he let out, stumbling backward. "I need at least eight," he called out.

I rolled my eyes. "Whatever you have to tell yourself," I threw over my shoulder as I walked away.

Later that night, we were back on the road, the bus asleep except for Jaxon and me. We were cuddled up in the booth seat against the window, enjoying the silence postshow.

I felt him shift, causing me to look up at him. "Tell me about your cousin," he said softly.

My brows furrowed slightly, being taken a bit by surprise at his words.

"I watch you night after night being swept up by the music and the overall experience. You give yourself up to it. I love watching you embrace this journey the way that you do. I find myself wondering if it's because of her. The way you immerse yourself into every experience."

I nodded my head, processing his words. We'd talked briefly about Sarah before. Clearly it stuck with him.

I shifted so that I could see him. "Sarah. Her name was Sarah. She was my best friend and my most favorite person that I have ever known. Despite everything she faced, she was always positive, and kind, and the brightest light in the room. She was loved by everyone. She was brave, and bold, and would never settle for mediocre. She always had to go big. She was determined to live her life to the fullest, with no regrets. She wasn't afraid of anything." I smiled thinking of her and all the silly and crazy things she had done and that she had talked me into.

Jaxon smiled at me. "She must have been something else for you to love her like you do."

Love. He said love – in the present tense. It made my heart swell because no one ever says love. It's always loved. Like she died, so my love for her had to as well. Only it doesn't work like that. She's been gone for years, and I miss her the same today as I did then.

I love her still today as much as I did when she was breathing here on this earth. The only change is that it doesn't hurt as much when I think about her. I can remember her and smile and not be paralyzed in a debilitating grief like I experienced when she was first taken from me. But my love for her, that will always stay the same.

We were more like sisters than cousins. We were inseparable.

I laughed to myself as I shook my head. "You know. Even in death she managed to teach me something."

"How do you mean?"

"At first, I was angry at her for leaving me. For going. It tainted the memory I had of her. And then I was mad at myself for being mad. I – know that doesn't make sense."

"Not everything has to make perfect sense," he offered.

I nodded. "Yeah. Anger is funny like that. It really doesn't have to make sense. It takes root in you, grabs ahold of you, and it eats you alive from the inside out. I blamed her for the rot that I was feeling. Even though, deep down, I knew my anger was misplaced, I couldn't let go of it."

He sat there absorbing my words.

"You're not angry now."

"No," I confirmed.

"How'd you move past it?"

"Forgiveness."

Jaxon's eyebrows pulled together, his lips parting like he was trying to process those words.

"Forgiveness?"

I nodded. "I had to forgive her. And then I had to forgive myself. It is a special kind of anger when you turn it inward. When it's yourself that you're mad at. When you're angry that you're angry. Even when a rational part of your brain knows it doesn't fully make sense."

Jaxon just stared at me.

"She lived her life the best she could. The only way she knew how. Boldly and fiercely. Yeah, it might have been helpful if she had been more cautious and careful. Playing it safer and staying closer to home when she was by herself. But that wasn't her. And I wouldn't be who I was today if she had lived like that. I had to forgive her. And then myself. Because the anger I was holding on to was slowly eating me alive."

Jaxon blinked. "Sounds easier said than done."

"Ha. Yeah. Forgiveness is like grief. It's not instantaneous. It takes time. It's a process. A choice you make over and over. But once I did that. Once I forgave her for leaving me." I swallowed.

"And myself – for being angry. It was like a weight was lifted off my chest and I could breathe again. Every day I felt a little lighter. Until one day I looked up and realized there were no bitter feelings left. I just missed her. And I was able to smile when I thought about the time I had with her."

"That's what she taught you. Forgiveness."

"It's one word. But it's so much bigger than that. Forgiveness is a powerful thing. I physically couldn't move forward without it."

I let him absorb my words because I could see the thoughts spinning in his mind, mulling it all over.

He looked into my eyes and took in a long breath. "You're incredible."

I pursed my lips together and grinned.

He reached out and cupped my face and the words just spilled out.

"I told you about her phrase 'just today,' and how it became our motto."

"Mmhm."

I licked my lips. "It's um, it's more than a motto. It's a way to honor her and her life. A way to honor her big, bold, unapologetically fearless life. This life that I get that she doesn't. I'm alive and she's not…It's not something that I can just forget."

Jaxon narrowed his eyes.

This is the conversation I usually try to avoid. The one that inevitably makes everyone give you that predictable pity look and then treat you like you're fragile – delicate. I'm not delicate and she wasn't delicate. Sarah had a freaking stroke of bad luck. Monumentally crappy bad luck.

I hated this conversation. I don't know why it was poised on my lips. Why I wanted to share it with him.

"You can tell me, you know. Whatever is sitting on the tip of that tongue of yours. It's not going to change anything."

"It will," I said assuredly. "You won't mean for it to, but it will. It always does."

He squeezed my hand. "Try me."

I took in a breath. "They said that my grandmother was dizzy a lot. The third time she passed out they went to the doctor. She had always contributed her racing heart spells to her three busy boys. Turns out she had Long QT syndrome. Which is when your heart has an abnormal feature in its electrical system." I said the next part as I carefully watched his face. "It can have a genetic component to it, so the doctors recommended her sons get tested as well. Two out of the three brothers had the condition. My dad is a carrier, he didn't have it. His brothers did. But you would never know. It hasn't impacted their lives hardly at all. I think one of them experiences occasional dizzy spells, but that's it."

I studied Jaxon's face as I explained my family's history. "Knowing this, every time one of the brothers had a baby, it was just understood that we would be tested in our adolescence. Only two of our cousins have it."

"Your cousin and – you," Jaxon supplied.

I nodded. "Yes. Me and Sarah."

"What does that mean for you?"

I lifted my hands, my shoulders shrugging. "Well, I'm here and she's not. I eat a diet higher in potassium and try to avoid excess caffeine levels. Though I'm really freaking bad at that one. She had to be on beta blockers. She lost her life because she went into sudden cardiac arrest. She fainted on a hike alone. A hike that she had invited me to go on but that I turned down because I had to finish writing a paper I had put off until the last minute. If I would have just been there, I could have called 911 before the people who found her did. I could have had her to the hospital sooner and potentially saved her life. She died while I continue to live a pretty stinking normal life. How messed up is that?"

He squeezed my hand. "Cam, you can't…"

I held my hand up. "Please don't. Don't tell me not to feel guilty. Don't tell me life isn't fair or doesn't always make sense. Don't tell me not to live in debt to a ghost."

He pulled his top lip between his teeth. "I think she would be proud of you."

I sucked in a slow breath. I was expecting the list of what I couldn't do. Not that.

"That night I met you, there was a fearlessness about you. From the moment you dragged that stool back, making your presence known to everyone, I couldn't keep my eyes off you. You were interesting from the very first moment. I was there that night to be alone. But after meeting you, I didn't want to be. I spent the whole night with the most fascinating stranger that I had ever met. I watched you live an evening to the fullest. All with a complete stranger. From what you've said about Sarah, seems to me like she would have been smiling the whole night."

He said her name. Sarah. I watched him a moment, focusing on every inhale and exhale that left my body. "Thank you," I said in a small voice. "Thank you," I said again. "She would have loved that night, jumping in a puddle and dancing in the street. Except she wouldn't have left you in the end. She had this determination about her to always push forward. Leave nothing unfinished. To experience everything. No regrets."

"I wouldn't change one thing about the night I met you," he said with a strong conviction. Like he needed me to feel the seriousness behind his words. And I did.

I moved onto his lap, straddling him. I cupped his face with my hands, and he gripped my waist.

"And you're good? There's nothing I need to be aware of?"

"Nothing." I shook my head. "I get a checkup every year to monitor it. Sometimes my heart races a bit, but that has always been it."

He moved his hand to cover my heart. "Is your heart racing right now?"

I smiled through a nod. "Yes."

He trailed his hand down my core, resting his hand on my waist, tightening his grip. "And now?"

I nodded while biting down on my lip.

He moved his hand further down until he was pressing his thumb against my center. I could physically feel my heart pounding in my chest.

"What about now?" he asked, moving his thumb in a circular motion.

I let out a breathy, "Yes," as the need took over.

"Do I need to be concerned?"

I pressed my hips into his hand. "Only if you stop."

I rocked my hips into him, and he let out a groan.

"Cambri Norwood." He said my name like a prayer. He gave me a look and then managed to flip me around, pressing my back into him, unbuttoning my pants and sliding his hand down the front. He began moving his fingers, finding the rhythm that had my eyes falling shut as my head rested against him.

"Right now, I'm about to show you that the only way I like to view you is with a satisfied look on your face. No matter what you tell me, that will never change. Got it?" he asked me.

No reply. I couldn't form words.

"Got it?" he demanded, his fingers moving faster.

"Y-yes," I let out, feeling the tension building inside of me.

"Good." He placed a kiss on my head. "But if you ever need reminding of that," his free hand moved inside of my shirt, slipping inside my bra, "of how much I like to make that heart of yours race…" he pinched my nipple, sending both pain and pleasure shooting through my body. "You need only to say the word." He moved his hand to my other breast, giving it the same attention before he had me falling apart in his arms.

I let out a satisfied sigh, resting fully against him.

"Look at me," he instructed. I turned my head toward him. "I want to see both of your eyes." I flipped fully around, sitting on my knees, arms resting out in front of me.

"Better?" I arched an eyebrow. He grinned.

"This. This is how I view you. A strong independent woman who goes after what she wants. And how I feel about you…I'm not even sure I have the words."

I sank back onto my heels. My heart slipping down into my stomach, setting off tiny flutters across my chest.

He didn't look at me with that pity look. There was emotion brewing behind his eyes, but it wasn't pity. And his words. Those were going to repeat in my mind for a while.

"'Roses.' The Chainsmokers."

He sat up, leaning toward me. "Cam." He ran his thumb across my thigh. "I never have any intention of letting you go."

I leaned forward and kissed him.

* * *

During the boys' sound check in Baton Rouge, I caught up on emails and updated their social media. Their fan base was growing. With each show that they played they gained more and more followers. Their songs that we had released before the tour were continually getting downloaded. They had that special something and the world was noticing.

Baton Rouge welcomed us with a sold-out show, and amazing food and weather. Country music fans came out strong for the Back to Texas show, but it was apparent that more than just a few were also here for the boys. You could hear them singing along in the crowd. People were singing along to the boys' music, the stuff they wrote.

The guys were more than an opening act. They were holding their own. It felt surreal to be right here with them, witnessing their rise to stardom.

I blinked and another show was played and then done. Then, we were back on the bus and headed to our first stop in Texas.

Houston.

The stop that every time it was mentioned, brought a storm in Jaxon's eyes. He'd get so quiet that the closer it got, even Everett stopped razzing him about it. I didn't know what it was about his home state that haunted him, but something sat heavy with him, and I wondered if he would ever tell me why.

I just hoped that for his sake, he could get through it. I didn't want to see him fall apart during this stop, giving more power to whatever was weighing on him.

Houston was a two-show stop, so we got to unload from the bus into a hotel again. Which meant I got to have Jaxon to myself again. We didn't even bother with the charade of separate rooms. There was no point.

We barely made it into our room before Jaxon was pushing me against a wall, trailing kisses down my neck.

"It has been actual torture being close to you without being able to have you," he breathed against my neck.

"Then what are you waiting for?" I managed to get out through the erratic breathing pattern his touch caused.

We stumbled toward the bed, peeling off layers as fast as we could manage. Laughing when a foot or arm got trapped in a piece of clothing. We made it almost to the bed before Jaxon groaned. "Fuck it." He stopped moving and bent me over the table instead, leaving me panting and calling out his name.

Collapsing onto the floor after, I sat between his legs, drawing shapes on his thigh. He lazily kissed his way across the nape of my neck before resting his head on top of mine.

"'White Horse' – Chris Stapleton," he uttered.

I stared ahead as I let those lyrics pour over me. Sifting through the words he chose to share in that moment. I craned my neck around. "There's no pressure or expectations here. Just – know that. Okay?"

He nodded.

I turned around, straddling his lap. "All there is is this moment. And each one that we choose to live after that." I cupped his face with my hands, searching his eyes. I didn't know what emotion was dancing behind them, but there was a storm swirling in them. "'Heart Like a Truck' – Lainey Wilson."

His hands gripped my waist as he nodded again, as if words were failing him. This town. This place. It set heavy with him. His wall not only going up, but him crouching down behind it in the corner. Like a child trying to hide from the thing that scared them.

"Jaxon Hastings, I don't want anything more from you than what you can give." I kissed his cheeks, his eyes, his nose, and across his jaw. "I don't even know what I have to offer."

"Are you sure?" he asked.

I kissed him in response.

"Just today?" he said over me.

I touched my forehead to his, nodding.

We spent the next half hour right there on the floor. Tangled up in each other. Call it what you want. Love, lust, hiding, healing. Whatever it was, I couldn't get enough. I was happy to be right where we were.

Peeling apart enough to stand, we moved to the shower in a continuous sea of limbs. Taking our time washing away the day, we were never far from the next kiss, touch. Our bodies seeking out one another.

After, I slipped on one of his T-shirts, and we finally made it to the bed. Laying on his chest, I traced the notes of his tattoo with my finger while he stroked my hair.

I debated whether I should try to talk to him about this Houston stop, chickening out several times.

It didn't help that my thoughts kept drifting back to the way his mouth covered my breasts under the warm stream of water. His teeth biting down on each peak, almost painful, but then pressing his tongue against the tender flesh, diluting the pain response.

I will never be able to take another shower without feeling him on every part of my body. This man. He has etched himself into my mind in a way I will never be able to erase.

I took a deep breath, focusing my thoughts on what I knew we needed to discuss. "We can talk about it you know. This stop. Whatever it is about this place."

"Nothing to talk about."

I pushed to sitting and looked at him. "We don't have to. Talk about it. But don't lie to me."

He met my gaze with his own. We breathed, neither of us moving. "I didn't lie. There's nothing to talk about. But I'll tell you whatever you want to know. Just ask."

I searched his eyes. His emotions hard to read. "Why does this stop steal your light and make you put up walls it feels like I can't break through? What's so bad about Houston?"

"I just don't like this town." He sat up against the headboard, leaning his head back against it. "It's where the sperm donor lives."

"Your dad?"

His head popped up; his gaze turned to stone. "He doesn't get that title. A dad is someone who sticks around, gives a shit."

I nodded. I wanted to pry more on this. To say I was sorry that he got a crap dad because I only knew what it was like to have a great one. But I knew he wouldn't want to hear that. The sympathy.

I scooted closer, my legs tucked underneath me. "Houston is a very big city. Don't give him all of it. Don't give him that privilege. You have come so far. Look at what you've done. What you all have done. You should feel proud of that. You should go own this show and own this city. Leave your presence here in such a way it can't be removed. Make this your place."

He reached out for me. "I fucking love you, Cambri Norwood." His eyes widened at his admission and my heart fluttered like it might actually burst from my chest.

He looked down, a nervous laugh passing through his lips.

I crawled onto his lap, resting my head against his. Savoring this moment. I don't know what this is. I don't know where we go from here or what we are after this whole thing is done. I just know how I feel right here, in the present. In this moment we are choosing to live together.

I nuzzled my head into his, bringing his head up. "I love you too, by the way," I said against his lips.

"You don't have to say it back," he said, like he genuinely couldn't believe that came from my lips.

"I know."

He searched my eyes, like he was trying to work something out. "Say it again."

I grinned. "I love you, Jaxon Hastings."

I could barely get the words out before he pulled me back in, crashing his lips to mine. He flipped me onto my back, peering down into my eyes. "I..." He shook his head. "'Watermelon Sugar.'"

I reached up, wrapping my arms around his neck. "See. I told you. That song is versatile."

Our first full day in Houston was spent exploring the city and eating a ton of what I learned was called Tex-Mex. Halfway through a bowl of queso I sat back and grinned. "After eating this magic Tex-a-fied orange goop, I'm afraid I don't understand how you guys could leave Texas. This stuff is amazing."

"Just wait until you try the enchiladas!" Ridge exclaimed as my phone beeped.

I checked my phone and saw the notification about our sound check moving.

"Welp, we are going to need to eat fast guys. Y'all's sound check just moved up by two hours."

We went from a leisure lunch to inhaling the food once it arrived. Lunch eaten, check paid, and we were hopping into an Uber on the way to the Toyota Center to get the boys prepped for their portion of the show.

At this point of the tour, sound checks were smooth sailing. The crew ran a tight ship and the boys sounded great.

I was going over a couple fine tuning things with the sound engineer when Jaxon walked up, rubbing the back of his neck. "So uh, my sister texted me asking if we could score her and a couple friends some tickets to the show tonight."

"Yeah, of course, let me see what I can do."

"Alright. Alright. Thanks. I just didn't know if that would be weird."

"Why would it be…ohhh." Realization dawned on me.

"It would be my sister, possibly her boyfriend, my buddy Jake, his girlfriend Emma, her – little sister, and her boyfriend."

"Let me guess, the little sister is the summer roommate?"

"Well, yeah. I uh. I just didn't want you to feel weird about it."

I gave him a look walking over to him. "Jaxon, I am going to find you five tickets for your friends, six if your sister will also be bringing a date. And it's not weird. You have a past. I have a past." I looped my arms around his neck and his hands found my waist. "But here in the present, 'I Got You Babe.' Sonny and Cher." I shrugged a shoulder.

"Cambri Norwood, you are without a doubt the best."

"Hmm," I lilted. "Don't you ever forget it."

I reached up and gave him a quick peck on the lips before releasing my hands from his neck. "Okay, you go finish whatever you need to do and let me work my magic," I said, stepping back with a wink, pulling out my cell phone and walking away.

Chapter Twenty

Jaxon

Not even a half hour later, Cambri was walking up to me beaming.

"Who's the best PR rep a guy could ask for?"

I pretended to think about her question, scratching at the scruff on my chin. "I'm guessing you."

She smacked me on the chest on a laugh that quickly died on her lips after I captured her hand under mine. I recognized that look. It's exactly how I felt right now. I couldn't wait to get her out of those clothes tonight after the show.

Releasing her hand, I did us both a favor by creating space between us. I didn't know if I would ever get used to this electricity I felt with her.

After last night, the way she helped chase away some of the darkness, that spark felt even more charged.

Voicing a bit of why I hate this place, her absorbing it without judging me or having pity on me, it made it feel less heavy. It felt smaller once I stopped holding onto it so tight, keeping it buried within me.

I dunno. It didn't fully make sense to me.

I still hated the guy.

She cleared her throat. "You have six tickets waiting for your people at will call. Tonight's show is technically sold out, but I managed to work my magic and score backstage passes for your Texas crew. I know, hold your applause."

"It's official. You really are the best PR rep a guy could ask for," I told her, wrapping her in my arms. I placed a kiss on top of her head. "Thanks, babe."

She leaned back. "Oh. Yeah. No."

I chuckled. "That really didn't sound right, did it?"

"No. Definitely not." She grinned.

"I just thought." I held my hand out dramatically. "After the song drop earlier…" I teased.

She scrunched up her nose. "Yeah. No. Doesn't land the same."

"Guess I'm going to have to detour to the Galapagos for a while."

She nodded her head. "I have seen people enter witness protection for less."

I shrugged my shoulders.

"But you know," she went on. "Then you risk being consumed by the iguanas and then the band won't have a lead singer. And well, I'm sure you can imagine how difficult that would be for the rest of us."

"Mmm. I hear you. So, you're saying that I shouldn't detour just yet."

"Yeah… better not."

"For the good of the group."

She nodded again. "For the good of the group."

"It won't be easy, but I suppose I can hang around a bit longer."

She placed a hand on her chest. "So selfless."

"What can I say? I'm a giver. In fact…" I nuzzled my nose in her neck, causing her to shiver in my arms.

She created space between us, her lips pursed together. "How about you go get show ready?" She patted my chest, then turned and sauntered off.

"But I'm a giver," I called out.

She threw a grin over her shoulder as she continued to walk away, leaving me standing there smiling like an idiot.

Vultures.

The energy tonight had everyone circling like vultures. But we were ready. I shook my arms out as I tilted my head from side to side trying to shake the rush I was feeling. I needed to ground myself before we took the stage. T-minus thirty minutes.

Cambri walked up to me. "You good?" she whispered. I nodded. "Okay." She paused, giving me a chance to speak. "Go out there and own that stage tonight, Jaxon. This is your moment." I nodded again.

Cambri touched her earpiece. "Yep. Copy. I'm on my way." Looking at me she said, "Your friends are here. I'll be right back." She was out the door before I could say, "I'm coming too."

Panic surged through me. The thought of Cambri meeting everyone without me, meeting McKenzie without me, was an unsettling feeling. I didn't know what was going to happen.

I was hot on her heels, but she was dangerously difficult to keep up with, weaving through all the people on the way to the roped off section.

I hadn't seen McKenzie since the night I left. I needed to catch up to Cambri, to slow our roll so we didn't go bulldozing in like a pack of hyenas.

This wasn't how I'd envisioned seeing Kenz again for the first time. I wanted to appear like the cool musician, not however we were about to look after this frantic game of chase.

Too late.

Cambri was impossible to catch. She moved as if the hallways weren't like navigating a minefield. I came to a sudden stop behind her. Skidding to still like this walking bit was new to me.

Wonderful.

"Hey guys! I'm Cambri," she shouted over the noise at the group. "Come on back." She waved them through the rope, turning so quickly she ran smack into my chest. "Sh–" she let out, catching herself before she could get the rest of her word out.

"Wow. Okay. Let's take it back to the room." She signaled for me to turn and head back.

I gave a curt nod. Smooth, Jaxon.

She recovered, looking completely unfazed. She was solely focused on getting everyone to where they needed to be. I don't know why I was nervous. Cambri was in business mode. Of course, she wasn't going to stop and make idle small talk before bringing them back.

We filed back into the room that held us preshow. Cambri closed the door once everyone was inside, shutting us in to drown out the noise from all the preshow prep.

"Welcome to the chaos." She greeted the group with a smile that stretched ear to ear. "We're glad you guys could make it."

"No! Thank you! I'm so glad I get to see my baby brother perform!" my sister shrieked as she wrapped her arms around my side, giving me a hug. "I'm Jade, by the way."

Cambri looked back and forth between my sister and myself. The confusion written all over her face.

"Cambri. Nice to meet you…baby brother? But you look exactly the…wait. How much older?"

I rolled my eyes. "Five minutes and some change. That hardly makes me her baby brother."

Cambri shook her head. "You're twins? I mean, clearly, you're twins, but – how do you not mention something like that? You were just casually like 'My sister needs tickets blah, blah, blah.' Not 'My twin sister who looks exactly like me needs tickets.' I feel like that's something one would mention. Just saying."

My sister was beaming. Turning to me she smacked me upside the head. "Yeah, ya birdbrain. Why you no mention I was your twin?" She winked at Cambri and Cambri laughed. Jade pinched my cheek before turning back to Cambri. "If it wasn't our twin powers that got us the tickets, what did?"

Cambri popped a hand onto her hip. "I have my ways," she teased. The girls exchanged a grin.

"Thanks again. We really do appreciate it. And sorry for the extra ticket left over. My boyfriend couldn't step away from his project." Jade rolled her eyes.

"It's not a problem. You guys are standing room only near the stage, so no seat is left unused."

It was happening. My sister and my uh – Cambri. My Cambri? My PR representative? My girlfriend? Hell, I didn't know what she was at this point. We'd never actually talked about it. We'd never put a label on it. One day we just were.

A mutual understanding that this was a thing, that being apart wasn't even an option. I didn't care about any of the labels that the social construct would ask of us. We just were. That's all I needed. She was all I needed.

Mine. She was mine.

That's it. I wasn't above beating my chest and claiming what was mine in front of any dickhead that thought she wasn't. Regardless, my twin and Cambri were clearly bonding, and I didn't know how I felt about that. Good? Fine? Relieved? Something else?

"Seriously though. Thanks so much for the hookup," Emma piped up, unable to hide her excitement. "I've never been backstage before. This is crazy cool," she let out. Turning to face me she said, "Thanks, Jaxon. Really."

I forced myself to look at them, sucking in a breath and making myself man up and look at the rest of the group. I still hadn't met McKenzie's eyes. I wasn't sure what the protocol was for this. Like, "Oh hey. How are you after we shared a summer and I fought not to lose you to your soulmate? Have I mentioned that I think I found mine?" Yeah, that's what completely sane people say to each other while seeing one another for the first time after an intense goodbye.

I smiled at Emma. "Of course, Em. I'm glad y'all could come see us play." I moved to give Emma a hug, forcing myself to try to act normal. Though this felt incredibly uncomfortable.

I hoped I didn't look as uncomfortable as I felt.

I extended my hand. "Jake. Ryan." I shook each of the guys' hands. Then I turned to McKenzie.

"Hey, Kenz." I did it. I nodded at her with a smile. See there. Easy-peasy. That actually wasn't too bad at all. Turns out I was just being an idiot. Shocker.

Relaxing, I pulled Cambri into my side. "This one is incredibly persuasive when she wants to be. That's why we pay her the big bucks."

I shot her a wink and she smiled up at me. I could see the challenge forming on her face, her brow arching up, before she opened that mouth of hers. "Is that right?" she said with a concerning amount of amusement.

"Abso-fucking-lutely," I replied quickly, leaning down to give her a quick peck on the lips.

She pressed her lips together, eyeing me like she was trying to decide what she would say next. But then her hand went up to her earpiece and she started nodding at whatever was being said. "Be right there," she spoke into the mini mic.

She leaned into me. "This is your night. You got this," she whispered, giving me the reassuring hug she knew I needed before excusing herself to take care of whatever was said in her ear.

I looked over to see McKenzie beaming at me. I took a deep breath in and then walked up to her.

"I like her," she said, gesturing in the direction Cambri had taken off. "I like seeing you like this," she told me.

I shoved my hands in my pockets. "Yeah?"

"She's good for you. It's written all over your face. You look happy."

I reached back and rubbed my neck. A sheepish grin spreading across my face. "Yeah. I think I am. I can't explain it."

"Something just fits, right? Like you feel more alive than you knew you could. That if she walked away, you would never be the same."

I held her gaze. "Pretty much. Crazy, right?"

She shook her head. "Nope."

"I can't explain it. But she feels vital. Like if she were gone, a part of me would be too."

McKenzie pressed her lips together. Nodding as if what I said made perfect sense to her. She stood up on her tiptoes and placed a kiss on my cheek. "You did it," she whispered in my ear. "You found your happy. I'm so very happy for you, Jaxon."

She stepped back and into Ryan's arms and I got it. What I'd missed over the summer. That thing that tied them together. I got it now. I saw it now. I felt it with Cambri. I can't explain it. It just is.

Cambri popped back into the room, excited energy swirling all around her. "Showtime," she announced.

Her eyes met mine, and I answered her silent question with a nod. I was ready. I could do this.

There is no way to explain the rush of taking the stage in your home state. The way it felt to be welcomed and cheered on by your people. Having my twin and my friends experiencing this journey with us was surreal.

I thought being back in Texas would be weird and difficult, and in a way it was. But Cambri was right. I needed to get out of my own head, to not give the sperm donor power over this city, because there was nothing like the way it felt to come home and play my music.

Tonight, I owned the stage. I didn't think about the man who had abandoned us. That was somewhere here in this city. I didn't worry about strained friendships and awkward relationships because everything worked out exactly how it needed to.

We came back to Texas with Back to Texas.

The irony was not lost on me.

After the show I brushed past everyone, needing Cambri's arms and lips to help bring me down from the insane adrenaline high I get out on that stage. She grounds me. She is what I need, what I crave at the end of every performance.

Breathing easier, I rested my forehead against hers. "Just today," I whispered. "Just today," she echoed. I grabbed her hand

and turned to my sister and my friends who'd come out to support us and see the show.

"You guys have to come out with us tonight. We go get food postshow in every city."

"After party with the band," Emma scoffed sarcastically. "I mean, I guess. If we have to." She attempted to look like the very thought was taxing but failed miserably. Emma was beaming like a kid the night before Christmas.

I laughed. "Enjoy the show, guys. We will meet y'all back up here in a bit."

We made our way backstage, taking time to shower, a necessity after being under the lights and giving it our all out there, taking a minute to relax and hydrate. Then we made our way back to my sister and the gang for the last couple songs.

Show over, we filed into cars that took us to get our postshow meal.

"How'd you guys meet?" McKenzie asked Cambri, sipping her soda.

Cambri glanced at me, knowing that question was more loaded than anyone knew. I sat back into my seat, crossing my arms, wondering how exactly she was going to answer this.

The smirk on my face giving way to the challenge in her eyes. "That is a good question." She cut her eyes back to me, the corners of her lips curving up. "The short story, I was assigned to the band after they signed to the label."

"And the long story?" McKenzie probed.

I leaned forward, placing my elbows on the table, clasping my hands in the air. "One for another time."

"Boo! That's no fun!" Kenz protested.

Jade threw a fry at me, which I caught. "Yeah. Give us the goods!"

I popped the fry in my mouth and my sister narrowed her eyes at me. I grinned.

"Well, if you must know. This one," I bumped my shoulder into Cambri's, "lured me in with a siren song. She's managed to drag me down deep." I turned to Cambri, wrinkling my nose. "Even if she was more Grimm fairy tale siren at first."

Cambri rolled her eyes, smiling as she shook her head. "Charming, isn't he?"

Jade shrugged a shoulder. "When he wants to be."

Cambri rustled her fingers in my hair. "I guess he does have a weird way of growing on you."

McKenzie grinned at her. "Yeah. I get that." She looked back and forth between Cambri and I before leaning her head against Ryan's shoulder, a content smile on her face.

"Where to from here?" Jake, Emma's boyfriend asked.

"A couple stops around Texas and then we dart around, slowly make our way to the West Coast," I informed him.

"I'm counting down the shows for that," Ridge interjected. "Cali is gonna be sick!"

"How's it been?" Ryan's voice cut through. "Singing night after night. Ever feel like you need a minute to rest?"

I nodded, taking a drink of my water. "It's been a crazy ride. But I couldn't imagine doing it any other way. I try to rest my voice as much as possible, lots of water and humidifiers. As well as lubricating things like shots of olive oil. We have break days between shows that are nice. But for the most part, I just do what I can."

"Makes sense," he agreed.

"Well, this evening has been truly great. One for the books. But I for one am exhausted," Emma informed us. She turned to Jake, looping her arm around his neck. "Take me home, my love. I need fuzzy PJ pants and my pillow."

"Good God, man," Cambri let out. "Get this woman home and to her softies!"

Jake looked at her, an eyebrow lifted in question. "Softies?"

"Uh, your favorite soft, comfy clothes. AKA her fuzzy PJ pants," she explained.

"She gets it!" Emma exclaimed, high-fiving Cambri.

Bellies full, we said our goodbyes, and the group made their exit, waving one last time at the door. I hung back with Cambri as she ran to the bathroom.

I stood there and found myself smiling. I didn't realize how much I needed this. This closure. Seeing everything through full-circle with my friends, with McKenzie. Seeing everything how it was meant to be.

A throat cleared. "Son?"

I whipped my head to the side, the smile on my face vanishing as I recognized the man standing before me. I stood up straighter, my back going rigid. "You don't get to call me that." I clenched my jaw together.

He nodded, shifting back on his heels.

"If I could just have a moment of your time. To talk. To explain."

I would have barked out a laugh at that if I weren't in such utter shock.

"Nope." I shook my head. "No."

"Okay. Ready?" Cambri asked, stepping up to me. She noticed my posture and glanced at the man in front of me. Her brows pulling together.

"Yeah. Let's go." I grabbed her arm and pulled her to the exit. I was fucking thankful that she didn't fight me as I did.

Outside, she stepped in front of me. Ignoring the confused stares from my waiting bandmates. "That was him, wasn't it? Your dad." She placed her hands on my chest when I didn't meet her eyes. Slowly, I looked down at her. All I could manage was a nod.

She searched my eyes. "Don't give him this power over you. This ability to steal your joy." I just looked at her. I had no words. She reached up and cupped my face in her hands. "Forgiveness is a powerful thing, Jaxon." She looked over my shoulder and then brought her eyes back to mine.

She took a deep breath in and then lowered her hands, sliding them down my chest. She patted my chest twice before turning toward the guys.

I clamped my eyes shut. I wanted to scream, "Fuck." I wanted to yell and lash out at everyone around me. But there was no one to fight. Cambri wasn't forcing me to do anything. No one was even standing close enough to blame for how I was feeling other than myself.

The person to blame was right on the other side of that door. The person responsible for abandoning his family, for living easy while money was tight for us, was right there, a door away.

I clenched my fists at my side. Did he even know that meals looked like shared ramen noodles from time to time? How hard it was that one winter when we didn't have heat for a while?

I didn't want to go back in there and talk to him. Hell, I never wanted to see the sperm donor again in the first place. He fucked up. He left. He abandoned me, my sister, my mom, all of us. He didn't deserve anything but my anger, my hatred.

I was so tired of this. Of feeling like this helpless little boy because of him. Of feeling unwanted and unlovable because of him. I had held onto this anger for so long I didn't know who I was without it.

Maybe if I could tell him that he was to blame. That he was responsible for this brokenness I felt, I might just feel a little better.

Sharing a piece of this darkness with Cambri made it feel lighter. Maybe getting to unload a part of this onto the man responsible for it all would make it feel even lighter. At the very least, he would be aware of the damage he caused.

The idea of that seemed fair. Because if I had to carry this. He should too.

It was desperation that had me turning back toward the door and storming inside. It was the desperate way I needed to feel anything other than what I had felt my whole life because it was fucking terrible.

Maybe Cambri was right. The only way forward, the only way to move past this, was to take back the power I had given him all these years. He didn't deserve to have that. He didn't deserve to have anything other than an understanding of everything he took from us.

I made my way toward him. His head snapping up, eyes wide when I approached. I shoved my hands into my pockets like I was a little boy, and I hated that I allowed him to make me feel small in this moment. Because I wasn't small. I was on tour with one of the biggest bands in country music. And I did that without any help from him. I was anything but small.

"You fucked up." Were the words that came out of my mouth.

He nodded. "I know."

"You really fucked up." Apparently, those were the only words I knew.

"I know," he said again. Eyes filling with tears. Oh hell.

"The biggest regret of my life was walking away from you three. From you. It's not an excuse, but I thought I was a better father that way."

I laughed. I actually laughed. "You weren't a father at all. You weren't there. You abandoned us, and then you went and found yourself a shiny new family. What kind of a man does that?" My lips curled down in disgust.

I watched a grown man's heart shatter in that moment. I hated that I felt anything other than hate as I did.

"I wasn't sober then, Jaxon. I wasn't a good man. But I got clean. I got my life together. I thought so many times about going back to you all once I was. Beg for your forgiveness. I got close once. I watched you play at a park. Watched your smile, your joy. I was so scared of messing that up, I walked away and never tried again. I was too chickenshit to face my own family after the demons that tore me from you all."

My eyes hardened. "We needed you then. I needed you then." I shocked myself at the admission. Despite how true it was.

"I am so sorry, Jaxon." He reached for me, and I flinched. His hand froze midair, pain sweeping over his face before clenching his fist and bringing it back to his side. "I'm sorry for any pain and hurt that I have caused you."

I gave an incredulous laugh. "Just not sorry enough to mind replacing us. Find family 2.0 and stick around for them. Huh?"

Hurt and regret flashed in his eyes. "I did get a second chance at being a dad. And I hope and pray that I have been better this time around. But they never replaced you and your sister. Your mother." His voice broke. "I have to carry what I did. How I was too weak of a man to take care of y'all how I should have. I have to carry that regret. That shame. With me the rest of my life. And I will, because not a day goes by where I'm not haunted by the mistakes of my past."

"I have hated you for longer than I remember not hating you."

He nodded, looking me in the eye with his mouth clamped firmly shut like he understood there were things I needed to say. Things I had to say.

"We made it. The three of us. We survived. There were times that we were literally freezing and starving. Times I thought it would be easier to not be here, but I wouldn't walk away from them. Leave them. I. Stayed."

His chest filled with air, but he didn't move. Didn't speak.

"I was the man that you should have been. And Mom, she is so tough. She is the strongest person I know besides Jade. She turned out great by the way. She's artsy and full of life. The three of us, we did it. We made it." My brows pulled together as I shook my head. "I look at you now and I wonder…a lot of things."

I took a deep breath in, letting my words stop because I didn't need to explain anything else. He knew. I could see that he understood more fully than I ever imagined. He didn't get angry or make excuses. He stood there and absorbed every word despite the fact that he looked as if he was about to crack right open.

I wondered how I gave someone who looked so fragile so much power.

Seeing him standing here now, he isn't at all what I pictured. Viewing him like this, rather than this larger-than-life entity my mind has always made him out to be. I don't know. It's confusing, and disorienting, and alarmingly disarming. It's like turning on the light in a dark room to discover the monster is just a coat hanging on the back of the door.

I raised my shoulders tall. Peering into the eyes of a broken man. A man possibly more broken than myself. Unexpectedly, something in me shifted and I heard Cambri's voice inside my head.

All the pain I'd ever felt toward him was still there. But there was something else too. Seeing him like this. As just a man.

Just a man.

In the next moment, I did something I'd honestly thought I would never do. Never wanted to do. I reached out and placed a hand on his shoulder. My chest filling with all the hurt I had carried with me my entire life. I took another deep breath in, trying to stabilize what I knew would be a shaky voice.

"I forgive you."

He inhaled sharply as the confusion in his eyes turned to processing the words I had spoken over him. His shoulders slumped forward, and sobs wracked through him.

Then I turned and walked away. Because forgiveness doesn't mean forgetting. It doesn't take away the pain. It doesn't mend a relationship or mean I was ready for anything other than what this moment brought. But it sure as hell took away the power I had given him over me for all of these years.

I walked out the door and straight to Cambri, looping my arm around her waist. Pulling her close to me, needing to feel the comfort of her as I guided her to the car they had waiting.

Chapter Twenty-One

Jaxon

Before

I trudged down the school hallway holding on to the straps of my backpack. It always felt heavier with my library book inside. Today it was even heavier because I had brought the giant dinosaur footprint book back with me.

My sister was talking a mile a minute, but I had no idea what she was saying. Something about how she hoped Santa would bring her the rainbow unicorn stuffy her friend had brought to school for show and tell.

I was too busy trying to find my friend who said he would save me some of his blueberry muffin his mom made this week.

I never turned down an offer of free food.

I heard my name behind me, and I turned, a smile forming on my face as Griffen held the prized possession outstretched in his hand. I reached for my sister, slowing her down. If I wanted that muffin, it would have to be outside of class. Once we got inside, our teacher would have us unpack into our cubbies and start morning activities.

Griffen caught up to us, and I thanked him before eating the entire muffin in a few bites. Today was already starting out great because he had remembered to bring me a muffin!

We walked in the class door to give Ms. McCallister a high five before finding our cubbies. She was such a nice teacher. Every morning she was there waiting by the door to offer a high five or a hug. I loved that I knew she would always be there waiting with a smile on her face.

I found the paper and markers I needed for morning activity on the counter by the wall, and then waved at my sister before heading to my table. Jade sat at a table on the other side of the room this rotation.

I didn't mind. Secretly, I liked having a little space sometimes. But I would make sure and sit by her at lunch. I didn't want her to get her feelings hurt.

The morning bell rang, and Ms. McCallister asked us to put our supplies away and get ready to start the day. We listened to the morning announcements, and then Ms. McCallister stepped in front of the class with a smile on her face.

"Good morning boys and girls! I have some exciting news to share today. Next week is bring your father to school day. You can have your dad come and meet all of our friends and have him share what he does for work." She clapped her hands together in delight.

My sister's hand shot up in the air. The moment she was called on she asked, "What do we do if we don't have a dad?"

Giggles rippled through class and several people brought their hands in front of their mouths as they laughed. I looked around confused. It was a good question. I didn't understand why it was funny.

Ms. McCallister's face fell along with her clasped hands. I didn't like the way she was standing. "Well, that's alright. You can bring an uncle or your mom." She nodded enthusiastically.

I slumped down in my seat. My cheeks burning red for some reason. I knew we didn't have a dad. But this was the first time I remember feeling embarrassed about it.

Different.

Did everyone else really have a dad at home? Were Jade and I the only ones that didn't?

Chapter Twenty-Two

Jaxon

I didn't have words. The level of emotionally exhausted I felt was shocking. I didn't know whether to laugh or cry. I did neither. I drifted, ghosting through the motions.

I didn't know how to articulate what I was feeling. There was so much spinning in my mind. Coupled with postshow exhaustion and being full bellied. It was overwhelming and I didn't know how to process any of it.

I just knew I needed Cambri.

She got it.

Completely.

I let her take my hand and guide us up to the hotel room.

I kicked my shoes off and sat in a chair, resting my head in my hands. I ran my hands down to my neck and peered up at her.

"You okay?" she asked me.

"Yeah."

She arched a brow like she didn't believe me. Hell, I didn't believe me.

"Want to talk about it?"

"No." Pause. "I don't know."

She nodded. "I know going back inside was not easy. For what it's worth, I'm proud of you."

A strangled laugh left my lips. "For what? For all you know I went in there and tore into him."

She pressed her lips together. "It was huge. Facing a demon that has haunted you. Stepping back inside tonight was huge. It took courage. You faced it. You faced the sperm donor."

My lips cracked a smile. She didn't call him my father.

I ran my hand across the back of my neck. "Yeah. That I did. I faced the sperm donor."

"Are you glad you did?"

I blew out a breath. "Honestly, I don't know. It wasn't what I expected. He wasn't what I expected."

"Oh?"

I stared at her, looking into her bright blue eyes. "He was so – broken. He was just so broken. I don't know how to explain it. It's hard to place all the blame that I always have on him when… When you see a grown man wrecked with regret." I shook my head. "I don't know."

She nodded again. "So, you didn't punch him square in the face? Because that wouldn't have been a completely invalidated reaction." There was a lilt of humor in her voice despite the heaviness of her question.

"No." I shook my head. "I forgave him."

Her eyes went wide. She watched me with a shocked expression as silence passed between us. "You did? Jaxon that's – astronomically huge. How–how'd it go? Do you feel alright about it?"

I shrugged. "I didn't stick around for a heart-to-heart if that's what you're asking." I paused, trying to find words I did not possess. "Seeing him like that. This mess of a man. As if I was really seeing him for the first time for who he was and not who I've always made him out to be. What I've always made him out to be. I don't know. I just – I heard your voice in my head and the words just came out."

Cambri walked up to me, kneeling in front of me as she placed her hands on my knees. "Jaxon Hastings. I am so proud of you."

"Yeah?" I asked in disbelief because I didn't know if I was proud of myself. If I forgave him, I didn't feel like I could still be as angry at him as I always had been. And if I didn't have the anger, what did I have?

"Yeah. I am." She squeezed my knees. "You took back the power you had given him. You faced your demon. You forgave your dad."

Dad. She called him my dad. My throat bobbed and I swallowed down the emotion that one word caused. I nodded because it was all that I could manage.

She stood, her body weight pressing forward. I leaned back in the chair. Slowly, she brought a knee up on either side of me, climbing into my lap.

She cupped her hands on my cheeks and tilted my head back to look up at her. "That's huge." She peered down into my eyes. I gripped her hips, needing to hold onto something. Needing to ground myself in her so the emotion didn't bubble over.

I pulled her toward me. She knew exactly what I wanted. What I needed. She sat back as she lowered her lips to mine. The gentle contact cracking my chest open. I rested my forehead against hers as I swallowed back another ball of emotion.

"Jaxon." Her voice sounded tender as I felt her thumb brush across my cheek. Swiping away a tear that had managed to fall. My eyes narrowed by the shock of it. I hadn't shed a tear over my father in more than a decade. I didn't think I even could.

I leaned into her touch. She brushed away another tear. Damn it.

"You are incredible, do you know that?" she asked, brushing her hand through my hair.

I closed my eyes, trying not to let myself break wide open.

"You are strong." She placed a kiss on my forehead, and I leaned into it. "And determined." She placed a kiss on each of my closed eyes. "And brave." She kissed the tip of my nose. "And talented." She peppered kisses across my cheek. "And I am so proud of you."

My chest was breathing heavy. Everything felt heavy.

"I don't feel strong," I admitted.

"You are. What you did tonight. It takes strength."

I wiped another tear from my face. "This isn't strength. A strong man doesn't cry. Especially over something that happened a long time ago."

"You're wrong." The tone of her voice had my eyes snapping to hers. "You don't measure a man's strength by what he can keep inside. A strong man owns every part of what he faces. He stands up and confronts it head on. He doesn't cower or hide. True strength is measured by being brave enough to take on what life throws at you. To work through it. To grow. To move forward. You were strong tonight, Jaxon. I am proud of the man that you are."

Her words reached something within me. I didn't deserve this woman, but I also wasn't about to let her go.

"'Save Me.' Jelly Roll," I uttered like a desperate plea.

I grabbed onto her face and captured her lips with mine. Hers parting for me, letting me kiss her deeply, maddeningly. She moaned into my mouth, her fingers tightening in my hair, and it cracked me wide open.

A sound rumbled out from deep within me, my grip tightening on her. Every part of me needed every part of her. I couldn't get close enough. Like an extension of my soul was trying to reach hers.

I was desperate for her. Clambering for all the layers separating us. I tore them off, ripping fabric as teeth clanged together. She matched my pace. Nails digging into my skin as she removed my barriers.

I gripped her thighs, standing up with her in one swift motion. Her arms clinging to my shoulders. I walked us over to the bed.

Laying her on her back, making quick work of yanking off anything left hiding her beautiful milky skin from my view.

She sat up on her elbows, scooting backwards, looking at me with expectant eyes as she watched me undo the button on my pants. Pushing them down. Heat dancing in her eyes as I sprung to attention. Showing her exactly how ready I was to get lost in her. Be healed by her. Loved by her.

I climbed up her. Watching as she bit down on her plump lip. I leaned down to free it. Sucking it between my teeth. She clasped her hands around my neck, pulling me closer.

I dipped my head to her neck, trailing kisses down, intermixing gentle nips. Her fingers dug into my skin with each one.

I kissed down her torso, pinching her hip between my teeth before biting down on her wonderfully rounded ass. Her back arched as she gasped in pleasure. My fiery siren enjoyed me marking her skin.

I kissed the spot, then ran my hand up her body with the firm grip I had learned she likes.

I pulled myself over her, using every ounce of restraint to not fuck her senseless, before making sure she was properly taken care of, with the way she was looking up at me with lust filled eyes. "You like that?" I released in a husky voice. "It's not too much?" I double checked that it was enjoyable for her.

Pure need radiated from her as she gripped my face, looking into my eyes. "Do your worst, Mr. Hastings." She yanked me back down, crashing her lips to mine.

We became a tangle of limbs. I made sure to give attention to every part of her. Devouring her body inch by inch. Until I was certain that she was fully satisfied.

Though I never would be. I would never get enough of Cambri. Enough of her taste. Feel. Scent. The way that mind of hers worked. No, I would never get enough.

I wanted her in a way that I have never wanted anything in my life. I didn't know what that meant, but as long as she was by my side, I was fine taking it day by day until I figured it out.

She lay in my arms, head on my chest, as she drew lazy circles on me. The feel of her touch satisfying in a way I've never experienced before her.

She pressed up on her arm, looking down at me. The look on her face and the way her hair fell over her shoulder had me wondering what in the hell I'd done to deserve this. Her.

"Keep looking at me like that and I'm going to be forced to flip you back over and bite you again." I winked and a blush spread over her cheeks.

My God she was beautiful.

"Yes. But not before I tell you that I was serious earlier." She peered down at me with those eyes. "I really am proud of you, Jaxon. I just wanted you to hear that."

I reached up and tucked her hair behind her ear. Needing a reason to divert my eyes from hers as I spoke. "The tears didn't scare you away?"

She shook her head. "No. Somehow they managed to make you even sexier."

"Is that so?"

She bit her lip as she nodded. "Mmhm."

This girl. Her mannerisms stirring things back to life like I hadn't just finished making love to her. I ran my fingers through her hair, fisting them at the base of her head.

Her lips parted and a heavy breath escaped.

"Do you have any idea what you do to me?"

She lowered down. "What do I do to you?" She ghosted her lips over mine.

"I'm not sure I can properly put it into words," I murmured.

Her forehead rested against mine. "What is this?" she whispered. She didn't need to elaborate. I knew she was talking about us.

"I don't know," I answered honestly.

I could feel her nod as she accepted my words.

"But I don't have to know. Or understand it. I just need you. With me. By my side. As long as I have that. You can call it what you like. I just need you."

Her lips found mine and we expressed everything words couldn't in a kiss. I sat up, pulling her onto my lap, so that she was straddling me. Our kiss never breaking.

"Are we crazy? Is this crazy?" she asked against my lips.

"I have never felt more sane in all my life."

She let out a small laugh and I captured it with a kiss.

"You're mine, Cambri. As long as we agree on that, I don't care what we fucking call it. Girlfriend. Couple. Queen of my heart." I explained through kisses because removing her lips from mine didn't even seem possible right now. "Can we agree on that?"

She grinned against my lips. "I like the sound of that."

"Which one? It's yours."

"The first one."

"Done. You're my girlfriend."

She shook her head and I pulled back. Eyes narrowing in confusion. "No?"

"No." She confirmed, and my brows went up. "I want the first part. Where you said I'm yours."

"You just want to be mine?"

"Yes. Because you're mine."

Mine. She just wanted to be mine. I wanted to beat my chest like a Neanderthal. Her saying she just wanted to be mine ignited the man inside. A growl rumbled up from within me.

I crashed my lips back to hers and kissed her in a way that didn't leave any room for words. There was no need for them. She was mine and I was hers. Nothing else fucking mattered.

Chapter Twenty-Three

Jaxon

I don't know who plans tour routes, but there has to be some method to the madness. My brain always assumed it would be linear in motion. Then again, I'd never thought too hard on it.

Now that I'm experiencing it, it makes sense that it doesn't move in a straight line from state to state. Good Lord, the entirety of the United States couldn't even be covered if you only toured cities moving in a straight line.

It's just surprising to me that sometimes we travel straight, and sometimes we ping around like a ping-pong ball going clink, clink, clink from city to city.

Welcome to the endless musings of a musician trapped on a tour bus.

The longer we were on this thing, the more my mind wondered over different topics, especially when I couldn't distract myself with Cambri when she was working on that iPad of hers.

I'm not complaining about tour life, but it definitely starts to wear on you. The constant travel. Only getting a few days off the bus at a time.

Even on the long days, the hard days, I still wouldn't trade it for anything. This life. This experience.

Now, what they don't tell you about going on tour are about the random little stops you get to make along the way. The rest stops in some states, that showcase the beauty of that state, are amazing.

Then, there are the hidden gem finds that Cambri finds a way to secure. Like a peach orchard, farmers markets that are straight out of a picture book, old bridges along a river, etc.

We've been able to experience so much on the road. I'm trying to store away these memories the best that I can.

The longer we're on tour, the more non-music-playing obligations we acquired. Kentucky was the first time we sat down at a radio station, guest hosting a segment of a show. The radio host making it easy enough. Asking the right questions that were simple to answer and move through.

It was cool to have people calling in and interacting with us. Even when we got questions that were aimed at Back to Texas; what it was like touring with them and how they were behind the scenes.

We were in New York, about to guest host a segment on a radio station in preparation for the Madison Square Garden show, when I got a text from Jade.

Jade: Mom said you talked to Dad.

I shoved my phone in my pocket. I could not do this right now. It buzzed again.

Jade: Did you not think that was something you should mention????

I shot back a quick reply.

Jaxon: Life has been crazy. I'll tell you about it later.

I got three frowning devil emojis as response.

Jade: Being on tour does not excuse you from omitting LIFE CHANGING announcements from your twin. But fine. We'll talk when you're ready.

Jade: I love you, Jaxon

Jade: For what it's worth. I'm proud of you, baby brother.

A lump formed in my throat. I hearted her text and texted "I love you" back. I turned my phone off and then shoved it in my pocket. Swallowing as I tried to reel in the thoughts racing through my brain.

How did my mom know I talked to my dad? Are they in contact? How long has that been going on? Why does this forgiveness thing feel easier some days than others? Why does the thought of my dad talking to my mom make me want to punch someone in the face?

Fuck.

I glanced up and made eye contact with Cambri through the glass. She gave a nod and then mouthed the words, "Just today," before her attention was required elsewhere. Somehow just knowing I needed her reassuring words.

I did. More than she knew.

I made it through the show. Thankful Everett was able to take the lead on this one. Apparently, New Yorkers loved a "bad boy member of the group" as a few callers pointed out.

Everett ate it up.

Madison Square Garden was sick. New York welcomed a bunch of country music playing boys with open arms.

More and more we were beginning to hear crowds singing our lyrics along with us. More and more we were starting to feel less like an opening act and more like the headliner.

I felt like I needed to pinch myself to make sure this wasn't all some crazy dream.

Back on the bus, I texted Jade. Knowing she had a sea of questions for me. We went back and forth on what happened, and how she was sorry that I'd had to do that alone. Her leaving just before it all went down weighing heavy on her.

I'm glad she didn't call. I don't think I would have made it through that conversation, and I think she knew that. Jade wasn't one to have big conversations via text. But it was good being able to work through it like that.

In a way, it felt good talking to my sister about it. Another weight lifting from my chest. Another moment of going down this journey of forgiveness, letting go of more of the anger I had held tightly to.

Telling my sister goodnight, I walked to my bed space and crawled in, falling asleep from the emotional toll I felt.

Sometime later, I felt Cambri crawling into the space, my arm snaking around her and pulling her into me. Drifting back to sleep with the comforting scent of her.

In Chicago, my mom called. Mother's intuition. That or she just couldn't sit on it any longer.

I hadn't raised my voice at my mother since I was a child. Walking alone along the Chicago River, I was finding it difficult to keep my voice level reined in. This particular conversation opening up a flood gate of emotions. I felt betrayed that she obviously had contact with my dad and didn't tell me.

She stayed calm throughout our conversation. Explaining that my reaction right now was why she hadn't told me. She didn't want to upset me. That she had started working through her own demons years ago, but knew I wasn't ready to face mine.

"Healing like this, Jaxon. Healing from a deep hurt like you have. Isn't something me or anyone can force upon you. It's something you have to decide on and want for yourself. I love you, my sweet boy, but you're a grown man now. I can't coddle you and pretend I can kiss away all the bad. You have to trudge through this mud for yourself. And I hope that you do, Jax. Because I don't want you to live under this burden the rest of your life. I want you to find freedom from it. I want you to find joy, my son."

Apparently, it was a while ago that he had reached out to Mom to make amends, as part of his recovery steps of getting sober. But it wasn't until this past year that she was ready to have that conversation.

Facing Jade and me was a hurdle he was working up to. Some shame more difficult to face than others.

It was purely a chance encounter that had us crossing paths in Houston. My mother holding fast to her belief that things have a funny way of working out. I wanted to argue, but I held my tongue. Because hell, I just didn't know anymore.

The farther West we moved, the more I learned how beautiful this country was. How small I felt after seeing the vastness each state had to offer.

Wyoming brought a phone conversation with Jade where I explained my heart, my mindset of forgiveness. Only to experience a new wave of anger that caught me off guard. Voicing it out loud to my twin while seeing this part of the country, knowing we could have never afforded to see it growing up, cracked open new hurt that settled in anger.

I took it out on the stage.

I healed in Cambri.

Utah brought a peace that had me believing I was finally on the other side of this yo-yo of emotion.

Cambri was with me through it all. Loving me as I worked it out.

Arizona brought warmer weather. Along with another onslaught of anger. I didn't want to keep going back to this place. But forgiveness is easier said than done. It's hard to erase the memories that want to stick in place.

"Forgiveness is a powerful thing, Jaxon. Let it set you free." Cambri gave a gentle reminder in the desert. One I clung to and wrestled with. Wanting to set it all on fire. Willing it to burn away in the oranges and reds of the Arizona sunset.

Colorado.

There was a freedom I felt here. In the beauty of it all.

There was healing here. One I felt deeply as I played my music during the sound check, letting the massive red rocks absorb everything.

There was also laughter. Deep belly laughs that felt as good as they sounded. Though they might be what led to my untimely demise.

"I'd like to see you make that trek several times," Cambri let out, trying to catch her breath after her umpteenth time climbing the rock steps of Red Rocks Amphitheater.

"I would. But I can't risk being in your delicate state before the show," I teased.

She narrowed her eyes at me.

"Laugh it up, Jaxon. Laugh it up."

"Guys! You have not lived until you've seen the view of Denver from up there!" Ridge explained, jogging up to where we were standing. Not even slightly winded.

I cut my eyes to Cambri, amusement growing across my face.

She held her finger up. "Not. One. Word," she instructed.

I nodded, swallowing the laughter that tried to bubble up.

Backstage before the show, we listened as the sound of the crowd growing reverberated through the space.

Ridge was air drumming, his energy coating every inch of where we were stationed.

"The acoustics here are sick," Everett said from behind me, gaining my attention. "I cannot wait to experience it with the volume up and the crowd coming alive."

I grinned at him. "Yeah, Ev. It's gonna be sick."

Stellan sat, quietly picking at strings of the guitar he'd kept with him ever since the show with the rain delay. Needing to feel grounded in the knowledge that he was never too far from his music.

"You alright, man?" I asked, walking up to him.

"Just taking it all in, Jax. This place, there's something special about it. Do you feel it?"

I gave a nod because I didn't know how to respond. I just knew that he was right. There was something about these Red Rocks.

"Guys!" Cambri came busting into the room. "The place is almost full. People are sitting on boulders waiting to see the show. Boulders!"

Her eyes met mine and we exchanged a glance. The one that settled me before each show. The one asking if I was good.

I gave a nod and then she was herding us out to the stage.

On cue, we made our entrance, picking up instruments and taking our places. We exchanged large grins as we settled in. The smell hitting us all square in the face. Welcoming us full force to Colorado.

I strummed a cord on my guitar before grabbing the mic. "How ya doing, Colorado?"

The crowd erupted. Ready for music and an evening in this breathtaking place.

We played, soaking up the energy of this venue. Living right here in this moment.

It hit me. What I wanted to do. What I needed to do. Swept up in the music and overall vibe of being surrounded by earth. My body was buzzing with the energy.

I held up a hand to the guys, signaling for a moment before they jumped into the next song.

"We don't normally do this," I said into the mic. "But I'm hoping you guys might oblige this opening act in an impromptu moment here in this beautiful state of Colorado."

The crowd went wild, erupting in cheers.

"There's a song someone very special to me wrote. I was wondering if y'all might let me sing it here, in this space, with just this ol' guitar of mine."

The crowd again erupted in cheers and whistles. I looked around at the guys, meeting their curious glances as they followed my cue. Setting down their instruments and stepping off stage for a moment.

I strummed a couple chords. "Y'all let me know if you like it, alright?" I began playing, glancing over to meet Cambri's stunned face as I sang her words.

I wanted to play her song, her lyrics that came straight from her heart. I wanted to honor her bravery for sharing her soul and let the world see a piece of her and the amazing person that she is. The person that she is to me.

I wanted to show her just how important she was. How much I appreciated her presence in my life. I sang my heart out, hoping I was conveying everything I wanted to tell her in each strum of my guitar.

I finished the song and the crowd lost it. Glancing over to Cambri, I gestured to the roaring sea of people. Letting her take in how much her words reached them. I clapped along with the crowd, holding her gaze as I did.

When it quieted down, I leaned into the mic. "How about we get the guys back out here for one last song before we get to the part all you good people came out for tonight?"

The guys retook their places as the crowd welcomed them back out.

We played our last song, giving it everything we had. Sharing this moment with everyone who filled this space.

When it was over, I thanked the crowd for letting us play and then went straight to Cambri. I slung the guitar around to my back, not bothering to even pass it off. I walked straight up to her, gripped her cheeks in my hands and met her lips with my own.

I pulled back, looking into her eyes. "Your words. They moved them. I wish you could have seen what I saw as I sang your words over them."

She looked at me for a moment. "Thank you." She gripped the shirt at my waist. "Just today."

I dropped my forehead to hers, breathing her in. "Just today," I echoed back.

Chapter Twenty-Four

Cambri

Night after night. Show after show. It had all led us here. To California. Our last stop of the tour. It was bittersweet watching this come to an end. I planned to enjoy every last second of it.

Northern California's stop at Levi Stadium was magnificent. The weather was spectacular. We seriously lucked out weather wise. It was the perfect temp and not a cloud in the sky.

And the lack of bugs…I mean, it's not that there weren't any. But there were noticeably less than in Tennessee. Points for that alone.

On our way to Southern California, I had Bear pull over so we could take time to walk the beach. Each of us peeled off our socks and shoes, enjoying the feel of the sand between our toes.

As the guys strolled down the coastline, I turned and walked into the water. It was freezing, but I still managed to let the water cover my feet. I closed my eyes and breathed in the salty ocean air as the breeze blew my hair back.

Jaxon stepped up beside me, taking my hand in his. I heard him take in an inhale, breathing this moment in along with me.

I looked over at him, watching him stare out into sea. "Where's your head?"

He blew out. "'Something in the Orange.' Zach Bryan." He glanced at me as he squeezed my hand.

I squeezed his right back, searching his face. "Are you alright, my rock star?"

"As long as I'm yours."

I pursed my lips together, feeling a light blush spread across my cheeks, as I shifted my gaze back out to the sea, watching the water move in and out, shocking our feet with the cold each time it rolled back over them.

"'Wild.' Carter Faith," I said into the breeze, his hand pressing into mine, acknowledging that my words hadn't gotten lost in the sea.

We stayed that way for a while. Hand in hand. Staring out into the water. We both felt it, but neither of us wanted to acknowledge it.

The end. The way it felt for this experience to be wrapping up the same way a good book reaches its finality. It's bittersweet because it needs to end, but it was so good while it lasted.

The feeling of it all hit me. I released Jaxon's hand and walked further out into the water, soaking my rolled-up pants. I bent down and let the water run through my fingers, enjoying the way it felt to have the cool sensation pass between each one.

I stood up and closed my eyes. I took in the scent of the air, the wind on my face, all of it. I opened my eyes on a deep inhale, soaking it all up for as long as I could.

I turned to find Jaxon in the same spot I left him, watching me. I could feel the intensity of his stare. A smirk on his face. He wore it well. It would almost be annoying if he wasn't so pretty. But damn if him knowing he was sexy didn't make him that much more appealing.

It was interesting that someone so beautiful, so talented, could be wrestling with so much from a lifetime of hurt. I was proud of how far he had come. For not giving up when the pain resurfaced again and again.

He fought through it every time, the best way he could. Reaching for the freedom that came from releasing the type of anger that had held him so tightly in its grip.

I walked back to that face. Into his arms. I reached up, cupping his jaw with both of my hands, meeting his lips with my own as he leaned into me.

A spray of water, accompanied with the laughter from the other guys broke us apart. We took in the scene before leaping into action to join in the water battle.

I'm sure we were a sight to take in. A group of grown adults, running around the shallow water, kicking and scooping water up with cupped hands, throwing it at one another.

Laughter overtook each of us as we delivered each round of spray to whoever we could reach. It was infectious. It was incredible.

One by one we waded out of the shallows and lay down on the sand. Laughing through the cold, talking, sharing this moment. We needed this. This afternoon to just be. To just live. To enjoy just today.

We filed back onto the bus, and as we did, I paused to turn around and take in the scene one last time. The coast. Its vast expanse. The hint of endless possibility. It held the promise of everything to come.

Back on the road, I squished into my favorite spot on the bus. Right next to Ridge.

"Whatcha got there?" I asked him.

"Oreos." He wagged his brows, holding the package out to me.

I grinned as I reached in and grabbed one. Popping it into my mouth. Used to my antics, Ridge just shook his head as he relaxed back into the seat.

We drove the remainder of the day and into the night, stopping only for food. This was it. The last town and the last stop of the tour.

The boys had a few hours to kill before the final sound check, and we spent it walking around the city. Relaxing before being stationed in the venue for the duration of the time. After the sound checks began, it always seemed to be like a ball rolling downhill crashing into the start of the concert.

Tonight, everyone from the stage crew to the lighting and sound people were buzzing around trying to make sure everything was perfect. To make sure we went out in a blaze of glory.

The energy before the last show is hard to describe with words. It's like everyone was painfully aware that this was it, but wanting to marinate in it just a bit longer. Not quite ready to acknowledge the end looming right around the corner.

"How'd we sound, doll?" Everett hopped down off the stage, spiking his hair up with one hand.

My brows inched up my forehead.

Everett cleared his throat. "Cambri. How'd we sound, Cambri."

I eased up on him, though I can't say I didn't enjoy, at least a little, my ability to tame the beast that was Everett.

"Awesome. You guys sound really good. The crowd is going to eat y'all up tonight."

A wicked grin formed on his face. "I sure hope so."

I reached out and patted him on the shoulder. "Oh, Everett. There is a special girl out there that is going to love the special concoction that is you."

He placed his hands over his heart. "Aww, Cam. That may be the nicest thing you have ever said to me."

I couldn't hold it in. A laugh escaped my lips. Oh, how I was going to miss this time with these boys. Interacting with them the way I had during this tour.

Two warm arms came up behind me, wrapping me snugly against the man my body has memorized the feel of.

"Okay. Give it to me straight," he said, placing his chin on my shoulder. "What would you change about that sound check?"

"Honestly?" I craned my neck around to see his eyes. "Not a thing. You guys nailed it."

He pulled me back against him, addressing Everett. "I guess this is it then. What a ride it has been."

"That is for damn sure."

I was signaled over to make my rounds and double check that everything was squared away as the boys disappeared to get concert-ready. By the time I made it to their room, they were hyped and ready to go.

I watched as Jaxon shook off some energy down his arms and through his fingertips. When he stilled his eyes met mine.

He gave me that nod.

Then I glanced around at each of the guys, taking in the preshow scene one last time. I grinned at them. "Okay y'all, one last time. Get out there and show them who you are!"

The guys played their hearts out. You could feel the energy pass between them and the crowd. They were meant for this. They were born for this. They were natural at captivating the audience with their lyrics and performance. This is where they were meant to be.

With each song that passed, the weight in my chest settled in a little more. The looming goodbye drifting in like an inescapable tide. The end of their set drew near, and it felt like the end of an era.

They came off the stage this last night, emotion written over each of their faces. We attempted our usual celebration routines, but it turned into one big group hug. Ridge being the one who audibly choked up first. Sending the wave out to the rest of us.

I pulled him into his own embrace. "You played your heart out on that stage tonight. I hope you feel so proud of what you did out there."

"Thanks, Cam." His voice laden with emotion. He pulled himself together before walking away to watch them swap the set out for Back to Texas one last time.

I turned to face Jaxon. "That was it."

"That was it," he agreed. "What now?"

I gave a shrug of my shoulders. "We pack it all up and go home. Work our butts off to line up a tour that you guys headline. The music we released before the tour is being bought and downloaded like crazy on all platforms. You boys have caught on like wildfire. The label is wanting to move forward with the momentum right away."

"No shit?" His eyes shot up in surprise.

I laughed. "Yes, shit. Or whatever the appropriate response is to that."

Jaxon stood there shaking his head like he truly couldn't believe it.

"You better buckle up, cowboy. Mitch wants you guys in the studio as soon as we get back, cutting a record. That, and I will be lining up as many press outings as we can get our hands on. Local news, morning shows, et cetera."

His grin stretched from ear to ear. "Cambri, this is surreal."

I held up a finger, reaching up to hold my earpiece against my ear to focus on the sound. "Say that again," I instructed into the microphone. My eyes lit up, glancing back to Jaxon. "Come on," I motioned for him to follow me as I walked around gathering up the other guys. "Come with me. All of you."

I led them to the edge of the stage area where you could hear the crowd. They were chanting. For the boys. Vibrations of "Reckless" could be felt going off in waves around the room.

"Y'all did it. Y'all have fans. Drink it up, guys. Each one of you deserves it. Each and every one of you." I made eye contact with each member of the group, driving home my point.

I am insanely proud of them. The guys and their natural charisma had taken the country music world by storm. The possibilities and doors that were about to open for these guys would be amazing.

The video that went viral, the one that made them the solo opening act for this tour, had set off a set of shockwaves. Riding that momentum into this tour was the smartest thing we could have done.

Right now, the crowd, they weren't chanting for Back to Texas. They were chanting for the boys. I looked at them with a big goofy grin before I started clapping. I hope they relished in how this felt. How they felt right here, right now. This was going to be just the start for them.

These guys were going to be big time. I could feel it.

Jaxon grabbed my hand and twirled me around. Each of the guys beginning to dance around to the sound of the crowd chanting their name. Then he swept me up in his arms, leaning me back and pressed his lips to mine.

I never wanted to forget how this felt. How we felt. Right here. Right now.

Just today.

Jaxon

We watched the entirety of the last Back to Texas show right from the sideline. We sang and danced to the songs right along with the rest of the crowd.

Every new song left a piercing feeling in my chest as it started. Each one a familiar bittersweet sting of a goodbye.

The encore lit up the stage and we all subconsciously stepped together, screaming out the lyrics as if they were our last breath. Our eyes filling with tears as the song neared an end.

The crowd lost it when the stage went dark. Cheers and screams echoing throughout the stadium. Everyone around me gripped a shirt next to them. Tears streaming down our faces, no longer on the inside.

I wasn't prepared for this. None of us were prepared for the onslaught of emotions we would experience once the tour ended. The finality of it, it hit in an unexpected way.

Back to Texas dismounted the stage, a range of emotions all their own. But nothing like my huddled-up gang. I guess one day, the wrapping up of a tour won't feel like the crushing weight that it does to a bunch of first timers from a small town, thankful as hell to just be here.

The gratitude we each felt for this journey was unfathomable. And though I could taste the bittersweet end of the tour, there was also the hope of a new beginning.

The news Cambri shared was mind-blowing. That the label wants to move forward right away with our own tour. I still find that I am pinching myself that our short time in Nashville, and then the exposure from this tour, has caused our music to blow up like it has.

This is the dream.

This is what everyone dreams about, and it is happening for us. I wish I could go back in time, and tell that little boy that it gets better. That his dreams come true. That he gets the girl. That it all works out in the end. That his dad leaving and mom working night shifts just to put food on the table doesn't last forever. I wish I could hug him and whisper in his ear, "Just today."

Chapter Twenty-Five

Cambri

I blinked and it was all over.

The experience of a lifetime came and went, and then we were all thrown back into the daily grind of real life.

The tour was a dream. It felt fast and furious, demanding, and exhausting. But all in the absolute best way possible.

I couldn't wait to do it again. I couldn't wait to get swept back up into the exhilarating rush of it all. Experiencing tour life made being back home feel mundane and relentless. I was now hyper aware of every minute spent in the office.

The only saving grace of being back from the tour was that things had been busier than ever. It made pausing to miss it all difficult because there was always something to do. There was always some item to check off the to-do list, and a fire to put out.

The business side of the boys' band exploding has had me attached to my phone twenty-four hours a day from the moment my feet hit Nashville soil. I think I am averaging four to five hours of sleep per night.

It's been insane.

On top of that, I have officially taken Alyssa on as a client and have been swamped in building her from the ground up. Revamping social media, her brand, all the fine print.

I was right about her having that something special. I pitched her to the label, and they were all over it.

I'm currently working around the clock and am fully aware that this pace isn't sustainable long term. But right now, I am all in, in every way. I can sleep when I'm dead.

The tour was huge for the boys' career, but it was also groundbreaking for mine. I proved what I was capable of in such a way that my value to the label could no longer be ignored.

I landed the promotion and thought there was no way I could feel happier about it. Until I saw Easton's face contorted in an unnatural way when he tried to hide his shock and disappointment that the position was mine.

I think watching the way I ran the demands of the tour, while keeping up with things at the office, helped my dad finally view me more through the lens of a businesswoman and less like his little girl playing dress-up.

It's been fulfilling to feel more like an equal, like I belong in this arena. That I'm not here just because of who my father is.

"Welcome to the big leagues, baby girl." My dad wrapped an arm around my shoulders, pressing a kiss against the side of my head after that first joint meeting with Alyssa. My chest filled with pride as he walked away. I finally felt seen, like my seat at the table actually mattered.

But it has been nonstop. And if I'm being honest, it's finally starting to catch up to me.

I was given additional bands to reimage and revamp at the label. In this industry, image is everything. Your fans need to feel connected to you and like each individual matters.

Crafting the relationship between the artist and the fan and doing so in a way that feels authentic is not just a recommendation, it's a necessity to stay relevant.

Between those bands, getting Alyssa started, and keeping the boys' momentum from the tour going, it has had me spread thin. It's running me ragged, but also feeling more alive than I've ever been.

Sarah would have loved it. All of it.

I think that's what has kept me going. Owing it to her to see this through. Chase this down 'til the end. Until I've accomplished everything we said we would.

Business relationships have left little time for personal relationships. Which has left little time for me and Jaxon.

Me and Jaxon.

How to describe things with Jaxon…

Being home has certainly presented challenges in that area. We basically have zero time together other than when I meet with him and the guys for band-related things. Though even that has been few and far between recently as most of their time is in the recording studio, and most of mine is bouncing back and forth between bands and office requirements. So much is handled via email or text right now.

We've lost that uncomplicated ease from the tour that made us so good. Being back in Tennessee, back in the real world, we both jumped headfirst back into business mode and well – things have not been easy.

Complicated.

It has all been a bit complicated.

I miss him. I miss us. I miss the way we fit together so seamlessly on the tour. On the road, being with him felt like breathing. It was natural – instinctual. We didn't have to force anything or try too hard. There was no thinking involved. We just were. We just fit. We lived for the moment, enjoying the way it all blended together so organically. I miss that. I miss him. I miss all of it.

I pulled up to my condo as the sun was setting and noticed a particularly handsome shaggy blond sitting on the step by the front door. Jaxon. I forgot to text Jaxon. We were supposed to grab dinner.

The list of missed dinners was starting to pile up. One of us always getting caught up or stuck in something we couldn't get out of. Or, like today, being so dog tired, it just slipped my mind.

I opened the garage door and pulled my car into the oversized one-car garage. Inside, I laid my head on the steering wheel. Taking a breath in, I wondered how long he had been sitting there waiting on me. I lifted my head and took the elastic off my wrist, taking a moment to pull my hair back and out of my face.

I dragged myself out of my car, mentally and physically exhausted. Life currently was a lot. But it was everything. I was chasing my dream.

I shut the garage door and made my way to the front door to let Jaxon in. He stood and turned around at the sound of the door opening.

"Hey," I said, leaning against the door frame.

He had his hands in his pockets. "Hey."

We stood and took each other in for a moment.

"I'm sorry," I started at the same time he said, "Can I come in," each pausing to let out a tired laugh. His days have been long too. A fact that only added to the guilt I was feeling as it was never fun waiting around on someone.

Though he looked more ready to curl up and pass out rather than angry with me.

I stepped back to let him in. "I'm sorry. I got caught up digging into the fine print of a contract and everything slipped my mind."

He pulled me into him and kissed me in response.

"Jaxon…"

"Uh-uh," he uttered, more like a sound than actual words against my mouth.

I knew we needed to talk about the way it'd been lately. The crazy, relentless, busyness of it all. The long list of missed texts, dinners, and conversations.

Him kissing me the way that he was kissing me, with his hands pressed into my skin the way that they were, made it difficult to remember exactly why that was. I gave into the sensation of him, one of us reaching over to close the door before we began climbing the stairs to the second floor.

Despite it all, my body craved him in a particular sort of way. Craved the unique cocktail that was Jaxon Hastings. The electricity I felt when he was near me, touching me, made everything else fade away.

When he looked at me with that hungry look in his eye, like he wanted to devour me, I didn't stand a chance. It made everything go fuzzy and flooded me with a raw need to be consumed by him. A need to be kissed by him, touched by him, until there wasn't an inch of me left that hadn't been marked by him in some way.

Several steps up and my back hit the wall on the stairs, my breathing heavy as his lips traveled along my neck, both of our fingers busily undoing buttons and removing layers. We peeled off the wall and made it almost to the top before a foot caught. We went down seemingly in slow motion. Arms going out and bracing for the inevitable blow, my backside taking most the impact.

I hardly noticed.

His lips were traveling down my torso causing my breaths to grow ragged in anticipation.

He shoved my skirt up around my waist, then yanked down the thin barrier that stood in his way. He ran his hands up the middle of my thighs, pressing them apart while he settled in front of me. My fingers tangled in his hair as he placed a kiss on the inside of my thigh.

His grip on me tightened, and then he buried himself in my center, finding that rhythm that had my head falling back. A moan escaped my lips, and he became more ravenous in response. Swirling his tongue until my body coiled up, begging to break free.

I ground my hips into him, my grip tightening in his hair, causing his own groan of pleasure to sound from his lips. The small vibration giving me what I needed to let go. I cried out as I tumbled over the edge, his name spilling from my lips in ragged breaths. His determined movements only stopping when I pushed against him forcefully.

He made quick work of his pants. Then he was over me, holding himself up with an arm while lining himself up with my entrance. He pushed inside of me in one thrust, my body ready for him.

He made love to me, crashing into me again and again while our eyes were locked onto each other's, letting the action replace all the unsaid words between us. It was rough, and desperate, and needy. Both of us clinging onto each other; my fingers digging down his arms as we moved. We got lost in the feeling, lost in us, lost in the way we felt without all the complications taking the front and center.

He grabbed onto my thigh, running his hand up to cup my backside, pulling me against him as he thrust into me, finding his own release.

I cried out his name, feeling him exactly where I needed to to find my own reprieve as my eyes clamped shut, unable to stay open. He clung onto me, not stopping until I was able to open my eyes again. Steadying my breathing, I came down from the high he ignites within my body.

He collapsed onto me, and I held him close. My hands working their way through his hair as I focused on his breaths. He placed a kiss on my collarbone and then my neck. He brushed his lips across my cheek, and I placed a gentle kiss on his jaw.

We traded these delicate exchanges, slowly coming up to sitting. He pulled me into him, and I savored the feeling of just being held in his arms.

We stood up from the stairs. Our hands fitting together, fingers intertwining.

Our feet padded across the floor as he led us down the hall and into my room. We crawled into the covers, his arms engulfing me as we snuggled into the warmth. My eyes grew heavy, and I gave into the darkness pulling me under, allowing myself to fall into a deep sleep in the comfort of his arms.

Movement beside me roused me from my sleep the following morning. Jaxon shifted as his eyes opened. A smile growing on his face when his eyes met mine.

He was handsome. Devastatingly so.

I smiled back at him, running a hand through his hair as I took him in. I loved it, the way it felt tangling my fingers in it, and watching his eyes sparkle under my touch.

"Jaxon," I began.

He pulled me into him, silencing me with a kiss. With zero concerns for morning breath. I guess living in close quarters on a bus, for as long as we did, changes things.

He shifted and I turned, pressing my back into his chest. He wrapped his arm around me and nuzzled into my neck.

"We need to talk," I whispered. Afraid to say it out loud, afraid of what it might change.

"About what?" His warm breath on my neck releasing shivers where it touched.

"Dinner. Me missing dinner," I explained.

"You were busy. Work is crazy right now." He offered the explanation as my excuse.

"Me forgetting about the dinner," I reiterated.

"You were busy," he said again.

"Jaxon, I totally forgot. It slipped my mind."

"And I forgot about lunch last week."

"Your recording session went long."

"Still forgot."

"Why is this..."

"Cambri." I felt the excuse he was about to make.

"Okay fine. How about the dinner you missed?" I asked.

He chuckled. Chuckled – like it was nothing. Like he didn't feel the thread beginning to unravel.

"Is that what this is about? Me missing dinner? Rehearsal ran late that night. You know I would never choose to skip out on you." He placed a kiss on the base of my head.

I turned in his arms and let my eyes find his. "No. I'm not mad that you missed dinner, or the text, or anything else because you're chasing your dream. You should be chasing your dream. It's your dream." He shot an eyebrow up. I let out a sigh. "This all feels complicated. That's the point. I'm not mad about who missed what.

We are both busy. Our schedules are pulling us in so many different directions. It all just feels so…"

"Complicated," he filled in.

I gave a nod. "Yes."

His shoulder raised. "So, it's complicated. Hell, everything right now is complicated. Finding time to eat a sandwich is complicated. But this," he gestured between us, "the rest I feel when we can take five minutes to slow down together. This isn't complicated. This is a fucking lifeline."

I nodded, absorbing the conviction in his words, studying his eyes and the truth behind them. For now, maybe that's all I needed. All that we needed, five minutes to rest in each other.

The alarm on my cell phone went off, breaking the mirage of the reassuring silence that passed between us. I rolled over and turned it off, sitting up and placing my feet on the floor.

I looked around and then remembered that most of our clothes were on the stairs. I stood up, taking the comforter with me as I made my way to the shower.

"Boo," he complained as I walked away. I felt the gentle tug against the comforter, and I turned back to look at him, a smile forming at the sight of his pout. I dropped the comforter just past my shoulders and his eyes lit up.

I rolled my eyes. "You are such a man." I walked away letting the comforter fall to the floor.

"You say that like it is a bad thing," he called after me.

He met me in the bathroom, pulling his jeans up and over his hips, not bothering to button them. I spit toothpaste into the sink, while the fogging mirror indicated that the shower was ready.

My eyes naturally gravitated toward his gaping pants. The way his happy trail spilled out and gave way to his bare chest. He was yummy. And yes, I was aware of how that sounded, but it was the honest to God truth and there was literally no other word to describe him like this. The way his jeans hung low, unbuttoned, teasing everything that was unseen, was yummy. Every. Last. Inch of him.

I placed my toothbrush in the holder and watched as he picked up the one that he kept here and squirted toothpaste onto it.

After the tour, we each had a toothbrush that just showed up at the other's place. Along with a few other miscellaneous items of comfort such as an old pair of sweatpants, extra undies, etc.

It's something that just happened once we started finding ourselves crashing at each other's house after a late night at the office. You quickly learn that having a few personal items on hand is a simple luxury that you appreciate when you don't make it back to your house in order to see the other one after a long day.

I crossed my arms and leaned against the bathroom counter, standing quietly while he brushed his teeth. Jaxon Hastings found a way to make even the simplest action sexy.

The way his arm flexed while he ran his toothbrush back and forth across his teeth. The way his other hand made an effort to tame his bed head. Not that his bed head even needed taming. Honestly, even that worked for him.

He oozed male primal sexiness.

He spit out his toothpaste and placed his toothbrush next to mine, then placed a hand on either side of me, trapping me between his arms. "Your shower's ready."

"Care to join?"

He answered by sliding his jeans down and stepping out of them. I bit down on my lip.

"After you." He stood back and gestured with his hand. He followed me inside, hiding away in the warmth that waited in the small enclosure.

"You headed into the office or are you meeting with clients in the studio today?" he asked me as we dressed.

"Both," I supplied. "I'm gonna check in at Norwood Records this morning to get a few things done. I have a meeting at 10:45, and then I'm off to the studio. Alyssa and Wyatt Logan have overlapping studio times. So, I'll probably be there for the remainder of the afternoon once I arrive."

He nodded, running his fingers over the scruff on his chin.

"What about you? What's your day look like?"

Crossing his arms, he shrugged. "Studios are booked, and my PR rep is busy with other clients. We may rehearse a few new songs, but other than that today is fairly light."

I deflated. "It feels like our light days never line up," I whined more than I intended to, but I couldn't help it. Not having more than the late nights we could steal together was really starting to get to me.

"I'm sorry." I clamped my eyes shut for a second before meeting his eyes. Forcing myself to sound more like an adult and less like a whiny teenager. "I'm just tired and I miss you." I shrugged. "I miss us."

He pulled me into him and rested his chin on the top of my head.

"I know." He held me in his arms, and I focused on the inhale from his chest. "One day this will all calm down, and I'm going to whisk you away to somewhere warm and tropical. Where clothes will be optional, but certainly not encouraged." He peered back and gave me a devilish grin. "Right now, we are both just getting started so our time is being demanded at crazy levels. I know it's hard and exhausting." He ran his hand down my back. "But this won't last forever. Just today," he finished.

"Just today," I repeated back against his chest.

"For the record." He looked down at me, causing me to peer up into his eyes. "I miss you too."

I melted. Blame it on the exhaustion and relentless demand of my schedule, but my eyes filled with tears. I blinked them away, resting my head on his chest, and took a deep breath.

"You're going to be late, Ms. Norwood." He ran a hand down my back.

"I know." But I didn't care. The pace of it all was starting to feel overwhelming and I found myself wanting to push pause for a moment. Just long enough to catch my breath and stay here with him like this.

I peeled myself away from him and smoothed my hair into place with my hands. He watched me silently as I did.

"Want to try for dinner again tonight since your day is light? I should be able to sneak away since both of my studio bookings are earlier afternoon."

He shoved his hands in his jean pockets. "Let's leave it at I'll see you when I see you. Then no one is missing a dinner," he suggested.

I gave him a tight-lipped smile as I nodded once. "Yeah. Absolutely," I let out as I felt a crushing weight in my chest at his words. "*I'll see you when I see you.*"

I walked away before he could see the tears resurface in my eyes. I really needed to get more sleep. It was not like me to be this emotional.

I took a deep breath to steady myself as I made my way to the kitchen to grab a banana before descending the stairs to my garage.

I heard him following after me. Once I grabbed my things and was more in control of my emotions, I turned around. I forced a grin onto my face. "I'll – see you when I see you."

Tonight, tomorrow, a week from now. I hated that phrase. The nights we stole were already spreading further apart. It felt like leaving it like this was signing a death warrant to this love affair we had. Leaving him with that phrase felt like we were pulling that loose thread further apart. Unraveling what little remained that held us together in the first place.

He shoved his hands into his jean pockets. "Have a great day, Cambri."

"You too."

I turned and walked down the stairs that lead to my garage as I shook my head. "*You too?*" What the hell? I made it to the door that opened to the garage, grabbed the door handle, and then turned and faced the stairs. I thought briefly about stomping back up them and over to him. Informing him that I was not fine with leaving things at, "I'll see you when I see you." Insisting that we talk about how it feels like we're falling apart. That we find a way to fix it before we completely shatter. Slowly. Piece by piece. I wanted to pound on his chest and demand for him to explain why this wasn't killing him the way it felt like it was killing me.

I didn't do any of that. That's not how adults handle things, and I had already voiced my concerns. Though currently, I wasn't sure I cared how adults handled anything. I'd never experienced a love like this, and I was scared that I was losing it. It felt like I was losing my mind.

I scolded myself at the thought. Because I knew better. I knew my career goals and I knew his. I had worked so hard to climb this ladder, to reach where I wanted to be.

I was frustrated with myself. I knew better than to get involved with anything even remotely serious because this life is demanding. The only relationship I truly had room for was with the music.

Definitely not with someone whose schedule was as demanding as mine.

Definitely not with a musician.

I shook my head, tearing my gaze from the stairs, and made my fingers turn the door handle. I made it to my car, opened the garage door, turned on my car, and slipped on my shades all on autopilot. Because I was in way over my head.

Because I had gone and fallen in love with a rock star.

Somewhere, I knew Sarah was watching all of this and grinning like the damned Cheshire cat. It would be great if she could also manage to point me in the right direction. Give me a semblance of clarity because I felt like I was drowning.

I held my hands out wide. "A little help here would be nice."

I gripped the steering wheel and laid my head back against the headrest.

I began to back out of the garage when my eyes caught sight of something in my periphery. I looked at the floorboard on the passenger side and saw the metallic shine of a guitar pick. I undid my seatbelt and then leaned over to snatch it, my foot pressing into the brake as I did.

I held the pick between my fingers, twirling it around. I glanced up at my house door and thought seriously for a moment about going back inside. Calling the office and taking a personal day.

I shook the thought off. I had people waiting on me, depending on me to show. This was the job, the demands, the requirements. This was everything I'd wanted for as long as I could remember.

I took my foot off the brake and continued to back out of the garage. I wasn't that person. I didn't let people down. I showed up when I was supposed to. I did my job. I crushed the job.

I wanted this career more than anything. So why did it feel like I was making the wrong choice right now? Why did it feel like I was tearing a piece of my own heart away?

Jaxon

I thought I was helping ease her stress because she was juggling so much. Hell, I had just told her that being with her was the only uncomplicated thing in my life.

The look on her face when I told her let's leave it at "I'll see you when I see you" – I didn't know how to undo it. I had wounded her when I was trying to make it better.

I couldn't find the words to explain. I watched her walk away.

The next time her eyes found mine, she plastered on a brave smile. I told her to "Have a great day." I pinched the bridge of my nose. I'm an idiot.

I listened for the sound of the garage door to open and when I didn't hear it, I almost marched down the stairs, told her that this was nuts, and that we needed a day. I wanted to throw her over my shoulder and carry her back to bed.

I should have demanded that she call in sick and let me spend the day showing her all the ways that I in fact did not want to wait until I got to see her again. I should have sat her on her bed and made her watch as I emptied a dresser drawer beside her and insist that it was now mine. The same way that she was mine.

She was pulling away from me and I didn't know how to stop it. She had never once told me not to chase my dream. I couldn't be the asshole that told her not to chase hers. Even if it was what ultimately made her walk away from me.

I slid my hand down my face. I'm such a fucking idiot. I know better than this. To get this involved. To feel this attached. I know better.

People always leave in the end.

Maybe not out of your life like I was used to. Cambri was too embedded in our music for that. But she was leaving me on a personal level, and it felt like my heart was being ripped right out of my chest.

Cambri had believed in the band from day one. She had been our biggest cheerleader and supporter. I didn't want to be that guy. The one that told her not to chase her dream. But every time we separated, it was getting harder and harder not to. Her dream was keeping her away from me. Her dream was the thing that was tearing us apart.

She is incredibly career driven, if she thought for a moment that I was trying to stand in her way, it would push her too far and that would be it. So, I just let her walk down the stairs and away from me. Even if it was letting her do the very thing that I was most afraid of.

Leave.

When the door to her garage finally began to close, I ran a hand through my hair. It no longer mattered what I considered doing. I heard her car back onto the street, and I walked over to the window and watched her drive away.

My phone beeped, stealing my attention. I checked it and groaned. I had been summoned to Norwood Records. I was going to have to be quick if I wanted to make it back to the house the guys and I shared to get fresh clothes before my meeting. I found my shirt and the rest of my items that had gotten discarded in various places last night, and then let myself out. Making sure to turn the lock behind me before I shut the door.

I arrived at Norwood Records with the rest of my band. I texted Cambri on our way to see if she knew what this was about, and she replied that she was as in the dark as we were.

We filed into the room and took our seats. Cambri was the last to arrive, apologizing for the holdup as she took the seat opposite me. We all turned to Easton Davenport who was standing at the head of the table, next to where Alyssa was sitting.

"Thank you all for joining us on such short notice. I appreciate that each of you could make this work. I know your time is very valuable." He glanced at Cambri, who motioned for him to continue.

"My client and I," he began, motioning to Alyssa.

Cambri sat forward. "You mean our client here at Norwood Records?" she questioned.

Easton grinned. The fucker had the nerve to grin before he delivered the blow. "Actually, no. Alyssa has chosen to go with different representation as of late. Citing that she felt you were unable to give her the attention she needs to launch her career."

Cambri gave a tight-lipped smile, turning to Alyssa. "Alyssa, I wish you would have talked to me before making changes to your representation. I'm sure we could have found a way to make you feel like you were getting the coverage you deserve."

Alyssa at least had the decency to look remorseful. "It's not personal, Cambri. I am so grateful for you finding me and giving me this opportunity. It's just that Mr. Davenport made some really valuable points about the direction of my career and well..." She paused and looked up at Easton, who gave her a nod. "There are a few things that he is able to handle differently. To give me exclusive coverage like you were able to do with Reckless. That type of representation really launched their career." She quickly glanced back over at Easton. "I really hope there are no hard feelings. I'm just trying to do what is right for my music," she stammered.

Easton coughed. "Thank you, Alyssa. I'll take it from here."

Cambri turned her attention back to Easton. "You poached my artist. And clearly coached the conversation. Bravo, Easton."

"Cambri," Alyssa jumped in. "I really am sorry. I just wanted what they had," she said, gesturing to my band.

A placated smile plastered onto Cambri's face. A cool indifference masking the rage that I'm sure was burning inside. She had been excited about Alyssa. She'd worked hard to get her signed here at the label. Though I'm sure "Mr. Davenport" left out those details.

Cambri waved off Alyssa's comment. "You did what you felt was best for your career." Alyssa gave her a sheepish grin as she sunk down into her chair.

Turning back to Easton, Cambri pressed on. Assuming the professional role she was bred for after this apparent ambush. "Is there more to this meeting? I'm assuming so since you included

Reckless as well. Or is it that you have gone and poached them too?"

She briefly cut her eyes to me, and I gave her a look that said she was crazy if she ever thought we would go with someone other than her. Especially Easton Davenport.

Easton smiled again. He had no idea how dangerously close I was to launching out of this chair and wiping that grin right off his face. "Of course not. I will be focusing my time on Alyssa," he said haughtily. "I called this meeting because she and I wanted to approach you and Reckless about potential mutually beneficial business." Cambri quirked an irritated brow. "We would like to propose a photo op between Jaxon and Alyssa in a more intimate setting." He said the last part carefully.

"A more intimate setting?" Cambri questioned.

"Nothing too revealing. Just something that could suggest that there was a budding romance. The media coverage would be mutually beneficial for both parties." He enunciated the word "mutually," trying to drive home that he had everyone's best interests in mind.

"Reckless doesn't need fake media news. They are soaring all on their own. I'm afraid we aren't interested in your proposal."

"Cambri, I hope you won't let personal feelings cloud your judgement. I understand this not being the best timing after finding out Alyssa's business move, but for the sake of their careers…"

"I think I've heard enough," I interrupted, standing from my chair. "Like she said, we aren't interested."

The guys didn't need any encouragement to stand and follow.

Everett let out a smug laugh before turning to Cambri. "Cam, please let us know how it is possible to never have to meet with this joker again. And since sharing helpful information isn't something you two seem to do before meetings, it may also be mutually," he said pointedly, "beneficial to let him know that even a shark knows when to retreat into deeper water." Everett said the last part cutting his eyes over to Easton.

I stood in the door with a smug grin on my face as the guys filed out one by one.

"Is your client threatening me, Cambri?"

I really wanted to be done with this meeting, and I certainly didn't want to step on Cambri's toes, but this guy got under my skin and made it very difficult not to puff out my chest and shut him the hell up.

"Nah, man." I stepped back into the room. "We just wanted to make sure we didn't have any misunderstandings about any future mutually beneficial business opportunities." I shook my head, turning to exit the room. Leaving Cambri with an amused grin on her face.

"Well, I think that about does it. As always, Easton, it was a pleasure," I heard her say as I made my way down the hall.

I walked straight to her office and leaned against her desk, waiting for her to appear, crossing my arms in front of my chest. I only had to wait a few minutes before she sought the solitude I knew that she would after being ambushed by one Easton Davenport. Her eyes found mine, that polished professional front dropping.

"What the hell?" She made her way to her desk, tossing her iPad onto it.

"The guy is an asshole," I supplied.

She paced back and forth. "The only reason he went after Alyssa was to get at me. He's pissed that I landed the promotion."

I gave a sideways nod as I shifted my weight. "It certainly seemed calculated."

She stopped pacing, moving to my side. She leaned back, placing a hand on her desk and the other against her forehead while clamping her eyes shut. "How did this happen?" She opened her eyes and placed both hands on the desk behind her. "How did I not see this coming? We were good. Everything was good. We were working on her album in the studio."

"Cam." I nudged her shoulder with mine. "I honestly don't think it has anything to do with you, and that it has everything to do with Easton being a special kind of snake. He's in a position of power. Attractive." She bobbed her head back, craning to look over at me. "All I'm saying, is that I'm sure he knew all the right things to say to her to make her question everything."

She blew out a breath. "But what would make her jump ship without at least talking to me first?"

I shrugged my shoulders. "Like I said, Easton is a special kind of snake. I bet he preyed upon her and her innocence with the promise of all her dreams coming true. Dangling that kind of nugget in front of someone who is young and hungry would be dangerously tempting."

"Oh really?" She quirked a brow.

"Yes. Really." I nudged her shoulder again with mine. "You could tell she was visibly torn on whether or not she made the right decision. She was extremely uncomfortable. I think you hit the nail right on the head when you said that he coached her. Coached her, tempted her, seduced her..."

She looked at me with disbelief. "Seduced her? You don't really think he'd…"

"Seduction comes in many forms. It's not always physical."

She shook her head, staring out in front of her. "This sucks. I have been working my butt off to make sure that everyone had a piece of me and…" She paused, inhaling a long steady breath. "This just sucks."

I moved my hand to cover hers and I gave it a squeeze. "Fucking shithead."

Cambri's head whipped over to mine. "What?" she laughed out, taken off guard.

I met her eyes with my own. Calmly and controlled I let out, "He's a fucking shithead." A smile threatened her face. "Maybe we can find him a new office name plate that reads 'Easton Davenport: Fucking Shithead'."

She snorted out a laugh, and a tight feeling spread throughout my chest as a ghost of a smile formed on my lips. I loved that I could do that to her, make her laugh unexpectedly. A reaction like that does funny things to a man.

I wanted to bottle it up and keep it with me. The easiness that swept back in when we were like this. The two of us against the world. Jaxon and Cambri.

I turned toward her. "Fuck this morning." Her brows raised. "Nothing came out like I wanted. I want you. Tonight. Okay?" She nodded. "Good." I placed my lips on hers, letting my tongue slide against hers as I deepened the kiss.

I grinned, taking a step back. "I'll see you tonight."

Her grip tightened on the edge of the desk. "See you tonight."

I gave a nod before turning and walking out of her office, a grin on my face. We would find it again. Our rhythm. We just needed to adjust to life back home and the pace that it moved. We all did.

The rest of the day slipped by painfully slow as I waited to hear from Cambri about this evening. As the dinner hour approached, I grew increasingly antsy. Checking my clock every so often, trying not to let disappointment creep in.

At 9:00 PM my phone rang. I picked it up on the third ring after my brain took a moment to stare at her name on the screen.

"I'm sorry," she said the moment I answered.

I took a deep breath, not wanting my voice to give away any of the frustration I felt about another day getting taken away from us. Pinching the bridge of my nose, I tilted my head up. "It's fine, Cambri. We had nothing set in stone." I offered the excuse up to her on a silver platter.

There was a pause. She knew as well as I did that it was a load of crap. That this morning, I'd told her that I would see her tonight right before walking out of her office feeling fucking elated. That feeling expired hours ago.

"Right." I could hear her tight-lipped expression even though I couldn't see her face.

I sounded like a dick. Worse, I knew that I did. It just – it all felt piled up. I didn't mean to be short with her. That wasn't my intention.

I'm tired. And damn it, I'm only human. I'm allowed to feel frustrated. Even if it makes me sound like a dick.

I would be lying if I said I didn't miss the reckless ease that consumed us while we lived life on the road. While we lived in the moment. When all we had was "just today."

"So um." She took a pregnant pause. "I'm just gonna call it a night. I'm exhausted."

"Yeah. Me too."

"Talk to you – tomorrow?"

"Sounds good."

"Okay."

"Okay," I repeated into the phone.

"Night, Jaxon," she said, a reluctance coming through in her voice.

This was hard. I knew this was hard. Trying to live life and have it all. I was starting to wonder if you could.

"Goodnight, Cambri." I ended the call and stared at the phone. How had this become something that felt so difficult?

I walked to the shower and placed both of my hands on the wall inside as I let the water run over my head and down my back. Going through the motions, soap, rinse, repeat before turning off the flow. Stepping out, I wrapped my towel around my waist while I brushed my teeth and combed through my hair.

Slipping on a pair of boxers, I climbed into bed and eventually drifted off to sleep.

My eyes popped open. I relaxed back into my bed, running a hand down my face.

It was just a dream.

I gripped the covers, turning over onto my side. I closed my eyes, willing myself to fall back asleep, but the image of Cambri stepping into a car with someone else, offering me only a polite wave you give to someone you once knew, had my mind alert.

I knew it was just a dream, but there was that voice in the back of my mind reminding me that eventually – everyone leaves.

Chapter Twenty-Six

Cambri

Another week went by, and I managed to see Jaxon alone only once as I ran around trying to put out the firestorm that Easton had caused by poaching Alyssa. All while maintaining my other bands, making sure they both had and felt like they had everything that they needed.

There had been so much in motion with Alyssa. It threw everything off when Easton slimed his way into her corner.

I was working double time as I got ready to officially pass the torch to Easton on all things Alyssa. The legal side of the business was insane. All the paperwork and signatures it took to hand over an account.

The entire thing was frustrating. I wanted to scream, and yell, and ball up the contract and throw it in Easton's slimeball of a face. Instead, I plastered on a smile as I handed over the folder while silently cursing his name.

Legally, this was a preference choice that Alyssa was able to make as stated in the fine print of her contract. Something that had been outlined to give the artist a way out in the event that someone wasn't doing their job well.

This was entirely in the parameter of her rights within her contract at Norwood Records. It just didn't happen very often. Especially when the representative was working their ass off for the artist.

There was a relationship of trust and loyalty that formed between an artist and their representative. To break that felt like a slap in the face. Easton knew that.

He clearly did his homework to sway her.

The silver lining here (because let's face it, finding a silver lining is what is keeping Easton's balls intact) is that this was an excellent learning opportunity.

Moving forward, I will take extra care in customizing client contracts. All fine print is important, down to the exact way things are worded. If there is any room for interpretation, people like Easton will find a way to exploit it.

In the future, I will be prepared for little hiccups like this. I will be better prepared for little snakes who try to back me into a corner that leave no option for escape.

The following week, I briefly considered putting a cot in the corner of my office. It felt like I was practically living there already as it was. If there was shower access, who knows, maybe I would've.

I shook off the thought. Then I really never would see Jaxon.

I honestly didn't know how much longer I could maintain this. Which was still something I was wrapping my mind around because this life was all I had ever wanted. Climbing this ladder, being on top, this was what I had worked for for as long as I could remember.

It's funny how things change. How you change. I still wanted this job. This life.

It's just, I wanted to figure out a way where I could have it all. This life. This job. The guy.

I needed to feel the comfort of his arms around me and the satisfaction of his lips on mine. I needed a break. I needed him.

I walked into my office, closed the door behind me, and then found the seat at my desk. Pulling out my phone, I opened the text thread between us and then thought better of it. Instead, I found his number and hit call. I wanted to hear his voice. Needed to hear his voice on the other end of the line.

He answered on the first ring.

"I miss you," I said, not caring about the sound of desperation in my voice.

"I miss you too," he said reflexively, putting a smile on my face.

"I'm thinking about entering into the witness protection program and signing up for the tropical division so that I can secure a spot with you and the iguanas. As it appears, that is the only way I will get to spend quality time with you any time soon."

I could hear the smile in his voice when he replied. "Thank God you said that. I would have insisted on the Himalayas and found myself cold and alone with nothing to keep me warm except for the snow monkey hell-bent on mating with me in the first snow ritual."

I snorted out a laugh.

I took a moment to enjoy the way his words felt. "I miss you," I said again into the phone. Not caring that I was repeating myself or sounding borderline manically desperate.

"I know. This feels terrible, doesn't it?"

My smile grew at his words.

"Yes. It feels catastrophically terrible. And no, before you say anything, that's not dramatic at all. It's just the facts."

"I want to kiss you," he said after a beat. I smiled wider. "I want to kiss you from your head to your toes." I let out a sigh because that sounded wonderful. "I want to kiss down your back, and then I want to bite your perfectly rounded ass." That got my attention, causing heat to begin spreading through my body, pooling low in my belly. "And after I leave a little mark, I want to kiss where I left me on you. Smoothing my palm across your tempting rear."

"Jaxon," I whispered into the phone. His words filling me with warmth, sending need radiating through my body. Those damn words. My cheeks flushed and my mouth hung slightly ajar as my brain filled with the images of the moment Jaxon described.

"Cambri, where are you?" he asked. The demand in his voice sending a shiver down my spine.

"In my office," I replied in a husky tone.

"Is the door shut?" I could hear the smirk on his face. And damn if it wasn't hot.

I nodded before supplying my words. "Yes." I let out on a heavy breath.

"Are you sitting?" His voice was rough, letting me know he was enjoying this as much as I was.

"Yes," I breathed again.

"Good. I want you to…"

There was a knock on the door causing me to startle and drop my phone as the door swung open.

"Hey Camb…" Bexley from HR froze in the doorway, watching as I bent down, scrambling to pick up my phone and pull myself back together.

Sitting upright in my chair, I held the phone to my ear. "Hey, someone just walked into my office. Can I give you a shout back?"

"Have dinner with me tonight," he said. He didn't ask, he didn't say I could call him back, he just told me to have dinner with him. It sent more delicious shivers through me.

I bit my lip. "I uh," I managed, while trying to form an actual reply. He had me completely flustered. I cleared my throat, suppressing the grin on my face as I attempted to gain composure. Knowing Bexley was bearing witness to this entire thing. I fought the blush forming on my cheeks.

"Have dinner with me tonight," he said again into the phone.

I swallowed, holding a finger up to Bexley to let her know I would be right with her and not to leave. "Yes. I will put it into the calendar." I tried to sound professional and less like I was stuck on a personal call since I was keeping HR waiting.

"8:00," he said into the phone. "Set a reminder for it. Because tonight, I will come get you and throw you over my shoulder if I have to."

"Yes. That should work. Thank you."

I could hear the smile in his voice as he said, "You will later."

I did my best to will away the fire his words caused. I took a deep breath to attempt to cool the burn on my cheeks as I gave my attention to the head of HR standing in my doorway wearing an amused grin.

"Bad time?" she teased.

"Hey, Bexley. Sorry about that. No, not at all. Please take a seat." I gestured to the chair across my desk.

She walked over and placed a file onto my desk before taking a seat.

"I come bearing some good news. This is the last thing you need to sign to get Alyssa all squared away as being fully covered by one Easton Davenport. Then you can get back to business as usual."

I opened the file and found a couple papers that had yellow sticky tabs marking places my signature was needed. I grabbed a pen and made quick work of the sheets. I closed the file and handed it back to Bexley, who took a moment to thumb through it before closing the file.

With a grin she said, "Alright, that takes care of that. Thanks, Cambri."

"Sure. Don't mention it. Glad to have that all taken care of."

I don't know if it was the look on my face, the tone in my voice, or both that gave away how I was feeling about the Alyssa situation, but Bexley looked over her shoulder to the open office door before leaning forward. "As HR, I don't take sides. I am a neutral third party who helps manage difficult situations in hopes of finding the best outcome for all parties." I nodded because what was the correct reply to that? "However, health concerns are not typically HR business. And if you were to find yourself in need of a laxative that can be completely dissolved in, say, a latte, and you were to go one floor down and look in the first aid cabinet in the far back right-hand corner, that would be your business."

I quirked an amused eyebrow up at her and nodded again. "Thank you, Bexley. That is very informative information." I wondered how many enemies Easton had managed to make for himself.

She sat up straight and grabbed the file with both hands. "Great. Always happy to help." She stood up, still looking my way. "Let me know if you need anything else from the HR side of things."

I let out a small laugh. "Will do."

On that, Bexley turned and walked out of my office. Easton clearly had done an impeccable job at maintaining office relationships if even Bexley wasn't his biggest fan.

I worked the rest of the day with a grin plastered onto my face. Between looking forward to dinner with Jaxon and Bexley's helpful health knowledge, it really provided the energy I needed to sail through the remainder of the workday.

I was packing up as I took out my cell phone to give Jaxon a ring to decide on a place to meet for dinner when I noticed that it was at 3% battery life. "Crap," I said out loud to myself. I plugged in my phone to give it a little charge and headed out of my office to use the bathroom. I had no sooner walked out of the women's room when I literally almost bumped into Easton, who was coming from the direction of my office.

Taking a deep breath to find a voice that didn't sound like I was plotting his impending doom, I plastered on a grin. "Easton, what a pleasant surprise."

"Your smiling face is always a pleasantry," he said in the same manner the serpent probably used in order to lead to the downfall of man.

"What are you doing on this floor?"

"Looking for you, actually. I'm afraid I messed something up and need you to take a look at it. I hate to do this to you as you were clearly getting ready to head out for the evening."

I gave him a questioning look.

He pointed over his shoulder toward my office. "I went to your office first while I was looking for you and noticed that it looked like you might be all packed up for the day," he supplied.

"Uh-huh. And what exactly does that look like?" I questioned.

"Pardon?"

"You said it looked like I was all packed up for the day. What gave you that impression?"

"Oh. Right. Your purse. It was on your desk, so I figured that meant you were about to head out."

I thought for a moment. Had I placed my purse on my desk? I really didn't know if I had or not. I shook off the thought because giving that any more attention only prolonged the amount of time I had to spend with Easton.

"What can I help you with, Easton?"

"I really should show you. It would probably be easier."

"Just run it by me and let's see if I can offer a solution."

"This is something that I must insist you place your eyes on."

It took serious willpower not to clamp my eyes shut in frustration at his persistence, but I was determined not to let him know that he was capable of unnerving me.

"Okay," I said with a grin. "Let's see it."

"It's down in my office. After you?" he gestured to the elevator.

I gave him a tight-lipped smile. "Of course."

We made it into the elevator and then walked down two halls toward his office. "Shoot," he said, one hand on the doorknob and the other patting his pocket. "I locked my door on the way out since I didn't know if I would catch you or not and I didn't want to leave sensitive paperwork out for prying eyes. I must have laid my key down on your desk."

It was getting harder to maintain composure around him. I was ready to be out of here and at dinner with Jaxon, and Easton kept finding ways to prolong my office hours.

"I'll just run up and get it for you."

"No. No. You stay here. I'll be right back. My mistake. No need to have us both tracking back through the office. I know exactly where I left it. I'll grab it and be back quick like a rabbit."

"Splendid," I let out, not necessarily wanting to be forced into more small talk with him on the key retrieval mission. That and I thought he might make better time if I let him run up without me. No way he would run down any halls if I were present.

"Be right back."

"Okay."

I made my way to the kitchen area around the corner to grab a water while Easton headed back upstairs. I took my time filling my cup with ice and water, knowing it would take Easton a minute before he was back on this floor.

I made it back to his office door and to absolutely no one's surprise he wasn't back yet. I took a sip and then cupped my water glass between my hands like a baby bird as I not-so-patiently waited for his return.

I was ready to see this item of importance that he had to show me and then be off to meet Jaxon for dinner. A few more minutes passed, and Easton was still not back downstairs. I began to grow antsy as I shifted my weight back and forth between my feet.

Another minute or two passed, my impatience growing. What could possibly be taking this long? I began pacing in front of his door, checking the hallways on either side for movement. Right when I was about to call it quits and just leave, I heard him moving swiftly in my direction. I looked up to see him power walking with a look of disbelief on his face, holding his key out in front of him.

"Sorry for the delay," he let out, exasperated. "I looked everywhere for this little booger. At one point I was literally crawling on my hands and knees in your office trying to see if it had fallen to the ground. I'm sure it was quite the sight."

"I bet," I quipped with a forced tight-lipped grin. Easton needed to move quickly. I was all out of patience and definitely out of time.

"Anyhoo," he said quickly. "Would you like to know where it was the whole time?" he asked, but clearly meant it rhetorically because I was not given time to respond. Not that I minded. Anything we could do to get the show on the road at this point was fine by me. He patted his other pocket as he looked up, shaking his head side to side. "It was right here the whole time. Just hiding in my pocket. I totally forgot I slipped it back there while I was on my mission to find you."

I was trying really hard not to let the frustration I was feeling show in this moment. I did not want to let Easton Davenport know he was getting under my skin, but man oh man were his antics making it tough to rein it all in. Forcing another tight-lipped grin I said, "I hate it when that happens. Shall we?" I gestured to his door.

"Oh. Right," he said like I had caught him by surprise, then slid his key into the lock on the door.

I inhaled a deep breath to steady myself. Easton was clearly in no hurry to be done with whatever this matter was. I, on the other hand, was like a teapot that was about to reach its boiling point. I needed to be out of this building.

We stepped inside his office, and I followed him over to his desk where he had a couple files neatly stacked. Moving the top file over to the side, he picked up the file underneath and held it up. "One can never be too careful." He grinned his sly grin that caused a shiver to run down my spine, and not in a good way.

Easton has always been a slimeball and something about him has never sat quite right with me. But that might just be his general off-putting persona. He is too confident, in a way that says he thinks he is better than everyone. He also looks at women like he wants to own them, not be their partner. And his smile says he is trying to be friendly, but looks entirely too forced. As if being compassionate and a good human is a concept he isn't fully familiar with.

"Quite right." I waited a beat for him to fill the silence. He didn't. "So, what do you think you fudged up?"

He opened the file and laid it flat on his desk. "It's the wording in this paragraph. I was tired when I was writing it, that has to be how this happened. I am not usually one to make mistakes. I value attention to detail."

"I can attest to that. Let me see this blip. It may be nothing that even needs our attention."

I took the spot beside him and placed a hand on his desk as I read over the part he said contained a mistake. He was right. It was wrong. And not a slight oof we could just roll with, but one that required our attention. Especially because this was also a page that contained my signature saying that I'd signed off on it.

My heart sank as I realized I would not be leaving the office right away and heading to meet Jaxon.

I reached for my phone to call Bexley and then remembered I had left everything in my office. Easton had caught me leaving the bathroom on my way to gather my things. I pinched the bridge of my nose, finally letting slip an outward display of frustration.

"I do apologize for this, Cambri. I knew you would want to lay eyes on it since you signed off on this page. I hope I am not keeping you from anything."

I waved a hand. "It's fine. I'd rather get this handled now. Do you have Bexley's number in your phone? I left mine upstairs."

"Of course." He took out his phone and pulled up Bexley's number, placing the phone in my outstretched hand.

It rang twice. "Hey Bexley, it's Cambri."

"Cambri? Why are you calling me from Easton's phone?"

I sighed, glancing over at Easton. "It's a long story. Let me cut to the chase. There is an error in the paperwork transferring Alyssa's representation over to Easton. I signed off on it and everything. I apologize, I was in a hurry and well – missed it. How do you want us to proceed?"

"Listen, Cambri. Don't stress too much about this. This is fixable. I'm walking into my daughter's recital as we speak, but if you guys can draft up the correct document, I will make it my top priority tomorrow morning once I get to the office. Sound like a plan?"

"Yep. Okay. Thanks for being understanding about this. We will fix it and have it ready for you to look at tomorrow."

The call ended and Easton jumped in as soon as I handed his phone back to him.

"What did she say? Are we in the hot seat?"

"No. No. She didn't think it was that big of a deal. We just need to fix what we can on our end and then she said she will make it her top priority once she gets here tomorrow."

Thirty minutes later (because Easton had managed to accidentally delete the first corrected draft) we finally had a new document drafted and sent over to Bexley to look at first thing in the morning. He had said I could leave after he deleted our progress, but at this rate I wanted to see it through myself, not trusting him to handle this on his own.

I ran my hands down my hair, smoothing it in place, as I did a quick mental recap of it all. Making sure that this time we got it right. Making sure, that this time we had our I's dotted and T's crossed.

I took in a deep inhale.

"I think we are all squared away."

"Agreed," he said, like he was as glad to be done with this as I was.

"Unless you need anything else, I'm going to head back to my office to grab a few things and then be on my way."

Pushing off his desk with his hand, he stood up straight and met my eyes. "Nope. I think we are ready to go in the morning."

"Great. Then I'll be on my way."

I made my way over to his office door, ready to get the heck out of there, when he said, "Cambri, sorry again about this. I do hope I didn't spoil anything for you this evening."

There was something about the way he said it that caused me to stop in my tracks, narrowing my eyes reflexively. Fixing my face to a neutral expression, I turned toward him. "It happens. Glad we could get it all squared away," I told him, plastering a forced smile to my face. Turning back around, I let the smile slip as my eyes grew wide in a sort of unsettling disbelief.

I made it back to my office, grabbed my phone, and called Jaxon, hoping my delay wouldn't terminate our dinner plans. No answer. Crap. I threw a couple things in my purse and slung it over my shoulder as I texted Jaxon while heading to the elevators.

C: Hey. Sorry it got late. Something popped up at work, but I'm headed out now. We still on for tonight?

No reply.

Dang it, Jaxon. Where are you?

The elevator doors opened, and I made a beeline for my car.

C: Almost to my car. Call me.

My phone rang and my heart relaxed momentarily before realizing it wasn't Jaxon. It was Mallory. "Hey," I said, bringing my phone to my ear on an exhale.

"Hey," she said carefully. "Where are you?"

"Still at the office. Don't ask. It was a whole thing," I told her as I made my way across the parking garage.

"Have you, uh, been on social media recently?"

"No. I have been furiously working on fixing an issue here so I could meet Jaxon for dinner. Why? What's up?"

"Yeah…about that. You may want to pull up the 'gram."

Reaching my car, I unlocked the door and slipped inside.

"Why? Can this wait? I'm sort of in a hurry."

"Just. Just do it."

"Mal, why are you being so cryptic? Just tell me," I said, putting the call on speaker and then checking on whatever it was that had her acting so weird.

I sat frozen, staring at the picture in front of me. I didn't have to ask her what I needed to look at. It was everywhere. Several accounts had posted the picture.

Jaxon. And Alyssa. Jaxon with his hand on Alyssa. On her lower back as he shielded them from paparazzi as they appeared to be making their way to a car. She was turned toward him, tucking herself into his chest while doing a poor job of blocking her face from the camera.

The captions were all the same. Posing suggestions about a budding romance between the two rising country stars. One account had managed a picture of them sitting side by side, drinks in hand, as Alyssa had her head thrown back in laughter.

The comments were exploding. People expressing their excitement over this possibility. There was everything from people saying how much they loved them to how they were country music's cutest power couple. It was nauseating. People were vultures.

I scrolled back to the picture with Jaxon's hand on the small of Alyssa's back. I couldn't stop staring at it. Why was this picture taken? Why were they together? And why the heck was his hand on the small of her back? The questions were racing through my brain as my mind tried to piece it all together. I wasn't able to land on anything that made any of this make sense.

I kept staring at the picture. They were leaving a restaurant. Did they grab a meal together, share a table? Did he have dinner with another woman because I got stuck late at work?

I grabbed my temples and pressed. Think, think, think. There has to be a reason. There has to be something to make what I'm seeing make sense. I'm just currently struggling to find that reason because I can't stop seeing him touch her. Why. Was. He. Touching. Her? And not just a friendly handshake or gesture. It was protective. It was intimate.

I'm about to have someone hold my earrings because this photo has my claws coming out. I never knew I was the jealous type, but this photo makes me insanely jealous. All I see right now is red and my gosh…why does my chest hurt?

"Cam? Cambri?" Mal said from the other end of the phone. I forgot she was still there.

"Mal, I need to call you back."

"Cam, I'm sure that there is…"

"I – I just need to call you back." I hit end on the call and then dropped the phone into my lap. My hands were shaking. This was awful. This felt awful.

I knew Mallory was about to tell me that there was probably a perfectly logical explanation for what I was seeing, I just couldn't hear that right now. Right now, my head was spinning, and I was having to remind myself to breathe. Right now, I was mad, and hurt, and tired. I was so stinking tired and - and I didn't know what was happening.

The first tear fell and then I did an inhale-hiccup thing that made way for lots more tears. A part of me recognized that I was overreacting, that I was just tired, and that things had just been hard, and that this was simply the icing on the cake that did me in. Yet, I really needed Jaxon to explain this to me right now. To tell me that what I was seeing wasn't real and to make it make sense.

My phone rang and bless Mal's heart, I just couldn't right now. With my eyes closed I answered the phone and brought it to my ear. "Mal, I'm fine. I just need a minute, okay?"

"Cambri." Jaxon's voice cut through, causing me to look at the screen before bringing it back to my ear. "Cambri?" He said my name again.

"I'm here," I said in a shaky voice.

"Fuck," he uttered through the phone. "You've seen it. Let me explain."

"Somebody better fucking start explaining this to me. Why were you with her, Jaxon? What is going on?"

"You texted me to meet you at Pinosh. But you didn't show. I ran into Alyssa at the bar and we had a drink while I waited for you. I was about to come get you at the office when you texted again saying that you were wrapping up and about to head my way, so I stayed. We got another drink. When I realized that you stood me up, I paid and was getting ready to leave. She asked if I could walk her out to her car and we were met with a sea of paparazzi. That's it. None of this would have happened if you didn't stand me up."

"What are you talking about? I never texted you."

"Yes, you did," he said, clearly frustrated.

"No. I didn't. I think I would know if I texted you." I blew out a breath. "Are we really doing this? Do you really think I'm that big of an idiot?"

My phone beeped. A text from Jaxon. He'd sent me the screenshot of our text thread. Sure enough, I had in fact texted him. Except, I hadn't.

"This doesn't make any sense," I said slowly, trying to process it. "I never texted you."

"Looks like you did. Cambri, what is going on?"

"Jaxon – I didn't even have my phone on me. I was..." My voice trailed off. No. How did he? He would have had to enter a password.

"Cambri?"

"Easton. It was Easton."

"Easton?" he said in disbelief.

"Yes. That is the only person it could have been. He was coming from my office when I left the bathroom, and then he went back to my office while I was at his."

"Slow down. What were you doing alone in Easton's office?"

I started from the beginning and explained how it all unfolded from the moment I first bumped into Easton.

"Well, you have to hand it to him. He found a way to get his photo op."

I scoffed. "Yeah. Um. I'm not really seeing anything other than him being the literal worst kind of person."

"Don't get me wrong. He's not getting away with his little stunt."

"I wish that were true." I felt queasy. Who goes out of their way to sabotage someone? Not to mention the invasion of privacy. He got into my phone. "Jaxon, he had to know my password. How did he know my password?"

"I don't know. I really don't. What are you going to do? Take this to HR?"

"And say what? That you got a text from me, but that it wasn't from me? That I think my coworker bypassed my password and made dinner plans with you?"

"Yeah." He said like it was that simple.

"I have no proof. There was nothing out of line or out of character said…I have no proof. All I have is how terrible it made me feel. When I saw your hand on her, Jaxon. I wanted to rip her eyes out."

"Cam, were you jealous?" he teased. I'm sure attempting to calm my rage, but only managing to feed it instead. I was in no way able to laugh about this.

"Damn straight I was jealous. How would you feel if you'd seen another guy's hand on the small of my back?"

"He probably would no longer be standing."

"See?"

It was quiet for a pause.

"I didn't kiss her back, for the record."

The world came to a screeching halt. *Didn't kiss her back?* Meaning she had kissed him. Meaning her lips had been on his. I gripped the steering wheel firmly while the air around me evaporated and everything started spinning. A new type of rage settled under my skin.

"You kissed?" My voice dripping with anger as it became abundantly clear that I hadn't known that part.

"Fuck," Jaxon growled through the phone. "It was hardly a kiss. I opened her door and when I stepped back, she stepped into me. Placing a kiss on my lips before I could stop it. It didn't mean anything. I didn't kiss her back. I quickly shut that shit down. I wouldn't have even said anything, but I assumed you had seen a picture of it."

My heart was ping-ponging all over the place and my mind was having difficulty catching up to the idea of the whole thing.

"You weren't going to say anything?" My voice was rising. "You let another woman put her lips on yours, and you just weren't going to say anything if you were confident I wouldn't find out?"

"Cambri…" he began, but the floodgates had opened, and I was a wall of water that couldn't be stopped.

"So, what, Jaxon? Next tour if a girl happens to fall on your dick, you're just not going to tell me? As long as you can have plausible deniability and be sure I won't be any wiser?"

"Cam," he said firmly.

"No. No. I don't even know who you are right now."

"Funny. Coming from the girl who just spent the last hour canoodling in her coworker's office. Conveniently not having your phone on you. Blowing me off. Did you blow him too?"

I scoffed. "You're an asshole! Maybe you would have seen through the ironic convenience of me not showing and Alyssa just happening to be there if it wasn't stroking your rock star complex so much having a girl fawn all over you."

"You mean enjoying someone making time for me and not being so damn consumed by work all the time," he seethed.

"Screw you, Jaxon. Why don't you go running back to her tonight if your ego is so fragile that you need to fall into the comfort of somebody else the moment things aren't smooth and easy," I bit out. "I never once attempted to hold you back from chasing your dream or tried to make you feel bad about it."

"That's not fair," he barked. His own temper rising.

"It sure the hell isn't." I clicked end to the call and dropped my phone, my hands shaking with anger and hurt.

Once my heart stopped racing and I could manage a calm breath, I put my car into reverse and drove. I needed away from here and this place.

Chapter Twenty-Seven

Jaxon

I threw my cell into the lawn before kicking the bushes. "Fuck," I growled out. I ran my hand through my hair, pacing out front of our house.

"Feel better now that you've assaulted that shrub?"

I stopped moving, looking up to see Everett standing in the door with his arms crossed across his chest.

"Don't start right now." I began moving again, unable to stand still while my mind was racing with the clusterfuck that tonight turned out to be.

"Says the guy picking on tiny little twigs." He casually hit the cigarette pack in his hand before taking one out and placing it between his lips. Lighting it up.

I took in a deep breath. "Everett, not now."

"I assume Cam was upset about the photos. Given your pleasant demeanor."

"Everett, I said not the fuck now."

He let out a smug laugh. I whipped my head toward him, my fists balling up at my side.

"Woah, settle down, Casanova." I stepped toward him. He was at least smart enough to take a step back. "Take a breath, Jax."

I scoffed. "Take a breath? Take a fucking breath? You have no idea how much things have just gone to shit, or you would not be telling me to take a breath."

He nodded. "Fair. But I can assume it's not great given this." He gestured toward me.

I looked up at the sky, trying to think of a way to salvage this. I had nothing. The evidence was too damning. And now she'd never trust me again. The shock and hurt in her voice potent when she asked if I wouldn't tell her something if I thought I could get away with it. Damn it.

"Jax. Buddy." He stepped forward. "Let's calm down, alright?" Everett took the front steps and walked toward me. "Talk about this."

"It's too late. I fucked up." I held my arms out wide. "This cannot be undone and now she's going to leave."

"Okay. That might be a little dramatic."

"You didn't hear how upset she was. You don't know what she said."

He nodded. "True. But she's not going anywhere."

I laughed, almost maniacally. "Yeah. Okay. She's going to choose to stay even though I hurt her. Even though I fucked this up."

"Exactly."

"Don't be a dick, Everett."

"Will you calm down a minute? Look at the whole picture. Why would she leave? How can she leave when we are all under the same label?"

"She'll pass us over to Easton or someone."

"Why the hell would she do that? The guy's an asshole."

"Because I blew it, Ev. I messed this up like I mess up everything. And now she's going to leave me. Us. And it's all my fault."

I looked away, trying to settle the storm raging inside.

"Not everybody leaves, Jax."

I cut my eyes to him. I scoffed before running my hand through my hair.

"I mean it, man. I'm still here. The guys are still here. We're with you through it all."

I blew out a breath, shaking my head.

"Your mom and sister aren't going anywhere."

"They're family," I spat.

"So was he."

I reached out, placing my hand on his chest firmly. "Don't."

He pushed me off him. "You wanna go?" He threw his cigarette to the side.

I clenched my jaw, thinking for mere seconds before I used both hands to shove him back.

He laughed. "That all you got, Jax?" He shoved me harder.

Stepping into it, I pushed him back, causing him to stumble a few steps.

Recovering, he stepped toward me. "Out of your system now?"

"Fuck off, Everett."

"When are you going to realize that you have people in your life that love you? That are going to stick by your side no matter what. You're my brother, Jax. And if you will pull your head out of your ass and listen to me for a goddamn minute, you'll see that that girl of yours isn't going anywhere. That we." He pointed back to the house. "Aren't going anywhere. Even when you are a pain in the ass."

I just looked at him.

"We're not him, Jaxon. And I'm sorry that he fucked you up. But you've got to man up and fix this."

"I don't know how," I snapped.

"You go find her. Talk. Work it out."

"What if she won't let me?"

"Cam loves you, you big idiot. I've never seen two people linked the way that you guys are. I've never seen you look at someone the way you look at her. You're happier than I've ever seen you. And I'm not going to sit around and watch you self-destruct because you can't move past your own demons."

I hardly blinked while he spoke.

"We all have demons, Jax. Don't let yours ruin the best thing that ever happened to you."

"How do I know that she won't leave? That she won't rip my heart out?"

"You don't."

I coughed out a laugh. "That's reassuring."

"All you can do is trust her enough to put everything out in the open. Allow her to lay it all out, and then choose to move forward together."

I ran a hand through my hair. "I don't even know where to start."

"You go find her. Before I'm forced to find her myself and steal her away from you."

"That's the least of my worries."

"I do like mine rougher around the edges. And commitment free."

"You're an ass."

He smiled, tilting his head to the side. "I know."

Everett placed a hand on my shoulder. "Go find your girl, Jax. Acknowledge the shit. Apologize. And be honest."

"About what?"

He smirked. "That you can't live without her."

Chapter Twenty-Eight

Cambri

I drove around trying to clear my head. It was all too much. Before I realized where I was going, I ended up here.

I sat at the bar, sipping a cosmo, when Bill crossed his arms across the counter, leaning toward me.

"Darlin', you know I always love to see your face. But tonight, you look exceptionally miserable. Want to tell me about it?"

"No." I slumped forward, resting my weight on the bar in front of me. I most certainly did not want to get into how hectic life was home from the tour, the terrible human that Easton was, and then the fact that Jaxon had his lips on someone else tonight. I buried my head in my arms.

"Alright," he chuckled. "You let me know if you change your mind." He drummed his fingers on the counter. "Want some tots while you wallow?"

I gave a thumbs-up because I literally could not meet Bill's eyes. I was in a state of wallowing in my own pity. My brain was yelling so many different things at me.

Be mad. Don't be mad. It's not what it seems. Hear him out. Screw him for being in that situation in the first place. Get some sleep and then deal with it all. There's no time for sleep. What kind of a person sets something like this up? Why did he let her get so close?

He let her kiss him. Alyssa's lips had been on Jaxon's tonight. And the only thing I could think to do about it was get drunk enough not to remember. I sat up and took a drink of the ice-cold numbing pink elixir.

I glanced out the corner of my eye and found Bill watching me. "Do I need to teach someone a lesson?" he asked like an overprotective father.

"No. Just another one of these." He raised a brow. "Please," I added.

Bill shook his head and turned to make the drink.

I placed my head in my hands.

"I know I make a damn fine drink, my dear. But take it from me, these won't fix whatever you're going through right now." I cut my eyes to him, causing him to chuckle again. "They certainly help numb it down for a minute though."

"No one tells you how complicated life gets when you grow up."

Bill stopped moving and looked at me. "Hmmm."

"What? That's all you got? You've been dropping little tidbits since I've been here and now you're speechless?"

Bill casually shrugged a shoulder. "I don't think you really believe that is all."

"What's that supposed to mean?"

He walked the drink he finished making over and placed it in front of me. "You've never lived a life with the wool pulled over your eyes. You, better than some, know that life can be very complicated."

"Oh, yes. The hardships of growing up in private schools and having two parents that are happily married," I quipped.

He stopped moving and looked at me. The disappointed look cutting straight through to my core. I at least had the decency to wince.

"I know your father, and he instilled the value of hard work in you from an early age. Yes, life has been kind to you overall, and from the outside it all looks picturesque. But you know the hardships and sacrifice it takes to make that life. As well as that things aren't always exactly how they seem from the outside looking in. You also know that's not what I was talking about."

I stared at him for a moment. "I know." I paused. "Sometimes I wish I hadn't been aware of life's gray areas so young."

Bill leaned forward, crossing his arms on the bar in front of him. "Everything life offers you teaches you something, molds you in some way. It's what you do with those lessons, those curveballs, that shapes the person you turn out to be. You either wallow in it, letting life crush you down. Or you fight through it. Letting what you learned add fuel to the fire that pushes you forward."

I glanced up on an inhale. I knew he was right, but it didn't make any of this feel better currently.

"Your gray areas in life taught you resiliency. Taught you how to double down and work harder for what you wanted. It helped you appreciate this gift that life can be. You didn't take the easy way out, Cambri. And it would have been very easy for you to shove it all down and choose not to deal with it. Distract yourself by jet-setting or with whatever substance could numb what you didn't want to feel. But that's never been who you are. You're a fighter who doesn't let life circumstances excuse your bad choices."

"What if I'm tired of being the responsible one. What if I just want to say 'To hell with it all,' and be young while I still can. Wallow a bit in the curveballs."

He pursed his lips together, studying me. "You've never been one to make excuses, Cambri. For bad choices and easy outs. It'd be a damn shame if you started now." He glanced over my shoulder and then tapped his fingers on the bar. "I'm going to go check on those tots."

I watched him go. Mulling over everything he said. My jaw set tight as my gaze settled back in front of me. Movement from my side disrupted my line of thought.

A barstool, two down from me, screeched back before being filled with a heavy plop. Great. So not what I needed right now.

I cut a glance at whomever had decided to make the boisterous entrance and then did a double take.

Jaxon.

"What are you doing here?"

"Ah, back to pleasantries I see," he said with all the cocky swagger of a rock star.

My jaw dropped open.

He smirked. "You know, if you took a picture, it would last longer."

I furrowed my brows as he turned to Bill, who was approaching with my tots. Bill placed the tray in front of me and Jaxon scooted over, plucking one from the stack. He gently placed one in his mouth, moaning in pleasure as he took his time licking the salty goodness off his fingers.

"Help yourself."

"Thanks." He took another one and popped it into his mouth. He turned his attention to me. "You should really have one. They're amazing. I swear, you will not regret it."

I narrowed my eyes at him.

He stole another tot, grinning at me as he placed it between his lips. "So good. Perfectly salty." He crooked his head to the side. "And somehow crunchy despite the mountain of toppings they possess."

I let out an exasperated laugh. He thinks he's so smooth.

He turned to Bill, trying to hide his grin at being pleased with himself with his little spectacle show.

"Bill, will you make me one of those drinks I like? And make it strong."

I gasped. Actually gasped. Recovering, I pointed my finger at him. "You think you're so smooth, mister."

"Ugh." He threw his head back. "Where are my manners?" He held his hand out to me. "I'm Frankfurt. But my friends call me Fronk."

He winked.

He had some nerve. I'll give him that.

I looked at Bill who was trying to stifle his own laugh. He placed a whiskey in front of Jaxon. "I'm just going to go check on something in the back."

I whipped my head toward Jaxon. "What is it that you think you are doing?"

"You're right. That was rude of me. I should have let you have the first tot."

I scoffed.

"I hear Colorado is great this time of year. The weather in Aspen, so crisp and refreshing."

"Cut the crap, Jaxon."

His façade fell. "No. You cut the crap, Cambri."

"Rich, considering that I'm not the one kissing other people."

"It's not kissing someone else when they turn into you, when you're just trying to get them safely away from the paparazzi piranhas."

I turned away and crossed my arms across my chest.

He placed his elbows on the bar and scraped his fingers across his head. He craned his head toward me. "Why are you refusing to see tonight for what it was? A setup. We were set up."

I took in a slow breath. I will not cry. I. will. Not cry.

"So, what if it was. Who's to say it won't happen again and again? As you guys get bigger, girls are just going to want to throw themselves at you more." I started shaking my head. "I don't know if I can do that. I – I don't know if I want to do that. This feels terrible."

"Cambri, look at me."

I continued to shake my head.

"Look at me. Look at me, damn it."

Slowly, I turned to meet his gaze.

"This isn't how things fall apart. Over a stupid act from two conniving morons. We are stronger than that." He said it with such conviction I wanted to believe him but didn't know if I could.

"How can you say that? How can you be so certain?"

"Because it's you and me. It's Jaxon and Cambri. Not everything makes sense to me. But this." He gestured between us. "This feels right. Even when it's fucking hard, this feels right. On tour, here in Nashville. It doesn't matter. You and me. This is what I want. It's the only thing that matters."

My eyes welled up at his words, and I looked up at the ceiling, trying to suck the tears back in. Trying to get ahold of them before the first one could fall.

He scooted closer, and I felt his knee brush mine. "Cam," he said on a breath.

I turned to look at him and he scooted closer, grabbing both sides of my face with his hands. "I love you, Cambri Norwood. From the moment you screeched that stool across this floor, I couldn't take my eyes off you. You captivated me with that fiery mouth of yours. And you bore yourself deeply into the fabric of who I am when you shared your soul with me. You lured me in with your siren song. So, you either keep me afloat or drag me down to the deep. Either way, I won't let go. 'Cause I can't go back to the me without you."

He swiped his thumb over my cheek as I realized I was crying.

"I'm scared," I admitted. All of this feeling like too much. Too real.

He grinned. "Me too. Loving someone like this. Letting someone in like this terrifies the shit out of me."

"I'm scared of losing you. I don't think I could survive that again. Losing someone I love so deeply."

"Then don't lose me. Fight for me, baby. With me." He swiped his thumbs against my cheeks. "There's never going to be anyone else for me. Not here, not on the road, not anywhere. You taught me to live in this moment. Live with me, Cambri."

"And when they come for us? The media, the sharks, the – temptations of life on the road. I wasn't prepared for a stunt like this to sting so much."

He dropped his hands into his lap, shrugging both his shoulders slowly on an inhale. "Let them come. As long as we have each other to come home to, to rest in, we can overcome anything. Together."

I closed my eyes as I took in a steadying breath.

His hands gripped my sides, and he rested his forehead against mine.

"'Iris.' The Goo Goo Dolls," he said over me. The warmth of his breath comforting.

I nodded.

"I love you, Cambri."

"I love you too," I whispered.

"I don't want to do this life without you. You make every day better. You make me better. Stay with me."

I released the slowest breath. When I could trust my voice, I let out, "Okay."

He tilted my chin up, his eyes searching mine. I gave the faintest nod, causing the corners of his mouth to crook up.

He crashed his lips to mine. Kissing me with everything that he was. Everything that we are. Because he is right. Life is better with him. Even the hard days, the longs days, when I know he's there in the end, it pushes me through.

"Just today," he whispered against my lips.

I looked into his eyes. "And every day after."

He grinned and then pressed his lips to mine.

Epilogue

Jaxon

After

Life is funny. At first it feels like you're never going to grow up. Never going to reach the end result you've always wanted. You blink, and then you've headlined tours. You have more awards than you can count. And your face no longer looks like that eager boy you were when you first started.

It hasn't all been easy. Life on the road. This industry. Getting here. There have been bumps and bruises, more than I care to admit. But that's life. We're not guaranteed easy. We're not even guaranteed tomorrow.

All that exists is today and what we choose to do with it. Right now, I'm choosing to be grateful. For this life and for this woman that has taught me so much.

Over the years, I've slowly talked to my dad more and more. It was uncomfortable at first, but it was something I needed to do for myself. What I needed to do to fully move past the anger and resentment I'd held onto for so long. To accept the man he is now and who he is striving to be.

Forgiveness is weird like that.

It's a process.

To let go of all the anger and negativity was the first difficult choice in a long path of choices. Along the way, I've learned that I also had to forgive myself and love myself in order to be the best me. To be a man worthy of respect. Worthy of Cambri.

Worthy of the little human we created together. He was a bit of surprise, but I've learned the best things in life usually are. His sister came next. She is as fiery as her mother. Lord help the man that falls for those bright blue eyes one day.

I'm not fooled into thinking that things are only going to be easy from here on out. And I'm okay with that. I'm okay with facing the good and the bad because that's what life is. It's a series of ups and downs. At the end of the day, this life is what we make it.

After that night at the bar. The one where I chased her down, hoping like hell she wasn't calling it quits. Calling us quits. I went to her house. I went a little overboard. I wanted to make sure she knew I wasn't going anywhere and that I didn't want her to. I emptied a drawer in her bedroom and bathroom, declaring them as mine as she laughed with tears occasionally running down her beautiful face.

I may have even cleared space in kitchen cabinets, insisting it was for my spices and cups before collapsing on the floor with her in a tangle of limbs. Like I said, it was a bit overboard.

I don't regret a thing.

Every day, I wake up to Cambri. Every day, we choose to love each other and fight for this life together. Every day, I am grateful for each moment I get with her by my side.

Because we aren't promised anything other than the present moment we live in. So, I choose to make the best of it. Live it fully for as long as I can, every minute that I can. For just today.

Acknowledgements

It takes a village to bring a novel to life. I am so grateful for mine!

First and foremost, thank you to the good Lord above. Without whom there would be no way I could have accomplished any of this.

To my wonderful boys, thank you for your love and support while I was tucked behind this ole computer of mine. Writing is a labor of love not only for the author, but also to the family whose lives are affected by my absence. Y'alls support and encouragement are everything!

My husband, baby daddy, best friend, twin flame, etc. – ect., you encourage, support, inspire, and drive me crazy. I truly don't know how I would do this, chase this dream of mine, without you. Thank you for providing a way for me to see this through, creating a life that allows me to be both mom and writer. For making my dream important to you as well. I look forward to our word + idea sparring at the end of each novel. You push me. You make me better. I am so grateful for you, my love.

Lindsay Stokey. Where to begin?! You were with me from what feels like the beginning of this one. Jaxon and Cambri's story would not be what it is today without you. You pushed me to think outside the box, to dig deeper and shape these characters into who they are. You saved me from breakfast tacos and educated me on Nashville culture. Possibly most importantly, you saved Cambri from a wig when you insisted "absolutely not." I cringe thinking about that original version of the chapter. Thank you for reading along with me during the first drafts, for starting many a day with Jaxon and Cambri. Thank you for brainstorming with me, analyzing the story line as we walked the streets, and for answering all my texts and calls with enthusiasm. I am forever grateful for you.

My betas: Ashleigh Scott + Brittany Allread. Y'all were my cheerleaders! Thank you for taking time out of your lives to read this novel. I appreciate your time and your feedback. Y'alls encouragement always made me smile. Especially when emojis were involved toward the end while I was polishing up certain scenes. You both kept me going during the final stretch with your words and enthusiasm. Thank you. Thank you. Thank you.

To the immensely talented Murphy Rae, thank you for creating beautiful cover designs, and for sharing your art with the world! It makes a novel feel extra special when you begin with one of your cover designs!

My editor, Lilly Schneider, thank you for taking my words and making them as pretty as possible! Thank you for polishing up my manuscript until it, "Shine bright like a diamond." (You sang that, didn't you?) I am so grateful for your skill and feedback.

Last, but certainly not least, a big THANK YOU to my readers. Without you, there would be no reason to put words onto a page. **I appreciate each and every one of you!** Thank you for reading my words and getting lost in this world. Thank you doesn't even begin to feel like enough, but I will say it again, THANK YOU! THANK YOU!

Playlist – J+C ♥

(Listed as appears in novel)

1. Fancy – Reba McEntire
2. Watermelon Sugar – Harry Styles
3. Have You Ever Seen The Rain – Creedence Clearwater Revival
4. Going to Mars – Judah & the Lion
5. Exile – Taylor swift
6. Find Another Reason Why – Judah & the Lion
7. Castle on the Hill – Ed Sheeran
8. I'm Gonna Be Somebody – Travis Tritt
9. Don't Threaten Me With a Good Time – Thomas Rhett
10. We Are Young – Fun
11. Lover of the Light – Mumford & Sons
12. Georgia – Vance Joy
13. You Know It – Colony House
14. I'm Gonna Be Somebody – Travis Tritt
15. Iris – The Goo Goo Dolls
16. I'm Gonna Be Somebody – Travis Tritt
17. Photograph – Ed Sheeran
18. Pretty Little Poison – Warren Zeiders
19. Look I Like – Alana Springsteen
20. Shivers – Ed Sheeran
21. Lose Control – Teddy Swims

22. Not Finished Just Yet - Bernard Fanning
23. Sun to Me - Zach Bryan
24. Roses - The Chainsmokers
25. White Horse - Chris Stapleton
26. Heart Like a Truck - Lainey Wilson
27. Watermelon Sugar - Harry Styles
28. I Got You Babe - Sonny & Cher
29. Save Me - Jelly Roll
30. Something in the Orange - Zach Bryan
31. Wild - Carter Faith
32. Iris - The Goo Goo Dolls

About The Author

Brittany Wynne was born in Odessa, TX. She attended Texas A&M University where she graduated with a degree in education. She now lives in The Woodlands, TX with her husband Chris, their two sons (Hunter and Lincoln), and a fur-baby, named Hank.

A self-proclaimed book addict, she contributes her love for reading as to why she developed the writing bug. When she's not brainstorming new character and story ideas, she can be found reading, blogging, playing tennis, spending far too much time on instagram, and binge watching her favorite shows with her husband and pup.

www.ingramcontent.com/pod-product-compliance
Lightning Source LLC
LaVergne TN
LVHW100503110826
845146LV00002B/501

9798990363724